Somewhere in France

ALSO BY JENNIFER ROBSON

After the War Is Over

Moonlight Over Paris

Somewhere in France

Jennifer Robson

HARPER LUXE

An Imprint of HarperCollins*Publishers*

This is a work of fiction. Names, characters, places, and incidents are products of the author's imagination or are used fictitiously and are not to be construed as real. Any resemblance to actual events, locales, organizations, or persons, living or dead, is entirely coincidental.

HarperCollins books may be purchased for educational, business, or sales promotional use. For information please e-mail the Special Markets Department at SPsales@harpercollins.com.

FIRST HARPERLUXE EDITION

ISBN: 978-0-06-249704-8

HarperLuxe™ is a trademark of HarperCollins Publishers.

Library of Congress Cataloging-in-Publication Data is available upon request.

16 17 18 19 20 ID/RRD 10 9 8 7 6 5 4 3 2 1

This book is dedicated to my father, Stuart Robson.
You are the finest historian and
the best teacher I will ever know.

Somewhere in France

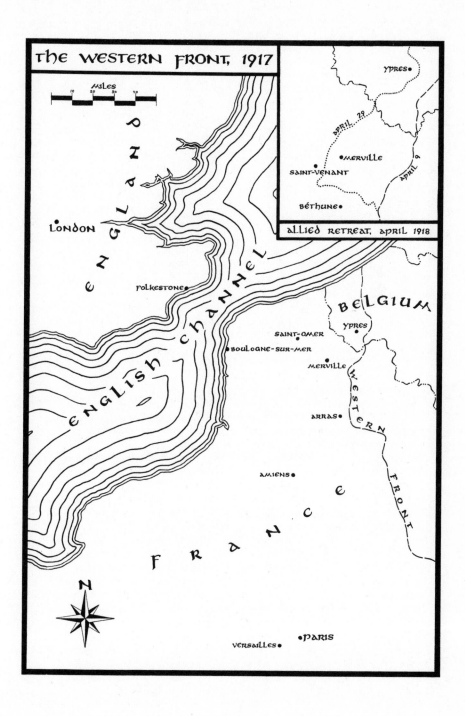

THE WESTERN FRONT, 1917

MILES

ENGLAND

LONDON

FOLKESTONE

ENGLISH CHANNEL

SAINT-OMER

BOULOGNE-SUR-MER

BELGIUM

YPRES

MERVILLE

WESTERN FRONT

ARRAS

AMIENS

FRANCE

N

VERSAILLES

PARIS

ALLIED RETREAT, APRIL 1918

YPRES

APRIL 29

MERVILLE

SAINT-VENANT

APRIL 9

BÉTHUNE

PART ONE

*The lamps are going out all across Europe;
we shall not see them lit again in our lifetime.*

—SIR EDWARD GREY, *foreign secretary
of Great Britain (1905–1916)*

Chapter 1

Belgrave Square, London
July 1914

It was past nine, past time, for the sun had set, the orchestra had begun to play, and hundreds of guests were streaming up the grand central staircase, their voices rising in an ebullient, ever-swelling chorus to the floors above. Past time to call for Flossie, and array herself in the gown her mother had chosen. If only there were armor for occasions like this.

A scratch at the door; then: "Lady Elizabeth?"

"Flossie. I was just about to ring for you. I've left things rather late."

"Your hair's done already, so we've only to worry about your gown. We'll have you ready in no time at all."

After shedding her dressing gown, Lilly stood in her chemise and stockings, still as a mannequin, as Flossie tightened and tied her corset. Then the maid fastened several petticoats around her waist, just enough to support the modest fullness of her skirts.

The gown itself had been set out on the floor, on top of a clean sheet, its bodice drawn wide so Lilly might step into it with Flossie's help. Made of palest pink satin, it was overlaid by cream-colored net lace embroidered with lilies of the valley. Although it had not been her first choice, it was a pretty gown, and she loved the way the light caught and reflected the seed pearls and crystals of its embroidery.

She drew on her gloves, their kid leather so paper-thin it took forever to smooth them up her arms, and bent her head while Flossie fastened a pink sapphire and pearl choker at her throat; it was followed by a tiara, bracelet, and earrings from the same parure.

She'd never be the belle of the ball, for that role fell to mahogany-haired beauties like her sisters. But she could admit, assessing her appearance with a critical eye, that she looked passable tonight. Pretty, even. In her favor was her complexion, glowing and clear, without even a hint of freckle, an acceptably rounded bosom, and an abundance of shiny brown hair.

It had been an age since she'd attended a ball. After her debut, two Seasons ago, she'd avoided such grand occasions whenever possible. Fortunately, this was the last event in honor of her brother Edward and his fiancée that she was expected to attend, at least until their wedding drew near. After tonight she could retreat to the quiet of Cumbria and enjoy what remained of the summer in peace.

The carriage clock on her mantel chimed the half hour. She had wasted enough time already.

"Thank you very much, Flossie. I'll ring for you when I come back upstairs."

"Yes, miss. You do look lovely."

"You're very kind. I'll see you soon."

Lilly took a steadying breath, as deep as her corset allowed, and hurried downstairs to the library via one of the back staircases.

At her arrival, Edward rose with alacrity from one of the wing chairs that flanked the fireplace. His fiancée's father, Lord Halifax, was clearly suffering from gout and took longer to extricate himself from his seat.

Dropping a kiss on Lilly's cheek, Edward moved past her and surveyed the empty hallway. "Where on earth are they? Shouldn't they be here by now?"

"I spoke to Helena and Lady Halifax not long ago," Lilly reassured him. "I'm certain they'll be here presently." Seeking to divert his attention, she caught sight of the evening paper on a side table. "Has there been any news?"

"Nothing from the Austrians, though it's only a matter of time." Edward picked up his glass of port, drained what was left of it, and grimaced. "We'll all be at war before the summer is out."

"Is there truly no hope that an agreement can be reached?" she asked, already knowing the answer.

"Best to get it over with," Edward said. "Like—how did you put it, Lord Halifax?"

"Lancing a boil."

"Yes, that was it. Quick and sharp; that's how we'll do it. We're sure to prevail, and once we do we'll finally be certain of peace."

A dismissive harrumph from the library door told Lilly that Lady Halifax had arrived. "None of your war talk this evening, gentlemen," the countess commanded. "You'll alarm the young ladies."

Edward smiled apologetically. "You're quite right, of course." Stepping forward, he kissed Lady Halifax's hand with a flourish. He then turned to his fiancée, who had been hovering behind her mother, and bestowed upon her the full, dazzling effect of his smile and regard.

"Helena, my darling, you look utterly beautiful tonight. I'm so very proud." He reached into his coat and pulled out a slim leather box from the inside breast pocket. "A small token of my esteem. I do hope you like it."

Helena opened the box, her gloved fingers fumbling with the catch, and gasped as she saw the diamond bracelet inside. She looked up at Edward, her heart in her eyes, and Lilly felt a brief, and disquieting, spark of envy. Was that what it felt like to love, and to be loved in return?

A discreet tap at the door announced the butler's arrival. Resplendent in his silk tailcoat, Mr. Maxwell led them up the grand staircase to the ballroom. As they approached the ornate double doors to the room, the orchestra inside fell silent and the accompanying din of voices grew hushed.

Mr. Maxwell's sonorous baritone was perfect for such occasions. "The Earl of Halifax and the Countess of Halifax," he proclaimed. "The Viscount Ashford and the Lady Helena Montagu-Douglas-Parr."

Lilly stood well back, waiting until the watching eyes of the crowd were elsewhere, then slipped into the ballroom all but unnoticed. She made her way around its perimeter, greeting those guests to whom she'd already been introduced, repeating the same inanities of weather and health each time. And each time, as she met their eyes and shook their hands, she was beset by the conviction that the interior life of the person to whom she spoke was utterly unknown to her. They might as well have been animated silhouettes, so profound was the effect they had on her. Not that she was likely to have made any more lasting an impression on any of them.

She made her way to the blue drawing room, intent on finding a quiet corner where she might sit and sip at a glass of lemonade. Then she saw him.

Robert Fraser. Robbie.

She had only met him once before, when her brother had invited his best friend from Oxford to stay for the long Easter weekend. Her parents had disapproved, of course, appalled that Edward would choose to associate with the son of a Glaswegian dustman. But Edward had insisted on bringing his friend to Cumbermere Hall for the holiday, and what her brother wanted he very nearly always got.

Though seven years had passed since that weekend, she recognized Robbie straightaway, though she could discern little of the boy he'd once been. He was as fair as ever, his hair the color of honey, and his eyes were the same bright blue of her memories. But he carried himself like a man, with none of the gracelessness and bluster of youth, and held himself so confidently that he overshadowed every other person in the room.

He looked wonderful in formal dress. Worn by a lesser man, the conventional ensemble of black silk tailcoat and trousers, stiffly starched white shirt, waistcoat, and bow tie was frequently unflattering. Lilly had seen more than a few oversize penguins tonight. But not Robert Fraser.

Heads turned as she approached him, one hand outstretched in greeting. "Good evening, Mr. Fraser."

He didn't respond. Just stared at her, his gaze quizzical. "I beg your pardon," he said at last. "I don't believe we've been introduced."

He didn't remember her.

"I'm Edward's youngest sister. Elizabeth."

Comprehension dawned on his face. Ignoring their whispering, gawking audience, he took her hand in both of his and held it as gently as if she were made out of porcelain.

"Lilly?" was all he said. He had the oddest expression, as if he were pleased to see her, but also, somehow, perplexed. "Of course. I do beg your pardon, Lady Elizabeth. How lovely to see you again."

"Thank you, Mr. Fraser."

He smiled, his eyes crinkling at the corners, and her heart skipped a beat or three. "I feel as if we're on display," he explained, leaning toward her fractionally. "Is there anywhere . . . ?"

"I agree, it *is* excessively warm in here," she said in a carrying tone. "Would you be so kind as to escort me to the balcony?"

At his nod, Lilly offered her arm and led him through the crush of guests to the sanctuary of the balcony. Stepping outside, she let the cool evening air wash over her for a moment before speaking again.

"That's better, isn't it? Now we can talk and have no fear of interruption, at least for a few minutes." She walked to a bench at the far end of the balcony and sat, hoping she looked more composed than she felt. He sat next to her, his eyes never leaving her face.

"You must think me the worst sort of fool," he said presently.

"Of course I don't—"

"You grew up. You were a wee girl when I saw you last."

"Not so wee as that. I was nearly thirteen," she reminded him.

"You wore your hair pulled back in ribbons," he insisted. "Your face was covered with freckles."

"That was seven years ago."

"As long as that? How have you been?"

"Very well, thank you. And you? I believe you're a physician now, are you not?"

"I'm a general surgeon at the London Hospital in Whitechapel. I've been there for a little more than six years."

She already knew, for Edward talked about his friend from time to time, and she was an attentive listener. Once, she had looked up the hospital on a map of the city, and had been surprised to see it was hardly more than five miles from Belgrave Square. From the way people talked about the East End, she'd have thought he lived and worked in a foreign country.

"You never thought of returning home to Scotland?"

"Once or twice. But I'm happy enough at the London."

"What sort of work do you do at the hospital?"

"I spend one or two days a week in surgery, learning from the senior doctors at the hospital. The rest of my time is divided between the postoperative wards and the receiving room. But I don't want to bore you. Tell me how you've been."

"Quite well, thank you."

"I feel sure your brother would have told me, but you haven't married, have you?"

"Not yet. Rather a disappointment to my—"

She broke off, her words catching in her throat as she saw her mother advancing purposefully toward them, her gaze sweeping from one side of the ballroom to the other. As Lady Cumberland drew ever closer, Lilly realized she wasn't alone. "Oh, no," she groaned under her breath. "Not him again."

"Who?"

"The young man with my mother. Bertram Fitzallen-Carr. He's a cousin of my brother-in-law Louis."

"He looks like a pleasant enough fellow."

"Pleasant, yes; interesting, no. He's absolutely hopeless at conversation, to begin with. No matter what one says to him, his response is either 'oh, really,' or 'you don't say.'"

She was suddenly aware of the pressure of her tiara and the hairpins that secured it. Massaging her temples with her forefingers, she willed the thrumming pain to subside. In a moment her mother would be at the doors to the balcony and there would be no escape from Bertram's bland ministrations.

Just then, the orchestra finished the sedate waltz it was playing, and almost immediately began a second waltz, this time in the livelier Viennese style. Robbie stepped back and extended his hand to her.

"May I have this dance, Lady Elizabeth?"

In a heartbeat they had stepped through the French doors and were drawn into the throng of couples swirling around the ballroom.

Chapter 2

With each step Robbie felt his grasp on reality slip further away. He'd always hated dancing, for he'd never, by his own estimation, been much good at it, but this was sublime.

Lady Elizabeth could not have been more different from the girl he'd met seven years ago in Cumbria. The Lilly he'd known then had been all freckles and pigtails, elbows and knees, hesitant and gangly and endearingly unpretentious. If he'd ever thought of her in the intervening years, it was as that awkward child. Never like this. Never as a woman grown, a woman so beautiful she stole the breath from his lungs.

Memories crowded upon him. They'd gone on a picnic the weekend of his visit to Cumbermere Hall, a picnic so colossally elaborate that he had, at first, been dumbstruck by the sheer extravagance of it. High in the fells above the great house, an army of servants had erected an enormous pavilion, which had been furnished with tables and chairs and even a chaise longue; underfoot, priceless Oriental rugs had been scattered over the rough ground of the heath. The entire two-room cottage where he'd lived as a child, where his mother still lived, could have fit inside with room to spare.

A second, smaller pavilion had been devoted to the food for their luncheon. There'd been platter upon platter of beef, chicken and game, innumerable pies and salads, and even, he recalled, a silver tray piled high with chilled, dressed lobster. For those with a sweet tooth, there were cakes and custards and mountains of exotic hothouse fruits. And everywhere there had been footmen, perspiring in their livery, with bottomless magnums of champagne.

After the meal, he and Lilly had gone for a walk to some nearby ruins. She'd confided to him her dreams for her future, her eyes bright with delight and anticipation. She had talked excitedly of Marie Curie, Elizabeth Garrett Anderson, Beatrice Webb. She had told him that she planned to travel the world, attend university, and then become a scientist, or perhaps a crusading journalist; she hadn't yet made up her mind.

The trouble was that her parents were unwilling to even think of her going away to school, but she was certain she would wear them down in time.

He had listened, yes. Listened and hadn't dared to tell her the truth, for he'd seen what happened to the pedigreed sisters of his schoolmates. Girls like Lilly didn't go to school. They didn't go on adventures and they didn't grow up to be women like Marie Curie. They made their debut, they married, they had children, and that was more or less it.

Unwilling to be the one to deflate her dreams, he'd instead suggested she ask her parents for an academically minded governess, one who would implement a more rigorous course of study than her existing feather-brained tutor could manage. He'd even gone with her to talk to Edward about their plan. But then he'd returned to Oxford and had forgotten all about her.

His insides curdled with shame. What kind of man had he been, to listen and sympathize and then walk away without a backward glance? Though he was ignorant of the details of her life in recent years, he was all but certain that her youthful dreams had not come true.

The proof was in her eyes. Their remarkable light had dimmed; certainly he saw little evidence of it tonight. Caution, not hunger, now informed her gaze.

The waltz finished with one final flourish, and he noted with relief that the formidable Lady Cumberland was nowhere in sight. "Let's go sit in the blue drawing room," Lilly suggested. "We can talk there without being overheard."

They found a window seat at the far end of the room, wide enough for them to sit at an acceptably remote distance from each other.

"I gather there is no fresh news from Vienna," she began.

"No, not tonight. What do you think will happen next?"

She looked surprised, as if no one had yet thought to ask her opinion. "I'm not sure. Edward thinks war is inevitable."

"It's only inevitable if enough people believe it to be so."

"Yes, of course. I only wish . . . it's just that everyone seems so set on it. As if it will somehow be the solution to our differences with Germany. As if it's something that will make *us* better."

"Only men who've never been to war can think it noble. And as it's been more than a decade since South Africa—"

"I know. But it's not only the young men who think so."

"You mean Kipling and the like."

"They speak of it as something beautiful, but how can it be beautiful? Has any war ever been fought where no one was killed?"

"You don't think it noble to die on the battlefield?"

"Nobler to die in one's bed after a long and happy life."

"I agree with you. Likely I'm the only person here who does."

"What will you do, if it comes to war?"

"I'll join the medical corps. What else could I do? I'd make a terrible soldier. What will you do?"

Once again, his question appeared to take her by surprise. "I beg your pardon?"

"Will you do any sort of war work? Join a voluntary aid detachment, that sort of thing?"

"I hadn't . . . I mean, I've never considered it. I doubt *I* could do anything to help."

"Because you're a woman? Rubbish. This is the twentieth century. Women can achieve anything they set their minds to do. Once we're at war and the men are off fighting, women will be needed here at home to do all sorts of important things."

"I should love to help, really I would, but—"

"Elizabeth! There you are!"

Lilly's mother was advancing upon them, her voice glacial with irritation. "I have spent an entire *quarter* of an *hour* searching for you, Elizabeth."

Robbie stood, offering his hand to Lilly as she rose, then turned to Lady Cumberland. "Good evening, ma'am." Seven years had not served to improve the countess's temperament or character, he thought dispiritedly. If anything, she was even worse than he'd remembered.

"Mr. Fraser," she greeted him. "How good of you to join us this evening. Pray forgive me for the interruption," she continued, "but I cannot allow Elizabeth to waste her evening in idle chitchat." Lady Cumberland turned to the young man at her side. "Mr. Fitzallen-Carr, I believe you've been searching for a partner for the next dance. Be so kind as to escort my daughter into the ballroom."

There was nothing to be done. The odious Bertram took Lilly's hand and propelled her across the room, though it was clear she didn't want to go; was, in fact, resisting with every step. And all Robbie could do was stand there, impotently, and watch as she was led away.

As she and Bertram began to waltz, Lilly strained to catch a glimpse of Robbie and her mother. It was difficult to see them at this distance, but they seemed to be speaking. Or were they? Mama was not even looking at Robbie, and actually seemed to have turned away from him. He was looking straight ahead, his eyes unseeing, his expression set and grim. Lilly craned her neck, straining to see more, but only succeeded in stumbling badly.

It took several minutes for her to extricate the heel of her shoe from the train of her gown, then further precious seconds to successfully plead exhaustion and make her escape. She tried not to run as she entered the blue drawing room, only to find that her mother and Robbie were nowhere in sight.

Telling herself not to panic, she moved from one reception room to the next, scanning the crowd for a glimpse of his golden hair, hoping against hope to find him in the green drawing room, or perhaps the hall, or the far side of the ballroom, or the balcony. But he was gone.

Disappointment, acute and bitter, rose in her throat. Was it something she had said, or done? Why on earth had he left without saying good-bye? Longing, now, for the evening to be at an end, she returned to the ballroom, intent on making her way upstairs. She'd only taken a few steps when she heard her name being called. She turned, her heart pounding, and saw that it was Edward.

"There you are, Lilly. Champagne?"

"Yes, please." She took the glass he offered and downed its contents in a few gulps.

"Steady on. I don't want to end my evening by carrying you upstairs. Is anything the matter?"

"I'm fine," she reassured him. "Just thirsty. I was wondering . . . have you seen Robbie?"

"Oh, right. I was supposed to tell you."

"Tell me what?"

"He was very sorry, but he had to leave."

"Did he say what it was?"

"No, just that he had to go, wished me and Helena all the best, would see me soon, et cetera. Why do you ask?"

Lilly inspected her champagne coupe, wishing intensely that it weren't empty. "No reason, really. It's only that . . . did he seem at all upset?"

"No, not at all. Seemed perfectly fine." Edward looked at her closely, his interest piqued. "Is anything the matter?"

"I can't help worrying . . ."

"About what?"

"Mama saw us sitting together, and of course she interrupted. She had that awful Bertram Fitzallan-Carr with her—"

"Louis's cousin? The one with practically no chin?"

"Yes, him. She sent me off to dance with him. And I'm almost certain I saw her speaking to Robbie after we left."

"They could hardly stand next to one another and not exchange a word."

"Yes, I know. But he had the oddest expression on his face. It was almost as if she'd struck him a blow."

"And now you're concerned that Mama might have said something unfortunate?"

"Yes, and that ruins everything, because we were only having a friendly chat with one another."

"I shouldn't worry about it. Most likely he looked upset because of something entirely unrelated. Perhaps he remembered something he was supposed to do, or some patient that needed his care?" He squeezed Lilly's hand reassuringly. "You'll soon see him again. There's the wedding, to begin with, and after that I'm sure we can contrive a meeting or two."

"But once we're at war, and you're all gone to Europe—"

"For a matter of months, no more. We'll all be home and wreathed in glory by Christmas at the latest."

"I suppose you're right."

"Of course I am. So stop fretting and go dance with someone."

"I don't know, Edward. I'm feeling very tired. Would you mind if I said good night?"

"Not at all. I'll cover for you with Mama if she comes looking."

"You are a dear."

"I try, Lilly. I do try."

He'd found Edward and made his excuses; had retrieved his coat and hat and made his way into the street. Had walked the half mile to Victoria Station, produced tuppence for an Underground ticket, and boarded the first District line train heading east. He would have preferred to take a taxi home, but finding a cabbie who could be persuaded to make the trip into the East End, he knew from experience, was next to impossible.

The stations blurred by, a tangle of fizzing electric lights, garish advertisements, and the impassive faces of strangers.

St. James' Park. Westminster. Charing Cross.

Lady Cumberland had been polite enough, but he'd seen the spark of triumph in her eyes. Her daughter's engagement would be announced soon, once the festivities for Edward and Helena were concluded. The young man, Quentin Something-Something, was the son of dear friends. Practically family already. So very suitable for Elizabeth.

Temple. Blackfriars.

He ought to have expected it. Lilly was beautiful, charming, and sociable, the sort of woman any man in possession of his senses would wish to have at his side. Perhaps she had simply forgotten to mention her fiancé. Perhaps he'd only imagined the glimmer of discontent hiding behind her smile.

Mansion House. Cannon Street.

He'd stammered his congratulations. Known he couldn't bear to stay for another minute.

Monument. Mark Lane.

Almost home now.

Aldgate East. St. Mary's.

He'd look in on his patients. Write up that stack of charts on his desk. Try to forget. Put from his mind the memory of Lilly's beauty, the sound of her voice, the warmth of her lovely eyes.

Whitechapel.

At last. He was back where he belonged.

Chapter 3

5 October 1914

My dear Lilly,

Yes, this letter still finds me in the delightful surroundings of Barrow-in-Furness. What could be more charming than a wet, cold, and very smelly encampment full of men who are bored senseless of drills, drills, and yet more drills? Every last one of us is champing at the bit to be done with this. We know it won't be long—it can't be long, given the state of affairs in France and Belgium. But still we wait for our orders to pack up and take ship for France, and an endless wait it is.

I've been promoted up to captain—no idea why, really. Likely they thought the lieutenants were a bit thick on the ground and needed thinning out. I only hope it doesn't mean they're fitting me up for a desk job behind the lines. Of course I wouldn't put it past Mama to try to ensure something of the sort, but I'll fight it to my dying breath. My place belongs alongside my men and she ought to know it.

Thank you, my darling girl, for the parcel of books and magazines and the seedcake from Cook. I have the scarf you made tucked around my neck as I write. I know you said you aren't a champion knitter, but I think it's perfect, dropped stitches and all.

If you are speaking to Helena, please apologize that I haven't yet responded to her letters. Though bored, I am nonetheless very busy and haven't as much time for correspondence as I would like.

Almost forgot—you asked after Robbie. Lucky man is in France already, working at a hospital in Versailles. (Not the palace proper!) No doubt he'd be glad to hear from you. Capt. Robert Fraser, RAMC, No. 4 General Hospital, 1 boulevard de la Reine, Versailles, France.

I'll sign off now—will let you know straightaway when we get our marching orders.

Love to all at home,

Edward

It was difficult to believe that little more than two months had passed since the declaration of war. When Lilly's father had announced the news to the family, at breakfast that August morning, her instinctive reaction had been one of horror. She didn't know much about war; had no memory of it, for she'd been a little girl at the time of the hostilities in South Africa. But she was certain its outbreak should not be an occasion for rejoicing, despite her parents' delighted reaction to the news.

It was a relief, to be sure, after all the months of waiting and wondering. And it was hard not to be pulled along by the joy that greeted the war's arrival. Cheering crowds and marching bands, and even poets proclaimed it glorious, so who was she to doubt?

Before the week was out, Edward had joined up. Deaf to their parents' protests that he might safely wait out the war, he became a lieutenant in the Cumberland battalion of the Border Regiment and was posted forthwith to Barrow for his training. Mama had taken to her bed for an entire two days after his farewell.

Lilly had been fearful, too, but had done her best to hide it when Edward had said good-bye. He, and all his friends, seemed to regard the war as a great lark. To them it was a blessed chance to do, to act, to be forged by the crucible of war into better men. An improbable notion, Lilly was sure, though she could understand its appeal. What had any of them actually *done* with their lives thus far, despite the riches and privileges heaped upon them?

She wasn't surprised to learn that Robbie had joined up and was putting his considerable talents to use. If there were one man she knew who had made something of his life, it was Robbie. And she wasn't alarmed to learn that he was in France, for he wouldn't be fighting; would, instead, be working behind the lines in a hospital, as safe as any man might be in a country that was at war.

It would be imprudent to write to Robbie. Her parents would be appalled by her audacity, should they ever find out. Busy as he must surely be with his work at the hospital, he might be none too pleased to receive a letter from a near stranger.

And there was the sticky question of what she would actually say in a letter. What did she have to impart that would be of interest to him? Descriptions of bandage-rolling parties and the sudden scarcity of petrol hardly made for a fascinating correspondence.

She hardly knew him. He was Edward's friend, not hers. He'd thought so little of her, the night of the ball, that he'd left without saying good-bye.

But he'd been so kind. On that Easter weekend so long ago, he had treated her not only as an intelligent person but also, astonishingly, as an equal. His words, his confidence in her abilities, had inspired her.

With the help and encouragement of Miss Brown, the governess Edward had found for her, she'd applied herself to her studies. She'd read as widely as her parents' limited library and her even more limited pocket money had allowed. When her father had objected to her unseemly interest in his daily newspapers, she'd convinced Mr. Maxwell to have them rescued before they were put in the rubbish. Cocooned in her room, she had read *The Times* and the *Daily Mail* and daydreamed about journeying to the exotic, far-off places described in their pages.

None of her dreams had come true. She hadn't traveled the world. She hadn't gone to university. She had yet to do an honest day's work and probably never would. If Robbie thought of her at all, it was probably as a failure. She'd been graced with every imaginable material and social advantage, and what had she done with such good fortune? Nothing. Nothing at all.

And yet . . . he had seemed delighted to see her again. He'd welcomed her questions and her interest in his life. Surely it couldn't hurt to send a brief letter, one that asked after his health, his work. It wouldn't take him long to read and it might, just might, offer him some small comfort at the end of a long day.

31, Belgrave Square
London SW1
7 October 1914

Dear Captain Fraser,

Just now I received a letter from Edward with your direction in France, and as he suggested you would be happy to receive a letter or two from home, I thought you might be glad to receive this. Of course I am sure you are terribly busy taking care of the wounded and haven't much time at all to yourself, but all the same I hope you know how very proud we all are of you and your colleagues.

Life here goes on much the same as always, though the streets are full of men in uniform and the cost of things such as petrol and sugar and meat have increased out of all expectation. Still I suppose it is the price we must pay if our troops are to have the foodstuffs and equipment they require.

Edward is keen as mustard to be over in France, as I imagine are most men in uniform right now. The papers still seem quite certain that the war will be over soon, but it seems to me that such a prediction is unlikely to come true, though of course I know little of such things. If the war is to end, one of two things must happen: both sides must come to the mutual conclusion that the fighting must stop (this I think impossible given the level of enmity) or one side must conclusively prevail over the other on the battlefield. One hardly needs to be a major general to know that has not yet happened nor is it likely to occur anytime soon.

I do hope you are well and not too exhausted by your work. Are you in need of anything to read? I only just sent Edward a parcel of books and magazines and should be delighted to do the same for you.

Yours faithfully,
Lilly

Chapter 4

"Captain Fraser?"

"Yes, Corporal?"

"You've some letters from home, sir. I popped them on top of the other papers on your desk."

Another stack of post, God help him. He'd only been here six weeks and the letters from home had been unceasing. All well meaning, all blissfully ignorant of what was really happening in France and Belgium, and he'd had to force himself to reply.

After a while he'd begun writing essentially the same letter over and over. Thank you for your good wishes. Yes, I am busy, but the hospital in which I work is a fine one and handsomely equipped. No, there is nothing I require by way of personal items or supplies for the hospital. Thank you again for thinking of me, yours faithfully, and so on and so forth.

He'd known it would be bad when he signed up, having read enough about the commission of recent wars to expect the worst. The problem lay in his expectations and the way in which they'd been flattened by the reality that faced him in the wards each day.

As a surgeon, he knew how to right what was wrong, repair what was injured, and find a way to create something whole out of something broken, even if the damage at first appeared irreparable. But how could he fight against an enemy that was invisible?

Some called it gas gangrene. Some called it enteric fever. No matter the name, it was his enemy, and it was killing his patients, one after another, no matter how long and carefully he labored to repair their wounds.

A day, a week, a fortnight after surgery, often for the most minor of injuries, the fever set in. Then came the infection, feral and relentless, poisoning its victim inch by agonizing inch.

They'd tried everything to eradicate it, scrubbing the wards from top to bottom every day, burning the uniforms the men arrived in, washing their skin with carbolic solution before surgery; they'd even set up special isolation wards for men who showed signs of fever. All to no avail.

He sat at his desk and took up the bundle of letters. One from his mother, two from colleagues at the London, and the fourth . . . he didn't recognize the handwriting. Feminine, almost calligraphic. He turned over the envelope and saw the address embossed on the back: Ashford House, Belgrave Square, London.

Now, this was something entirely unexpected. A letter from Lilly.

He tore it open and read it through, too quickly. Why had she written to him? Was it out of a sense of duty or Edward having asked her to do so? Or had she taken it upon herself to write, to establish some kind of contact with him?

He read it again. No mention of the fiancé.

No matter the reason. She had written, she seemed to be sincere, and so he might as well reply.

No. 4 General Hospital
Somewhere in France
16 October 1914

Dear Lady Elizabeth,
  Thank you for your letter. You do find me well, and not especially tired, although I'm at a low ebb because of some difficulties we are encountering

in the postsurgical treatment of soldiers at our hospital.

I've been in France for a little more than a month, having been sent here via Le Havre after three weeks of officer training. Drill, endless rules and regulations to memorize, and, worst of all, target practice, at which I took great pride in my poor showing. When I left for France I packed my service pistol into my locker and I earnestly hope it remains there for the duration.

In our spare moments we performed medical inspections on recruits, with only the finest physical specimens accepted for duty in France. His Majesty's Army is choosy now, but the day will come when it will gladly accept any man between sixteen and sixty, no matter his height, health, or accomplishments. Mark my words.

The hospital where I work is located in a hotel that's been taken over by HM Forces for the duration. It's by far the grandest building in which I've ever lived or worked, not the equal, of course, to your father's houses but at least a thousand times nicer than my little flat in Whitechapel or the aging wards of the London. Certainly the supply of hot water to the bathrooms is far more reliable.

All the furniture and artwork was removed before we set up here, but the building itself is beautiful, with high ceilings and immense windows (well taped in case of stray enemy munitions) and gardens that stretch nearly as far as the eye can see.

As quarters, I have a smallish room, set on a high floor, with a fine view that I do not admire as often as I should. I share it with one other surgeon, a decent fellow, but he talks in his sleep and has a snore that would wake the dead. Fortunately most nights I'm tired enough that I have no difficulty falling asleep.

The food here is good—cooked, alas, by RAMC canteen workers and not the kitchen's original French staff—but there is plenty to eat and they always have something available when we work into the wee hours.

With that I'll say good-bye for now. We have another lot of wounded coming in and I should probably take care of some paperwork before I go into theater again.

As I said, I am delighted that you wrote and I look forward to our correspondence.

Yours faithfully,

R. Fraser

31, Belgrave Square
London SW1
27 October 1914

Dear Captain Fraser,

I was delighted to receive your letter, all the more because we are just now returned from Portsmouth, where we bid farewell to Edward yesterday. We were only able to visit with him for a few minutes, it was so busy at the port, but I was glad of the chance to see his face and hear his voice before he embarked for France. He told us his battalion was likely to be attached to one of the Indian brigades, as several have recently been recalled to Europe, but beyond that he had little notion of where he was to be sent next. Simply "somewhere in France," as the saying goes.

It was pretty hard to see him go, though as Edward deplores tears or any kind of fuss, I was careful not to allow myself to become overset. But knowing what he faces in the coming months, the kind of danger he will encounter, the horrors he will see—all of that weighed upon me quite dreadfully as I said good-bye.

Of course my troubles are as nothing compared to your present worries. You mentioned some

*difficulties regarding the care of patients. Do you
have all the equipment and supplies that you need?
Are there enough doctors and nurses to care for the
wounded? I so wish there were something I might
do, some way in which I might help. Even if it is
only to listen, and in some way bear witness to the
hardships you are suffering.*

*I do have some welcome news, for yesterday I
received a letter from Miss Brown, my former governess and my dear friend for many years. She
became a part-time nurse with the VAD before the
war, in the spring, when the call first went out for
volunteers, but recently decided she ought to be
doing more. So she gave her notice to Miss Rathbone (a city councillor in Liverpool for whom she
has worked since leaving me) and, with that lady's
blessing, has been accepted as a nurse trainee at the
Great Northern Central Hospital on the Holloway
Road. It is rather a leap of faith for Charlotte, leaving a secure (and paid) position to work for nothing
as a volunteer nurse, but she hopes to be offered a
paid position once she has qualified.*

*I don't believe you have ever met Miss Brown,
but I'm certain you would like her immensely. She's
of an age with you and Edward, I believe, and terribly well read and knowledgeable about so many*

things. But it hasn't made her tiresome or pedantic at all; quite the contrary, for she has such a warm way about her and is endlessly curious about the people she meets. No matter where she goes she is always making new friends—a person need only sit next to her on the omnibus and within five minutes she has learned their entire life story. I imagine this will serve her in good stead as a nurse.

My own contributions to the war effort remain embarrassingly modest. Mama and Papa will not allow me to join any of the relief agencies, although both my sisters hold positions in the VAD. Once a week I'm allowed to attend a gathering of worthies as we pack parcels for the BEF, roll bandages, or unravel old jumpers to scavenge yarn for knitting. I've nearly finished knitting my third scarf— anything more complicated, such as socks or mittens, is sadly beyond my limited talents.

I thought of sending you a scarf but presumably your mother keeps you well supplied with such things. In lieu of that, I enclose a jar of damson plum jam. I helped (a very little) when Cook made it last week and I do hope you enjoy it. The plums were from the weekly hamper of produce sent from Cumbermere Hall, and were sweet enough to eat out of hand.

And now I shall say au revoir. Please let me know if there is anything else I might send that would aid in your comfort or that of your colleagues and patients.

Yours faithfully,
Lilly
(as I do hope I can encourage you to
address me from now on)

No. 4 Gen. Hosp.
Somewhere in France
2 Nov. 1914

Dear Lilly,

It's nearly midnight as I write this, having discovered your letter waiting for me when I finished rounds just now. As I will be up with the larks tomorrow, I thought it best to reply straightaway.

Thank you very much for the plum jam. I am tempted to open it now, just to sample it, but on second thought will keep it for breakfast.

Today was endlessly long and utterly disheartening. In answer to your question about the difficulties to which I alluded in my last letter: no, unfortunately, there is nothing you can send or do that can help. Though I thank you for asking.

The difficulties are being caused by what some here are terming an epidemic of enteric fever, although I don't believe it can be so easily classified. No matter its name, it is a terrible thing, this fever and infection that kills men who ought to live, men whose injuries simply are not severe enough to be fatal—but still they die.

I believe (as do most others; I am no visionary) that this disease originates in exceedingly small organisms, bacilli, which live in the soil. When men are injured and their wounds are contaminated with this soil, the bacilli take over and render ineffective whatever other care we may offer. It is, I fear, as simple as that. We have no vaccine, no drug, no course of treatment that can halt the disease once it has set in.

Today I saw a man at eleven o'clock in the morning; to all appearances he was recovering well from surgery two days earlier. By one o'clock he had begun showing symptoms of infection. By midnight he was dead.

The frustration I am experiencing is quite terrible, Lilly, and I am very sorry to burden you with the knowledge of it. I hope you will write to me again; if you do so, I promise to answer with prettier words.

Let us talk instead of the work you are doing. You said your mother won't let you become a full-fledged member of any of the services, which is unfortunate, but perhaps you might consider less formal channels? Once Miss Brown is established in London, for example, you might ask her if there's a need for volunteers to read to the wounded, or help them write home to their families. The days pass slowly for men in the convalescent wards, particularly those whose families live far away and are unable to visit.

As I have scarcely set foot outside the hospital for some weeks now, I have no souvenirs to offer you. But I thought you might like this sprig of leaves from one of the linden trees that grow in the hotel garden. Not in bloom at this time of year, so there isn't any scent to speak of, but the trees themselves are lovely.

Yours faithfully,

Robbie

(no more "Captain Fraser," I beg you)

Chapter 5

North London
November 1914

Lilly surveyed the remains of her and Charlotte's afternoon tea. Only crumbs were left where, minutes before, there'd been a tower of ham and tongue sandwiches and, on a second plate, a small mountain of Dundee cake. But there was still plenty of tea left in the pot.

Charlotte looked very well, though as usual her clothes were at least a year out-of-date, and much plainer than anything Lilly herself would have chosen. Her simple white shirtwaist with middy collar was unadorned, as was her slim-fitting, ankle-length skirt. But her felted wool hat was pretty enough, its wide upturned brim faced in navy corduroy, and her overcoat was of a smart military cut.

It was the first time the women had seen each other since Charlotte's arrival in London a fortnight earlier. At first her weekly half days off had been occupied in finding lodgings and getting settled, but once that was accomplished, she had written to Lilly and asked if they might meet at the A.B.C. tea shop, just down the Holloway Road from the hospital, on Wednesday next.

Lilly's mother made only a token protest at the notion of her traveling all the way to north London for tea, although she did insist that Lilly take along one of the maids. After recovering from the excitement of the taxi ride, Sarah Jane had settled herself at a nearby table and had happily accepted Lilly's offer of a pot of tea and a slice of seedcake.

"Do you want anything else, Charlotte? Would you like a cream bun?"

"No, I mustn't. Otherwise Matron will find me sleeping in the linen closet before the end of the afternoon. Never mind that I had the entire morning off."

"Is she very fierce?"

"Not at all. Crusty on the outside, of course, otherwise she'd never keep all of us in line. One has to respect her for that. She's very fair, I think, especially to those girls who work hard."

"I can't imagine how one could be a nurse and *not* work hard."

"There are some who try, but they don't last long. They take one look at a really nasty wound, or at some of the messes they're expected to mop up, and they either faint dead away or scurry for the exit."

"I expect you're better off without them."

"I expect so, too," Charlotte agreed, pouring them both another cup of tea.

"How far is it to your lodgings?"

"Not far. I found a room in a little house in Camden Town, just two miles down the road. Clean and not too dear, and the landlady is a character. One of those busybodies who means well. You know the sort."

"Have you heard from your parents?"

"Like clockwork. I write every few days, mainly to reassure them I haven't been corrupted by my new profession, nor have I fallen victim to some rogue contagion. It's the least I can do, given that they're supporting me. So embarrassing to be accepting money from my parents at my age, but it is for a greater good."

"And it's only for a short time, you said. Just until you're qualified, and then you can hope for a proper position."

"Yes. Though there are no guarantees."

"I'm very proud of you. To have left everything behind, your work and friends, all to come here and work so terribly hard."

"Thank you, but it's nothing more than tens of thousands of other women are doing." She fixed Lilly with a penetrating look that was intensified by her dark brown eyes and the lenses of her spectacles. "Which brings us to the question of what *you* plan to do. You've talked and talked about war work, told me again and again that you want to do your part to help, but you haven't done one single thing toward that end. At least, not so far as I know."

"I want to, I do, but—"

"But?"

"Mama won't hear of it. If I so much as say two words on the subject, she cuts me to shreds. And I've no qualifications, no actual skills to offer. What could I really do? I could never become a nurse like you. I know they would never take me."

"How do you know? Have you ever asked?"

"Well, no," Lilly began, feeling rather beleaguered.

"Then do it. I'm not saying this to make you feel badly, or to shame you in any way. I know very well how obstructive your mother can be. But if you want this, truly want this, then you have to *act*."

"You're right. Of course you're right."

Charlotte took several sips of tea before speaking again. "What does Captain Fraser say?"

"He's offered some suggestions. He thought I might read to the wounded, or help them write letters."

"An excellent idea. Though you'll need to start by joining the VAD."

"Mama is quite opposed to that. I don't understand why, since both my sisters belong."

"They're married, and presumably answer to their husbands. So she wasn't able to forbid them."

"I suppose."

"Perhaps you should just find yourself a husband. That's the easy solution. And your mother would be so pleased."

"*Charlotte.* You, of all people—"

"What do you mean, 'of all people'? I've never said I don't wish to marry."

"But I thought . . ."

"You and everyone else. My parents included. I've nothing against marriage, I'll have you know. The problem is that I've never met anyone I wanted to marry."

"Never?"

Charlotte looked away, out the window to the busy road beyond. "Not anyone I *could* marry. Which is different, I know."

"I could marry Captain Fraser," Lilly burst out. "I mean, that is, if I ever were to marry, he is the sort of man I would like. Not that he's interested in me, for I'm fairly certain he's not. But if he were . . ."

Charlotte abandoned her contemplation of the traffic on the Holloway Road. "In all those letters, he's said nothing? Intimated nothing?"

"We truly are nothing more than friends. I ought not to have said that just now. It was silly of me."

"Not at all. And it seems to me, though I've never met him, that he is exactly the sort of man who would suit you. If you were ever to decide to marry."

"He's so different from other men I've met. My parents think him common, because of his family, but he's nothing of the sort. He's brave, and terribly intelligent . . . and he hasn't let anything hold him back."

"Exactly. Just as you should be doing."

"You know, he said something to me, the night of Edward and Helena's engagement ball. He said it was the twentieth century and that women could and ought to do anything they wished to do. I've never forgotten it."

"But you did forget. That's why you're still under your mother's thumb, and why you're still sitting at home feeling sorry for yourself instead of doing what you know is right."

"You're right."

"Of course I am. So what shall you do?"

"I . . . I'm not certain."

Charlotte peered at Lilly over the top of her spectacles, fixing her with a steady, disbelieving stare. It was the same look she had often employed when they were still governess and pupil and Lilly had offered an unconvincing or ill-thought-out reply to a question.

"But I will think on it, I promise. Perhaps the VAD or the FANY to start."

"Excellent. And if their response is disappointing?"

"Then I shall think of something else."

Chapter 6

Belgrave Square, London
December 1914

L illy could always tell when her mother was approaching. It was something about her footsteps; they were so precise and clipped. Relentless, even.

"Elizabeth! There you are."

"Yes, Mama. I've been here since breakfast."

Lilly folded her book into her lap, but not before it caught her mother's attention.

"I see. *Reading.*"

"Yes, Mama."

"Why do you persist in burying your nose in a book all day long? Learning is all very well, Elizabeth, but you cannot expect to find a suitable young man if you hide yourself away."

Lilly bit back her instinctive response that every suitable young man she knew was presently occupied elsewhere, having taken up the call to arms, and counted to ten before responding.

"If I were busy with war work, doing my duty like others are, then I wouldn't need to fill my days with reading."

"Your duty begins and ends with your family."

"But, Mama—"

Lilly's mother walked to one of the windows overlooking the formal gardens, her spine rigid with disapproval. "Pray allow me to continue, Elizabeth. Your father, you and your siblings, our homes; that has been my life's work. And I have devoted the same energy and dedication to it as men bring to their own endeavors. Surely you appreciate what I have done."

"Of course I do. And please believe me when I say that I am grateful. But—"

"But what, Elizabeth?"

What could she say? Of course Lilly felt grateful, but she also knew, to the core of her being, that her mother's life was not for her.

"Only that you make it sound as if I'm rejecting everything. As if I don't want to be a wife, or a mother. And I do, but not yet. I'm too young—"

"Nonsense. I was eighteen when I married your father, and nineteen when Edward was born."

"Mama, please let me finish," Lilly implored. "You know that's not what I want, not yet. Perhaps I will, when the war is over. Until then—"

Her mother crossed the room and sat next to Lilly, taking her hands in a fervent grasp. Lilly was astonished; Mama never touched her, apart from the occasional kiss on the cheek.

"I realize it is difficult, my dear. I do. Practically every girl your age seems to be wearing a uniform. But they are ordinary girls, common girls. And you are not. You are meant for *more*."

Before Lilly could answer, her mother rose from the sofa and moved across the room, taking a moment to compose herself. Lilly knew, from many years of observation, that this was essentially an internal process, a swift reordering and leveling of her mother's mental equilibrium. Another woman might be so crass as to smooth her hair, or straighten her stays, but not Mama.

"Enough of this, Elizabeth. We are expected at luncheon with Lady Walsingham, or have you forgotten?"

"No, Mama."

"Then I shall expect you downstairs at half-past twelve and not a moment later. It will take at least a half hour to drive there."

Lilly's imagination sparked to life at her mother's words. "Yes, Mama. May I ask if—"

"Yes?"

"Will we be spending Christmas in Cumbria?"

"Of course we will. Why wouldn't we?"

"Would you mind very much if I stayed on at the Hall after? Rather than return to London with you and Papa?"

"Whatever for?"

"It's quiet there, with less talk of the war. It would be easier, for me, if I were in Cumbria."

"Very well. I suppose you do have a point. Is that all?"

"Yes, Mama."

In Cumbria she would be free to spend her time as she wished. And what she wished, she had only now decided, was to learn how to drive.

Christmas at Cumbermere Hall was a quiet affair, with Edward in France and her sisters in London with their families. Her younger brother, George, had come home from school for a week, and it seemed to Lilly that he had grown at least a foot since the summer.

Her parents stayed until New Year's Day, her brother a day longer, but she let another week pass before she made her move. By then it was clear to Lilly that the household staff had little interest in policing her whereabouts, which meant she could walk and ride the estate grounds without a chaperon. If anyone were to notice that she was spending nearly every afternoon in the company of her father's retired chauffeur, it was nothing out of the ordinary. Certainly she had always tagged along at John Pringle's heels when she was little, so what harm could it do now?

Always known by both names, for reasons Lilly now couldn't recall, John Pringle lived with his elderly parents in a tied cottage on the estate grounds, their reward for a lifetime of service to Lilly's father and grandfather. He was a quiet man, painfully shy, and suffered terribly from the rheumatism that had forced his early retirement from full-time work.

She began by joining him in his tiny garden, helping with the winter crop of vegetables and preparing the beds for spring. And then one day, late in January, the weather was cool and wet, and too miserable for gardening.

"You might as well head back to the big house," John Pringle told her when she knocked on his cottage door. "There's no use going out today."

"What will you be doing instead?"

"I'm thinking to visit the garage and check on the motorcars," John Pringle answered. "The weather's been that damp. If I don't mind them, it'll be the devil's own work to set them to rights again."

"May I come with you?" she asked, her heart pounding. If he were to say no . . .

"Suit yourself. I'm only going to turn over the engines a time or two, make sure they'll still run."

That's how it started. She followed John Pringle around as he looked after the motorcars, watching what he did, listening carefully. When she asked, after a week, if she might try her hand at driving, he didn't say no.

Instead, he ushered her into the stable annex where the estate vehicles had been mothballed for the duration. Surveying the row of motorcars, he circled round each of them, muttering to himself. And then he turned to her, a wide smile on his face, his choice made.

"We'll start you on Lord Ashford's old coupe. A Vauxhall Prince Henry and a real beauty. Dead easy to drive, though the engine is another story. Come on, now. I'll take her round back and we can get started."

John Pringle was the best of teachers, patient and gentle and utterly unflappable. It must have been frustrating work, given that the essential step of getting out of first gear took her nearly a week to master, but he seemed to relish the challenge.

Slowly, over the days and weeks, he taught Lilly how to drive, first on the Vauxhall, then on the other motorcars. He also insisted she learn how to drive the estate's sole lorry, a temperamental four-ton Thornycroft that had a disconcerting habit of slipping the brake and lurching forward just as she was about to finish hand cranking the engine.

Considerably less enjoyable were her lessons in vehicle maintenance, but John Pringle insisted. So she dutifully learned how to strip down an engine and rebuild it, part by part; learned, too, how to change a punctured tire entirely on her own.

Soon she felt quite confident behind the wheel of all the cars; the lorry, too. Past time, then, to apply to the VAD and the FANY for work as a driver. Surely one of them would need her assistance and would offer her a position. Once it was settled, she would tell Edward, for with his support her parents were all but certain to give in, just as they'd done when she'd asked for a governess of her own.

By the summer she'd have found a place for herself in this war. She was certain of it.

Chapter 7

Cumbria, England
March 1915

It had been three weeks since Robbie's last letter. Not an unprecedented length of time, given how erratic the post from France could be, and it was perfectly likely that he had been busy with work at the hospital and hadn't been able to find the time, in recent days, to write to her. But it was worrisome all the same.

As soon as she finished this row, she would set aside her knitting and write to him again. He might not have the time to write to her but she could boast of no such excuse. And he had told her, any number of times, that he keenly anticipated the arrival of her letters.

At first Lilly didn't notice the faint ringing noise in the distance. Only when Mr. Petrie, the underbutler, knocked on the door of the morning room did she recall the existence of the telephone in the library. It had been installed years before but no one ever used it; the post was efficient enough for most occasions, and for anything more urgent a telegram might do.

"I beg your pardon, Lady Elizabeth. There is a telephone call for you from London. From Mr. Maxwell."

An icicle of dread slithered down Lilly's spine. Mr. Maxwell would never place a telephone call without a direct order from her parents. And her parents would only use the telephone in case of dire emergency.

Edward. Something had happened to Edward.

She threw aside her knitting and sprinted along the corridor to the library, to the low table in the corner where the homely apparatus had been installed.

She picked up the receiver, her hand trembling, and held it to her ear.

"Yes?"

"Is that you, Lady Elizabeth?"

"Yes, Mr. Maxwell."

"Lady Cumberland has asked me to inform you—"

A blizzard of static obscured his next words.

"I'm sorry, Mr. Maxwell. I couldn't hear you. Could you repeat what you just said?"

"I beg your pardon. I said that Lady Cumberland has asked me to inform you that she and Lord Cumberland will not be going to Cumbermere Hall for Easter. Her ladyship asks that you return to London instead."

This was the reason for the telephone call? She was being summoned home?

"Very well. Did my mother say anything else?"

"Only that she wishes you to come immediately. On the eleven o'clock train if there are any seats left in first class. You are to bring one of the maids with you, she said. Doris will do."

"I see. Will I be met at the station?"

"Her ladyship says you are to take a taxi from the station. Mr. Petrie will provide you with sufficient funds for the journey."

"Is that all, Mr. Maxwell?"

"Yes, Lady Elizabeth."

"Then I expect I'll see you this evening. Thank you for calling."

Of all the insensitive ways to effect her return to London. Her mother ought to have known that anything beyond a simple letter would be certain to give Lilly a fright. Mama ought to have known, but likely hadn't cared.

Lilly checked the clock on the fireplace mantel: a quarter to ten already. She had precious little time to pack and dress for the journey, alert Doris that they were leaving, and run down to the stables to let John Pringle know she was returning to London.

It was raining, so she threw on her battered old mackintosh and rubber boots and ran across the back courtyard to the stable annex. Though she couldn't see John Pringle, she could hear him fussing away with something in the back. Likely the lorry's carburetor was clogged again.

"John Pringle? It's Lilly."

He emerged from the bonnet of the Thornycroft, a wire brush in one hand and the offending carburetor in the other, an expression of grim satisfaction on his face. "Took me ages to loosen this. Look at all that carbon."

"I can't stay, but I wanted to tell you. I've had a tele-phone call from London."

His face paled. "Not Lord Ashford?"

"No, nothing like that. Thank goodness. No, my parents have asked me to come to them for Easter. I'm not certain when I'll be back. I hope in a few weeks, no more."

"Miss Lilly . . . there's something I need to tell you."

"Yes, John Pringle?"

"The other day, when we were out in the lorry, the vicar saw us. I think he'd been fishing in the stream when we drove over the bridge. He was none too pleased to see you at the wheel."

"He is rather old-fashioned about these things."

"The problem is, Miss Lilly . . . he came to see me after. Said he was going to write to your father. Tell him what you were up to. I didn't think any harm could come of it, when he told me. Thought he was making a fuss over nothing. But now . . ."

"I see."

"Do your parents know about the lessons?"

"I hadn't thought to tell them," she said. A lie: she hadn't wanted to tell them. "That is, I didn't think they would care." Also a lie.

"It might be nothing, you know. They might just be wanting you with them for Easter."

"That's probably it. But all the same . . . I won't let you be blamed for this, John Pringle. I swear I won't."

"Never you mind about me. You've a train to catch. Be off with you now."

"Have a very happy Easter, and please pass on my best wishes to your parents."

"The same to you, Miss Lilly."

She ran back to the house, packed a few things into a valise, and arranged for a carriage to Penrith, her anxiety mounting with every passing minute. Why on earth hadn't she been more careful? Anyone might have seen them. It was a miracle no one had written to her parents before now.

And though she had tried to make light of John Pringle's concerns, she knew very well what was waiting for her in London. Nothing less than disaster.

Lilly had scarcely set foot inside Ashford House before Mr. Maxwell was rushing up to her.

"Lady Elizabeth! Thank goodness you've arrived."

"Is anything wrong, Mr. Maxwell? Surely I'm not that late."

"No, Lady Elizabeth. It's your parents. They're waiting for you in the blue drawing room."

Lilly ascended the stairs, her movements hampered by choking tendrils of dread. Her parents never bothered to greet her when she returned from a visit away.

Her mother was sitting, motionless, at a table in the center of the drawing room while her father paced fretfully behind.

"Mama, Papa—what is it? What has happened?" The room spun before her, and she had to reach for the doorframe to steady herself. "Edward?" she asked, the hollow echo of her voice fracturing the silence of the room.

Her father, hurrying forward, guided her to a chair across the table from her mother. "No, your brother is fine. As far as we know, at least," he clarified. "I'm afraid it is something else."

At last Lady Cumberland looked up, and it seemed to Lilly that her mother now saw her for the first time. From her lap, she produced a stack of envelopes, which she tossed onto the table. "What are these, Elizabeth?"

Lilly picked up the topmost letter and was horrified to see that it, like its fellows, was from Robbie.

"So this is why I haven't heard from him recently. Have you been stealing all my post, or only my letters from Captain Fraser?"

"Be silent!" her mother commanded. "I am saving you from a most unfortunate entanglement. The less you have to do with that man, the better. How long have you been writing to him?"

"You have no right to ask me such—"

"How long?" The vehemence of her mother's voice, so at odds with her typical demeanor, was startling.

"Since the autumn. How long have you been taking them?"

"I have read all your incoming and outgoing post since January, when one of his letters to you was delivered here. I opened it, naturally, and I was appalled. He addressed you by your Christian name, he described things no decent young woman should even know about—"

"He's being honest with me. He respects me."

"He's hardly more than a tradesman, you silly girl. I am acting in your best interests. For you to settle on some nobody—"

"Captain Fraser is worth ten of any of the foppish, empty-headed, chinless dolts you have paraded me past, year after year. If you had any idea of the work he's doing, you wouldn't discount him so easily," Lilly interrupted angrily.

Her mother stared at her in astonishment, unaccustomed to hearing her daughter speak with such passion. Lilly decided she needed to return the discussion to a more even keel.

"I apologize for my outburst, Mama. Yes, I admire Captain Fraser. Yes, we've exchanged a number of letters over the past months. But surely you could see for yourself that they were completely innocuous."

"They were nothing of the sort, which is why your correspondence with him must end."

Before Lilly could protest, her mother launched a fresh salvo. "There's also the matter of this letter from the vicar. Mr. Burgess says he saw you driving the estate lorry."

There was nothing for it but to put on a brave face. "I didn't think it would trouble you, quite honestly. Certainly you've never forbidden me to drive."

"It may not have been expressly forbidden, but your silence on the matter tells me you were quite aware of what my feelings would be. Once again you have demonstrated how duplicitous, how ungrateful—"

"Oh, Mama. Only you could regard something as harmless as driving a motorcar an act of duplicity. Perhaps I should have been more forthcoming with you, I admit. But the two of you persist in treating me like a child, and an empty-headed child at that. I'm twenty years old, nearly twenty-one. It's past time you allowed me the same freedoms as other girls my age."

"Do not attempt to turn the conversation away from your misdeeds, Elizabeth. You realize of course that we shall have to let John Pringle go."

Long seconds passed before Lilly was able to reply. "He's done nothing wrong, and you know it."

Her mother no longer looked at Lilly directly, her eyes focusing instead on a point on the far wall. "Your father and I have agreed to extend him and his family two weeks' notice on their cottage. That is more than generous."

"John Pringle has worked for our family all his life. His parents, too. Yet you mean to turn them out over something so trivial?"

"He ought to have thought of that before blemishing his family's record of service in such a fashion."

Desperate beyond measure, Lilly approached her father, setting a hand on his sleeve. "How can you stand by and let this happen? The Pringles have served you faithfully for generations. To treat them like this is beneath contempt."

But her father, unwilling to intervene, turned away.

A rush of shame swept over Lilly, bitter as gall, poison-sharp in its intensity. That her actions should have resulted in such calamity for the Pringles, that those carefree hours with John Pringle should be responsible for their ruin . . . why had she not seen how her mother would react?

And then, oh God, the realization that she *had* been hoping for just this sort of confrontation with her parents. Had known, but hadn't acknowledged to herself, that it was only a matter of time before open battle commenced.

How could she have been so thoughtless, so selfish? Even worse was the knowledge that there was no going back. No matter how she humbled herself, no matter how she begged for mercy for the Pringles, her mother would never relent.

Her mouth had gone so dry that it was an effort to speak. Somehow she forced the words past her lips. "Will you not reconsider? Allow me to prove I can be trusted? Allow me to show you that John Pringle is innocent of any disloyalty to you and Papa?"

"What would that achieve? You have already proven, time and again, that you cannot be trusted."

"Then I suppose there is nothing more to be said."

"Indeed," snapped her mother. "Return to your room at once."

"I will, but only to collect my things."

"What on earth are you talking about?"

"I am sorry, more sorry than you will ever know. But I cannot live with you like this. Not after what you plan to do to John Pringle and his family. Not when there is so much else I could be doing with my life."

She paused at the door, her knees shaking so hard it was a wonder she still stood upright. Another step and it would be done.

"Good-bye."

Chapter 8

Anger fueled Lilly's retreat upstairs, along the corridor, and into her bedroom, a room that would, in a matter of minutes, be hers no longer. After turning the key in the lock, she collapsed in the slipper chair that had sat by the hearth for as long as she could remember.

Precious minutes evaporated as she fought against a rising tide of panic. Calm down, she told herself. You are not entirely without means. You *can* manage. You *can* do this.

A soft knock sounded at her bedroom door. "Lady Elizabeth?"

"Yes?"

"It's Mr. Maxwell, Lady Elizabeth. Her ladyship has, ah, explained that you will be, well, leaving us. May I offer any assistance? Shall I ring for a taxi?"

Unlocking the door, she took one look at Mr. Max-well's kindly face and found herself blinking back tears. "Yes, a taxi would be very helpful. I'll need a few minutes; I have to pack my belongings."

"Of course, Lady Elizabeth. And if there is anything else I can do, or the rest of the staff . . ."

"Please don't worry about me. I shall be quite all right. I promise you that."

A half hour was all it took for Lilly to parcel her life into one large carpetbag and two small valises. Her plainest skirts and blouses went in the carpet-bag, together with an extra pair of boots and two nightgowns. In the first valise she packed two day gowns, the simplest she had, and enough undergar-ments to see her settled. The second valise held noth-ing but books; she had restrained herself to ten, but the case was still as heavy as an anvil. And that was all, apart from the contents of her jewelry box, which she secreted at the bottom of the carpetbag, together with a bundle of letters from Edward, Robbie, and Charlotte, and a framed photograph of her brother in his uniform.

It was time to go. Gathering up her bags, she left her room for the last time, not allowing herself the luxury of a backward glance.

Seeing her struggling with her luggage on the stairs, Mr. Maxwell rushed forward. "Pray allow me, Lady Elizabeth—"

"Thank you, Mr. Maxwell, but I must learn to manage on my own."

The taxi was waiting outside. As the cabbie loaded her bags into the motorcar's boot, she prepared to say farewell to Mr. Maxwell.

"Do you know where you're going, Lady Elizabeth?"

"I shall go to Miss Brown. I know she'll take me in. And, Mr. Maxwell?"

"Yes, Lady Elizabeth?

"Thank you for everything. You've always been so kind to me. Please say farewell to Flossie and Cook and . . . and everyone else."

He nodded solemnly. "Good-bye, Lady Elizabeth."

The journey to Charlotte's lodgings took much longer than Lilly had expected. Just as she was beginning to fear the driver had lost his way, they turned a corner and pulled up in front of a row of neat Georgian town houses.

"Here we are, miss. Was it number twenty-one you were wanting?"

"Yes, thank you. Would you mind waiting for a moment, just until I see that my friend is home?"

Lilly crossed the street and knocked on the door. There was no answer at first, so she knocked again, this time more forcefully.

"Hold on, hold on!" She heard a voice from somewhere near the back of the house. "Give us a minute, won't you?" At last came the sound of a key being turned, rather laboriously, and of bolts being drawn back.

"Do you have any idea what time it is?" The door, open little more than an inch, revealed nothing of the speaker.

"I beg your pardon, but may I speak to Miss Brown? Is she home?"

"Of course she's home. Who wants to know?"

Best not to use her title, she decided, else risk making an awkward moment even more uncomfortable. "My name is Lilly, ah, Ashford. I'm a friend of Miss Brown's. I do apologize for the lateness of the hour—"

"You might as well come on in, then. No point having the entire street know our business."

Charlotte's landlady opened the door and beckoned Lilly in. With a frantic look back at the waiting taxi, she took a step inside. She'd thought to bring her reticule with her, but all her other belongings were in its boot. If the cabbie were to tire of waiting and drive off—

"Lilly? Is that you?"

Her friend appeared at the top of the stairs, saw the look on Lilly's face, and immediately took the situation in hand. "But you're not late at all! Come in, come in. Is your taxi still waiting?"

"Yes—"

"I'll just run out and pay him. I won't be a moment."

It was one of the longest moments of Lilly's life, made even more excruciating when Charlotte's landlady realized that three pieces of luggage had been removed from the taxi and were being carried in the direction of her front door. Before the landlady could object, the cabbie had deposited the bags in the front hall and was walking away.

"What's with all this?" the woman asked, her round little figure puffing up like a startled pigeon.

Charlotte stepped in front of Lilly, as if to protect her from the onslaught to come. "I'm so dreadfully sorry, Mrs. Collins. I *had* meant to ask you. And then, I must confess, I quite forgot."

"Forgot what?"

"To ask if my friend might stay with me. Only for a few days. She's a lovely girl, Mrs. Collins. Just your sort of person. And so quiet."

"Is she now?"

"Of course I insist on covering any additional costs you may incur."

"How long's she staying?"

"Oh, not long. Isn't that correct, Lilly?"

"Yes, not long at all. Just until . . ."

"You see, Mrs. Collins? And I swear she won't be any trouble at all."

The landlady's expression brightened fractionally. "Stay if you must, then, but keep the noise down. Your friend can sleep on the settee in your room. I'll fetch sheets and a blanket now." She grumped off down the hall, her retreating figure the very picture of indignation.

"Charlotte, I—"

"Hush, now. Wait until we're upstairs."

Charlotte's room, which faced the street, was much larger than Lilly had expected. At one time it must have been the sitting room for the house, and was graced with tall windows and a prettily tiled fireplace. It was sparsely furnished with a single bed against one wall, a narrow settee on the opposite wall, and a sturdy table and two wooden chairs in the center of the room. A Morris chair, its tapestry upholstery faded and slightly threadbare, had been drawn up to the hearth.

Charlotte shut the door decisively, hung up Lilly's coat and hat, and guided her to the seat by the fire.

"Perch here while I get the kettle going. I think we're both going to need a cup of tea."

She lit the flame of the spirit kettle that sat on the table, measured a spoonful of tea leaves into a waiting teapot, then carried one of the chairs across the room so she could sit next to Lilly.

Lilly took one look at her beloved friend, who was regarding her owlishly through the gold-rimmed spectacles she hardly ever took off, and had to blink hard to hold back a rush of tears.

"There, there," Charlotte murmured. "You'll have time for that in a bit. First tell me what happened."

"Mama has been intercepting my post for weeks now. Possibly longer. She admitted to taking Captain Fraser's letters, and I suspect yours as well."

"I was wondering why I hadn't heard from you. Did you only just return from Cumbria?"

"Yes, today. And that's the worst part. You know how John Pringle had been teaching me to drive?"

"Yes, and I couldn't be more pleased. It's exactly the sort of thing you should be doing."

"I'd been making such progress. But then, the other day, our vicar saw me driving the estate lorry."

"Not good. If it's the same vicar I remember."

"Yes, still Mr. Burgess. He wrote to my parents. Mama was so incensed, you'd have thought they'd caught me planning an elopement with the gamekeeper's son."

"Or a dustman's son—"

"Charlotte! This is serious. They're going to sack John Pringle. Turn him and his parents out of their cottage."

"My God."

"We argued. I said the restrictions she and Papa were placing on me were unfair, and unbearable. And that blaming John Pringle was terribly wrong. They disagreed, of course."

"And so?"

"I left. I went upstairs and packed my bags. And then I came here."

"Oh, Lilly."

"I'm so sorry to be inconveniencing you like this."

Charlotte waved off her apology. "Nonsense. I'd have been very hurt if you'd gone to anyone else."

"But your landlady—"

"Isn't bad at all, once you get to know her. You'll have her wrapped around your little finger before you know it."

The kettle was singing, so Charlotte hurried to turn down the flame and fill the teapot. "I shall sort things out with Mrs. Collins. The room down the hall has been empty since her other boarder moved to Brighton a fortnight ago. She charges ten-and-six a week. Will you be able to manage?"

"I think so, though I don't have much money at all. Just a few pounds, perhaps a little more." Lilly went to her carpetbag, unlatched it, and delved deep inside. "But I do have *these*."

A tangle of necklaces, bracelets, earrings, rings, and combs spilled out of the scarf she'd wrapped them in, nearly covering the table, an entrancing array of gold and platinum filigree, glittering gemstones, and luminous pearls.

"Birthday gifts, some pieces I inherited when my grandmother died, one or two things from Edward . . ."

"Do you have any idea how valuable these are, Lilly? I'm no expert, but they must be worth hundreds of pounds, even thousands."

"I know. But I can't keep any of it for myself. It must all go to the Pringles. I am the author of their misfortune, after all."

"Not you, Lilly. Your parents. Remember that."

At that point Charlotte declared a halt to serious discussion, at least until they'd had their supper. Lilly had never eaten so informally: her plate of cheese on toast propped on her knees, a mug of tea at her elbow, her fingers shiny with butter. Even in the nursery she and her siblings had been expected to sit perfectly still at their little table, linen napkins across their laps, sterling silver cutlery clutched in their hands.

"Do you want any more?" Charlotte asked after Lilly had finished her third slice of toast.

"No, thank you. That was lovely. My first meal as a free and independent woman."

"That's the spirit. Now, tell me: What are your plans? What sort of work do you want to do?"

"I was thinking I might find a position with the VAD, or the FANY. Assuming Mama doesn't have me blacklisted."

"You could work as a driver," Charlotte suggested.

"That's my hope. But I'll do anything if it helps Edward. I don't mind how difficult the work is. I'll clean privies if I have to."

"What are you going to tell him?"

Lilly had heard Charlotte speak with that tone of steady and utterly serious purpose many times before. "The truth, I suppose. Although I can't bear the idea of upsetting him further, not when he's so far from home. He has enough to worry about without my adding to his woes."

"For heaven's sake! Why do you persist in wrapping him up in cotton wool?" Charlotte's words felt like a dash of cold water against Lilly's face.

"Wrapping him . . . ?"

"You know perfectly well what I mean. 'Oh, poor Edward, we mustn't upset him. How will he manage? How on earth will he survive?' He's a grown man, and stronger than any of you give him credit for."

Lilly couldn't think of a thing to say. And Charlotte did have a point. Edward had always been the golden child, adored by all, pampered and coddled and indulged by those who professed to love him the most, herself included. It was a miracle that such treatment hadn't turned him into a first-class oaf.

"Lilly?"

"Yes, Charlotte?"

"Please forgive me. I spoke quite out of turn."

"You were right. Are right. And I will tell him the truth. I'll write to him tomorrow."

"And what about Captain Fraser? Will you write to him?"

"Of course. Though he may have given up on me, after writing so often and never receiving anything in return."

"I'm sure he will understand. And I very much doubt he'll have lost interest."

"What do you mean by 'interest'? We're friends, nothing more."

"Are you certain of that? You no longer have your mother standing between you. Why can't there be more?"

"He thinks of me as a sister, that's all. I'm sure of it."

"Well, then. Write as many sisterly letters as you wish. But don't be alarmed if he decides he'd rather have you as his sweetheart than his sister."

"Charlotte!"

"Just you wait. When this war ends, I wager he'll be beating a path to your door."

"I honestly don't think—"

"Shush, now. I have decided to propose a toast." Charlotte raised her mug of tea and tapped it against Lilly's. "To your newfound freedom."

"To my freedom. And to the end of the war. May it come sooner than any of us dare hope."

PART TWO

It had to be got through somehow.
Action, doing one's best, rightly or wrongly,
mistakes or no mistakes, precluded all thought of self,
and drove out fear and anxiety.

—CAPTAIN JOHN A. HAYWARD, Royal
Army Medical Corps

Chapter 9

51st Casualty Clearing Station
Aire-sur-la-Lys, France
October 1916

Robbie stood just outside the operating hut, swaying a little, trying to find his bearings in the thin half-light of dawn. He longed for sleep; was desperate for it. Could almost taste the respite it offered from blood and gore and the agony of others. But the ambulances would be back soon, he needed to see how his patients were faring, particularly the ones just out of surgery, and he had a mountain of case notes and official correspondence to conquer.

So he dragged his weary carcass over to the ward tent, greeted Matron and her nurses, and somehow managed to focus on their reports of his patients' progress. Only one man had died during the night, a stretcher-bearer shot in the neck while helping to retrieve the wounded from no-man's-land. Another letter for him to write to a grieving wife or mother. Another life lost, and to what end?

He'd been quick to volunteer when the first casualty clearing stations had been established, last year, to cover the gap between the frontline aid stations and the base hospitals. He'd worked in the receiving room at the London, after all, attending to victims of motorcar crashes, gas explosions, knife attacks, collapsing buildings, dockside accidents, and nearly every imaginable infectious disease or ailment. There, he imagined, he'd seen the worst.

He had been wrong.

He'd arrived at the 51st CCS one sunny afternoon in June 1915, in the aftermath of someone's asinine decision to send a platoon of Canadians over the top on a bright, clear, moonlit night. Every last man had been felled in a matter of minutes.

After introducing himself to Colonel Lewis and Matron, both of whom appeared exceptionally composed despite the frenzy of activity around them, he was ushered into the operating hut, shown where to gown himself and scrub up, and was presented with his first patient.

It was the Canadians' second lieutenant, hit by grenade fragments, and it had taken Robbie what felt like forever to pick through the wreck of the man's bowels to find the scraps of jagged metal that had torn him apart, and then to repair his viscera and abdominal cavity. It was a miracle the man hadn't died on the table.

As soon as the Canadian had been taken to post-op, another man had been placed on the table in front of Robbie. And then a third, a fourth, a fifth. He'd operated on eighteen men in twenty hours, more surgeries than he would have done in a week at the London, and when the ambulances finally stopped coming, he'd had less than a day to recover before the reception marquee was again filled with stretchers.

He'd never worked so hard, had never been so tired. It was worth it, he knew it was. This was where he belonged, where he could do the most good. So why did he end each day feeling as if he could teach Sisyphus a thing or two about frustration?

Tonight was no different. An hour passed, then another, and still he lingered on in the ward tent, laboring to reduce the pile of military paperwork that threatened to collapse his portion of the surgeons' shared desk.

"Captain Fraser?"

It was Colonel Lewis, likely come to chivvy him to bed, though the OC had been on his feet for every bit as long as Robbie.

"Yes, sir?"

"When was the last time you had leave?"

"I can't recall. Sometime last year."

"Right. Which means you're long overdue for some time off. I can give you ten days, starting on the twentieth."

"But we're shorthanded, sir—"

"Captain Mitchell will be back from leave."

Well, then. He could trust Tom to keep on top of things. "Thank you, sir. I'll just finish off this paperwork."

"Bugger the paperwork. Get to bed, get a decent night's sleep, then send a telegraph to your mother and tell her you're coming home."

"Yes, sir."

Ten days. The most leave he'd had since signing up more than two years ago had been three days. Not long enough to do anything more than take the train to Paris. But ten days was enough for a trip to Scotland, and then . . .

Perhaps a visit with Lilly? Only lunch, or tea, or whatever was considered proper with the youngest sister of one's dearest friend. Certainly not dinner at a restaurant or dancing or an evening at the theater.

Telegraph forms were kept in a pigeonhole above Matron's desk, and ordinarily were reserved for official use. But the OC had told him he might send one to his mother.

He took one and then, hesitating a moment, pulled out a second. The post to England could be unreliable, and he knew there'd been times when Lilly received a bundle of his letters all at once, some of them weeks old. If his letter went astray, and she weren't able to secure a few hours off work, it didn't bear thinking about.

He glanced at the calendar above his desk. If he left on the morning of the twentieth, he'd be back in London by late the following day, in time to take the night train to Glasgow. That would give him six days with his mother and, allowing at least twenty-four hours to return to Aire from London, a slender window on the morning of the twenty-eighth for him to see Lilly.

He couldn't, in good conscience, allow any more than that; not only for his mam's sake, but also for Lilly's. Though she would, he prayed, be happy to meet him for a cup of tea, he had no illusions that she wanted anything other than friendship from him. And there was the matter of that fiancé, God rot his soul, though she'd never once mentioned him in her letters, and he'd never been bold enough to ask. Was it too much to hope that Quentin Whatsit had cried off when Lilly had broken with her parents?

He took up his pencil, schooling his doctor's scrawl to the neatest block letters he could manage, and began to write.

DEAR LILLY. HAVE BEEN GIVEN LEAVE. HOME TO SCOTLAND FIRST. THEN BACK TO FRANCE VIA LONDON VICTORIA MORNING OF OCT 28. LET ME KNOW IF ABLE TO MEET. SEND REPLY TO MRS GORDON FRASER, LANGMUIRHEAD RD, AUCHINLOCH, NORTH LANARKSHIRE, SCOTLAND. WARMEST REGARDS. ROBBIE

Chapter 10

The sun was long gone by the time Lilly trudged up to the door of 21 Georgiana Street and let herself in. It hadn't been up either when she'd left for work that morning.

Not counting the journey to and from work at the Willesden Garage, or her half-hour midday break for dinner, she'd spent ten hours hanging off the back platform of a motorbus, clipping tickets and finding change and offering directions and ignoring the comments, some of them shockingly lewd, from a minority of passengers who were still disconcerted by the sight of female conductors on the trams and buses.

Now all she wanted was a hot bath, assuming Mrs. Collins was in a good mood and let her run one, a plate of hot toast, and an even hotter brick at her feet when she fell into bed. That, and as much sleep as she could manage.

Charlotte was working late, as usual; she'd been transferred to a new hospital that summer and was well down on the pecking order when shift assignments were made. It had been days and days since they'd had a chance to talk, but it did mean that Lilly could go straight to sleep after she'd bathed and eaten, without being tempted to stay up late.

"Is that you, Miss Ashford?" came her landlady's voice from the back of the house.

"Yes, Mrs. Collins. How was your day?"

"Terrible. Boiler stopped working again. And me halfway through the household wash!"

So much for a hot bath. "I'm sorry to hear that. Were you able to get anyone to see to it?"

"Not yet, but I've asked Mr. Pruitt down the road if he might pop by and have a look. He'll come round tomorrow."

"Good luck, Mrs. Collins. I'll be off to bed."

Lilly climbed the stairs, her regulation boots weighing down her every step, and let herself into her room. Switching on the light, she hung up her coat and hat and bent to unlace her boots. Only then did she notice the telegram that had been pushed under her door.

Toast and tea forgotten, she retrieved the envelope from the floor, then sat on her bed and stared at it. Please, oh please, let it not be about Edward, she prayed. And then the realization: it couldn't have anything to do with her brother, for the War Office would send news only to her parents. And Mama and Papa would never bother to contact her, not now.

Could it be?

She tore open the envelope. Yes; it was from Robbie. He was coming home and would be in London the morning of the twenty-eighth. A Saturday, not one of her days off, but she might be able to persuade one of the other girls to take her shift.

Where might they meet? He was returning to France via Victoria Station; there was a Lyons tea shop nearby, she recalled. A perfectly respectable place to meet.

16 October 1916

Dear Robbie,

Such a wonderful surprise to return home from work and find your telegram waiting for me. I am so glad your OC feels able to spare you and that you will be able to see your mother.

I am free the morning of the twenty-eighth. Let's meet at the Lyons tea shop on Victoria Street (at Palace Street) at eleven o'clock. If either the venue or time doesn't suit, do let me know.

Please pass on my regards to your mother.

Your affectionate friend,
who is very much looking
forward to seeing you again,
Lilly

It had been harder than she'd thought, finding someone to take on her shift, but Betty had agreed eventually, with the added inducement that Lilly would cover two additional shifts at any such time as Betty asked.

She'd barely slept last night and had scarcely been able to eat a thing at breakfast. Before that, there'd been the question of what to wear. After extensive consultation with Charlotte, Lilly had decided on her plain gray wool skirt, which she had recently shortened to a more fashionable calf-grazing length, and a simple white blouse. Over it she wore her best coat, a gray wool, which buttoned tightly at the waist. Bought secondhand from the dressmaker around the corner, it still looked like new. Crowning it all was her hat, a recent extravagance, made of black felted wool and trimmed with a wide ribbon of charcoal-colored satin that Charlotte had unearthed from her mending basket. Nothing about her ensemble was particularly stylish, but it looked well on her and was suitable for the occasion.

A few years before, she would have turned up her nose at such simple clothes, but she had changed since then, and thank God for that. The Lilly of two years past had been oblivious to her actions and the effects they had on others, as evidenced by the disaster that had befallen the Pringles.

She'd done her best to atone for that, selling her jewelry and insisting that John Pringle use the proceeds to buy a cottage in Penrith. With the additional help of a character reference from Edward, he had found work at a motor garage and the family had avoided destitution, though not before suffering weeks of agonizing uncertainty and public humiliation.

Those first months after she'd left home had been exceedingly unpleasant; a fitting punishment, she told herself, for her misdeeds. To begin with, it had taken much longer than she'd expected to find work, for none of the women's services would accept her without formal qualifications and proper references. When she was finally hired on by the London General Omnibus Company, more than a month after leaving home, it was as a painter and not as a driver.

Of course she'd been terrible at the job, absolutely ham-fisted, and it was a miracle of sorts that she hadn't

been sacked after her first week. But she had perse-
vered, had become friends with some of the other girls,
and had been punctual and attentive enough that after
a year her supervisor had recommended her for a cov-
eted position as a bus conductor.

Work as a clippie, as the female conductors were
called, was ever so much easier than painting, and it
had been heaven to finally wake up without the smell
of oil paint and turpentine clinging to her hair, but it
still fell far short of what she had hoped to be doing.
She was freeing up a man to fight, that was true, but
was she truly making a difference? Was her work
actually helping Edward and Robbie in any mean-
ingful way? She knew the answer, and it wasn't an
inspiring one.

But she hadn't complained in her letters to Robbie,
not once. Instead, she'd written long, carefully composed missives, full of what she hoped were amusing
anecdotes about life at home. She was pretty certain he
didn't want to read about zeppelin raids or American
neutrality or German U-boats, so she wrote of the craze
for jazz music among her friends at work, her well-
meaning but inept attempts to knit socks for the troops,
her Sunday-morning walks on Primrose Hill, and her
occasional trips to the theater with Charlotte, most recently to see the musical comedy *Theodore & Co.*

His replies, always prompt, weren't nearly as long as hers, were often scribbled in pencil, and were strangely barren of detail compared to the letters he'd written while first in France, at the hospital in Versailles. Presumably he had little time to himself at the clearing hospital, which accounted for the brevity of his letters. Likely he didn't feel she was capable of appreciating the finer points of his work, hence the lack of detail. But it would have been nice to have a better sense of how he spent his days.

Today she walked the four miles to Victoria from Camden Town; it was a fine morning and she hadn't been able to bear the wait, fretting, sitting alone in her room. As always, she was struck by the changes that war had brought to the city.

Everything was shabbier, for a start; an artist would need little more than gray and brown on his palette to capture the scene. There were fewer automobiles than before the war, and fewer horses, too. Nearly every man she saw was in uniform, some of them alarmingly young; surely they were not yet eighteen? A khaki-clad boy passed her, brushing so close that she could see the down still softening his face.

She continued south on Palace Street, crossing at the junction with Victoria Street. Just ahead was the distinctive white-and-gold lettering of the Lyons tea-shop facade. She stepped inside, scanning the tables to see if Robbie was waiting.

"May I help you, madam?"

"Oh, yes, thank you. I'm meeting a . . . a friend. But he hasn't arrived yet. I'm not sure if I ought to take up a table; you seem so busy."

The waitress smiled understandingly. "We've been busier, madam. You go on and sit down wherever you like. I'll come along to take your order once your friend is here."

Lilly walked down the center aisle of the tea shop, finally selecting a smaller table, only big enough for two, near the back. She sat, facing the door, and tried to make herself presentable. Not that there was much she could do: tuck any stray curls under her hat, straighten the lapels of her coat, take off her gloves and tuck them in her reticule. She checked she still had her change purse and noticed she had forgotten her handkerchief. If only she had thought to bring something to read.

Pulling the bill of fare from its little metal stand, she leafed through it slowly, the lines of text blurring before her unfocused gaze. Three pence for a pot of tea, tuppence for lime cordial and soda, a penny each for scones, jam tarts, or ginger cakes. The bell hanging above the shop's front door jingled loudly; she looked up, her heart racing, but saw only the back of a departing customer.

Perhaps Robbie had forgotten. Perhaps his train had been delayed.

Better to think of something else, anything else. What of the people surrounding her? At one table, a group of young women talked excitedly, their chairs pulled into a companionable circle. They were fashionably dressed, their skirts even shorter than hers, and one of them had rouged cheeks and lips. Lilly decided they probably worked in a nearby office or shop, doing the work of men who'd been called up.

She turned her attention to an older couple, the husband clearly too infirm for service. They'd ordered tea and crumpets, and seemed to be relishing every bite. At one point the wife reached out and gently brushed a crumb from her husband's coat, a gesture born, Lilly imagined, of long years of love and companionship.

Nearest to Lilly was a young couple, the man in uniform. The woman held his hand, ignoring her tea, her eyes fixed on his as he spoke slowly, softly, his words indistinct but their murmur infinitely soothing. *I promise I will be fine*, he must surely be saying. *I will be fine; I will return to you; you mustn't worry about me. I will be fine.* Lilly said a silent, fervent prayer that it would be so.

The bell jangled again, knocking against the glass of the shop's front door. She looked up, telling herself it couldn't be him; it would only be another stranger, come for tea and toast and a warm refuge from the sharp chill of the day. But it was Robbie, politely holding the door so the elderly couple, finished with their crumpets, could depart.

He surveyed the shop interior, then, seeing her, smiled crookedly. The shopgirls, silent for a moment, turned in their chairs to look at him, their expressions nakedly admiring. He walked toward her, unbuttoning his greatcoat; under it she could see the khaki of his officer's tunic and trousers. Someone, his mother probably, had polished his leather gaiters, boots, and Sam Browne belt, and she saw, as he removed his hat, that his beautiful golden hair had been cut very short.

"Hello, Lilly. I hope I haven't kept you waiting."

Chapter 11

"No, not at all," Lilly answered, her voice even sweeter than he'd remembered. "I only just arrived." She rose from her chair and, unexpectedly, stood on tiptoes to brush a kiss against his cheek.

Light as it was, the caress burned like a brand on his skin, lingering after even the memory of her scent had faded. She was so very pretty, her hazel eyes shining, her creamy skin adorned with a constellation of freckles that she probably detested but which he found delightful.

"Do sit down," she prompted, and only then did he realize he was still on his feet, looming over her, his coat slung over one arm. Belatedly he sat and tried to gather his thoughts.

Lilly smiled at him, seemingly unconcerned by his awkward response to her greeting. "How was your journey from Scotland?"

"Quite pleasant, thank you. It was hard to say good-bye to my mother, though. My wee cabin felt rather lonely for the first few hours."

"I've never been on a sleeper train. Do they give you a proper bed?"

"More of a bunk, really, that pulls out of the wall. I slept very well; I think it must be the rhythm of the train. Rather like being a baby in a cradle. Before I knew it, we were pulling into Euston."

The waitress, noticing that Lilly was no longer alone, approached them. "Good morning. May I take your order?"

"What do you want, Robbie?"

"Just a cup of tea, thank you."

"May we order a pot of tea between the two of us?"

"Of course, madam," the waitress said, smiling encouragingly. "Would you like something to eat?"

"Robbie?" Lilly asked, but he shook his head. "No, thank you; just the tea for us."

"Very good, madam."

The tea arrived in short order, in a stout Brown Betty teapot with a chipped spout. Lilly poured hers immediately, but when she went to fill Robbie's mug, he shook his head.

"Thanks, but I'll wait a minute or two. A legacy from my days as a resident at the London. We'd drink our tea so strong you could stand a spoon in it.

"So tell me," he continued, determined to stick to neutral topics, "about your work as a clippie. How long has it been since you started?"

"A little more than six months. It's certainly an improvement over being a painter, I can tell you that." She smiled, her eyes bright with mischief. "Mr. Burns, the man who supervised our crew, was forever shouting at me. I got drips of paint everywhere, I never cleaned the brushes properly, and I was ever so slow compared to the other girls. He suggested I apply for the training course for bus conductors. It was kind of him. Certainly it would have been easier to sack me."

"You don't say much about your work in your letters."

"There's not much to tell. I stand on the back of the bus, find out where people are going, tell them how much for their fare, make change, and give them their ticket. The only difficult part is the maths."

"How do people react to seeing a woman doing what is usually a man's job?"

"Most are lovely about it. Tell me I'm a good girl, am doing my part for King and Country, that sort of thing. But some clearly can't abide the sight of me. You'd think I was dressed for the Dance of the Seven Veils, the way they stare."

Then they're swine, he wanted to say, but thought better of it. "You're not wearing your uniform today."

"We aren't supposed to when we're off duty. I think they're worried we might be seen drinking in public houses or kicking up our heels in dance halls. I don't mind. I'm happy to wear something else on my day off."

"You look lovely."

The compliment seemed to fluster her. "Thank you. You too. I mean, you look very fine in your uniform. Very impressive."

At this his sense of amour propre flickered to life. So she liked the way he looked? Could that mean . . . ? No, now was definitely not the time to be exploring such thoughts. Best to steer the conversation in another direction.

"Have you heard from your parents? From any of your people?"

She blanched at his words; he'd been too successful. "Only Edward. I assume my sisters are siding with Mama. And George is away at school. Likely he has no idea of what has happened."

"What about Quentin?" he asked without thinking.

"I beg your pardon?"

"Quentin . . . I'm sorry, I can't remember his surname. I thought you and he had an understanding."

"Oh, no. No, Robbie. I mean, I do know a Quentin. Quentin Brooke-Stapleton. But I haven't seen or spoken to him in . . . oh, it must be two years. Likely longer. Certainly not since the war began. And he was never more than an acquaintance."

"I beg your pardon. I spoke out of turn."

He was an idiot not to have realized straightaway. Of course her mother had concocted the fiancé, just as she had censored his correspondence with Lilly. Anything to keep her daughter well away from the street urchin, as she no doubt regarded him.

Robbie wasn't a man given to anger, or indeed to acts of violence. But at that moment he could have strangled Lady Cumberland and taken grim pleasure in the act.

"Is everything all right?"

"Yes, of course. I was woolgathering just now," he answered, struggling to regain a measure of composure.

"I understand. You must be very tired."

"Not at all. I've been on holiday for a week now."

"A very short holiday, if you ask me."

"It's better than nothing. Have you had any holidays?"

"A few days, here and there. But I'd rather be working," she said with a smile.

"Forgive me for asking, but have you been able to, ah, manage? I don't mean to be crass, but I can't imagine that clippies are paid very well."

"I'm quite comfortable, Robbie. Don't worry about that. And working is good for me. When I think of how I lived, how I used to spend my allowance on books and clothes and whatever else took my fancy, when there were so many who hadn't enough even to eat, I feel so ashamed of myself."

"You were never like that, Lilly."

"You're too kind. Did Edward ever tell you what happened to the Pringles?"

"In one of his letters he said your parents sacked Mr. Pringle, then evicted him and his family, but that you sold your jewelry to provide for them. He was very proud of you."

"I helped them because it was *my* fault they lost their home. My carelessness was responsible. They said it wasn't my fault—Edward, too—but I know it was."

"I think you've been too hard on yourself. Life is short, you know. I see the truth of that every day."

"Of course it is, which is why—"

"Let it go, Lilly. You've atoned for what you believe you did wrong. Let it go, and stop punishing yourself. Promise me?"

"I promise. But if you ever think I'm behaving like a spoiled child—"

"I'll be the first to let you know."

"That's enough of me. I want to hear about your trip home. Auchinloch, was it? Did I pronounce it correctly?

"You did. It's a small village not far from Glasgow."

"Your mother has a house there?"

"A cottage. Known as a 'but and ben' in my part of Scotland. Two wee rooms, with the privy at the bottom of the garden."

"That's where she lives? Even now . . . ?"

"That I'm a professional man, and presumably can afford to move her to something grander? I've asked, believe me. But she won't move, won't even consider it." He searched her face carefully for signs of disgust, but saw nothing but sincere, unprejudiced interest.

"Your father died when you were little, didn't he?"

"Yes, when I was six. Run down in the street by a wagon."

"Do you remember him at all?"

Robbie poured his tea, checked to see it was dark enough, and drank deeply from his mug. "A little. None of it good. I remember his being drunk. He was a mean drunk. Would lash out if we so much as looked at him. Did terrible things to my mam. He never hit my sister, though."

"You have a sister?"

"Had. Her name was Mary. She died when I was seven. Diphtheria. We were both sick from it."

"I'm so sorry," she said, her voice warm with sympathy.

"It was a long time ago. Why don't you ask me about my visit home?" he asked, hoping to paper over the awkwardness that had arisen again.

"Yes, of course. Well, ah . . . your mother must have been delighted to have you home."

"I suppose she was. She certainly made a fuss over me. But then, she hadn't seen me in a long time."

"How long?"

"Not since just before I left for France . . . two years? I've had leave since then, but never enough to manage the journey back to Lanarkshire."

"She must miss you."

"I haven't lived with her in donkey's years; not since I was eight, when I won that scholarship and went off to school in Edinburgh. But I know she worries. I doubt she's had a moment of peace while I've been in France."

The expression on Lilly's face told him she understood exactly what his mother endured.

"I haven't been much of a son to her," he continued, drawing strength from her empathy. "Before the war, I hardly ever visited, hardly ever wrote. But I'm all she has."

"How did she react when you asked for the transfer from Versailles?" Lilly asked.

"If you're thinking I was playing the hero, I wasn't. I was bored, that's all. My talents, such as they are, lie in trauma surgery. All those years spent in the receiving room at the London. I felt I could do more good in a frontline unit."

"There was an article in *The Times*. Last year, I think. It described the line of evacuation for our wounded. It said the enemy keeps shelling our field hospitals."

"I'm not convinced it's deliberate. Bear in mind we treat German prisoners as well as our own men. But, yes, some of the clearing stations have been hit, mine inclu—"

So she had been thinking of him. "Were you worried about me?"

Would she answer honestly? Or would she laugh off his question with a flutter of eyelashes and a demure smile? The minutes were ticking by; soon he would be gone from her again.

"No. That is . . . I mean, yes. Yes, I was." She was blushing now, the merest flush along her cheekbones. "Is it . . ."—and here her voice faltered—"is it very bad?"

How could he answer such a question? The truth was too cruel. He could not burden her with it.

"Robbie?" she prompted.

He tried to collect himself, began to say something, but the words died in his throat. At last he spoke, his voice hardly more than a whisper. She leaned forward, straining to hear above the din from the surrounding tables.

"It's so bad that I'm not sure I can talk about it. I'm not certain I want you to know."

Silence fell between them, lingered painfully. Then he felt her hand upon his, holding it securely, the warmth of her touch the benediction he sought.

Chapter 12

"Why don't you begin by telling me about where you work?" she prompted. "Where is it? Your letters only say 'somewhere in France.'"

"Just outside Aire-sur-la-Lys, a small village a few miles from Béthune. Though there's been talk of moving us east, closer to the Front."

"How close is it?"

"About seven or eight miles. But the guns are so loud you'd swear we were nearer than that. At first I couldn't sleep for the noise, but now I hardly hear it."

"What do you do?"

"We're one of dozens of casualty clearing stations along the Front. If I had to sum it up, I'd say we save the men who can be saved. If their injuries are minor, we patch them up and send them back to their units.

If they're badly wounded, we stabilize them and send them on to a base hospital for further care. And if they're too far gone for help, we keep them comfortable until they die."

She nodded carefully, taking it all in. "What do *you* do?"

"I'm one of seven surgeons. As the wounded are brought in, one of us assesses them. If surgery is required, we perform it immediately, day or night.

"Before I came to France, I thought I'd seen everything. After all, I'd worked at a hospital in the East End. I'd operated on stabbing victims, people who'd been trampled by horses, men who'd been crushed by falling crates on the docks. But none of that comes close to what I've seen at the Fifty-First."

He hesitated, wanting to give her a chance to ask that he change the subject to a safer, more anodyne topic.

"Go on," she said, squeezing his hand.

At that moment he'd have given every shilling he possessed to be somewhere else, somewhere private, and to be free to embrace her. Just hold her gently, carefully, and in her arms know the bliss of forgetting.

"Since July, we've hardly had a break. The ambulances come in, and if I'm on triage, I assess the condition of the wounded. I only have seconds to decide who will get a chance to live and who will die. A straight amputation, you see, is quick; I can get through two or three in an hour. But anything more complicated . . ."

He took a fortifying gulp of his tea. "A man is brought in and there's hardly a scratch on him. But his pulse is shallow, his breathing is labored, his color is poor. Clearly he's in trouble. So the orderly and I look him over, examine him from top to bottom, and we find it: a tiny hole where a bullet, or a piece of shell casing, has gone in. His only hope is surgery. For me to cut him open and find out where it's gone. When I do, I find that it's ricocheted off a rib, or his spine, and has ripped open every vital organ, every artery, in its path. Damage like that can take me hours to repair, assuming the wounded man doesn't die of shock or straightforward blood loss while I'm working on him. We are able to transfuse blood, after a fashion, but it takes ages and there aren't always enough men who are well enough to act as donors.

"Yet while I'm busy trying to save that *one* man, half a dozen are dying in the pre-op tent. Boys, no more than eighteen or nineteen years old, calling for their mothers. And our nurses and orderlies are so overrun they can hardly spare a moment to hold their hands as they die."

He looked up, did his best to meet her steady gaze. "I've seen terrible things, Lilly, but that's the worst.

Hearing them cry for their mothers as they die. And they try so hard to be stoic; would you believe they even beg my pardon for it?"

He looked away then; had to, or else reveal the hot, shaming tears that had gathered behind his closed eyes.

"I wish I knew what to say," she said softly, her voice tremulous with emotion. "I had no idea it was so bad. You never said . . . in your letters you never said."

Of course he'd never written of it. Why would he do such a thing to her? He blinked hard, praying she hadn't noticed his pitiful lack of composure. And then he found the strength to look at her again. She was weeping silently, her cheeks marked by the tracks of her tears.

"I'm so sorry, Lilly. Truly I am," he said, his guts churning with guilt. "I shouldn't have been so frank with you. It was unforgivable of me to tell you such things."

"It was nothing of the sort." She dashed at her eyes with her sleeve and opened her reticule to search, unsuccessfully, for a handkerchief. He reached into the breast pocket of his jacket, found the worn square of cotton his mother had tucked there the day before, and pressed it into her hand.

"Thank you," she said after she'd finished wiping her eyes. "You mustn't mind these silly tears. I did tell you I would listen, no matter what. And I promise I can bear it."

That was true enough. She was the sort of woman who could bear anything. But he knew himself to be a coward, at least as far as it came to Lilly, and so he took the easy way out and changed the subject.

"Has Edward mentioned anything of what he's been through?" he asked, then cursed himself silently. How did that constitute a change of subject?

"In his letters? Very little. Just the usual jolly Edward sort of remarks. I've thought about pressing him on it—"

"For his sake, don't. Life in the trenches makes my experiences look like a weekend at Cumbermere Hall. At least I have a reasonably comfortable bed to sleep in, with warm, or nearly warm, food when I'm hungry." His voice shook with anger now. "And I don't have to worry about being shot by a sniper, or drowning in a flooded shell hole, or getting tangled up in barbed wire and bleeding to death. That's how they're dying in this god-awful fucking mess of a war—"

He broke off, horrified. "I beg your pardon, Lilly. My choice of language was indefensible."

"It's not the first time I've heard that word. Remember where I work."

"All the same, I ought to have minded my words."

What a fool he was, to ruin what little time they had together. All he'd done was blather on about himself, terrify her with stories of the Front, curse like a navvy, and no doubt ensure she'd have nightmares of the worst sort for weeks to come. Well done, indeed.

In the distance, the chimes at Westminster called the quarter hour. He pushed back his greatcoat sleeve and checked his wristwatch with a sinking heart.

"It's a quarter to twelve already. My train leaves in half an hour. Walk with me to the station, won't you, and see me off?"

He beckoned their waitress, settled the bill, and escorted her outside. He felt a jolt of satisfaction when she took his arm, and resolved to enjoy every last moment of their time together. There would never be enough time to say what really mattered, to tell her how he really felt.

In a matter of minutes they had arrived at Victoria Station. He collected his kit bag from the left-luggage counter, slung it over his shoulder, and swung round to examine the departures board high above them. The train to Dover was leaving from Platform Three in ten minutes.

"Will you come with me as far as the barrier?" he asked. She nodded shyly, likely feeling as awkward as he.

When they reached his platform, he set down his kit bag and turned to her. "Write to me, Lilly?"

"Of course. But before you go, Robbie, there's one thing—"

"Yes?"

"I've always wanted to know . . . on the night I saw you last, at the ball to celebrate Edward's engagement, why did you leave without saying good-bye?"

God, no. Not now.

"I thought Edward would have told you. Something came up."

"I was worried my mother might have said something, might have offended you in some way. Is that what happened?"

"Please, Lilly, not here—"

"I'm right, aren't I? You must tell me."

"She did speak to me. She told me you were engaged to Quentin Brooke-Stapleton."

"It was a lie."

"I see that now. I think we both know why she invented a fiancé for you."

"If only I'd known. If only you'd mentioned it, I would have told you straightaway. There was never anyone else. Never. You do believe me, don't you?"

"I do," he promised, wishing in vain for time to say more.

At the far end of the platform, a whistle blew. "Lilly, I must go."

He reached out, smoothed a curl from her brow, and bent to kiss her cheek. But she turned her face at the last moment—by accident or by design?—and her mouth brushed against his.

So soft. That was all he could think, at first. Her lips were so soft. When had he last touched anything so perfect?

He framed her face with his hands, stooping as he deepened the kiss. At last her mouth parted under the insistent pressure of his, and he dared to trace his tongue along the delicate, satin-smooth interior of her lower lip. Her hands, clutching the lapels of his great-coat, had begun to tremble.

"Ahem."

Reality descended in a chilly blast. They were standing in the middle of Victoria Station. Kissing. Not a yard distant from the platform attendant, who didn't trouble to hide his amusement. In front of, oh hell, at least a score of Tommies, all clearly delighted to be witnessing such a scene.

Robbie took a step back, gently divesting Lilly's hands from his coat, and attempted a reassuring smile.

"Good-bye, Lilly," he whispered, and turned away. He managed to find his ticket, was waved past the barrier by the attendant, and made it through to the platform.

He knew she was watching and it killed him not to rush back to her, abandon all propriety, and kiss her again. He strode along the platform; every bloody car he came to was full. Kept on walking, his heart pounding, desperate to turn back and see her one more time. And then, finally, an empty compartment.

He climbed in, stowed away his kit bag, and let the train bear him away. Away from Lilly, back to the nightmare of his life in France.

Back to a war that had lasted so long he could no longer imagine its end.

Chapter 13

16 December 1916

Dearest Lilly,

Have been given leave for Christmas—just enough to get me home for two days. You must have Christmas lunch with me at the Savoy. Miss Brown, too, if she is free. Shall we say noon?

Love, etc.

Edward

Lilly arrived at the Savoy a half hour early on Christmas Day, expecting she would have to wait alone at their table, but to her delight Edward was already there, pacing back and forth in the lobby. He was thinner than when she'd seen him last, his cheekbones and high-bridged nose cast into stark relief by the electric lighting, his uniform hanging off his tall, too-slender frame.

"Edward!"

He turned and saw her, then swept her up in his arms and showered kisses on her hair. "Lilly, my Lilly. If you only knew how I've missed you."

"In spite of all my letters?" she teased, laughing as he finally set her on her feet again.

"Yes, in spite of your jolly tales of life as a clippie. I couldn't wait to see you today—I've been awake for hours. Happy Christmas, by the way."

"And the same to you. When did you arrive home?"

"Yesterday afternoon. Just in time for a gruesome dinner *en famille*."

"You poor thing."

"I did my duty, no more. Shall we see if there's a table free for us at the Grill?"

It was a rhetorical question, of course, for the moment they entered the restaurant the maître d'hôte appeared out of nowhere, greeted Edward by name, and ushered them to their table.

"Isn't Miss Brown going to join us?" Edward asked as they were being seated.

"She is. But her shift at the hospital didn't finish until eleven, and then she had to change and travel here from Kensington."

A discreet cough alerted them that their waiter had arrived. "Happy Christmas, Lord Ashford, Lady Elizabeth. May I offer you an aperitif?"

"Yes, please. How are your champagne reserves holding up?"

"Very well, your lordship. May I suggest the Moët et Chandon Brut Impérial 1907?"

"Splendid."

"And to follow, Lord Ashford?"

"Nothing just yet. I'll let you know when we're ready to order." As soon as the waiter had departed, Edward turned back to Lilly.

"Let's drink all the champagne straightaway. That way when Miss Brown arrives we'll be three sheets to the wind and she'll lecture us on proper deportment and behavior in public."

"She's not like that at all, Edward."

"Yes, yes. But I do love getting under her skin. She takes everything so seriously."

"And you make a game of everything."

"Used to," he muttered, not meeting her gaze. "Hard to play the fool when you're standing knee-deep in mud and blood."

"Robbie told me how bad it is. That is, he told me how horrible things are at his hospital, and then said it was much, much worse for you." She reached out and took his near hand in hers, clasping it warmly. But he didn't seem to notice.

"Oh, I don't know about that. I wouldn't last long if I had to do some of the things he does. Lopping off people's legs and arms, for a start."

"You know what I mean."

"I do. But I only have today and part of tomorrow before I go back, and the last thing on earth I want to do is talk about it. Think about it, even."

"So what shall we talk about?" she asked, deciding to be cheerful for his sake.

"Help me make the most of these few hours. Laugh at my jokes, complain about Mama, that sort of thing." He grinned at her, and for a moment she saw the carefree, privileged, aimless boy he had once been.

A boy who had returned to her from school, not from a distant, nightmarish battlefield; a boy whose departure, when it came, would be to the safe, if boring, confines of Winchester or Oxford, where the worst thing awaiting him was a stern tutor and the prospect of punishing examinations. She blinked, and the boy was gone.

"Would you like to hear how difficult I was at dinner last night?"

"On *Christmas Eve*?"

"I enjoyed myself enormously, of course. I began by asking after the Pringles. That put rather a damper on the conversation. Then, when Mama began to complain about how difficult it is to find decent help, I rhymed off the names of the men from Cumbermere Hall who were killed at the Somme. We're all in the same battalion, you know."

"*Edward.* You're too old to be playing the scamp."

"But you love me for it. I even managed to work Robbie into the conversation," he added.

"You didn't."

"I sang his praises for all to hear. And I may have happened to mention that the two of you had tea when he was last in London. No; don't protest. Mama needs to know she hasn't managed to keep you apart."

"It's cruel of you to taunt her that way."

"Compared to what she did to you? To the Pringles? I think not."

The champagne having arrived, he filled both their coupes to the brim and drank deeply, draining his glass. "Let's talk no more of Mama, else you'll put me off my food. What about Robbie? How was he when you saw him?"

"Well enough, I think," she answered. "But tired and frustrated. I persuaded him to tell me about his work at the clearing hospital."

"You said so earlier. Not a pleasant subject for tea-time."

"I was glad to listen, though it was awful in the details. Far worse than anything in the papers."

"So was that all you talked about? His work?"

"No. I know you don't want to talk about Mama, but . . ."

"Go on."

"Well, when we were at the tea shop Robbie mentioned Quentin Brooke-Stapleton."

"How would he know that layabout? He wasn't at Oxford with us."

"He doesn't. For some reason Robbie was under the impression that Quentin and I had an understanding. Possibly even that we were engaged. I meant to ask him why, but we got on to another subject. And then, when we were at the station, I realized who must have told him."

"Mama."

"Yes. He admitted it. She told him, and I just know how she would have said it. In that dreadful voice that leaves one feeling about an inch tall."

"I've heard it often. Robbie too."

"But they only spoke the one time, so how—"

"People have always spoken to him like that. I can't say what it was like when he was a boy at school, but it was pretty bad when we were at Oxford. Practical jokes, mainly. There was a hamper of laundry delivered to our rooms, with a note asking him to send it on to his mother. She was a laundress, you see. Or the time his books were taken from his table in the library while he was at lunch, and left at a pawnbroker down in Jericho."

"What did he do?"

"Nothing. He never reacted. Never so much as blinked."

"Did it ever stop?"

"It petered out, mostly. Not much fun when the object of your scorn doesn't appear to notice anything you do."

"And now? I mean, was it bad when he was working in London?"

"His colleagues respected him, so I don't think he was chaffed much while at work. But I know he couldn't abide the do-gooders. You know the sort—philanthropists, politicians, bored society matrons. His hospital was perpetually short of money, so was always having dinners and teas and so forth. He hating attending, but if it meant more money for the hospital . . ."

Edward paused to drink down the rest of his champagne. "So he'd go and they'd trot him out as living proof that the great unwashed could, on occasion, drag themselves out of the gutter. '*Dear* Mr. Fraser, *do* be so kind as to tell us about your life in the *slums*. It must have been perfectly *frightful*.'"

"Slums? I thought he was from a village outside Glasgow. Auchinloch."

"They moved when he was seven or so, after his sister died. I think he and his mother went to her parents'. But before that, they lived in the nastiest, dirtiest, most dangerous slum in Glasgow, and that's saying a lot. Take the worst description of squalor you've ever read in Dickens, multiply it by a hundred, and you have the Gorbals. That's where he was from."

"He never said—"

"He doesn't hide it. Never has. You had only to ask."

"He must know that I don't care. That it means nothing to me."

"But it means something to *him*. How can it not? No matter how far he rises in the world, no matter how accomplished a surgeon he becomes, there will always be someone like Mama who feels the need to put him in his place. Or treat him like a sideshow at a traveling carnival."

"Even now?"

"Even now. Have you ever wondered why he works so hard? Because it's his escape. You might even call it his salvation. Any sense of worth he has comes from his work."

"He is worthy. You've only to meet him to know the sort of man he is."

"That's just it, Lilly. He's a *man*. Not a saint and not a hero. Just an ordinary man who is awfully talented at the work he does, and awfully insecure about his origins. Never forget that."

"I must tell him, when I write to him next. I'll tell him how proud I am, what a talented doctor he is—"

"Christ, no. That'll only make it worse. Better to pretend none of that happened. It will only be salt in the wound if you do mention it again."

"I suppose you're right . . ."

"I am. Tell him about your work as a clippie instead. I know *I* find your stories vastly entertaining."

"I'm glad you do."

"I wish you would let me help you. You don't have to work, you know, nor live in lodgings. You could stay at my house in Chelsea. Miss Brown, too, if you think you'd miss her. And it would be no trouble to set up an account for you at my bank."

"Thank you, but no. I'm very happy in my lodgings and I'm very happy with my work."

"How can you like it? Punching tickets in the rain, day after day?"

"Because I know I'm doing something to help. What was the poster I saw the other day? 'Do a man's job here so he may fight.' That was it."

"More like 'do a man's job here so he can be turned into cannon fodder.'"

"Oh, Edward. I didn't mean it like that."

"I know, darling girl. And I'm sorry for being such a bore. Have some more champagne."

She waited for him to refill her glass and took a large and fortifying sip. "You haven't said a word about Helena. When are you going to visit her?"

"I've scarcely been home twenty-four hours, my dear."

"Is everything all right between the two of you? She hasn't been put off by my break with Mama and Papa, has she? I'd assumed they kept it quiet, so as to avoid any scandal."

"No, no. She hasn't said anything about you. I doubt she even knows. It's not as if the two of you were bosom friends, after all."

"I know. Though I did enjoy her company on the few times we did meet."

"And when you see one another again, you will see that she and I are still very much in accord. I was planning on paying her a visit this afternoon, after I take my leave of you and Miss Brown. And look now—here she is. Miss Brown, that is."

They both stood as Charlotte approached, escorted by the maître d'hôte. After kissing Lilly on the cheek, she and Edward shook hands somewhat tentatively. If Lilly hadn't known better, she'd have sworn they were meeting for the first time.

"Do have some champagne, Miss Brown," Edward offered once they were seated.

"Thank you, Lord Ashford. Happy Christmas."

"And to you, Miss Brown. You look very well today."

Charlotte had evidently put some thought into her ensemble, for she was wearing her best dress, made of a fine dark blue wool, and a close-fitting black velvet hat that framed her face quite winningly.

"Have you ordered?"

"Of course not," Lilly answered. "We were waiting for you."

It had been ages since Lilly had gone out for a meal, only excepting the pot of tea she had shared with Robbie at the Lyons tea shop. Not having access to a proper kitchen, she and Charlotte subsisted on meals of toast, whatever tinned foods went well with toast, and cups and cups of tea. So this was a rare treat indeed.

Her tastes must have changed in the past year, however, for she found little on the menu that appealed. Lobster soufflé, Dover sole in oyster sauce, roast pheasant with truffles, filet mignon stuffed with foie gras and cèpes; all of it was much too much. She looked up and saw that Charlotte and Edward both appeared to share her lack of enthusiasm for the food on offer.

Edward summoned their waiter to the table with an almost imperceptible nod.

"I have a favor to ask."

"Yes, Lord Ashford?"

"What I would really love is something rather more pedestrian. Some roast chicken if you have it, no sauce, with perhaps some potatoes alongside? And something green, too?"

"It would be our pleasure, Lord Ashford. Do you require a first course of any sort?"

"No, thank you. Just the main."

"Very good. Shall I call up a bottle from our cellars for you?"

"Do you have any of the 1910 Chevalier-Montrachet la Cabotte left?"

"Of course, your lordship."

"That will do. But not too cold."

Now that they'd decided on their meal, another topic of conversation had to be found. Lilly was the first to wade into the fray.

"How was work today?" she asked Charlotte.

"Uneventful, which is the best sort of day. I expect you would say the same, wouldn't you, Lord Ashford?"

"I do wish you would call me Edward."

"And I prefer to address you in a formal manner. So please do stop asking."

"But Lilly calls you Charlotte. Why mayn't I?"

"You know very well why not."

Charlotte was acting in a most unusual fashion. Normally she was the very soul of polite and agreeable behavior, but for some reason she appeared to be at odds with Edward. And on Christmas Day, too. Lilly determined to return the conversation to a more harmonious subject.

"Just before you arrived, Charlotte, we were talking about my work at the LGOC," she began. "Isn't that correct, Edward?"

"Quite correct," he agreed. "In fact, I was about to share some interesting news with Lilly. At least it has the potential to be of interest."

"Out with it, then," Charlotte said, swallowing the last of her champagne.

Edward raised an eyebrow at her abrupt tone but continued on without comment. "On the train home from Dover I ran into an old friend from Oxford. David Chamberlain. He's with the War Office now, though I can't recall in what capacity. At any rate, he'd been over in France and was on his way home for Christmas."

"And?" Charlotte prompted.

"And he told me that plans are afoot to create a new women's corps."

"You can't be serious," Lilly said. She must have misheard him. Or perhaps those two glasses of champagne on an empty stomach were to blame.

"I'm quite serious. Certainly Chamberlain was. The army badly needs women workers to take the place of men who are working behind the lines so those men can be freed up for frontline service. They'll be looking for ten thousand women, if not more."

"I can't believe it. When?"

"As soon as February, I gather. And I think you should consider applying as soon as it's announced."

"Do you think they would take me?"

"I do. They're sure to need drivers to ferry about officers, supplies, that sort of thing. You would be helping out but wouldn't be doing anything dangerous."

Lilly looked to Charlotte. "What do you think?"

"I think you should apply. I'd miss you, of course, but isn't this what you've wanted all along?"

"It is . . . but it's been ages since I did any driving."

"I'm sure it will come back to you," Charlotte assured her. "You don't have to become a driver, for that matter. Most likely they'll be looking to fill all sorts of positions. There's certain to be something you can do."

Edward reached across the table and took Lilly's hand in his. "Please forget what I said earlier—my remark about cannon fodder. The truth is that we're desperate for more men. My battalion hasn't been at anything like full strength since the summer."

"Wouldn't it worry you? My being so close to the fighting?"

"Most likely you'd be posted somewhere in England. Although I rather like the idea of your being in France. We could see each other, you know, when I have leave. Experience the heady thrills of Boulogne-sur-Mer together, and all that," he joked.

Somewhere in France. Close to Edward; close to Robbie.

"You are certain?" she asked, still not quite believing.

"Chamberlain was certain enough. So keep your eyes and ears open, and be ready to apply when the call goes out."

Their food arrived just then, prepared exactly as Edward had requested: roast chicken, potatoes Lyonnaise, and tiny new Brussels sprouts. Lilly concentrated on her meal, allowing her brother and Charlotte to carry the conversation with their spirited and, at moments, barbed debate over the relative merits of modern art.

As she ate, bite after methodical bite, she let her imagination soar, borne high by Edward's news. If it were true, and if she were accepted, she'd have a chance to make something of herself, become someone worthwhile to know, even to love.

February couldn't come fast enough.

Chapter 14

It was no trouble to find a copy of *The Times* among the discarded newspapers on the bus at the end of the day. Strictly speaking, she wasn't supposed to keep anything she found, but she couldn't justify spending tuppence on a daily paper, not when she had to be so careful with her money. And the papers would end up in the rubbish anyway.

Her shift was over, and after ten long hours it was her turn to sit, feet aching, head pounding, on a series of buses as they traced a meandering route east from Willesden to Camden Town. Opening her scavenged *Times*, she went straight to the casualty lists on page five; force of habit compelled her to read through them line by line. Relieved to find only unfamiliar names, she turned to the front of the paper and began to read the articles in earnest.

And then, on page nine, she found it, the article she had been awaiting eagerly since Christmas Day. As Edward had promised, a women's corps had been established. WOMEN'S WAR WORK IN FRANCE was the headline. *Posts to Be Filled Behind the Lines.*

She read on, and was heartened to discover that women were required in a number of categories, one of them a motor transport service. Interested applicants were instructed to obtain the necessary forms from Mrs. Tennant, the director of the women's branch of the National Service Department.

As soon as the bus arrived at Camden Town, she jumped out and ran home, not able to wait another minute to share her news with Charlotte. Dashing through the front door of her lodgings, she shouted out a hello to Mrs. Collins and ran upstairs to knock on Charlotte's door without even taking off her coat.

"Is that you, Lilly? Do come in."

"They've announced it, just as Edward said!"

"Announced what?"

"The women's corps. It's right here in *The Times.*" She handed the paper to her friend, who was still sitting in her chair by the fire, her darning forgotten on her lap.

"So it is. This is exciting!"

"I must apply immediately. There's no time to waste."

"Of course you must. But first take off your coat and hat and change out of your uniform. I'll make you some sardines on toast and a cup of tea, and *then* you can get started."

"You're right, you're right. I won't be a moment. Do you have any stamps? I think I've run out."

"I have plenty of stamps," Charlotte assured her. "Now stop marching around my room in those muddy boots or Mrs. Collins will have both our heads!"

A week later, Lilly arrived home from work to find a packet of papers waiting for her. Standing in the front hall, rain dripping from her sodden coat and hat, she tore open the envelope, which contained an application form as well as a letter.

Devonshire House
Piccadilly
London W1
Monday, 5 March

Dear Miss Ashford,

Thank you for your letter of 28 February. You are requested to present yourself for an interview with Dr. Chalmers-Watson, our chief controller, on Monday, 26 March, at ten o'clock in the morning. The interview will take place at the Women's Army Auxiliary Corps headquarters at Devonshire House, Piccadilly.

Please complete the enclosed forms and return them to my attention at your earliest convenience. As well, please note that if you are successful in your application, you will be required to pass a medical examination.

Yours faithfully,
Miss Annabelle Hopkinson
Assistant Administrator
Women's Army Auxiliary Corps

The application form didn't seem especially alarming, although she was required to state her father's occupation—how should she answer? member of the House of Lords?—as well as details of her education, scant as it had been. It asked her to specify what sort of work she sought, and also to provide the name and details of people who could act as character references.

Charlotte could certainly provide one of the references, but a second was sure to be difficult. The problem, of course, was that she'd led such a sheltered life. She'd only ever worked at the LGOC, had never gone to a proper school, had never really moved beyond her parents' circle of friends and acquaintances. She read the form again: one reference was required from "a lady," while the second had to come from a "mayor, magistrate, justice of the peace, minister of religion, barrister, physician, solicitor, or notary public." She had no personal physician, hadn't established any kind of relationship with the vicar at St. Michael's Church, where she and Charlotte went to Sunday services, and she'd never consulted a lawyer of any description.

But she did know a surgeon.

Surely it wasn't possible that most of the night had passed by while he attended to his patients' charts, filled in forms, wrote letters to the bereaved, and filled in yet more forms. Robbie stole a look at the clock on the far wall: nearly four o'clock in the morning. He decided to admit defeat for now and leave off the final pile of papers that awaited his attention.

While he'd been working, another delivery of post had come in from home. He went over to the bank of pigeonholes by Matron's desk, extracted a wodge of papers from his compartment, and sorted through them rapidly. Asinine directives and demands from higher-ups went straight into the rubbish. There was a notice from his bank, probably to confirm the additional funds he'd asked them to send to his mother. And, last of all, a small, thin envelope, addressed in handwriting so familiar he didn't need to turn it over to confirm the sender.

He hurried back to his quarters, hoping against hope to find them empty, and was rewarded by the sight of an empty tent; Tom must still be working away on the compound fracture that had come in earlier. Only then did he tear open the envelope.

21, Georgiana Street
London NW1
Monday, 5 March

Dear Robbie,

I hope this letter finds you well. I have some exciting news: this morning I received an application form from the new women's corps. They've asked me to come for an interview on March 26. The one difficulty is that I require two letters of reference, one from a lady (I shall ask Charlotte) and the other from some sort of official. I apologize in advance

for the imposition, but could I prevail upon you to
provide the second reference? I will leave off now
as I want to send this out with the evening post.

Lilly

P.S. The reference should be sent to Dr. Chalmers-
Watson, Women's Army Auxiliary Corps,
Devonshire House, Piccadilly, London.

P.P.S. Thank you!

So the women's corps Edward had told her about at Christmas hadn't just been talk, after all. He told himself he was glad, for Lilly's sake, that it had come to pass. As for how he felt about it? That was a thousand times more difficult to gauge.

He was delighted for her, of course; this was exactly the sort of work she had been hoping to do all along. And it was doubtful that the War Office would knowingly expose women to danger, so he didn't have to fret about her safety as such.

He had to admit he was nervous about her joining the motor corps, for driving was filthy, backbreaking, dangerous work. The few friends he had with automobiles, Edward among them, seemed to spend half their time fiddling around with engines that had blown a gasket, or mending punctured tires at the side of the road. As for accidents, he'd had to patch up victims of motorcar crashes when he'd been at the London, and it had been grisly work.

Might she be posted to France? Just the possibility was enough to overcome his reticence about her choice of occupation. She wouldn't be sent anywhere nearby, of course, but he might dare to visit her on his next leave, if only to see that she was well, and happy, and not too homesick.

Altogether, it was the best news he'd had in a long, long while.

He heaved himself up, rummaged in his locker for a pencil, writing paper, and envelopes, and sat at the tent's lone table, a rickety affair with one leg distinctly shorter than the rest. A few minutes of work to write the reference and his reply to Lilly, another minute or two to drop off the envelopes with Matron, who'd see they went out with the next post, and then he could sleep.

March 16
51st CCS
France

Dear Lilly,

   Your letter of the fifth arrived with the post today and I am about to write a letter of reference to Dr. Chalmers-Watson as requested. I have every

hope that it will arrive in London before your in-
terview. Before long you will be writing to me from
Boulogne or Calais—I am certain of it. I must go,
as I have been working for many hours now and
need to get some rest. I promise to write again soon.

Robbie

Less than a week after receiving Robbie's reply, Lilly found herself seated on a hard chair in a gloomy corridor, one of more than a dozen young women who were waiting for their interview with Dr. Chalmers-Watson.

Every ten minutes or so, a terrifyingly efficient-looking aide would open one of the double doors at the end of the corridor, call out a name, then close the door behind the candidate. None of the women called in had, thus far, reappeared in the hallway. Lilly found this disconcerting, mainly because there was no way to judge what the interview was like by the demeanor of the departing applicants.

"Miss Ashford? Miss Lilly Ashford?"

Lilly stood hurriedly, smoothed her coat and skirt, and marched down the hall. The aide, who seemed perfectly friendly at closer range, directed her to a seat in front of a long oak table. On the other side of the table were three women, with Dr. Chalmers-Watson, whom Lilly recognized from a photograph in the newspaper, at the center.

"Miss Ashford, I believe?" The doctor had a lovely voice, clear and warm, with a hint of a Scottish burr.

Lilly found she had to clear her throat before answering. "Yes, ma'am."

"I see that you wish to join our motor transport service. Is that correct?"

"Yes, ma'am."

"But I also see from your application that you have been employed by the LGOC as a conductress for the past year. Where were you before that?"

"I worked as a painter at the LGOC. Before that I was at home with my parents, ma'am."

"Very good. Now, your references. Miss Brown was, I believe, your governess?"

"Yes, ma'am. She taught me for almost five years. I'm afraid I have no formal education as such."

"Quite a number of our applicants have little in the way of formal education, Miss Ashford. That is not an immediate concern, to my mind. As for the other reference: how do you know Captain Fraser?"

"He is a close friend of my eldest brother. I've known him for ten years."

"He writes most compellingly of your capabilities and your very real desire to aid in the war effort."

"Yes, ma'am."

"Both these references do you great credit. But I do have my doubts, Miss Ashford. Or should I more properly call you Lady Elizabeth?"

Lilly squirmed in her seat, feeling like a butterfly at the end of a botanist's pin. At last she found her voice again. "I do not seek, or expect, any kind of preferential treatment, Dr. Chalmers-Watson. I only want to work, and do what I can to help us in the war effort. I promise I will not be a burden. I'm a good driver and I'm not afraid of hard work."

"But this work will be harder than anything you can imagine, Miss Ashford. Even harder than your work as a bus conductress. You can expect long hours, difficult conditions, plain food, and even plainer living arrangements. You will be working with women from exceedingly modest backgrounds. Women who, if I may be quite frank, will be rough in their habits and their talk. Are you prepared for all of that?"

"I am," Lilly insisted. "I truly am. And it doesn't matter to me. You see, my brother has been in a frontline unit since almost the beginning of the war. I know he has endured terrible hardships. I know my work will help him, and that will make everything worthwhile. I beg you, please let me help."

Silence fell over the room, and Lilly sank back in her chair, feeling more than a little mortified at her outburst. Turning to one another, the officials spoke quietly, then Dr. Chalmers-Watson finally turned to look at Lilly. "Thank you very much for your time, Miss Ashford. We will contact you in due course with our decision. Miss Hopkinson will show you out."

"Thank you." Lilly considered making a further plea, but the doctor had turned her attention to the next applicant, who was already being shown in. Instead, she meekly followed Miss Hopkinson to a door at the far end of the chamber.

"Turn right as you exit, and follow the stairs to the bottom floor. That will return you to the entrance hall. Thank you very much for your time, Miss Ashford."

Chapter 15

Devonshire House
Piccadilly
London W1
Monday, 26 March

Dear Miss Ashford,

Further to your interview with Dr. Chalmers-Watson, I am pleased to offer you a position with the Women's Army Auxiliary Corps. You have been assigned the grade of Worker and will be attached to the motor transport division in France after you complete your training at our facility in Shorncliffe, Kent. Your pay will be 35 s. a week, including accommodation, with a weekly charge of 12/6 deducted for food.

Before you commence your service with the WAAC, you must pass a medical examination. I have scheduled your examination for Thursday, 29 March, at 2:00 P.M. It will take place at our offices in Devonshire House; please ask the official on duty at the front desk for directions.

You are requested to report for duty on Monday, 2 April, at WAAC headquarters, the Connaught Club, near Marble Arch. From there you will be provided with transportation to Kent.

Enclosed is a list of required clothing and personal items, as well as details of the uniform provided by the corps.

Kindly respond by return post to advise me if you intend to accept this position with the WAAC.

Yours faithfully,
Miss Annabelle Hopkinson
Assistant Administrator
Women's Army Auxiliary Corps

The grand entrance hall of the Connaught Club, stripped of its finery for the duration, was a hive of activity, with queues of young women, some in uniform, some in civilian clothing, crisscrossing the chamber. Lilly had just stepped forward, looking for someone whom she could approach for advice, when she felt a brisk tap on her shoulder. Turning, she felt a twinge of anxiety as she took in the severely tailored uniform and no-nonsense coiffure of the woman who now faced her.

"I believe you are one of the new girls. May I help you?" The woman's voice was friendly, however, and she had a reassuring smile.

"Yes, please. Yes, ma'am, I mean. I was told to report here for duty today, but I'm afraid I don't know where to go next."

"That's simple enough, my dear. See the queue at the far right-hand side of the hall? That's where you belong."

Lilly thanked the woman, silently praying that everyone she encountered that morning would be as helpful, and joined the end of the queue. The other women were happily chatting with one another, sharing names and hometowns, and after a minute or so one of them grinned and held out her hand for Lilly to shake.

"Hello there. My name is Constance Evans."

"Oh, yes, hello. My name is Lilly. Elizabeth, really, but everyone calls me Lilly. Lilly Ashford."

Constance didn't seem to notice Lilly's nervousness. "Where are you from?"

"Cumbria, near Penrith."

"You don't sound like a northerner," Constance observed.

"I suppose I don't, do I? I've been in London for a while now, working at the LGOC." Better to gloss over the truth of her upbringing, at least for now. "Where are you from?"

"Peterborough. My father works in the head office of London Brick. I worked there, too, after I left school. As a typist. But I was never very good at it, so I've asked them to let me join the motor corps."

"That's where I'm assigned, too. When did you learn to drive?"

"Ages ago. My father taught me. We'd motor out into the countryside, switch seats, and I'd drive us back. At first I kept veering into the hedgerows, but I got better in time."

By the time the queue reached the back office, Lilly had learned a great deal more about Constance. She was twenty-one, an only child, a Methodist and teeto-taler, an enthusiastic walker, a cat lover, and a passion-ate devotee of Gilbert and Sullivan. It was impossible not to like Constance, with her round, freckled face, bright ginger hair, and warm but direct manner.

Of her own background Lilly said as little as pos-sible, just as she'd done with her fellow clippies in London. She did intend to tell the truth to her friends, one day, but it could wait. For now, she simply wanted to fit in, share the same experiences, share the same stories. And the only way she could do so was as plain Lilly Ashford.

Lilly also met some of the other women in the queue, most of them destined for jobs in the catering and clerical corps. They'd come from every corner of Britain, looking for work and adventure. They talked of the homes they'd left behind and their families. They talked of the work they had done since leaving school: long days in biscuit factories, weaving sheds, offices, potteries, and the parlors and kitchens of grand homes. Most movingly, they shared the names of their beaux and husbands, gone for many months, some gone forever.

At last they reached the front of the queue and it was Lilly's turn. A WAAC official took her name, disappeared into the back of the office, and emerged with a fat file. She then gave Lilly a sheaf of vouchers, as well as a timetable that told her where she ought to be, and when, for the remainder of the week.

Her next stop was at the quartermaster's office. Some of the other women complained loudly as they received their uniforms, but Lilly rather liked hers. The wool khaki coat had enormous pockets and smelled strongly of damp sheep, but it fit well, as did its matching skirt. She was also given a gabardine blouse and matching tie, and a small, tight-fitting khaki cap, which apparently was standard issue for drivers. The official on duty gave her a further voucher that entitled her to goggles and a thick sheepskin coat, explaining they would be issued once she was posted to France.

After dinner in the mess hall, Lilly and the other new recruits, about sixty altogether, piled into buses for the journey to Charing Cross Station and from there were ushered onto a train for Kent. Although they'd be spending their days at the training facility at Shorncliffe Camp, they would be lodged in rooms at several hotels in Folkestone.

Her quarters in the Burlington Hotel came as a shock to Lilly, though she tried hard to conceal her surprise. Her roommates were happy enough, however, and seemed not to care that the room was furnished only with six metal beds, six thin mattress rolls, and one lone electric sconce on the wall by the door. Her mattress, unrolled, had more lumps than actual mattress, but it looked clean. Disappointingly, Constance was not one of Lilly's roommates, although her room was on the same floor of the hotel.

The next morning began with roll call at Shorncliffe Camp, then the women were divided into their respective trades for training. Lilly and her fellows from the motor transport division were taken out to a large, open field, which had a track of sorts, gravel in some places, tarmac in others, laid out rather haphazardly around its perimeter. After queuing up, each woman, one after the other, had to take the wheel of the one vehicle available for training, an elderly Daimler that was wonderfully easy to drive.

The remainder of the day was taken up with drill, which Lilly quickly learned to dread, lectures, dinner, more driver training, more drill, and an early supper at camp. After their return to the hotel, roll call was completed and the women were given two hours before lights-out.

The next day was the same, and the next and the next. The only variation to this routine came on Sunday, their day off, when the WAACs were shepherded to church in the morning and then had the afternoon to themselves.

Late one evening, a fortnight after they'd all arrived in Folkestone, Lilly's roommates initiated a whispered discussion on the subject of beaux. Ada was the first to submit to the interrogation, which was led by Annie and Bridget, tough-as-nails millworkers from Birmingham. She happily answered a series of questions that rapidly escalated from the mundane to the intimate: "What's his name? Where'd you meet him? Has he kissed you? Have you let him take any liberties?"

Ada confessed that she loved a man called William, that they had been walking out together for two years, including the year he had been in France, and that, yes, they had kissed a number of times, and once she had let him reach under her skirts and touch her leg *above the knee*, but that had been all.

And then it had been Lilly's turn.

"Eh, there," Annie hissed at her. "We know you're not sleeping, so it's no use pretending. Come on now, tell us everything."

"There isn't much to say, I'm afraid."

"Listen to you, all prim and proper. As if you've never had a man of your own. A pretty girl like you."

"I . . . I'd rather not say."

Derisive snorts punctuated the close air of the hotel room. "Be like that, then. We was only trying to be friendly, like."

"I'm sorry," Lilly whispered, but they had moved on to Minnie, who seemed more than happy to regale her new friends with stories of her amorous adventures.

The following night, as soon as the light had been switched off, it began again. Lilly was pointedly excluded from the discussion, which now revolved around Annie and Bridget and their beaux. In fond and, to Lilly's ears, unimaginably salacious detail, they described their escapades with Jim and Gordon. Although nearly two years had passed since the men's departure for France, Annie's and Bridget's recollections made it clear that time had not dulled the flame of their collective ardor.

By the time the conversation petered out, well into the wee hours, Lilly had received a thorough education in the finer details of lovemaking, for Annie and Bridget had been most forthcoming in describing everything, simply *everything*, to the other girls in the room. She had learned of the many positions in which a man and woman might perform the deed, just how much men liked it when a woman "did for them," and the drama associated with Annie's once having been "late."

Lilly's mother certainly would never have enlightened her or her sisters in such a fashion, or indeed in any fashion. Thinking back, Lilly tried to remember what she had once imagined married people—or, for that matter, defiantly *unmarried* people—did in the privacy of their bedchamber. She'd often heard her sisters allude to something exceedingly disagreeable and undignified, something to which, as wives, they were bound to dutifully submit, but she had never dared ask them for a fuller explanation.

Well, now she knew, and she probably had a better idea of what lovemaking entailed than had either of her sisters on their wedding nights. Most surprising of all was Annie's assertion, contrary to everything her sisters had intimated, that lovemaking was a pleasant activity and something a woman might ardently anticipate.

Lilly's mind flew, unbidden, to those precious moments with Robbie at Victoria Station. He was stooping to kiss her, his hands encircling her face so gently. She was leaning into his embrace, standing on her tiptoes, and her trembling hands were clutching at the lapels of his coat. They stood so close that she could feel his warmth, smell the lingering scent of the soap he had used that morning, even feel the rush of his breath against her face.

Merely thinking of his kiss was enough to make Lilly feel feverish, yet also chilled to the marrow. Thank goodness she was hidden from prying eyes, swathed as she was in blankets and the blessed cocoon of night. Could *this* be desire, this unearthly sense of yearning, of emptiness, of longing for the touch of another?

And could it be that Robbie felt it, too, lying alone in his cot, kept awake by a mysterious hunger? It seemed improbable. To begin with, he hadn't meant to properly kiss her. She was the one who had, by accident, turned her head and caught his lips with her own. Yet he hadn't broken off the kiss straightaway, as he ought to have done. Instead he had deepened it, held her closer, and had ended it rather reluctantly.

She would give almost anything to know what he had thought of their kiss, of her, at that moment. But he'd betrayed nothing of his deeper feelings in his subsequent letters, telling only of his long days in surgery, his pride in her accomplishments, and his hope that they might see each other before too long.

He missed her; he hadn't said so outright, of course, but she felt certain of it. And that would have to sustain her until they met again.

Chapter 16

True to her name, Constance proved herself a loyal friend over the first weeks of their acquaintance, always saving a seat for Lilly at mealtimes and lectures, and making a point of including her on group outings on their Sunday afternoon half holidays.

Walking along the Leas cliff-top promenade, with its striking views across the Channel, was Constance's favorite outing, and nearly every week she persuaded her roommates, as well as Lilly, to join her.

When they'd first ventured out today, just after dinner, the weather had been blustery and chill, and the other girls had protested; but before long the clouds parted, the wind died to a breeze, and the sun emerged for the first time in days. Walking east along the promenade, they discovered a zigzagging footpath down to the beachfront far below.

The beach was deserted, apart from clusters of wheeling gulls. Abandoned by the others, who had walked ahead to the pier, Lilly and Constance soon fell into a comfortable silence, each woman lost in her own thoughts.

For her part, Lilly was preoccupied by the view across the Channel. From where they stood, France was only twenty, perhaps twenty-five miles away. Near enough, in clearer weather, to make out the blur of the coast, but not today.

Constance was the first to break the silence. "Promise me that you won't be offended, Lilly, but I'm concerned about you."

"What do you mean?"

"Don't look so alarmed! It's just that our conversations are always so one-sided. Me prattling on about my mum and dad, or some lark I got up to when I was at home, but I never hear you talk about your people. And I would love to know about them, truly I would. Is anything wrong? Anything that you'd like to talk about?"

Looking at Constance, her brow knitted in an anxious furrow, Lilly felt a surge of affection for her friend. Stumbling over her words, she answered as honestly as she dared. "Thank you, Constance. You're so kind to think of me. I'm quite all right. And I'm sorry I haven't said much about my family. It's just that . . . well, there isn't much to tell. I'm not very close to my parents, and my life, before I came here, was very dull. So there's not a lot to say." There, then. A few truths hidden amid the prevarications.

"So who is writing you all those letters? Oh, Lilly, come on. You should see your face when the post is handed out. It's all you can do not to tear open the envelopes straightaway."

"They're from my brother Edward. He's been in France for more than two years. And from Charlotte, a friend. I knew her at, ah, at school."

"Where is she now?"

"She's a nurse in London. Isn't one of your friends working for the VAD now?"

Constance rolled her eyes and laughed. "Good try, Lilly, but I'm not going to let you change the subject, not just yet. Are the letters only from your brother and Charlotte?"

Lilly made no reply, and somehow this only encouraged her friend. Constance reached out, took one of her hands, and squeezed it reassuringly. "Go on. You can tell me."

"My brother has a friend. His best friend, for many years. And also, I suppose, my friend. I'm very fond of him . . . in a sisterly way, of course."

"Of course." Constance couldn't keep the glee out of her voice.

"But my parents dislike him, and I've, well, I've grown used to not talking about him."

"Surely you can tell *me* about him," Constance pressed on. "What's his name?"

"Robert. Robert Fraser. But I call him Robbie."

"You said he's a friend of your brother's. Were they school friends?"

"Yes, they went to university together."

"*University.* My goodness. What does he do now? Or I suppose I should ask what he did before the war."

"He's with the RAMC, in France. He works at a field hospital as a surgeon."

"Even more impressive. Is your brother a doctor, too?"

This was a trickier question to answer. "No, just an infantry officer. He's with the Border Regiment, near Ypres."

That seemed to satisfy Constance, at least for the moment. "See how easy that was? All you need is a little more practice."

"I'll do my best from now on. I promise."

"And will you let me know if the chaffing from Annie and Bridget gets any worse?"

"It isn't that bad, honestly—"

"It sounds pretty bad to me. Ada let slip about their goings-on after lights-out. They should be ashamed of themselves. As if *that's* something to be proud of. You mustn't mind them, Lilly, really you shouldn't. They're just jealous."

"Of me? No, I don't think so."

"Of course they are. They'd kill to have your fine manners. You're a lady down to your toes. That's why they try to shock you with their off-color talk."

"I don't blame them. I ought to have been friendlier, back when we first arrived here."

"Then be friendly now. Offer to share something from home with them. Anyone can see they haven't tuppence to rub together. Now," Constance continued, her voice brightening, "what time does that fancy wristwatch of yours say it is?"

"Half-past four."

"Time to head back. Let's try and catch up with the others. Hallooo, there!" she shouted ahead to the rest of the group, then surprised Lilly by breaking into a run. It was so unexpected that Lilly could only stand and stare, then, clutching her hat, madly chase Constance along the shifting sands of the beach.

After a solid month of practice on the Daimler, Lilly and her fellow driver trainees arrived at the garage one morning to find Miss Davies, the unit administrator who was supervising their training, waiting with an unfamiliar instructor.

"Good morning, ladies. You have all made such splendid progress that I feel it is time you switched over to larger motor vehicles. Corporal Pike is our resident expert on the Crossley 20/25 lorry and has been seconded from his work with the ASC in order to teach you."

"Humph," said Corporal Pike.

"Now, has anyone here any experience with the Crossley? Anyone? Never mind; that's what you are all here for. Over to you, Corporal Pike."

Lilly's hope that Corporal Pike might be impressed by their collective mastery of the Crossley died as soon as the first WAAC climbed into the driving seat of the lorry.

"Stop right there!" the corporal bellowed. "There's your first mistake. Do any of you lot know what your friend here failed to do? What's your name?"

"Blythe, sir. Ellen Blythe."

"Don't call me sir; I'm not an officer. Corporal will do."

"Yes, si—I mean, yes, Corporal."

"Rule number one, Miss Blythe. Always check under the bonnet. The last driver before you might have topped up the fluids, or they might not. So get on down, miss, and make sure the petrol, oil, and water are as they should be. Go on, now, and tell me what you see."

"The radiator is full, Corporal."

"And what about the gearbox? Is there enough oil?"

"Um . . . yes, there is, Corporal."

"And what about the chassis? The clutch bridle? The brake-rod joints? Have they been greased?"

And on it went. By the time she finally clambered behind the steering wheel again, Ellen Blythe had been reduced to a red-faced, quivering wreck. Corporal Pike cranked the engine for her, muttering all the while about "useless females," and Ellen handily got the Crossley moving across the tarmacked courtyard. He seemed to be directing her toward an open area, presumably meant for parking in off-hours, when the vehicle shuddered to a sudden halt and the corporal could be heard shouting again. When the lorry returned to the group several minutes later, Miss Blythe had been relegated to the passenger seat.

"Look, you lot," the corporal began, evidently at breaking point, or possibly past it, "I don't have all day to waste. One of you must be able to handle a lorry— isn't that why you're here? To help us out? Otherwise you're only making more work for me and my mates!"

Lilly knew it was now or never. If no one volunteered, they all risked being reassigned to canteen duty or worse. She stepped forward, feeling her cheeks flush as everyone's attention fell on her. "Excuse me, Corporal. I am familiar with Thornycroft lorries, which I believe are similar to the Crossley. May I try?"

"Be my guest, miss," the corporal replied wearily. "Don't bother with checking her over; we've already done that. Let's skip to the part where you drive her."

"Yes, Corporal." Lilly hoisted herself into the driver's seat and felt for the foot pedals; the clutch was awfully far away, and she found she had to perch on the very edge of the seat in order to reach it. Her heart racing, she put the lorry in gear and slowly drove off.

Corporal Pike directed her to drive around the perimeter of the parking area, which she did, eventually reaching fourth gear. They were almost at the end of the pavement, so she began to switch down, carefully depressing the clutch to put the lorry in neutral, revving the engine a bit to better align the gears, then engaging the clutch a second time as she shifted into the lower gear.

The corporal let out a low whistle. "Well, I never. Thank God one of you knows what to do. Pull to a stop, now, and put her in reverse. Good job. Right, then. Time to take her back."

Lilly drew the lorry to a halt a few yards from the group of WAACs and swung her legs out to descend from the driver's seat. "Oh, no, you don't," ordered the corporal.

"Ladies," he continued, turning his attention to the other women, "your friend here is going to be your new instructor. I'll give you the rest of the day, and if you haven't figured out what you're doing by then, you've got no place in this war. Good luck to all of you." And then, under his breath, "You're going to need it."

Miss Davies made a few feeble sounds of protest, but to no avail; Corporal Pike had already marched away. "Goodness, gracious . . . I don't know what to say. I suppose we'll have to make do. Miss Ashford, how do you suggest we proceed?"

"It depends on what the others prefer, ma'am. Perhaps we should start with the preparatory steps?"

"Please do," Constance broke in. "I wasn't able to see what Corporal Pike was doing before." The other women also chimed in their assent, even Annie and Bridget, and at a nod from Miss Davies, Lilly switched off the engine and walked round to the front of the lorry.

"I might as well start at the very beginning. As the corporal said, it's important to check everything is topped up and well greased before you set off. Let's start with the gearbox. You'll need to fill it up to the center of the bottom shaft so that all of the bottom wheels are covered. Once it's filled, the oil should last for four hundred miles, but check it every time, just in case."

Step-by-step, Lilly ran through the checklist that John Pringle had insisted she learn by heart, making sure that all the other WAACs understood and were capable of following before she moved on to the next step. With maintenance of the vehicle mastered, Lilly decided to move to the driver's seat, where she mimed and described starting a cold engine, moving out of first gear, braking without skidding, and of course the all-important step of double-clutching when changing down gears.

They broke for dinner at half-past twelve, and as they walked back to the canteen Lilly felt a ridiculous sense of pleasure to hear the other girls thank and compliment her, one after the other. Even Annie and Bridget offered shy smiles, which Lilly returned wholeheartedly.

The afternoon's lessons were equally satisfying, with each woman taking a turn to drive the modest circuit. By the time they finished, early that evening, Lilly's arms and shoulders were numb from having cranked the lorry's engine so many times, and her throat was raw from shouting out instructions above its rumble and hum, but she felt strangely content.

It was a wonderful feeling, Lilly decided. Wholly unfamiliar, and simply wonderful. She'd done a really hard day's work, had helped her fellow WAACs, and was now so tired that she was about to do the unthinkable: she would go to bed, for the second day in a row, without writing a letter.

Today, Lilly had planned on writing to Robbie, and part of her yearned to put down on paper everything that had happened to her. But not tonight. Robbie's letter would keep for tomorrow; and if not tomorrow, then the day after. For Robbie, of all people, would surely understand.

Chapter 17

Nurse Williamson had only been at work for six-teen hours straight when she collapsed. She'd arrived from one of the base hospitals the week before, a good worker, uncomplaining, but unaccustomed to the long hours typical of a clearing hospital.

Robbie suspected the smell in the operating hut had pushed her over the edge. Even he had to admit it was pretty bad today. Ether fumes hung heavy in the stagnant air, mixing with the iron-sharp tang of blood, the unmistakable and nauseating scent of putrefying flesh, and the earthy stench of human excrement.

"Private Dixon," he yelled at the orderly. "My nurse has fainted. Get her to the ward tent and bring back one of their nurses with you."

"Shall I take over from Nurse Williamson?" asked the nurse who was acting as his anesthetist.

"No, stay where you are. Let me know if he goes into shock."

He'd almost finished debriding his patient's wounds. It was exacting work, and took forever, but without it the man wouldn't survive. Too many bacilli hid in the soil, and an injury like this, where shell fragments had ricocheted from place to place before ripping a path through the flesh of his patient's chest, was particularly dangerous. He'd excised every scrap of injured tissue, searched for and rooted out every last splinter of metal and shred of uniform, and flushed the wound thoroughly with disinfectant. In so doing he had guaranteed his patient would be left with the most god-awful scar across his chest, but the man would probably live.

A new nurse had arrived and stood expectantly at Robbie's side. "Good evening, Captain Fraser."

"Good evening, Nurse Greenhalgh." That was the end of pleasantries for now. "Hemothorax. Wound is debrided and flushed with Carrel-Dakin. I've stopped the internal bleeding. Shall we drain his chest and send him on his way? I'll do this without a trocar. Scalpel, please."

He made an incision between the man's fourth and fifth ribs; then, using a hemostat, he bluntly dissected through the muscles and entered the pleural space. Blood began to drain out of the patient's chest immediately. He opened the incision wide enough so he could insert his finger, then felt inside to ensure the ribs on either side were intact.

"Tube and forceps, please." He fitted the end of the rubber tube to the forceps and guided it gently into the pleural cavity. The other end of the tube sat in a basin, rapidly filling with blood, that Nurse Greenhalgh had placed on the floor.

It took him hardly any time at all to suture his patient's chest wounds; few seamstresses could match his skill with a needle and thread. The chest tube he'd leave in place for now, at least until the drainage abated.

He checked the clock on the wall behind him. It was half-past eight at night, which meant he'd been on his feet, in this tent, for nearly thirty hours. Not quite straight, for he'd visited the latrine twice, and had taken a minute to drink a cup of tea and wolf down a sandwich that morning. Or had it been yesterday morning?

"Anyone able to take on triage?" asked Colonel Lewis, who was, Robbie noted, halfway through a double leg amputation: he'd detached the patient's left limb, or what remained of it, and was now turning his attention to the man's mangled right leg.

"I'll go," Robbie volunteered. "How many shall I bring back with me?"

The colonel surveyed the hut; six tables, not including Robbie's, were occupied. From the look of it, none of the other surgeons would finish anytime soon.

"Just two for now. I won't be long with this one."

Robbie stripped off his gown, cap, and gloves and tossed them into an overflowing hamper by the door. Stepping outside, he was relieved to see that he and his colleagues had, miraculously, made a dent in the volume of patients waiting for care; earlier in the day, at least a hundred men had crowded the reception marquee. Some had even been left to lie on their stretchers in the open air. But now there were no more than two dozen Tommies awaiting aid. With any luck, they'd all be seen to before midnight.

He caught the eye of one of the orderlies. "How long have these men been waiting?"

"Last ambulance came in round about six o'clock, sir. Already sent the critical cases on to you."

Robbie walked through the tent, listening to Private Harris describe the wounded men's injuries. Apart from one man with a compound fracture to his tibia, all seemed stable and reasonably comfortable. All except one.

"What about him?" Robbie asked. He pointed to a stretcher at the far side of the marquee; its occupant was eerily still, his face ashen with shock.

"Beg your pardon, sir, I should've said so before. He came in about a half hour ago. Ambulance driver took it slow for his sake. Spinal injury."

"How high up?"

"Not sure, sir. High enough. Can't move his arms or legs. Having trouble breathing."

Robbie walked across the tent to the patient, who was no more than eighteen or nineteen years old, and knelt on the ground next to the boy's stretcher. "I'm Captain Fraser, one of the doctors here. I'd like to take a look at you now. Can you speak?"

"Aye, sir," came the whispered reply.

"What's your name, Private?"

"James Kerr, sir."

"From the sound of your brogue, I'm thinking you're from the same part of Scotland as me. Lanarkshire?"

The boy smiled weakly. "Airdrie," he murmured.

"That's no more than ten miles from where I grew up, Private Kerr. Have you heard of Auchinloch?"

"Aye. Captain . . . ?"

"Yes, Private?"

"What's wrong wi' me?"

"You've sustained an injury to your upper spine. That's why you're having trouble feeling your limbs. Can you remember what happened?"

"No, sir . . . sorry."

"How are you feeling now? Are you in any pain?"

"No pain. Hard to breathe."

"We'll give you some medicine that will help with that. I'm going to ask our orderlies to carry you into one of the tents so you can rest. I'll check on you in a while, and you can tell me all about Airdrie."

The boy wasn't going to last the night.

While they'd been talking, Robbie had tested his reaction to touch, and there'd been no response when he pinched the skin on Private Kerr's legs, arms, and abdomen. The note from the medic at the ADS, who'd examined and dressed the wound, had been quite clear: axial loading to the lower cervical spine, sustained when a shell blast had dashed him against a support beam. Private Kerr would die, likely by asphyxia, within hours.

Robbie stood up and turned to the orderly at his side. "Take him to the resuss tent. Who's on duty there now?"

"Nurse Bell."

"Tell her to give him morphia, half a grain, to keep him comfortable. And have her call me when things change."

"What of the rest of them, sir?"

"We've only got space for two, so I'll take the man with the tibial fracture as well as the fellow next to him."

"The one with the crush injury to his hand?"

"That's him. Colonel Lewis has a way with hands. Perhaps he can save it."

"Yes, sir. I'll just get some help from the ward tent for this here stretcher—"

"No need. I'll help you move him over to pre-op. But make sure you get Private Kerr to the resuss tent as soon as we're done. Might as well make sure he's comfortable."

It was half-past eleven, a mere blip of time, before Robbie finished his final surgery of the day and stumbled, his eyes burning, his head pounding, into the night.

In thirty-three hours, he had performed nineteen surgeries. Fourteen limbs and one spleen removed, three bowel resections, one hemothorax drained, and countless debridements of wasted, destroyed, pulverized human flesh.

"Captain Fraser?" It was one of the orderlies; Robbie couldn't remember his name.

"Yes?"

"Nurse Bell asked me to fetch you. The paralysis case."

Robbie set off at a run for the resuss tent. Inside, the lights were low, but he could make out the figure of Nurse Bell, sitting on a stool next to Private Kerr's cot.

"Nurse Bell? May I speak with you a moment?"

They stood at the foot of the bed, their voices lowered, their words carefully chosen.

"Prepare a syringe with another half a grain. Just enough to ease his breathing."

"Yes, Captain Fraser. It's not busy in here tonight; shall I sit with him until . . ."

"No, thank you. I'll stay."

Robbie perched on the stool and focused his attention on the boy. "What does your mam call you, Private Kerr?"

"Jamie, sir." His voice was so soft that Robbie had to bend close to hear it.

"Would you like me to write to her, Jamie? And your da? To let them know how you're getting on?"

"Aye," came the halting reply. And then, "Can't . . . breathe . . ."

Robbie took the syringe from Nurse Bell, who stood silently behind him, and injected its contents into Jamie's slender arm. "I'm giving you some medicine. It will make it easier."

The boy made no answer; he was beyond speech now. As the morphine took effect, Robbie was relieved to see his breathing become less labored, though increasingly shallow. His pulse was slowing, too. They were nearing the end.

"You know, Jamie, it's been a long time since I met someone from home," Robbie began. "I left Auchinloch when I was eight, to go to school in Edinburgh, but at half term and in the summer I would go home to my mam. I expect summers in Airdrie weren't much different. I remember how I'd go fishing for perch in the loch. The water was always so cold, even in the summer. And then, when I took the fish home to my mam, she would grumble about the state of my clothes. But I think she was happy enough to have fresh-caught perch for our supper."

He watched the boy's face intently. Seeing the shadow of a smile, he decided to carry on. Robbie kept up a comforting flow of reminiscences, as soothing to himself as to his patient, until his voice faltered and he found he could go no further.

Jamie's eyes were closed, his breathing so shallow that Robbie could no longer mark it by the rise and fall of his chest. With one hand he brushed the boy's hair off his forehead, rather as he imagined a loving father might do; with the other hand he felt for the boy's pulse.

Gradually it slowed, the space between beats lengthening: further apart, further, ever further, then ceasing.

Robbie sat for a minute, too tired to move. When he did stand he found himself staggering. Evidently the exhaustion of the day, and the emotion of the moment, had caught up with him.

Nurse Bell was at his side in an instant. "Captain Fraser! Are you all right?"

"Yes, thank you. I simply stood up too quickly."

"I will take care of the paperwork; you should get some rest."

"Thank you, Nurse Bell, but I'll do it. I don't mind."

Leaving her to prepare Private Kerr's body for burial in the cemetery adjacent to the hospital grounds, he exited the resuss tent and entered the ward tent next door. Sitting down at the desk he and the other surgeons shared, he drew a blank sheet of paper from the pigeonhole above and began to write. He left the address blank; the boy's OC would have to provide it.

14 June 1917

Dear Mr. and Mrs. Kerr,

I am very sorry to inform you that your son James died this morning, at twenty minutes past midnight. You will no doubt also receive official notification, but I felt I must write to you and let you know the circumstances of his death.

I am a surgeon with the 51st Casualty Clearing Station and received Jamie into my care late yesterday evening. He had suffered an injury to his upper spine that could not be remedied by surgical or other means, and it was this that led to his death. I should add, however, that because of the nature of his injury, he was insensible to pain and remained quite comfortable in the last hours of his life.

I remained at his side until the moment of his death. His final thoughts were of you and it was his express wish that I write to you.

Despite our brief acquaintance it was evident to me that Jamie was a courageous and honorable young man. I deeply regret that I was unable to save him.

Please accept my sincere condolences for the loss you have suffered. If at any time you wish to correspond with me further, I would be delighted to oblige.

Yours faithfully,
Cpt. Robert Fraser, RAMC
51st CCS
France

Chapter 18

Burlington Hotel
Folkestone, Kent
24 July 1917

Dearest Edward,

Let me begin by thanking you most sincerely for your letter and the birthday wishes it contained. I was so relieved to hear that you were finally given some leave and were able to enjoy two days of leisure in Saint-Omer.

It was a very great surprise to receive the hamper from Fortnum & Mason—there was no card but it could only have been from you. It arrived a few days ago and I am ashamed to say I opened it directly, rather than wait for the twenty-third. I have shared the books and magazines with my friends and they extend their thanks. The ladies' journals, with their illustrations of the latest fashions, were indeed a sight for sore eyes. The chocolates are all gone, I'm afraid, for we ate them straightaway, but several inches of Dundee cake remain, and we haven't yet opened the pots of jam and marmalade. I plan to ration the tea, reserving it for the rainiest days only. I doubt it will last long!

Last night my friends surprised me with an impromptu party after supper. Bridget had procured a bottle of champagne (I dared not ask whence it came) and we toasted my twenty-four years by clinking together our tin cups and tooth mugs. I think it was the nicest birthday party I have ever had, despite the absence of guests such as yourself and Charlotte.

Life here is much the same as it has been since my arrival in April. Breakfast at dawn, up to Shorncliffe Camp, drill, lectures, practice driving, a filling but tasteless dinner, more drill, another lecture if we are particularly unlucky, more practice on the Crossley, then back to our hotel for supper, with lights-out no later than ten o'clock.

This evening at supper our unit administrator told me and a number of my friends that she wanted to speak to us tomorrow. She didn't seem in the least perturbed, so I'm not overly concerned. Probably she wants us to volunteer for something tiresome—showing around new WAACs, or tidying the grounds in anticipation of a visit from a higher-up. I shan't lose any sleep over it!

It's lights-out in a few minutes, so I shall end this letter now and post it tomorrow. Do write again as soon as you can, for I treasure every scrap of news you send me.

With much love from
Your devoted sister
Lilly

Her letter complete, Lilly changed into her nightgown, washed her face, and brushed out her hair. Her uniform lay across the foot of her bed in readiness for the morning; with six women in one tiny room there were only so many hooks to go around.

She climbed into bed, willed herself not to notice the scratchiness of the blankets, which was all the more noticeable since there were no sheets, and waited for her friends to return from the hotel's dining room. It was there they spent most evenings, crowded together, the air heavy with talk and song and the smoke exhaled by several especially daring girls. Lilly had joined her roommates earlier in the evening, but had stolen away after an hour so she could write to her brother.

It astonished her to think of it, even now, but her impulsive decision to step forward and help the other women with the troublesome Crossley had turned the tide in her favor, particularly where Annie and Bridget were concerned. They still delighted in chaffing her at every opportunity, but now did so more gently, and with greater gentility, than previously.

For her part, Lilly now did her best to join in whenever invited, and if that meant endless evenings in the raucous, headache-inducing confines of the dining room, so be it. It was worth it.

"Good morning, ladies."

"Good morning, Unit Administrator Davies," the women replied in unison. They'd been finishing dinner when the summons had come to meet with Miss Davies. Eight of their group of sixteen drivers, Constance, Annie, and Bridget among them, now stood before her, shoulder to shoulder in the close confines of her office.

"At ease, ladies. I have been very pleased with your progress over the past three months, and I have the utmost confidence in your abilities. I want to be very clear on that point.

"The army needs your help. As you may know, until recently most ambulance drivers were drawn from the Army Service Corps. Now that more and more of the ASC drivers are being transferred to frontline duties, there are too few drivers for the routes between the advanced dressing stations and the casualty clearing stations."

Her words echoed in Lilly's ears. Surely Miss Davies had made a mistake; had meant to say something else entirely. Or perhaps Lilly herself had misheard and was imagining it all.

"I must now ask," Miss Davies continued, "if any of you are willing to drive those routes. While they are not, strictly speaking, part of the front lines, they are well within reach of the enemy's guns, and the Front itself is only miles away. It will be difficult and, I fear, emotionally trying work, as you can well imagine. I stress that this is a request only, and not a command. Those among you who choose not to volunteer will not be censured in any way."

Lilly stepped forward almost before Miss Davies had finished speaking. "I volunteer."

A heartbeat later, Constance joined her. "I will go as well," she said. From the corner of her eye Lilly saw Annie, then Bridget, then the remaining WAACs, step forward.

Miss Davies's eyes became suspiciously bright, and she cleared her throat again. "Your eagerness to help is most commendable, ladies. I shall be sorry to lose you."

"Do you know where we will be posted?" Constance asked.

"My aide is finalizing the details now. I expect you'll be somewhere in the vicinity of Saint-Omer, well south of the Ypres salient. I suggest you return to your quarters and pack your things. Miss Blythe will let you know as soon as possible. No need to wait here; she knows where to find you."

Rising, she shook their hands, one by one. "Each of you is a credit to the WAAC. I wish you the best of luck, and farewell."

The women filed out of Miss Davies's office and began to walk across the compound to their quarters, all except Lilly. "Don't mind me," she told her friends. "I'll be along soon."

Retracing her steps, she hurried back to the warren of rooms that housed the WAAC administration at Shorncliffe Camp. Just down the hall from Miss Davies's office was the room, hardly bigger than a broom closet, which had been allotted to her aide. Lilly knocked lightly on the doorframe.

"I'm so sorry to bother you, Miss Blythe. I just wanted to say hello before I left. Do you remember me? Lilly Ashford—"

"Of course I do. How lovely to see you again."

"Are you enjoying your work over here?"

Ellen Blythe beamed at Lilly. "I *adore* it. Why I thought I would be happy in the motor corps I'll never know."

"You were making some progress—"

"A *very* little progress, Miss Ashford, and only because you were helping me. But I'm forgetting myself; I should be congratulating you on your transfer. I'm just typing everything up now."

All you have to do is ask, Lilly told herself. Simply ask, as nicely as possible. The worst you can expect is a no. "Thank you very much. I was wondering . . ."

"Yes?"

"I have a very large favor to ask of you. So large that I will quite understand if you aren't able to help me."

"Go on," Miss Blythe said eagerly.

"I have a friend, working at one of the clearing hospitals. A very dear friend." She was careful not to specify the gender of said friend. "And I was hoping that, ah, if it's not too much trouble, you could—"

"Arrange to send you to the same hospital?"

"Yes. But only if it's not too much trouble."

"It's not any trouble at all. I haven't forgotten how you stepped in and took over from Corporal Pike that day. Such a disagreeable man," she said, wrinkling her nose at the memory. "Let's see if your friend's hospital is on the list."

"It's the Fifty-First. I believe they're located near Aire-sur-la-Lys."

"Hmm . . . Fifty-First . . . ah, here it is. But they're not in Aire anymore. Does Merville sound right?"

"I suppose. My friend had said they might be moved."

"There you are. Now, then, what does it say here? Ah, yes—they're meant to be receiving drivers from Boulogne."

"I see," Lilly said, her hopes deflated. "I'm so sorry to have bothered you."

"Don't give up so easily. I can easily change it around. I'll just need to telegraph our offices in Boulogne."

"Thank you so much. You don't know how grateful I am."

"It's the least I can do, Miss Ashford." Squeezing past Lilly, she disappeared down the hallway. "I won't be a minute," she called back cheerily.

Miss Blythe reappeared a half hour later, a sheaf of papers tucked under her arm. "I'm sorry that took so long. They were having some trouble with the direct lines, so the telegraph operator had to do some complicated kind of rerouting."

"And . . . ?" Lilly prompted.

"It's all arranged," Miss Blythe confirmed. "We'll send four drivers to the Fifty-First and they'll send four to the Twenty-Second, where you were supposed to go. Now, tell me, which of the other WAACs should go with you?"

This was turning out far, far better than Lilly had hoped. "Constance Evans, Annie Dowd, and Bridget Gallagher, if that's quite all right with you. Thank you—"

"As I've said already, Miss Ashford, it's no trouble at all."

The next morning, at nine o'clock on the dot, RMS *Invicta* departed Folkestone harbor, its decks crammed with troops as well as a modest contingent of WAACs. Lilly, Constance, and the rest of the women, thirty all told, were confined to a smallish dining room for the two-hour crossing. Ostensibly it was for their comfort, but Lilly suspected the intention was to keep them separate from the men for as long as possible.

Within minutes the air was foul with the unmistakable odor of seasickness, as well as the exhalations of nervous smokers. Constance had found a pair of seats near the windows, but the occasional waft of salt-sweet air did little to lessen Lilly's discomfort, and before long she was wondering if she would have to beg for one of the enameled pails that were being handed round to her indisposed companions. Even Annie and Bridget had been silenced, too weakened by mal de mer to do anything more than groan and retch into their shared pail.

Just as Lilly was certain she could bear it no longer, a shout went up from the men on deck.

"What is it? Has someone spotted a U-boat?" she asked Constance worriedly.

"No, you goose. We're coming into Boulogne harbor. If you'll only take your head out of your hands and look up you'll see what I mean."

Lilly peered out of the window nearest her, which Constance had wrenched halfway open when they boarded, and surveyed the promised view. It was true—they were in France.

"What time is it?" Constance asked.

"A quarter past eleven. Or, rather, a quarter past twelve. We're on continental time now." Lilly adjusted her watch, then slumped back in her seat as her nose was assailed, yet again, by the stench that permeated the cabin.

An unspeakably endless hour passed before they were released from purgatory and allowed on the upper deck, empty now of Tommies. A WAAC official marshaled the women, and they dutifully formed a neat column, two abreast, as they departed the ship and marched to the railway hub that had been set up some two hundred yards distant. It was a shock, as they walked along the docks, some of the women wobbling a little on their sea legs, to hear French being spoken around them. At last they were on foreign soil, and only hours from their destination.

"Attention, everyone!"

"Hush, girls—it's the deputy controller. Quiet, now, so she can speak." Constance ought to have been one of the officers, Lilly reflected, hearing her speak so authoritatively.

"A show of hands, please, for those of you who are being posted onward to Saint-Omer and points west. Ah—there you are. Please make your way to Platform Three. One of our officials is waiting for you there. As for the rest of you, I believe you are all staying in Boulogne? No one is being sent on to Étaples? Right, then. If you are going to Saint-Omer, walk ahead and follow the signs; everyone else, come with me."

And with that she turned her back and marched off with her charges, leaving Lilly, her friends, and four other WAACs where they stood.

"She said to follow the signs—"

"Did she say Platform Three?"

"I don't see any signs for Platform Three."

"What if we can't find it before our train leaves? What will we do then?"

"I know where to go."

Only Constance heard Lilly at first. "What's that, Lilly?"

"I know where to go. I can read French. We want a sign that says *'quai numéro trois,'* or words to that effect. It might be *quai* followed by a three with an *e* after it. Oh, wait—I think I see it!"

"What are you waiting for, then?" Constance laughed. "Come on, everyone. Lilly's saved us. Follow her."

In a matter of moments they had arrived at the correct platform, and were greeted by a young WAAC who was clearly relieved to see her charges appear more or less on time.

"Hello, everyone. Please take your seats on the train; your lockers have already been loaded."

She had a pleasant face, Lilly thought, and the clipped, rather nasal accent of someone who had attended a good school, and possibly even university. Just the sort of woman Lilly herself had once aspired to be.

Once they had settled in the carriage, which had banks of seats rather than compartments, the WAAC official clapped her hands and waited, her expression inscrutable, until everyone was silent.

"Thank you very much. As you all know, we are traveling on to Saint-Omer now. It's thirty miles from here, as the crow flies, so we won't arrive until the late afternoon. If you need to use the facilities, I suggest you do so while we are stationary. The lavatory is at the far end of the carriage."

More pressing, at least to Lilly's mind, was the question of what they would eat, although the hour for dinner had come and gone more than an hour ago. Probably they would have to wait until Saint-Omer for a decent meal. Her stomach rumbled but there was nothing to be done; even Constance, who was normally so organized, hadn't brought so much as a square of chocolate.

She hugged her arms about her middle and, gazing out the window, turned her attention to the French countryside, so similar to England, but still, some-how, indefinably unique. Perhaps it was the houses, she thought, with their tiled roofs and whitewashed walls.

The weather was fine, and it seemed to Lilly, as she admired the lush fields, dotted here and there with flocks of plump sheep, that the war must belong to an-other world entirely. How else could she reconcile this sylvan bliss, now slipping so gently by her window, with the fact that guns were blazing, shell fire was raining down, and legions of men were fighting, killing, and dying, somewhere in France, all less than a hundred miles away?

Chapter 19

A WAAC forewoman was waiting when their train pulled into Saint-Omer late that afternoon.

"I'm taking four of you to the Fifty-First and the other four to the Fifty-Fourth—correct? Good. I can take two up front with me; the rest of you will have to go in the back."

Ordinarily the journey ought to have taken no more than an hour and a half, at most, to cover; but the lorry they rode in, a decrepit three-ton Dennis, could only manage five miles at a stretch without overheating, so they spent many long minutes by the side of the road, waiting for the radiator to cool so their driver could refill it and safely restart the engine.

As much as Lilly longed to arrive in Merville, she was grateful for the respite provided by the stops, not least because it offered a break from the teeth-jarring, bone-crumbling confines of the lorry's smelly interior.

By the time they halted for the fourth or fifth time, she threw propriety to the wind and lay down on the road's grassy verge. It felt like the loftiest of feather beds in comparison to the lorry's unforgiving wooden benches.

Bridget followed Lilly's lead and, chuckling a little, flopped down in the grass as well. "Grand idea, this. Wouldn't mind staying here all day."

"If only we could," Lilly agreed. "Anything to avoid getting back in that lorry."

"You all right, duck?" her friend asked. "You aren't yourself today, if you don't mind me saying."

"I'm fine. Just wondering what things will be like for us at our new posting."

"You 'n me both. I dunno how I'll tell my Gordon. When I signed up I swore up and down I wouldn't let them send me anywhere dangerous—and now look at me!"

"Do you think he'll be upset when he finds out?"

"Ooh, yes. Gets as mad as a wet hen when I cross him! But he'll come round soon enough. Always does."

Lilly smiled but made no reply, instead tilting her face to the sun. How long now, she asked herself for the thousandth time that day, until I see him? And what will that moment be like? Will he be angry? Or, despite everything, will he be glad to see me?

The sun was giving her a headache, so she turned her face away and tried to focus on the crisscrossing leaves of grass beneath her outstretched hand. She felt a whispery tickle and saw that a ladybird had clambered onto her forefinger. It sat, folding and refolding its lacquered wings, appearing to enjoy the warmth of its perch.

Behind her, the engine sputtered to life. Lilly placed the little beetle on a dandelion bud, making sure it was well settled, then climbed into the lorry with her friends. With a bit of luck they would be in Merville before dusk.

After that final stop by the side of the road, the lorry had behaved, and had rumbled meekly along for the remainder of the journey. The women had fallen silent, tired of shouting to make themselves heard, and it was then that Lilly had become aware of an odd noise. At first she thought it must be thunder, but the timbre of the sound was disturbingly low, and its arrhythmic, discordant drumbeat never ceased.

To begin with the sound was so indistinct she could hardly make it out above the irritable hiss of the lorry's radiator, but with every passing mile it grew louder and stronger, and Lilly began to suppose she could feel the ground rumbling beneath them. She caught Constance's eye, and in that moment she understood.

It was the guns. Monstrous guns, German and British and French, spewing out shells to pound the fields and villages of this gentle landscape into ruination.

She knew that Edward could hear them, too. Not as a distant roar, but as a deafening curtain of falling, endlessly falling shells that exterminated every living thing in their path. And nothing, no shelter, no armor, could protect her brother, or any other man on the front lines, from the remorseless anger of those guns. Only fate.

It was a mercy she was already sitting, otherwise her knees surely would have buckled. She reached out, blindly, and felt Constance grip her hand, anchoring her to sanity.

"I expect we'll get used to it," she heard herself saying.

"Of course we will. Rather like having a train at the bottom of the garden," Constance offered. Lilly could only nod.

The lorry slowed abruptly, the driver struggling to change down, and Lilly saw they were entering a village. A shout from the front told them they had reached Merville. Peering out the back of the lorry, she could see a church, not especially grand, flanked by modest brick buildings, a forge, the clipped lawn of a common green.

The lorry continued along for another five minutes, then lurched to a halt in what appeared, from Lilly's perspective, to be nothing more than a fallow field.

"Is this it?" Bridget asked. "Are we here?"

From the front, Annie's voice could be heard, faintly, above the rumble of the engine. They'd arrived.

Lilly jumped down and immediately saw they were stopped behind a line of ambulances. Just beyond, a village-size group of huts and tents had been erected in the field, their entrances linked by yard after yard of mud-stained duckboard walkways.

There seemed to be no one about, so Lilly helped Constance, Annie, and Bridget lower their lockers to the ground. No sooner had they finished unloading their belongings than the driver shouted a perfunctory good-bye and drove off, much to the surprise of the remaining WAACs in the back of the lorry.

Lilly had begun to worry there must have been some kind of mistake, for there'd been no signs to mark the way, when a woman emerged from a tent at the far end of the compound. She waved to them, hastening over to where they stood. Lilly saw that she wore the uniform of a WAAC official, so did her best to stand a little straighter, despite her fatigue.

"At last you've arrived. We've been expecting you all day," the official said. "I am Assistant Administrator Diana Jeffries, and I will be your supervisor here at the Fifty-First. Simply call me Miss Jeffries; 'assistant administrator' is a bit of a mouthful. Now, let me show you to your quarters. Leave your lockers; you can come back and collect them once I've shown you around."

She set off at a trot, clearly a woman disinclined to waste time, and led them back to the tent from which she had emerged only moments before. "My quarters, as well as my office. I like to be close to my girls, and I want you to know that if you have any concerns, or difficulties of any kind, you should not hesitate to come to me."

She smiled at them brightly, then flung back the entrance flap of a larger tent, mere inches away. "This will be your quarters. Just poke your noses in for the moment. You'll be sharing with our other WAACs here. Cooks, both of them. Ethel Finlayson and Rose Thompson. Lovely girls. Has everyone had a look? Excellent. Now I'll take you to the mess tent. Supper is over, but I asked them to keep something warm for you."

The mess tent, capacious and light, with a high ceiling and duckboard floors, had four distinct banks of tables. Miss Jeffries directed them to the nearest, and smallest, table. "This is where you will eat. And of course you are welcome to come here when you are off duty."

"Where is everyone else, Miss Jeffries?" Constance asked politely.

"I expect most are at work in the wards. It's been nonstop here for the past few weeks. Our poor doctors and nurses are run off their feet. Enough talk, now. Sit down and I'll have something sent out to you."

That had been the extent of their tour. After a supper of tea, toast, margarine, and applesauce, even though it was only half-past seven, Miss Jeffries had whisked them back to their tent, pausing only to show them the latrine, separate from its fellows, that had been set aside for the nurses and WAACs.

"Off to bed, all of you. We get started bright and early here, with breakfast at half-past six." She began to leave, then turned back, her expression serious. "You are bound to notice that military discipline is rather, ah, relaxed here. One might go so far as to say it is somewhat slack. That, of course, is for Colonel Lewis to determine, and in his opinion it benefits morale here at the hospital if officers and other ranks are not prohibited from socializing with one another.

"That laxity does not, however, extend to the women under my care. I must tell you that I will not tolerate any infraction of our code of conduct. If any of you is so unwise as to engage in inappropriate fraternization with any of the soldiers or officers, you will be sent home immediately. Do I make myself clear?"

"Yes, Miss Jeffries," they replied.

"Very well, then. I am glad we understand one another. Good night to all of you. Sleep well."

Lilly woke with a start, blinking her eyes in the half-light of dawn. It had been a long night. She had slept fitfully, her dreams invaded by harrowing images, only half-remembered now, their dissonant score the rumble of distant guns.

Looking around sleepily, she assessed her surroundings, which she had been too tired to notice the night before. She and her friends were quartered in a canvas tent, not especially large, with rough deal planking on the floor. Two modest openings, now covered with flaps, served as windows. The center of the space was marked by a compact coal-burning stove. Their beds, actually folding cots, were arranged around the tent's perimeter, with the WAACs' wooden lockers at the foot of each cot. A single nail, hammered into one of the tent's support posts, held a kerosene lantern.

Lilly peered at her wristwatch: it was almost six o'clock. A little less than twelve hours, then, since they had arrived at the 51st.

"Constance," she hissed. "Constance, wake up. It's just gone six. If we want any breakfast before we start, we have to get up now."

"Mmph . . . all right. Are Annie and Bridget awake?"

"Not yet. I'll wake them. We daren't be late, not on our first day."

Lilly roused her friends, dressed hurriedly, then began the tiresome task of brushing and braiding her hair. After she'd coiled the plait into a knot at the nape of her neck, and secured it with her diminishing store of hairpins, Lilly made up her cot and waited, rather impatiently, for the others to be ready. The walk from their quarters to the mess tent, no more than twenty yards, seemed to stretch into infinity. Would Robbie be at breakfast, sitting with the other officers at their table?

The tent was busy, its tables crowded, but there was no sign of him. Lilly swallowed her disappointment and turned her attention to breakfast, a nourishing but bland meal of salted porridge, applesauce, and luke-warm tea. No sooner had she begun than Miss Jeffries bustled up, brimming with vim and vigor.

"Good morning, ladies! I trust you slept well?"

"Yes, Miss Jeffries," they replied.

"Do your best to finish, then I'll take you over to your ambulances. Eat up, now. You have a long day ahead of you."

Chapter 20

M iss Jeffries returned in short order to escort them to the group of ambulances they'd seen last night. Waiting for them was a private, about Lilly's age, whose neatly clipped mustache lent maturity to his young face. He smiled shyly as the women approached.

"This is Private Gillespie," Miss Jeffries explained, "one of our ASC drivers. I've asked him to answer any questions you may have about your ambulances and the routes you'll be driving."

As Miss Jeffries took her leave, silence fell as the WAACs contemplated Private Gillespie and he, blushing furiously, examined his boots. He cleared his throat once, then twice, but seemed at a loss for words.

Constance spoke first. "Could you tell us a bit about our ambulances, Private Gillespie? We've been driving lorries for the past few months."

"What kind of lorries, ma'am?"

The women giggled, and Constance reached out and gave him a friendly pat on the shoulder. "They were Crossleys, in the main. But please don't call me ma'am. I'm the same rank as you. Just call me Miss Evans. I'm Constance Evans. And these are my friends." One by one, they introduced themselves, shaking Private Gillespie's hand, and Lilly was relieved to see the hectic color begin to fade from his face.

"These here ambulances are Fords, straight from America," he began. "They're built on a Model T chassis with a wood-and-canvas frame, so they're nice and light. Easy to push or hoist if you get bogged down. Top speed is forty-five miles an hour, but you'll never get close to that here."

He approached the nearest ambulance and pulled up one side of the hinged bonnet so they could see inside. "Engine is four cylinders. Water-cooled, so you'd best keep an eye on that radiator. Oil needs topping up often; do it every morning, or at least check the levels." He reached across to the engine, pulled out a spark plug, and inspected it closely. "Four spark plugs; make sure you check they aren't bunged up with carbon."

"That sounds straightforward enough, doesn't it, girls?" Constance commented. Private Gillespie closed the bonnet and walked to the driver's seat, hoisting himself into it easily.

"This shouldn't be much different from the Crossley. Same setup for your clutch, throttle, brakes, and gearshift. Go easy on the brakes at first; she's apt to skid." He paused, considering the group looking up at him. "Did they give you any cold-weather gear? Not that you need it now," he clarified, blushing again, "but you'll freeze solid in winter without a decent greatcoat and gloves." He waved his arm, indicating the open sides of the driver's compartment, and the women shivered despite the warmth of the July morning.

He jumped down and walked to the rear of the ambulance. "You've got room for three stretcher cases, or six seated, plus you can usually cram one extra man up front between the two of you. You won't be expected to lift the stretchers into the ambulances; there'll be orderlies to help with that. But you will have to help the walking wounded. And you'll also have to swab out the ambulance after each run." He broke off, and Lilly realized he was considering how honest he ought to be with them.

"Go ahead," she encouraged him. "We volunteered for this work."

"That's good of you, miss. It's just that . . . well, some of the men, once they've been wounded, can't control their, ah . . ."

"Bodily functions?" Constance interjected gently.

"Yes, ah, that's it. So it's a right midden back here sometimes. Blood, of course, and sometimes they're sick to their stomach, or worse. But if you put off cleaning it up, the smell only gets worse.

"Now I'd best show you the route you'll take, and all of that. When you come back from the ADS—that's the advanced dressing station—you'll pull up there," he told them, pointing to an open area in front of an especially large tent. "Facing it is the reception marquee. The orderlies will unload the stretcher cases and you'll be left to help the men who can walk. Don't give them anything to eat or drink; that's for the doctors and nurses to decide. Once they're inside, the doctors will look them over and decide where they go next.

"Next to the marquee is the pre-op tent. That's where men who are strong enough for surgery are prepped. There's a wooden building just beyond—can you see it from here? That's the operating hut. On the other side of it is the resuss tent. That's where they stabilize the men who are too weak for surgery. Sometimes all they need is a warm blanket around them. It's also where they take the men who are, well . . ."

Lilly touched his arm, lightly. "We know. It's for the men who are dying."

He looked at her gratefully. "Thank you, miss. Seems wrong, somehow, saying it. But it's true enough." He rubbed the back of his neck, as if weary already, then continued his explanation. "Beyond it is the ward tent. That's where the men go after surgery, until they're strong enough for the trip to a base hospital."

"How many wounded men are here now?" Lilly asked.

"About a hundred and fifty, give or take a few, I reckon. We've fifty ward beds, plus room for another hundred and fifty stretcher cases. That puts us almost at capacity. When that happens, any new casualties will go to the Fifty-Fourth, just down the road, and we'll have a few days to catch up. Then, once we've moved most of the wounded on to Saint-Omer, the Fifty-Fourth will close and we'll be open again."

Bridget found her voice at last. "So how are the men moved to the base hospitals?"

"There's a railhead about five hundred yards from here. Didn't you come here on one of the hospital trains?"

"No, we were driven here from Saint-Omer," explained Constance.

"Hmm. Might've been a problem with the line somewhere between here and Saint-Omer. At any rate, when we have any men who are ready to be moved, you'll be taking them. I'll show you the way today or tomorrow.

"Now, if you don't have any other questions, we'd best be heading off. I'll drive in the lead, with two of you up front with me. Which of you wants to drive the second ambulance?"

"It should be Lilly," Constance answered. "She's the best driver among us."

"Right, then. Just give me a minute to fetch some cans of water for the radiators. We don't want to use any of their water up at the ADS if we run low."

Annie and Bridget took their seats in the lead ambulance, leaving Lilly and Constance to perch on its running boards. The minutes dragged by and Lilly began to feel rather warm in her woolen jacket and skirt. She loosened her tie a fraction, which seemed to help, and wiggled a finger under her too-tight collar.

On the far side of the clearing, the door to the operating hut opened and a group of men appeared, blinking in the morning light, their surgeon's gowns splattered with blood. As the last man emerged from the hut's darkened interior, he paused in the doorway, his fair hair gleaming in the sunshine, and directed a curious glance at the group of women by the ambulances.

It was Robbie. Even at this distance, she knew it was him.

Heedless of what her friends might think, she stood, took a step forward, another, another. She opened her mouth, tried to call out his name, but no sound emerged.

She'd drawn his attention. He began to walk toward her, his expression of stunned recognition transmuting into a grimace of stricken realization. He stopped short when they were only an arm's length apart.

"It can't be . . . Lilly, what on earth . . . ?"

"I know, I know. Robbie, I'm so sorry to surprise you like this. They told us two days ago that we were being transferred. That is, they asked us to volunteer, and I said yes."

"Are you insane?" he countered. "Didn't you listen to a word I said? When I told you just how god-awful it is here?"

"I did, of course I did. I know it will be difficult, and not just the driving. But I'm sure I can do it."

He reached out and grasped her shoulders, and she was taken aback by the torment in his eyes. "I'm not talking about that; I don't doubt for a moment that you can manage. Lilly, it's too dangerous. The road between here and the ADS has been shelled any number of times. Even the Fifty-Fourth, just down the road, was hit a few weeks ago."

"But those are just stray shells, falling wide. That's what everyone says—"

"Bugger what everyone says," he replied, truly angry now. "That red cross on the side of your ambulance—do you honestly think it'll protect you if the Germans decide to play target practice with this hospital?"

"Robbie," she pleaded, aghast at his reaction, "please understand. I had to come. Not because I think it's some kind of adventure, or for . . . for personal reasons. I'm here so I can make a difference. Just like you promised I would."

With that, the anger seemed to drain out of him, and he stepped back, his arms falling to his sides. She felt transfixed by the naked anguish in his eyes, bluer than any remembered July sky.

Looking beyond Lilly, he noticed their audience for the first time. "Splendid," he muttered. "Any chance that your friends didn't hear our disagreement just now?"

"They won't say anything, I'm sure they won't."

He smiled at her, briefly, then covered his mouth as he suppressed a yawn. "Lilly, I must get some sleep before the next lot of wounded arrive. And you clearly need to be on your way as well."

"Promise you'll come and find me when you have a chance?"

"I promise. And in the meantime, please take care of yourself. I've more than my fair share of nightmares to cope with already."

Looking past her, he jabbed a finger at Private Gillespie, who had returned with his water cans and was standing, slack-jawed with astonishment, next to Constance. "Gillespie, isn't it?"

"Yes, sir, Captain Fraser, sir."

"Miss Ashford is the sister of my dearest friend. If anything happens to her on the road today, there'll be hell to pay. Understood?"

"Yes, sir!"

Robbie now directed a weary smile at Lilly's friends. "For my lack of courtesy, ladies, I beg your pardon, and I hope you'll excuse me now." With a final nod to Lilly, he walked away.

"It's him, isn't it?" Constance asked Lilly, concern shading her voice. "Your brother's friend from school. The one—"

"Yes," Lilly interrupted, loath to share any more details with Annie and Bridget, not to mention Private Gillespie. "Yes, it's him. Edward's friend. I meant to say something, earlier, but I wasn't sure how he would feel about my coming here."

"None too pleased, by the look of it," Annie commented. "He took a right turn, he did, the minute he saw you."

"I know," Lilly admitted. "I feel wretched about that. But there was no time to send word ahead. I just hope he'll change his mind about my being here."

"Of course he will," Constance promised. "But none of us will be here for very long if Miss Jeffries decides we're slacking off. So let's be on our way. Lilly, do you want to drive or shall I?"

"I will, but thank you for offering."

Lilly walked to the second ambulance and heaved herself into the driver's seat. She'd never driven a Ford before, and although Private Gillespie had said it was similar to the Crossley, from where she sat, everything about the vehicle looked and felt different. Driving it, for the first time, she would have to muster every ounce of concentration she possessed. Today there would be no time to think about anything else.

Or anyone.

Chapter 21

P rivate Gillespie set a measured pace for their first
trip to the ADS, tracing a painstaking course
around the mud-filled potholes that had left the road
a stippled ruin. Lilly saw very little of the surrounding landscape, so intent was she on following in his
wake, but several times she was obliged to bring her
ambulance to a halt as his Ford inched past an especially large crater. In those moments, Lilly was able to
survey the devastation that war had visited upon the
countryside.

The farmhouses they passed were abandoned, tiled
roofs shattered, shutters swinging wide, their vegetable
gardens choked with weeds. Fields and hedgerows,
once green and lush, had been drained of color and life,
the skies above empty of birdsong. Where trees once

towered, only jagged stumps now remained, marking the graves of vanished groves and thickets.

The lead ambulance was slowing; they had arrived at the ADS. She parked her vehicle carefully, taking care to turn around, as Private Gillespie was doing, so the ambulance was ready for the return journey.

The ADS was unmarked and, from the roadside, appeared to be little more than an embankment of sandbags, not especially high, with a gap in their middle about a yard wide. The women now followed Private Gillespie through the gap, stepping down into a crude, poorly lit dugout, where men sat silently on wooden benches as medics worked to bandage their wounds. At the far end of the chamber, stretchers crowded the dirt floor. A crude field dressing, already soaked with blood, was wrapped around one soldier's head, covering his eyes and much of his face; another man, now mercifully unconscious, seemed to have been wounded in the abdomen. His dressings, too, were stained rust red.

"Where the fuck have you been?"

Lilly turned, her heart pounding, and attempted to formulate a reply. The man who had approached them seemed to be a sergeant, although it was hard to be certain in the chamber's dim light.

Before she could say anything, Private Gillespie slipped past her, once again crimson with embarrassment.

"These are the WAACs who'll be our new drivers. We meant to set off earlier, but I had to show them around first. Sorry we're late."

"WAACs? *Women* drivers?" The sergeant's face was, if possible, even redder than Private Gillespie's. He sighed, heavily, and Lilly's toes curled in her boots as she waited for the inevitable. "Bugger it, Gillespie, you could have warned me. Now I've gone and said 'fuck' in front of them."

"That's twice now," Bridget pointed out.

The sergeant sighed loudly, then held out his hand for them to shake. "Sorry about that. I'm Sergeant Barnes, ladies, but you can call me Bill. Now let's get these men loaded and on their way." He walked to the door and whistled loudly. "Just calling for some help with these stretcher cases. Who's going to take them?"

"I will," answered Private Gillespie. "The ladies haven't driven the route before, so—"

"Well, they'll be driving it soon enough. And better now than in the rain, or in the middle of the night. It's just the two ambulances, right?"

Muttering under his breath, Bill walked to the back of the dugout and surveyed the men who lay on its rough floor, their only cushion the thin canvas of their stretchers. "Him . . . and him . . . those two in the corner . . . the head wound there . . . and this one. Gutshot, but

Captain Fraser might be able to pull him through. Do you have room for anyone up front?"

"We do," Lilly offered.

"Then take this one. Shell fragments in the arm."

Constance had already taken the uninjured arm of the soldier and was gingerly leading him out of the dugout. Before Lilly could follow, she was brushed aside by two stretcher-bearers, who carried their patient up the rough-hewn steps with surprising grace. First one stretcher, then another, was loaded into the back of her ambulance, the wounded men groaning a little as they were deposited on the thinly padded benches. Last of all was the man, hardly more than a boy, with the frightful abdominal wounds. Tellingly, he made no noise as the stretcher-bearers placed him on the floor between the other two stretchers.

Lilly began to pull the ambulance's canvas covers into place, but a shout from the dugout stopped her. It was Bill, who for some reason was carrying a pair of battered tin canteens.

"They're filled with hot water," he explained, tucking the canteens under the blanket that covered the boy. "He's gone into shock. They'll keep him warm. And mind you bring them back—they're as scarce as hen's teeth."

Blinking hard, Lilly looked away, hoping she would not shame herself, here, by shedding tears. Her vision clearing, she saw that Constance was waiting for her; clearly their passenger needed some assistance to climb into the ambulance.

Together they settled him in the center of the front seat, and then Lilly sat behind the steering wheel as Constance cranked the engine to life. She put the ambulance into gear as gently as possible, and it rewarded her by rolling forward without so much as a hiccup. So far, so good.

If the drive to the dressing station had been challenging, their return to the CCS was doubly so. Try as she might, Lilly was unable to avoid all of the potholes, for it seemed as if there were more of them than actual road. With every lurch and bounce of the chassis, a chorus of groans could be heard from the back, a daunting reminder of the urgency of her task.

"How far, do you think?" she asked Constance after many long minutes, praying the man hunched on the seat between them would not notice the anxiety percolating behind her words. But he made no sign of having heard.

"It's so hard to tell. There's no odometer on this thing, is there?"

"Unfortunately not."

"Well, let's see what we can recognize. That farmhouse over there, to the right—do you remember it?

The whole thing is tilting at such a funny angle. I can't imagine why it hasn't fallen down yet."

"Constance," Lilly warned, gritting her teeth. "We're not meant to be sightseeing."

"Calm down! I remember it from earlier. We'd only been driving a few minutes when we passed it. So we're nearly there."

Constance was right. Ahead, Private Gillespie's ambulance rounded a bend in the road, passing the ruined house, which in other circumstances would have looked quite comical, and there, only a few hundred yards distant, was the CCS.

Chapter 22

I'm here so I can make a difference. Just like you promised I would.

He'd been lying on his cot for more than an hour, desperately tired yet miserably awake. Try as he might, Robbie couldn't erase the memory of Lilly's words. Or the look on her face as she'd stared him down. She was right; he *had* encouraged her to join the WAAC. So why should he oppose her now?

The answer was clear enough, and it shamed him. He was afraid. More afraid than he'd been for a long, long time.

Sickening visions crowded in on him: a shell flattening her ambulance on the road to the dressing station, a gas attack on the ADS, a German raiding party breaking through the lines and reaching the ADS or even the 51st. It had happened before, elsewhere along the Front.

And then there were the horrors that Lilly was certain to face each and every day. He'd described them, as graphically as he dared, when she'd met him at the tea shop last October. But no secondhand account could possibly convey the morass of suffering, despair, and limitless loss into which she and her friends were about to wade.

Yet he'd never experienced so much as a twinge of concern over any of the other women he worked with, nor would any of them have welcomed such sentiments. They were here to do a job, to win the war, and had no time for old-fashioned notions about the so-called weaker sex.

It was time to face up to his role in this. He had encouraged her to apply to the WAAC. Bugger it, he'd even sung her praises to the corps' chief controller.

She was here now; nothing he said or did would change that. He had to accept it. Would force himself to accept it. So why not embrace this twist of fate for what it was? A gift, pure and simple. The gift of time with Lilly.

He could see her lovely face whenever their paths crossed in the mess tent or the reception marquee. He could talk with her discreetly, share a cup of tea from time to time.

"Captain Fraser? Sorry to disturb you."

It was Private Dixon; most likely Matron was sending him from tent to tent to rouse the surgeons.

"What time is it?"

"Nearly half-past nine. You're wanted in surgery, sir. First lot of wounded just arrived."

"Thanks. I'll be right there."

Robbie sat up, swung his feet over the side of the cot, and began to lace up his boots and gaiters. He hadn't slept, hadn't eaten, hadn't washed, and he would stay that way—tired, hungry, and unshaven—for many hours more.

He would work until there were no more patients waiting in the reception marquee, and then he would eat. He would have a bath, possibly a warm one if the cistern hadn't been emptied, and would shave.

And then—he would have to be careful; he didn't want to get her in trouble already—he would seek Lilly out, apologize, and make everything right between them.

As the CCS came into sight, Lilly breathed a sigh of relief, fractionally relaxed her grip on the steering wheel, and promptly drove over a block of fieldstone that had become lodged in the mud of the road. From the back of the ambulance, piteous moans were her reward for a moment of inattention.

The road had smoothed a little, now, and she sped up as the tents and sheds of their destination grew closer. Private Gillespie had parked already, and she could see Bridget and Annie standing solemnly by as orderlies and nurses began their work.

Lilly pulled to a stop; even before she had switched off the engine, the canvas covers at the back of the ambulance were being pulled aside. By the time she and Constance had helped the soldier sitting between them to descend, all three stretchers had been removed from the ambulance; a flurry of activity surrounded each of their occupants.

"We'd best be off again, ladies," Private Gillespie said. "We've got to move out all those men we saw, back there at the ADS, before we dare take a break. I'll bring around a third ambulance so you have some extra help this morning."

With that, they were off again. Another load of stretcher cases, another mutely suffering Tommy squashed into the front compartment, and then the journey home.

And again.

And again.

By the time they had cleared the last patient from the ADS, the sun was descending in the sky. Bill bid the WAACs a cheery good-bye, instructing them to return at first light. "They try not to move the wounded men from the front lines in daylight," he explained. "Too dangerous. Most come to us overnight, so try and be here at dawn, or even earlier, if you can stand it."

Lilly nodded, too weary to answer, and put the ambulance into gear. Only that morning, the pockmarked road in front of her had been as unfamiliar as the surface of the moon. And now? Now she knew every crater, every rut, every splintered branch and shattered boulder as well as she knew the rooms and hallways of Cumbermere Hall.

The ambulance, too, felt like an old friend. It was much easier to drive than the Crossley, to begin with, displaying none of the temperamental eccentricities that had made the lorry so difficult to manage. Lilly decided it ought to have a name.

"I think we should call the ambulance Henry," she announced to Constance. On this trip, fortunately, they did not have a front-seat passenger.

"What was that? Did you say you want to name the ambulance?"

"Why not? Horses have names. Let's call it Henry, after Mr. Ford. From all accounts he's a detestable man, but his company has made us a fine ambulance."

"But shouldn't it have a female name? Like a ship?"

For the first time since that morning, Lilly felt her face relax into a smile. "Of course it should. What about Henrietta?"

"Henrietta it is."

Chapter 23

Lilly had been looking forward to a cup of tea, and perhaps even something to eat, upon their return to the CCS. But first there was the disagreeable business of washing out the back of the ambulance. By the time she and Constance had filled their buckets and found some brushes and soap, the water, not very hot to begin with, had cooled to lukewarm; but the soap, which smelled strongly of carbolic, did a fine job of erasing the stench that permeated the ambulance's interior.

At last it was done. Constance went off in search of some tea, though it was less than an hour until supper, while Lilly sat on one of Henrietta's running boards and tried to ignore her growling stomach.

Seconds stretched into minutes; where was Constance with that tea? Lilly leaned back, tilting her face to the sun, and closed her eyes. Only for a moment, though. She still had to refill the radiator, check the oil, clean the spark plugs—

"Lilly?"

Why now? Why did he have to seek her out now, when she was dirty and disheveled and completely out of sorts? If only she'd taken a moment to wash her face when she'd gone to the lavatory earlier.

"I'm not bothering you, am I?" he asked.

"Not at all. I was waiting . . . that is, Constance is getting us some tea. We've only just finished."

"Do you mind if I sit?" Robbie asked. "Is there room?"

Lilly shuffled to the end of the running board. "Of course there is."

"I owe you an apology. My behavior, this morning, was inexcusable. Your friends must think me a brute."

"No, they don't. And it was my fault. Seeing me, like that, must have been a shock."

"It was," he admitted.

"Do you forgive me?"

"Aye, but with one condition. Agree to start over. Pretend this morning never happened."

"How good to see you again, Captain Fraser," she began, trying not to giggle.

"Likewise, Miss Ashford. How has your day been so far?"

"Quite fine, Captain Fraser, thank you."

"Honestly?"

"Honestly? No. It's been awful. Every bit as bad as you warned me it would be. I'm exhausted, and hungry, and I look a fright—"

"You're wrong about that," he interrupted.

Lilly decided to ignore the compliment. "I'm not complaining, Robbie. I'm just admitting that it's bad. But I'll manage."

"Of course you will."

"It wasn't all bad. My ambulance is much easier to drive than the lorries we drove in Kent. So that's one good thing. I've decided to call her Henrietta. After Mr. Ford."

"I'm sure he would be flattered."

"Robbie . . . did that boy survive? He had ginger hair, and the most terrible wounds to his abdomen. We brought him from the ADS around nine o'clock this morning."

"I'm sorry, Lilly. By the time he arrived he had lost too much blood. We tried transfusing him, but it wasn't enough. He died before I could operate."

Tears sprang to her eyes, acid and unbidden. "I ought to have driven faster. If only I had known the road, I could have got him to you sooner . . ."

But Robbie was shaking his head. "No, Lilly. Even if I'd seen him hours earlier, he would have died. There was nothing that you, or I, or anyone could have done to save him. But he wasn't alone. We weren't very busy today, so one of the nurses was at his side to hold his hand, and make sure he was comfortable. Sometimes that's all we can give them."

She closed her eyes and pictured the soldier's face. He'd been so young. "Do you know his name?"

"No," Robbie replied. "But I'll learn it soon enough. As soon as I have some time, I'll write to his mother, since I doubt he was old enough to have a wife, and tell her what happened."

"Surely you won't tell her the truth?" Lilly asked, aghast.

"I'll tell her what I just told you. Nothing clinical. Just that he didn't suffer at the end, and that he wasn't alone. I expect I'll say something about his bravery, and the sacrifice he made for King and Country."

Out of the corner of her eye, Lilly saw a familiar khaki uniform moving toward them. If Miss Jeffries were to see them together—

"Is anything the matter, Lilly?"

"No, I . . ." The figure moved closer and she saw that it was Constance, walking slowly, her hands full. "I thought I saw Miss Jeffries, that's all."

"Is she as much of a dragon as she looks?"

Lilly couldn't help but laugh. "More, I think. I have to be careful. If she were to see us . . ."

"This is innocent enough, isn't it? Simply two friends sitting together and talking?"

"Of course it is. But I doubt she'd agree with you."

"Then I'd best be on my way. Before I go, may I tell you something?"

Her throat suddenly dry, she could only nod in agreement.

"I'm glad to see you here. In spite of everything I said this morning, I am glad." He turned to her, his eyes scanning her face, and it seemed to Lilly that he was trying to gauge her reaction.

Just then, a low "ahem" alerted Lilly to Constance's arrival. Her friend was carrying two mugs of tea, as well as a small packet of biscuits.

"My mum sent me these last week," Constance explained, "and since today was so long, and awful, I thought we deserved a treat."

"How very kind of you," Lilly replied cheerily, hoping her irritation wasn't evident. "Constance, may I introduce you to my friend Captain Robert Fraser?" Turning to Robbie, she completed the introduction. "Robbie, I should like to introduce you to Miss Constance Evans."

Their greetings complete, Lilly took one of the cups of tea and offered it to Robbie. "You probably need this more than I do."

"I'm fine, Lilly, but thank you all the same. I ought to be going. Enjoy your tea and biscuits, ladies. Perhaps I'll see you in the mess tent later on."

As soon as he was out of earshot, Lilly turned to her friend, who was now seated in the spot that Robbie had just vacated. "Don't say it. Please don't."

Constance sipped her tea delicately, then selected a biscuit and began to eat it. "Say what?" she asked between nibbles. "Say that it's such a fortunate coincidence? Because, you know, it really is. Out of all the clearing hospitals along the Front, somehow we end up at this one. The very same one where your Captain Fraser happens to work."

"Constance, I—"

"It was Miss Davies's aide who helped you, wasn't it? That poor girl who had such a hard time with Corporal Pike?"

"Yes. Please don't be upset with me."

"I'm not. Honestly, Lilly, I'm not. If I had a sweetheart, and there was a chance I could be nearer to him, I would take that chance."

"He's not my sweetheart," Lilly insisted.

Constance fixed Lilly with a hard look, her eyebrows raised. "Sweetheart or not, you understand that you're taking an awful risk, don't you? Think what would have happened if Miss Jeffries had come along just now."

"He only wanted to apologize, and see how I am."

"He's done that now. And let's be thankful you didn't get caught."

"Surely Miss Jeffries wouldn't consider *that* to be fraternization," Lilly protested feebly.

"I have no idea what she thinks. But do you really want to misjudge her and end up being sent home?"

Lilly knew Constance was right. "So what should I do? He's my friend, after all. I can't ignore him."

"I'm not saying you should. Say hello when your paths cross; even ask him how he is. But don't sit alone with him, and for heaven's sake, hide your feelings for him in front of everyone but me. Will you promise to try?"

Lilly nodded wearily. "I suppose it won't be that hard to avoid him. He spends most of his time in surgery or taking care of his patients, and I'll be driving back and forth to the ADS all day long."

Constance reached across Lilly's shoulders and gave her a brief hug. "That's the spirit. Now let's get

Henrietta settled for the night. I think we still have some time before supper."

Supper. He had said he might see her there. Would she be able to talk with him? Probably not. But she would be able to see him, exchange a smile or even a brief greeting. And that would have to do.

Chapter 24

Torture. Her presence at the 51st amounted to nothing short of torture for him.

When Lilly had first arrived, less than a month ago, he had smothered the protests of his better judgment and convinced himself that all would be well. He'd been wrong.

Since the day of her arrival, they'd not had a single conversation. He'd tried, at first, to speak with her when their paths crossed, but he never managed to do more than stammer a few quotidian platitudes about the weather or her health before Miss Evans would appear out of the blue, beg his pardon, and hustle her away.

After that, he'd tried to ignore her, or at least to put her out of his mind when she wasn't standing directly in front of him. That, too, was unsuccessful. For Lilly was everywhere.

In the mess tent at the crack of dawn, laughing with her friends. In the reception marquee, encouraging the walking wounded to lean on her as she saw them safely to a cot or bench. In the ward tent nearly every evening, reading Sherlock Holmes mysteries or Walter Scott or Tennyson to the men, or helping them write their letters home. He couldn't so much as step from one tent to the next without encountering her, and the sight of her and the sound of her voice never failed to affect him.

Even in the few hours he allowed himself for sleep she was with him. He dreamed of no one and nothing but her. Lilly laughing, Lilly whispering his name, Lilly standing before him, in the station, turning her face so his brotherly kiss might land on her lips and be transformed.

Only in the operating hut was he free of her. There, cocooned in his unlikely sanctuary, he could concentrate on the minutiae of surgery and put her tantalizing presence out of his mind. As the long hours he worked grew ever longer, his colleagues warned him to take care of himself, and Colonel Lewis began to make disagreeable noises about sending him on leave. Robbie ignored them all.

His one solace, a rather pathetic one, was the letters Lilly had sent him before her arrival at the 51st. He'd kept all of them, bundled together in a biscuit tin, and whenever he had a spare moment he would lie down on his cot and read one, just as if it had been delivered that day.

And then, early one morning, the idea came to him. He would write to Lilly, and he would ask her to write him back, just as they had done before.

It was risky; they would have to pass their correspondence to each other without anyone else noticing. And if anyone were to intercept a letter, and discover their friendship, then Lilly would certainly be sent home. She might well prefer not to take such a risk.

Yet he had to try.

13 August

Dear L,

I think I told you, some months ago, that reading your letters was one of the few pleasures left to me. Since your arrival I have had no letters from you, understandably enough, but your presence here in no way diminishes my longing for them. A glimpse of your face as you drive past, the sound of your voice as you read to the men in the ward tent.

But never a chance to talk, to hear your thoughts and opinions, to laugh with you about the bad food and endless rain. It's enough to drive me mad.

So it has come to this: either I write to you, and convince you to write back to me, or one of these days I am going to sit down at your table in the mess tent and begin to talk to you, in front of everyone, Miss Jeffries be damned.

I'm at my desk in the ward tent most evenings. It should be easy to leave your reply there.

R

He folded the single sheet of paper in three and stuffed it into an envelope, which, after a moment's hesitation, he left blank. He'd told her where she might deliver her reply, but where could he leave this?

Slipping into her tent and leaving it on her cot, not that he had the faintest idea which one was Lilly's, was too dangerous. Perhaps her ambulance? It was worth a look.

Dawn was approaching; he'd better be quick about it. He made his way across the compound, skidding once or twice on the dew-slicked duckboards thrown down over the muddy ground. He hesitated as he approached the row of ambulances next to the marquee tent. Lilly had parked her ambulance at the end of the row yesterday afternoon, when he had seen her last, but had she moved it since then?

He approached the vehicle: it looked exactly the same as its fellows, with nothing to distinguish it from any other American-made ambulance along the Western Front. He was about to turn away when he noticed the word that had been painted, in rather shaky script, on the bonnet. *Henrietta*.

She'd named the ambulance, he remembered. So this was the one. Now he only had to find a place to hide the envelope. Plucking at the seat cushion, he found it wasn't affixed to the bench seat. He slipped the envelope underneath, patted the cushion in place, said a silent prayer, and walked away.

Instead of going back to his tent, he went to the ward tent to see how his surgery patients had fared overnight, then tackled the heaps of paperwork on his desk. The clock chimed six o'clock; a good time, he judged, to go to breakfast. He'd have time to eat his meal and perhaps even spend a few minutes in conversation with his colleagues before Lilly and the other WAACs arrived.

Robbie had been cradling a half-empty cup of coffee for a half hour before the first of the WAACs walked in. He made his way to the mess tent's exit, standing aside so that Miss Evans might pass.

Lilly was just behind her. He stepped forward into the doorway and there was an awkward moment as each attempted to step aside. They exchanged murmured apologies and then, before she could move past, he bent his head and whispered in her ear.

"Look under the cushion on the driver's seat of your ambulance."

The look of astonishment on her face nearly made him laugh out loud. "Your ambulance. Under the seat," he repeated. She nodded, but did she understand?

Lilly had been in and out of the reception marquee all day, but always at a distance, and always with her watchdog, Miss Evans, in close proximity.

It was the end of the afternoon; the marquee tent had cleared and Robbie was standing outside the operating hut, trying to clear his head before returning for one final surgery.

A movement, just at the periphery of his vision, caught his attention. It was Lilly, carrying a leather bucket full of soapy water. She looked tired and disheveled and was probably desperate for her supper. But first she and Miss Evans were going to wash out the ambulance, as he knew they did every day. It was an unpleasant task, yet she seemed oddly cheerful.

He almost called out to her, but before he could say anything, she looked at him, held his gaze for an endless moment, and then, as bold as any music-hall actress, she winked at him.

That evening she came to the ward tent, as was her habit, and read to the men for more than an hour. She walked by Robbie on her way out of the tent, her only greeting a soft hello as she passed. An envelope slipped from her hand onto his desk; he covered it swiftly with one of his files in case anyone should pass by.

Robbie surveyed the tent: of his colleagues, only Lawson was on duty, and he was preoccupied with his charts. The nurses were at their stations and the wounded were asleep or unconscious, leaving him, for a change, alone.

He used his penknife to open the envelope. Only one sheet of paper inside, but then, she wouldn't have had much time to craft her reply.

13 August 1917

Dear R,

Thank you very much for your letter. I, too, have been feeling quite desperate about our lapse in correspondence, and not only because I miss re-

ceiving your letters. There is so much I want to tell you, for I know you will understand. I will send a longer response as soon as I am able. Until then, I remain,

Your devoted friend,

L

Chapter 25

The main thing, Lilly told herself, was to avoid sitting on her cot. That was the only way she would stay awake long enough to finish the letter.

She'd been at the 51st for six weeks now, and life had settled into something that resembled a routine. Awake at first light, breakfast, trip after trip to the ADS, a break for dinner, then back to the ADS, again and again, until it had been cleared.

Today had been no different. By noon, they had driven back and forth four times, working to empty the ADS of the scores of wounded men that had arrived in the wake of yet another Allied push on the Ypres salient. Four unspeakable journeys, punctuated by horrors that Lilly knew would be branded into her consciousness forever, no matter how commonplace they had become in this war of horrors.

A man so badly gutshot that his entrails were barely held in place by the field dressings that encircled his torso. Another, white-faced with shock, both legs shattered, pulling piteously at Lilly's sleeve as his stretcher was carried past.

"Please, miss, don't let them take me legs. Miss, please, you must tell them."

Lilly had patted his arm reassuringly, murmured some anodyne platitude, and felt like the worst sort of fraud, because of course they were going to take off his legs. For that was the only way he would live. That was the future that awaited him, now that he had done his duty to King and Country.

It was seven o'clock; her friends, sensibly, had made for their respective beds as soon as supper was finished. Annie and Bridget were snoring away peacefully, but Constance was still awake as Lilly sat at the wobbly table and chair at the far end of their tent.

"Put that letter away and get to bed. You know we've an early start tomorrow. And it's impossible to sleep properly with that lantern flickering away."

"I've only the one letter. I'll be done soon."

Monday, 3 Sept. 1917

Here I am again. I had hoped to finish this last night, but the lantern in my tent ran out of kerosene and it was too late to fetch any more. No—

that's not precisely true. I was too tired to fetch any more. I was in my cot by a quarter to eight and slept so soundly that Constance had to shake me awake at dawn.

I blame the mud. I do not think it an exaggeration to say it is the chief torment of my life here. The route to the ADS is awash in it, although "awash" gives the unfortunate impression that it bears some resemblance to liquid. It's more like molten wax, clinging to everything, making any kind of fluid movement impossible. But wax can be chipped away when it hardens, whereas this cursed stuff never dries. How can it? There's no sunshine, no warmth—just rain and rain and more rain. Even my trusty Henrietta balks at it.

Yet how can I complain? I sleep in a tent that is dry, walk on duckboards that (mostly) keep the mud away, am able to wash my person and my uniform in clean (if not hot) water, and eat meals that are warm and nourishing. The wounded men who ride in my ambulance have been wet, cold, dirty, and hungry for what must seem like forever to them. And they never complain. Or, if they do, they manage to make a joke of it. What sort of world is this, where men learn to joke about rats and lice and dysentery?

*They don't joke about the men who drown. I be-
lieved this war held no fresh horrors for me, until I
heard two men talking of what had happened to their
friend at Langemarck last month. He was shot, but
not badly enough to kill him outright. He fell into a
shell hole, at least a yard deep, filled to the brim with
mud and muck and gore, and they heard him drown.
Heard him begging for help, but could do nothing.*

*When this war is over I want to go somewhere
with no mud, a place where the people have never
seen mud—where they have no word to describe it,
even. Does such a place exist? In Arabia, perhaps,
or the central plains of Asia? I've never been much
of a traveler but I'm determined to go there one day.*

Lilly peered at the tent's ceiling, which had begun
to sag near the corners. She tiptoed to Bridget's cot and
reached underneath it for the old broom handle her
friend had managed to scavenge a few weeks ago, when
the rain first began to seep through the tent's worn
canvas. Using the handle to push at several strategic
spots, she heard the satisfying noise of water splashing
harmlessly to the ground outside.

*We just learned of the ceilidh that's being
planned. Would you believe Miss Jeffries has decided*

to relax her rules for the evening? Not only may we attend, but we may also dance with the men—providing, of course, that we ONLY dance. The slightest hint of anything more, and it's back to quarters for all of us.

The other girls are very excited, naturally, and I suppose I am, too. Certainly there will be no shortage of dance partners for us all, even though I'm the only one who knows how to do the reels. I've promised to teach them the basics, if we have any time beforehand. I wonder if I'll remember, for it's at least fifteen years since Nanny Gee took me to a ceilidh on the estate.

Now it really is getting late, and I must finish this letter. Please don't worry about replying straightaway—I know you will do so as soon as you have time. Until then, I remain,

Your devoted friend,

L

The letter, stretching to four closely penciled sheets of paper, was rather difficult to stuff into the envelope. Lilly tucked it into her jacket pocket, which she had kept on in deference to the chilly evening, tidied away her writing things in her locker, and extracted a book from its depths. She turned down the lantern and slipped outside, her footsteps hurried. Dusk had already begun to color the sky; the sun would set in less than an hour.

Matron was not on duty in the ward tent tonight. In her place, a younger woman sat at the nurses' station. Nurse Greenhalgh. Not especially friendly, and fond of reminding the WAACs, whenever their paths crossed, that she had been "in the thick of it" since 1915. But she made no protest when Lilly entered. Perhaps she looked forward to an hour of *Sherlock Holmes* as much as her patients.

Ever since her arrival at the 51st, Lilly had made a point of spending her spare time, usually an hour or two after supper each evening, reading to patients in the ward tent. Some of the men were so badly injured that she couldn't be certain if they even heard her voice. But most were grateful for the company, so much so that Lilly suspected she could have read from a telephone directory without complaint.

At the far end of the tent, well away from the men who were recovering from surgeries, was a group of patients who'd been at the 51st for several weeks; their injuries hadn't allowed them to be moved on to Saint-Omer. The men—a wagon driver whose pelvis had been broken when a horse had fallen on him, and two Australians who had been burned by incendiary grenades—had evidently been waiting for her arrival. They smiled shyly, returning her "good evening" with soft-spoken hellos.

Lilly found a stool and placed it between the wagon driver's cot and his neighbor's. Then, opening her much-loved copy of *The Return of Sherlock Holmes,* she found the page where she'd stopped the night before, roughly halfway through "The Adventure of Charles Augustus Milverton."

"When we left off yesterday evening," she began, "Mr. Holmes had just told Dr. Watson that he meant to burgle Mr. Milverton's house. Shall I reread a few paragraphs? Just to help us get back into the story?

" 'Watson, I mean to burgle Milverton's house to-night.'

"I had a catching of the breath, and my skin went cold at the words, which were slowly uttered in a tone of concentrated resolution. As a flash of lightning in the night shows up in an instant every detail of a wild landscape, so at one glance I seemed to see every possible result of such an action—the detection, the capture, the honored career ending in irreparable failure and disgrace, my friend himself lying at the mercy of the odious Milverton."

The ward tent was eerily quiet, the only sounds the scratch of the nurse's pen, an occasional moan from one of the men, and the measured tones of Lilly's voice. Quiet, and oddly peaceful.

She'd been reading for about a quarter of an hour when she heard footsteps, then the sound of someone sitting at the surgeons' desk immediately behind her. She stifled the urge to turn, focusing instead on the page before her.

She lost her place, briefly, when the unseen doctor and Nurse Greenhalgh began to discuss some detail of a patient's care. She knew, even before she heard his voice, that it would be Robbie.

When was the last time she'd seen him, heard him speak? Three days? Four? No matter. Soon she would finish the story, and then, only then, would she turn and look at him.

At last it was done: Milverton the blackmailer was dead, shot by one of his victims, and Mr. Holmes had refused to assist Inspector Lestrade in Scotland Yard's efforts to find the murderer.

Wishing the men good night, she tidied away the stool and approached the desks that flanked the tent's entrance. By a stroke of good luck, Nurse Greenhalgh was busy at the other end of the tent, conducting an inventory of the stores locker.

"Good evening, Captain Fraser." Lilly pulled the letter from her jacket pocket and placed it on the desk, sliding it toward him without comment. He set down his pen and tucked the envelope under a pile of charts that lay before him.

"Good evening, Miss Ashford," he answered, at last looking up at her. "I'm glad to hear that you and the other WAACs will be joining us at the ceilidh."

"Everyone is very excited, Captain Fraser. These, ah, diversions come so rarely."

What a ridiculous conversation; if only they—

"Captain Fraser? Could you assist me in lifting these crates at the top of the stores locker? We seem to have lost our orderlies."

"I'll be with you presently, Nurse Greenhalgh," he replied. Then, in a whisper, "Promise to save me a dance?"

As he moved past her, she felt his fingers brush against hers. For an instant he held her hand, her pulse quickening at the warmth of his touch. And then it was over, and he was striding across the tent, coming to the aid of the nurse, and Lilly was walking away, too, out into the dying light of the setting sun.

Chapter 26

At last the day of the ceilidh was at hand. The 51st had closed to new patients the day before, so Lilly and her fellow drivers had only to see to their vehicles and quarters before readying themselves for the dance.

Lilly's morning was occupied in scrubbing out Henrietta from top to bottom, replacing a valve spring that had broken the day before, tightening the spring clips on the back axle, oiling the magneto, and adjusting the ignition coils. Once those chores were accomplished, and dinner was eaten, Miss Jeffries directed the women to clean their quarters. What time remained in the afternoon would be theirs to enjoy.

Tidying, sweeping, and scouring of the rough deal floor of the tent took up little more than an hour, and no sooner had the WAACs finished than they learned the boiler in the women's washhouse was lit and there would be hot water for baths. It was a rare luxury, for normally they had to be content with sponge baths in cold water.

Lilly washed her hair twice, shivering a little as she knelt in the cramped wood-framed canvas washtub. Not wanting to take more than her fair share of time or hot water, she hurriedly scrubbed herself top to bottom with her last sliver of scented soap, a birthday gift from Charlotte. It was the first time in weeks that she had felt clean.

Before emptying the tub, she checked the water and was relieved to find no evidence of lice. A month earlier, she'd been horrified to discover nits when combing her hair before bed. Persian insect powder, mixed into a paste with petroleum jelly, had killed the lice in her hair, but then she'd inspected her clothes and found them infested with body lice, likely picked up from one of the walking wounded who sat next to her in the ambulance. Matron had given her a tin of NCI powder, which smelled simply awful, and had instructed her to lay out her greatcoat, jacket, and skirt on a white sheet, find and squash anything that moved, then rub powder into all of the seams. Since then, all the WAACs had been affected, and it was a rare night indeed when their quarters smelled of anything nicer than delousing agents.

After her bath, basking in the smelly but welcome warmth of the tent's little stove, Lilly felt as content as she'd been for months. But she'd promised to teach the other women at least a few of the reels, and only an hour remained before dinner.

"Why aren't we having a proper dance?" asked Rose. "I don't understand why it's these country dances. None of us know the steps."

"The men do," Lilly countered. "Most of the other ranks are from Scottish regiments. That's why it's nicknamed the 'Highland' CCS."

"How *couldn't* you notice? The kilties are as thick as flies here." Annie laughed.

"Don't worry, Rose. It's much more fun than waltzing," Lilly promised. "Now let's get our beds and lockers moved so we can practice."

"How is it you know the reels?" asked Constance as they were pushing the furniture out of the way.

The truth was that she'd learned at the servants' dances at Cumbermere Hall, which Nanny Gee had allowed her and the other children to attend when their parents were away. Once or twice a year, space would be cleared in one of the estate's ancient tithe barns, the musicians would take up their fiddles, and Lilly would dance and dance until it was so far past her bedtime that she could scarcely stay awake the next day.

She couldn't tell Constance the precise truth, but she could supply some of it. "I learned when I was a little girl. Children were always welcome at the dances where I lived." True enough, if the children in question were the progeny of the Earl and Countess of Cumberland. "I expect many of the people there were Scottish, or had family in Scotland. We were only thirty miles or so from the border."

It had been more than fifteen years, however, since Lilly had last attended a ceilidh. "I hope I still remember the steps."

"You know more than any of us," Constance said. "We've less than an hour, you know. We'd best get started."

"Let's try an eightsome reel. Though as we're only six, you'll need to imagine there are two more of us."

She directed the women to stand in a square, with Ethel, Annie, and Constance designated as men for the purposes of the practice. "First we join hands and dance round to the left for eight steps, then back again in the other direction for eight more. It's a little like skipping, see? Well done. Now Bridget, Rose, and I will go into the middle of the circle, since we're meant to be the women, and join our right hands so we're making a wheel. Put your left arm around the waist of your partner, then we all dance round in a circle, rather like the spokes on a wagon wheel. Then the women spin round like this. Our left hands are the center of the wheel, and then we dance back the other way. Now you dance in place for a few bars, just so, and then the men spin the women round to the right, so the women are back inside the main circle. Then we weave in and out, the men going one way, the women the other, until we're back with our partners."

The women were having a grand time already, all of them catching on easily; the eightsome was one of the easier dances to master, which is why Lilly had chosen it. Once they had repeated the first sequence a number of times, she showed her friends how each woman would take a turn in the middle of the circle, dancing in place before her partner, then turning to dance with the man at the opposite side of the circle.

Ethel and Rose had to leave then to help with the dinner service, but there was time still for Lilly to acquaint the others with Strip the Willow, the Gay Gordons, and the Dashing White Sergeant.

"You are right, Lilly," gasped Bridget, trying to catch her breath after the final reel. "This is ever so much fun. Only wish my Gordon was here. Jim, too. Did you know they're cousins?"

"I didn't. Perhaps we can all go to a ceilidh together, after the war is over," Lilly offered.

"Sounds a treat, that does. What do you say, ladies? Is that a plan? When the war is over?"

Who could say where they would all be when the war ended? All the same, it was a nice sort of plan to have, no matter how improbable.

They took their supper soon after, all six WAACs sitting with Miss Jeffries at their table in the mess tent. Lilly was only able to swallow a few bites of her shepherd's pie, filled as it was with indefinable chunks of gristly meat that had never been within a mile of an actual shepherd. It was filling, though, and hot, and she knew she ought to be grateful for it. Likely enough Edward's dinner that evening would be far less palatable.

As the ceilidh didn't begin until half-past seven, Lilly had intended to spend a half hour, possibly more, reading to the men in the ward tent. In this she was overruled by her friends.

"Not tonight," Annie ordered. "Otherwise how'll you have enough time to get ready?"

"I am ready. I had my bath, my hair is pinned up, my uniform is clean—"

"Listen to you! No, duck, you're not nearly ready," said Bridget. "Now sit yourself down while we get to work on you."

"What did you have in mind?" Lilly asked nervously. As fond as she was of her friends, she wasn't at all sure she wanted to look like them, with the exception of Constance. Bridget and Annie had partially bobbed their hair, which meant that when they pinned up the longer strands behind, the front section barely reached their earlobes. They had been known to wear cosmetics while on duty as well, in spite of official WAAC directives to the contrary. Not only had Lilly never cut her hair, apart from a minor trim to its ends, she'd also never used cosmetics, not so much as a wisp of face powder. Just the prospect of putting something on her face other than plain soap was as intimidating as it was exciting.

As Lilly watched, Annie lighted a small rectangular kerosene burner, then covered it with a metal frame. On this she placed a set of curling tongs, their metal dark from long use and, Lilly imagined apprehensively, the ashes of incinerated hair. As the tongs heated, a wisp of steam, or perhaps smoke, wafted up from one end. It was not a promising sight.

"I don't want you to curl my hair," she confessed. "I'm sorry, but I'd rather not."

Annie burst out laughing. "Not to worry. Anyone can see how curly it is already. Constance, do you want us to fix your hair? No? Then we're just doing up your face?"

"We can't. You can't," Constance protested. "Miss Jeffries—"

"It'll be dark at this 'kelly' thing. No way she'll see."

Lilly watched, unaccountably fascinated, as Bridget and Annie worked their magic, rouging Constance's lips, taking the shine off her nose, and darkening her lashes with a mix of soot and Vaseline.

"Your turn now, Lil. Come over here." Annie beckoned. "If you don't like it, you can wipe it off and I won't hold it against you. How's that sound?"

Fair enough. Lilly sat on the end of Bridget's bed and steeled herself to sit perfectly still as her lips were painted, her eyelashes were brushed with her friends' sooty concoction, and a haze of choking powder descended upon her face. As soon as she could see clearly again, she grabbed the mirror from Annie's outstretched hand.

How could so little paint make such a difference? Her eyes seemed bigger and brighter, her lips fuller, her skin luminous and fresh.

"See?" said Bridget. "You look a treat. Now out of the way so I can put meself together."

Arrayed in their pressed and sponged uniforms, shoes polished, faces powdered, and hair meticulously arranged, the women lacked only one final touch, Lilly thought. So she dug into her locker, brought forth a tiny bottle of perfume, and dotted the stopper to everyone's wrists. The tent was immediately filled with the scent of lily of the valley, a vivid and refreshing contrast to the prevailing odor of singed hair, disinfectant, and kerosene.

"If only we were allowed to wear civvies." Ethel sighed. "I look like a sack of potatoes in this uniform."

"You look lovely," Lilly insisted. "And besides, the men outnumber us six to one. You could be wearing an actual potato sack and it wouldn't make a lick of difference."

"Right she is," seconded Annie. "So stop your mithering and let's be off."

Chapter 27

Robbie could scarcely believe he was standing in the reception marquee. Normally it was such a grim place, crowded with stretchers, its floors dirtied by discarded dressings and drifts of blood-sodden sawdust. All that was gone, if only for one night. Benches had been brought in from the mess tent and were arranged neatly around the perimeter of the marquee, although hardly anyone sat on them. A small group of musicians was playing "A Soldier's Joy" from an improvised stage at the far end of the marquee, while a knot of kilt-clad soldiers performed an energetic hornpipe.

The arrival of the WAACs at the ceilidh coincided with the end of the dance, and within seconds the women were hemmed in by a crowd of potential dance partners, each man keen to capture a spare female for the next reel.

Predictably, Lilly looked enchanting. Like the other WAACs, she was in uniform, which did little to flatter her or any of the other women's figures. But her lovely hazel eyes were sparkling, her face was aglow with excitement, and her hair, normally pinned tight and hidden beneath her driver's cap, had begun to curl enchantingly at her temples and nape.

Before Robbie had even taken a step in Lilly's direction, her arm was seized by Andrew Harrison, one of the surgeons. Though Robbie considered him a friend, he could cheerfully have throttled him at that moment. The man had lived his entire life in the south of England, and it showed, for he hadn't the faintest idea of what he was doing. Lilly didn't seem to mind, though, and gamely led him through the reel, laughing gaily whenever Harrison led her in the wrong direction.

At the end of the dance, Harrison was elbowed aside by one of the orderlies, a Glaswegian named Murray. The musician calling the changes, a fiddle player, ordered the dancers to line up in two rows for Strip the Willow.

If he didn't act soon, Robbie realized, he'd never come within a yard of her. He saw Matron standing by the entrance to the marquee; she would do. He advanced on her, took her hand without so much as a by-your-leave, and escorted her to the dance floor. He'd beg her pardon later.

Robbie and Matron were near the beginning of the row, so it wasn't long before it was their turn to twirl from dancer to dancer, the faces that surrounded them a mere blur.

The touch of Lilly's hand ought not to have shocked him so much. At least he had some warning, for a heartbeat before he reached her, reached out to grasp her hand, he chanced to look up, and there she was. Laughing, clapping to the music, one foot stomping time as she waited her turn.

Then she was before him, their hands were joined, and he was pulling her into a spin. Before he had a chance to recover from the thrill of her touch, they were done. Time to return to Matron, continue down the line, and put himself back together.

The music swirled to a halt, with the accordion player gasping a little from his efforts. While he recovered, the fiddle player announced that the musicians would be taking a short break after the next dance.

"We hope our next selection will please the ladies among us," he announced. "The song may be unfamiliar to some of you, but it's in waltz time, so even our English friends will have nae trouble in joining in."

A fresh crush of admirers surrounded Lilly and her friends, and Robbie felt a tug of regret that he would have to stand aside and watch her dance, again, with someone else. He decided he was done with waiting.

He shouldered his way through the crowd, not caring if the others thought him a boor. Her back was turned, so he tapped her shoulder. She wheeled around, clearly irritated, though her expression softened as soon as she saw it was him.

"I beg your pardon, Miss Ashford. I meant only to gain your attention. May I ask for the honor of this next dance?"

She nodded. He took her hand, led her away from the throng of supplicants, and, never taking his eyes from her face, waited for the dance to begin.

As the keening notes of a single fiddle curled through the air, Robbie took her in his arms again, for the first time since that July night three years ago. Three years that had been stretched, by war and distance, into something that had often felt like an eternity. But tonight they were together, for however long this dance lasted.

He held her as a gentleman ought to hold his partner for a waltz, without a hint of any interest beyond the platonic. All the same, he was acutely aware of the points of contact between them. His left hand enveloping her right hand. His right hand at her back. Her left hand on his shoulder. Perfectly formal and proper, he told himself. So why was his pulse racing?

A man began to sing; it was Private Gillespie, the ASC driver who worked with Lilly. He sang in Gaelic, the language of Robbie's maternal grandparents, the language of his earliest happy memories.

"Do you know what this is called?" Lilly asked.

"Aye, I do. In Scots Gaelic it's 'Ho Ro, Nigh'n Donn Bhoideach.'"

"What does that mean?"

"Roughly translated, 'My Brown-Haired Lass,'" he answered. "Do you like it?"

"I do, very much. And Private Gillespie sings so well. What is it about?"

"I can't remember exactly. Let me listen as he sings."

He was surprised by how readily the lyrics revealed themselves, though it had been more than twenty years since his Nan had sung to him as she pegged out the washing in the backyard.

"'My sweet pretty girl, my sweet pretty girl,'" he murmured, bending his head so he might whisper in her ear. "'My lovely pretty lass, I'll marry none but you.'

"'I have fallen in love with you,'" he continued. "'Your face, your beauty, they are always on my mind.' That's what the words say, Lilly."

The song had ended; it was time for him to cede his place to another. But he'd forgotten that the band meant to take a break, and as soon as the musicians put down their instruments and lifted their mugs of ale, Lilly's would-be dance partners melted back into the crowd.

Not far away, Robbie saw, the formidable Miss Evans was engaged in earnest conversation with one of the surgeons, while Lilly's other friends held court on the opposite side of the tent. Surely if the other WAACs were able to converse so freely with the officers and men, then he and Lilly should be able to talk without causing a sensation.

"Come with me, over here, where it's cooler," he suggested, guiding her to one of the benches. "We'll sit for a minute and I can fetch you a cup of tea."

"No, thank you. I'm fine. I'd much rather talk."

"Very well, then. What do you want to talk about?"

"Do you remember the last time we danced to-gether?" she asked abruptly.

"I do. As if it were yesterday." He grinned, a little ruefully.

"Would you rather not speak of it?"

"I don't mind, not now. So much has changed since then."

"I know," she agreed. "But I've always wondered . . . what if my mother hadn't interrupted us, and told you I was engaged? What would have happened?"

It was a question he'd never asked himself. What good would it have done? All the same, she deserved an answer. "Shall we try and find somewhere more private to talk?"

"What about Miss Jeffries?"

"She has her back turned to us, and Miss Evans is busy with Captain Lawson. If we slip out now, no one will notice. Are you with me?"

"Aye," she answered, and he smiled at her attempt at levity.

"I'll leave now. Follow me in a minute." Taking a step back, he loudly wished her a good evening before turning and walking out of the marquee.

He moved away from the entrance and stood in the shadows, waiting for his eyes to adjust to the dark. Long seconds inched past before the flap covering the marquee entrance was thrown back and Lilly emerged.

"Robbie?" she whispered.

"I'm here. Just to your left."

"Where shall we go?"

He hadn't thought that far ahead. "Perhaps one of the storage huts? We can hope for some privacy there."

"What about the mechanics' garage? Private Gillespie never locks the side door."

"It sounds grand. Lead the way."

Chapter 28

They walked in silence, mere inches apart, their fingertips almost touching, the din and chatter of the ceilidh fading with every step. Lilly could hardly breathe; surely someone would emerge from the reception marquee and call them back.

They reached the garage. She led him inside, instructed him to wait at the door, and inched carefully through the darkness until she was at the back wall of the hut. She pushed open the first shutter she found, then its neighbor. Moonlight streamed in, revealing the garage's interior.

"Let's sit there," she suggested, pointing at the bench where the WAACs took their tea on rainy days. "I wish it were more comfortable—"

"It's fine," he interrupted, his beautiful face very serious now. "Where did we leave off, then, the night of the ball?"

"We'd just finished dancing, and were sitting in one of the drawing rooms."

"So we were. What were we talking about?"

"What you would do when the war came. What I would do, too."

"That's all?" He sounded intrigued.

"We weren't talking for long before Mama interrupted us."

"I remember your mother's arrival quite clearly. I don't know what I would have said next, though."

"Oh." She couldn't manage anything more.

"But I can tell you what I ought to have said."

"Really?" she asked, her voice squeaking a bit.

"I should have said you were beautiful, and that it was impossible to think of you as a little girl any longer."

Silence enveloped them. Would he say nothing more? Did he expect her to respond?

"May I?" he asked, and then he took hold of her right hand, his fingers easily encircling her narrow wrist. Then, shockingly, he unbuttoned the cuff of her blouse. Pushing her sleeve past her elbow, he began to massage her forearm with a sure and steady touch.

"Robbie, I—"

"I know. I've noticed you rubbing your wrists and arms. When you think no one is looking. It's all that driving. And those heavy buckets of water."

"This is . . . not what I expected," she said.

"Hmm. I'm sorry. Do you want me to stop?"

She shook her head, wondering if he could see her in the gloom. "It's only that . . ."

This was all she had dreamed of, for weeks and months and years. Why hold back now? "I can't remember the last time someone touched me," she confessed. "Apart from a handshake. Or a kiss on the cheek from Edward."

Instead of answering, he busied himself with the buttons on her other cuff, then began to massage her left wrist and forearm. It was a minute or more before he spoke again.

"No kisses from ardent young admirers back home?"

"Not a one. I was rather a failure during my one Season."

He looked up, his gaze shadowed in the ambulance's dim interior. Just then, a moonbeam escaped the cloud cover above, its quicksilver gleam falling across his face. His eyes glittered jewel-bright, their blue the only point of color in her universe.

"Why count that one summer a failure? Unless you'd been hoping to end up married to a complete stranger."

"I know," she admitted. "And I am glad things happened as they did. It's . . ."

"Go on."

"It's embarrassing. Twenty-four years old, and I've never been kissed."

"Aren't you forgetting something?"

"You mean . . ."

"In the middle of Victoria Station. In front of all those Tommies."

"But that was a mistake. You meant to kiss me on the cheek. And I moved. That's all."

"How do you know?"

"What? I mean . . . what?" He was serious now; she didn't need to see his face to know it.

"How do you know I didn't intend to kiss you?"

"But you've never—"

"Lilly, look at me," he insisted. "I wanted to kiss you then. I do now." And then, his voice hesitant, "Is that what you want?"

She nodded, incapable of saying anything more.

"I mean a proper kiss, you understand," he explained. "Not some brotherly peck on the cheek."

She nodded again, wondering if she would ever regain the power of speech.

"Close your eyes, Lilly," he murmured, leaning closer. "You're meant to close your eyes."

"Is that all?"

"No. You're meant to kiss me back."

His mouth touched hers, gently at first, and then more insistently, until he was coaxing her lips apart and Lilly felt a rush of certainty that this was what a kiss was meant to be. She'd always wondered why poets and playwrights and artists were so preoccupied with kissing; she had even asked Charlotte, once, but her friend hadn't seemed able to answer.

Now she understood.

She remembered, belatedly, that she was supposed to kiss him back. So she pressed her mouth more firmly against his, opened her lips a fraction wider, and prayed that she would not repel him with her ineptitude. His response was to deepen the kiss, his mouth pushing against hers with an urgency that was exciting and alarming at the same time.

His hands were at her waist now, and before she could protest, he had pulled her onto his lap, never breaking their kiss. Her hair had begun to fall around her shoulders, one heavy ringlet after another, and after a moment she realized that his hands, combing through her hair, were dislodging the pins that held it in place.

A sudden urge to touch him, while she could, rushed over her, and before she could think better of it, she reached up and swept her fingertips across his face.

Breaking their kiss, he turned his head in the direction of her hand, pushing his face into her palm.

"What is that scent you're wearing?"

"Lily of the valley."

"I should have known," he muttered, and she could feel the curve of his smile against her hand.

"Do you like it?"

"Yes. It smells like springtime. Like hope."

She thought he would kiss her again, but instead his hands rose to her throat, and before she had quite realized what he was doing, he'd unfastened the top button of her blouse.

Lilly told herself she ought to protest, for allowing him such liberties only meant one thing, could only lead to one thing. So why could she not bring herself to stop him?

Another button popped open, then another. Robbie pulled her close, bending his head to drop fluttering kisses at the base of her throat. A fourth button came undone, then a fifth and a sixth, and she shivered as a flame of night air chilled her bared skin.

He pushed aside her blouse, a hand stealing beneath the stiff gabardine to trace the curve of her breast. Only the veil-thin cotton of her combinations separated her skin from his touch, and the knowledge and delight of it emboldened her.

She ran her hands through his close-cropped hair, wishing there were enough light to make out its color, marveling at how soft it felt beneath her fingers.

"Robbie, I—"

His hand covered her mouth an instant before she heard his whisper in her ear.

"Hush, Lilly. There's someone outside."

There it was—a rustling, shuffling noise. Someone was approaching the side door. And the someone was singing.

"'*When dosh a soldier grumble? When dosh he make a fuss,* hic*? No one issh more contented,* hic*, in all the world than ussssh . . .*'"

"I think it's Private Gillespie," she whispered. "If he comes in . . ."

"Don't panic. He might just be taking a shortcut to his quarters."

Time stood still as they waited for Private Gillespie to move on. He'd paused just outside the side door of the garage, blocking their best avenue of escape, but after two more stanzas of "Oh, It's a Lovely War" and a round of fruity burps, the private continued on his way, a fading chorus of hiccups marking his departure.

"Lilly? Are you all right?"

Acutely conscious of her unbuttoned blouse and disheveled hair, Lilly steeled herself to look Robbie in the eye. What must he be thinking?

But he only smiled at her, the same reassuring, wise smile he'd always had, then gathered her tenderly into his arms. "I'm sorry," he whispered. "I let myself get carried away. I hope I didn't upset you."

Suddenly she became aware of how uncomfortable she was. She wriggled a little, trying to quell the pins and needles in her toes, and was alarmed when Robbie let out a soft groan.

"For the love of God, Lilly, please sit still."

She complied, hardly daring to breathe, the seconds dragging by. At last he looked up, his eyes meeting hers readily, without a shadow of shame or regret. She felt a tug on her blouse and was amazed to see that he'd already done up her buttons.

His hands were at her waist again, but only so he could place her back on the bench at a respectable distance.

He was breathing deeply, his head in his hands now, and Lilly felt a flicker of alarm.

"Is something wrong, Robbie? Did I do something wrong? You must tell me—"

"You did nothing wrong." He reached out, grasped her hand, and squeezed it to emphasize the truth of his words. "I'm fine. Uncomfortable, but fine. Just give me a moment." And then, as he stood, he muttered something to himself.

"I beg your pardon?"

"I said, 'Thank God I'm not wearing my kilt,'" he clarified.

"What on earth do you mean?" she asked, truly perplexed by his odd behavior.

"If you don't know, Lilly, then I have no intention of telling you. At least not tonight."

"Was it something I did?"

"Yes. And I mean that in a good way." He reached out and hugged her tight, dropping a lingering kiss on the crown of her head.

"What shall we do now?" Lilly asked.

"I need to check on my patients, and I think you ought to go straight back to your tent."

She nodded, her face buried in the scratchy wool of his uniform tunic.

"You leave first," he suggested. "Go directly to your tent. Don't rush; just walk normally. If you meet anyone, say your hair fell loose during the reels, and you're on your way to fix it. I'll follow in a minute."

He bent his head to kiss her one last time, and before she knew it, she was navigating the maze of duckboard pathways that led to her tent, her lips stinging a little, her heart racing.

Everyone else seemed to be at the ceilidh, for she encountered no one as she returned to her quarters. None of her friends had returned from the dance, so she had time to change into her nightgown and brush out her hair without having to answer any awkward questions. She'd only just settled in her cot when the others returned.

"Where were you, Lilly?" Constance asked, her face flushed after the exertions of the final dances. "Without you we were short a woman for the reels. We had to ask Matron to join in!"

"I had a headache. I would have said something, but you were all dancing."

"No harm done. Do you want a cool cloth for your forehead?"

Lilly nodded, feeling rather guilty for fibbing to her friend, but relieved that Constance seemed to believe her story.

It wasn't long before the other women were in bed, the lantern was doused, and silence enveloped the tent, apart from scattered giggles and whispers from Bridget's and Annie's cots.

If only there were someone she could share this with, Lilly thought, some confidante she could tell. But her friends here wouldn't understand, and Charlotte, despite her modern views on any number of subjects, would almost certainly disapprove.

No matter; she still had the memory of those moments. When she closed her eyes she could almost believe she was there again, in the uncomfortable and smelly confines of the garage, in darkness leavened only by stray moonbeams, with the man who had been at the heart of her dreams for so many long, lonely, solitary years.

And she had discovered he felt the same way. There, in that most unlikely of places, she had learned that he had missed her, had thought of her, and had yearned for her.

She knew then that she had been right to come here. The war would end soon, surely it would, and the day it was over, her life with Robbie would begin. It was simply a matter of time.

Chapter 29

Tonight she would try to break him down; he was certain of it. It had been a month and a half since the night of the ceilidh, and he was close to giving in.

The first time he'd asked her to come to the garage, he'd known he was playing with fire. He might tell himself that there was nothing improper in their meeting, and in so doing, he might convince Lilly, but it was a lie. He didn't want to be friends and he didn't want to talk. He wanted to make love to her, and the more time they spent together, the more difficult it was to resist.

At that first meeting, he'd sat at an entirely proper distance the entire time, had kept the conversation to suitably neutral topics, and then, after only a quarter hour had passed, had suggested she return to her tent.

"Is anything wrong?" she had asked him. "You haven't . . ."

"And I won't," he had replied. "I can't. We can't. If only so I can honorably answer, if asked, that nothing improper has occurred between us. Not recently, at least."

He hadn't relented. Week after week, she sidled close; he moved away. She reached to touch him; he took her hand and set it on her lap. She stood on tiptoe as they said good night, and made to brush her lips against his; he turned his face so the kiss fell harmlessly on his cheek.

It was killing him slowly, a death of a thousand cuts. All it would take was one spark—the hint of her smile, the brush of her hand—and he would be consumed by his obsession with her.

The day crept by, hour after endless hour, as he tried and failed to focus his mind on the work at hand. In the main it consisted of sorting through the mountain of paperwork that had accumulated while his days were spent in surgery, rounds to assess the postoperative condition of the men in the ward tent, and an hour spent catching up with his case notes. He ate his supper in near silence, scarcely aware of the conversations at the table, then returned to his quarters with the thought of writing a few letters. He went so far as to pull out some writing paper and a pencil, but they sat untouched on the table, his thoughts elsewhere.

Finally it was time. He made his way to the garage, taking a roundabout route around the pre-op tent and supply huts. Private Gillespie had been given three days of leave in Saint-Omer, thank God, and wasn't expected back until the morning.

He settled on one of the benches, in more or less the same place he'd sat with Lilly on the night of the ceilidh, and prepared to wait. Sometimes she was late, kept behind by requests from the wounded men in the ward tent: another letter written home, another chapter of *Sherlock Holmes* read aloud to leaven the tedium. So he sat in the still, cool half-light of the garage, hideously aware of the way his heart was pounding and his palms perspiring, and for the hundredth time that night he prayed he would find the strength to resist her.

Twelve minutes before nine. Eleven minutes. Ten minutes. Would she never come? And then, out of the darkness, careful footsteps on the duckboards outside, the door opening on hinges that he knew she kept well greased for just such a moment.

"Robbie?"

"I'm here. In the far corner."

She sat down, close enough that he could hear her breathing, feel the heat of her leg where it almost touched his.

"How was your day?" he asked. "Did you enjoy the quiet?"

"I did," she confirmed. "I hardly worked at all. How did you fare?"

"A good day. As days here go. But I missed you. I feel as if I haven't seen you for ages."

"We were in the mess tent at the same time yesterday," she said.

"Were we? How was it I didn't see you?"

"You were speaking with Nurse Ferguson. I gather you used to work together at the London."

"We did. She was a nurse in the receiving room when I was there. Just the sort of person we need here now. Nothing fazes her. Matron's already made a point of telling me how pleased she is with Edith."

"She seems very capable," Lilly said, her voice strained.

"She is that. A fine nurse."

"And she's a Scot, too, isn't she?"

"She is," he answered, mystified at the direction their conversation was taking. "From Edinburgh, though."

"I see. She seems nice."

"Aye, and she has a fine sense of humor, which seems to be a rare thing these days."

"I hope this doesn't sound silly, but I envy her. Having the chance to go to school. To make something of herself."

"I sympathize, Lilly, I do. God knows what would have become of me if I hadn't won that scholarship when I was a boy. But you did get a fine education from Miss Brown. You're far better read than most of my colleagues, for a start."

"Thank you. But it wasn't the sort of education that can lead to anything *more*. I'm fortunate to even be working as a WAAC."

"That's ridiculous. They're the ones who are lucky to have you. Look at what you do, day in and day out. It's demanding work, physically and mentally. I know any number of men who wouldn't last a day doing what you do."

"All the same . . ."

And then he realized what was bothering her. It wasn't a lack of self-confidence as such, for Lilly took real pride, justifiable pride, in her work. It was jealousy, and how could he blame her? He had been friendly with Edith, but only because he'd known her for so long. He certainly had never thought of her as anything more than a friend and colleague.

"Look at me, Lilly." He pulled her close, holding her carefully, fraternally, and dropped a kiss on the top of her head. "If you'd been given the opportunity to do so, I believe you would have made a fine nurse. Every bit as capable as Edith Ferguson or any of the other women here."

"I doubt it. I still get queasy, sometimes, when I see the state of some of the men waiting for me at the ADS."

"As would anyone. No one is born with a strong stomach for this kind of thing. You learn it, and sometimes it takes years. The first time we were allowed into theater, when I was a medical student, half the class was sick. I'd been warned by a friend in a higher year, so had skipped breakfast that morning. The others weren't so lucky. And for what it's worth—"

"Yes?"

"Edith is a friend, no more."

"But you must wish . . . I mean, don't you wish I were able to talk about your work with you?"

"We've talked about it many times. I don't mean the mechanics of it, so to speak. That's unimportant. That I can discuss with any of the surgeons or nurses here.

What I want to talk about, with you, are the things that really matter."

He paused, seeming to consider his words, weighing them before he spoke again. "The men I can't save, the bodies I can't mend. The misery of that, and how I can learn to bear it. I've never talked of it with anyone else."

"Thank you, Robbie. You honor me. I only wish there were more I could do. To help, that is."

"What you can do, now, is get back to your quarters before Miss Jeffries comes searching for us."

"I suppose you're right. But before I go, could you do one thing for me?"

"Yes?" he asked, keenly apprehensive of what she would say next.

"Kiss me. Like you did the night of the ceilidh. Just one kiss."

Before he could say no, before he could move away, she grasped his collar and pulled his head toward hers. She touched her lips to his, lightly, tentatively, and when he didn't respond she pushed her mouth more firmly against his.

He forced himself to do nothing, to simply sit there until she was finished, his hands resting lightly at her waist. Not pushing her away, yet not embracing her. Just waiting until she gave up.

"I must go," she whispered, her voice breaking. "I'm so sorry."

It was the catch in her voice that finished him off. His hands tangled in her hair, pulling her toward him almost roughly, and he was kissing her soundly, completely, his mouth pressing on hers so hard that he knew the stubble from his day-old beard must be rubbing her skin raw. There'd be no hiding what they'd been up to from her friends.

He pulled away, let his forehead rest against hers, and fought to regain the power of speech.

"This must . . . this must stop. Do you understand?" he said at last, his heartbeat sounding so loudly in his head that he could barely make out his own words.

She tried to embrace him, but he reached around and unclasped her hands, setting them firmly in her lap as he stood and walked to the far side of the garage.

"That was . . . it was my fault that happened." He raked his hands through his hair, pulling at it, reveling in the pain, and took one deep, measured breath after another. "If we can't control ourselves, we will have to stop these meetings. This is a matter of honor for me, and for you, too. Surely you understand."

"I do. Though honor is cold comfort at the best of times."

"I agree. But it's better than your being sent home in disgrace, and my having to confess the truth to your brother."

"I should go," she said again.

"Of course. Good night, Lilly. I am sorry." The garage door closed behind her. She was gone.

What was he to do? He had dug himself into a hole so deep, there was no getting out of it now. And this was all his fault, every last part of it.

He had encouraged her to join the WAAC, he had told her he was glad she had come to the 51st, and he had initiated their illicit correspondence. He had suggested they leave the ceilidh together and find somewhere private to talk. Had kissed her and would have happily done much more if Private Gillespie hadn't come so close to barging in on them.

Tonight, he had kissed her again, though he had promised himself he would find the strength to resist.

Worst of all, he wouldn't undo any of it, not a moment. He had dishonored both of them and would continue to do so as long as he was given the chance. That was the sordid truth of it.

That was what he had become, trapped by this war, mired in an existence that promised no escape, no respite, no release, only the gradual sapping away of every last grain of hope. And all that remained was a ghost, the ghost of the man he'd once hoped to be, one of millions of ghosts, both the living and the dead, who haunted the killing fields of Flanders and France.

Chapter 30

"Bugger of a day." Tom Mitchell had never been one to mince his words.

"Aye." Robbie was too tired to talk. Too tired to think, to eat, to do anything but sleep.

"Coming to breakfast?"

"What time is it?"

"Half-past five."

"No, thanks. I'd rather get a few hours of sleep."

"I'll be along in a bit. Will try not to wake you." Tom shuffled off in the direction of the mess tent, his head bent against the driving rain.

Robbie was soaked through by the time he reached their tent. He unbuckled his boots and gaiters, shrugged out of his jacket, shirt, trousers, and socks, and fell onto his cot, wearing only his singlet and undershorts. The blankets were damp and chill, and it was an age before he was able to stop shivering.

No sooner had he fallen asleep, it seemed, than he was being shaken awake.

"Captain Fraser, sir!"

"Um, yes?" he mumbled, wishing whoever it was would just go away and leave him in peace.

"We've another load of wounded in, sir, and the OC says you're needed."

Robbie sat up, shook the cobwebs from his head, and dressed rapidly. "How many?" he asked.

"I dunno, sir. Lots. Reception marquee's full already, and more're on the way."

"Christ Almighty. Just when we'd cleared out the last lot."

He followed the orderly through the night, squinting against the faint light of the kerosene lantern lighting their way, and braced himself for the hours to come. There was nothing about it that ought to faze or unsettle him in the slightest, for he'd long ago lost count of the number of times he'd been roused from bed and harried into an operating theater.

So why, this morning, did he feel as if he were riding a tumbrel on the way to the guillotine? Why was he assailed by a feeling of dread that began in his toes, wound snakelike through his guts, and perched as heavy and ponderous as a gargoyle over his heart?

The orderly hadn't exaggerated. The tent was bursting at the seams: scores of men on stretchers lined the floor, with half as many again sitting on the benches that stretched along the perimeter. Even with seven surgeons operating at full tilt, it would take an entire day, or more, to clear the marquee.

He was the first of the doctors to arrive, so set to work at triaging the stretcher cases. First up was a private, his skin pale and clammy to the touch, his respiration shallow, his pulse rapid and thready. Robbie bent to read the label that had been affixed to the soldier's jacket: single rifle wound, right lower abdomen, no apparent exit wound.

It was hopeless. Back in England, with all the amenities of a modern operating theater at his disposal, he could easily save this man. But here? It might be possible, assuming he could find a handful of walking wounded who were strong enough to donate blood, assuming the bullet hadn't nicked the man's spine, assuming he didn't die of shock before they got him into surgery.

"Where to?" asked Private Dixon, who was waiting for his orders.

"Resuss tent." He'd have ordered some morphine for the man, if there were any to spare, but they'd only enough at present to support the postoperative cases. One of the nurses would make sure he was warm, and she might even be free to hold his hand when death crept close. As long as she wasn't holding the hand of some other poor bugger at the time.

Next in line was a captain, his right arm shattered by a shell fragment. Straightforward amputation. "Pre-op," he instructed Dixon.

Resuss. Resuss. Pre-op. Resuss. Pre-op. And then a sergeant, young for his rank, no more than nineteen or twenty.

"Hello, Sergeant. Can you tell me what happened to you?"

He only shook his head, his eyes wide with terror, and pointed to the label attached to his jacket. *Simple fracture left humerus, superficial wounds to chest and abdomen, nervous shock.*

"Can you tell me your name, Sergeant?" No response. The soldier's eyes rolled upward, as if to heaven, and tears began to trickle down his face.

Robbie set his hand on the man's right shoulder, steadily and gently, and tried to make eye contact. "My name is Captain Fraser. Listen to me for a moment. You're away from it now. Do you hear me? You are away from it. Can you nod if you understand?"

The man nodded once, his eyes shut against the shaming tears.

"I'm going to see to it that you get a good long rest. That I promise you." Robbie turned to Dixon. "Send him on to resuss. I'll be along later to set his arm."

He'd discuss things with the OC later, make sure the sergeant was sent to the closest neurasthenia center, and pray he found a sympathetic ear.

On to the next man, and no need to read the label this time. His head was bandaged, the cloth soaked through with blood, there were thick dressings on his chest and lower abdomen, and his left thigh was in a Thomas splint. Robbie took a moment to peer under the dressings, and what he saw only confirmed his initial instinct. The soldier was already, mercifully, unconscious, his pulse barely discernible.

"Resuss."

On and on he progressed, up and down the rows, the wounded men becoming a blur of blood and mangled viscera and shattered bone. Tom had joined him; the other surgeons were already hard at work in the wooden hut that served as their theater.

From time to time he allowed himself to straighten, look ahead, wonder how long it would take to finish triage and move on to surgery. They were making headway, a little, and he decided when he came to the end of his present row of stretchers, he would take five minutes to visit the latrine and gulp down a mug of tea.

Resuss, pre-op, resuss, morgue—the man had died en route—resuss, resuss, pre-op, pre-op, pre-op.

He stood up fully; for the last hour he'd been crouching and shuffling, crablike, from stretcher to stretcher. His head spun and he had to bend forward, rest his forearms on his knees, and take a deep breath to right himself.

He stood tall, rubbed the sweat and grime from his eyes, and turned to look back at how far he'd come.

He was alone.

The marquee was empty, with not a stretcher left, not a single soldier sitting on its benches. No nurses, no orderlies, no Tom. Empty.

He swung round, dizzy again, unable to believe what he saw. Everyone was gone. Even the bloodstains had been scrubbed from the rough deal floors.

Silence descended on the marquee, though it was never quiet in camp. Even the guns were silent. All he heard was the thundering drumroll of his own heart.

He blinked, scrubbed at his eyes, tried to will the fantasy away. He had to settle himself, rid his mind of this bizarre vision, else risk being sent to the neurasthenia center with the young sergeant.

What was that sound? Someone was breathing, was struggling to breathe. He wheeled about and spied a stretcher, alone, abandoned at the far side of the marquee. Its occupant had been covered head to toe with a khaki blanket.

He stepped forward, surprised he hadn't noticed the stretcher before. Only then did he see the faint movements beneath the blanket. The soldier was alive, after all.

It wasn't the first time he'd known such a thing to take place; mistakes happened during a crush like this. He tried to move closer, but the floor was shifting and tilting beneath his feet, as unsteady as a ship in a gale, and after only a few steps he pitched forward on his knees and began to crawl.

He reached the stretcher, pulled back the blanket, and discovered that no soldier lay hidden beneath.

It was Lilly, his Lilly, and her wounds were the stuff of nightmares. Three huge field dressings, sodden and black with blood, covered her chest and abdomen, and as he scrabbled closer he saw that her hair, loose about her shoulders, was also wet with it.

He pulled back the dressings, his hands gone clumsy with terror, and saw the unmistakable evidence of bayonet wounds, deep and jagged and desecrating.

"Lilly, oh, Lilly," he howled, knowing he could do nothing for her.

And she knew it, too. Her eyes were wild with pain and fear and the horror of what she had seen and felt at the hands of her enemies. She knew he couldn't save her.

"Help me!" he screamed. "Will no one come and help me?"

But the orderlies were gone, Tom was gone, Matron was gone, and it was left to him to lift her, his hands slippery with blood, her body so terribly light in his arms.

"Don't leave me, Lilly," he begged, already broken, but the life was fading from her eyes, her face relaxing into the calm certainty of death, and he was falling, a deadweight through soundless skies, until he woke in a sweaty, gasping heap on his cot.

It had been the same dream for weeks now. A dream so vivid, so true, that the agony of it broke him anew each night.

It was still pitch-black outside, too dark in the tent to make out the time on his wristwatch. Less than an hour, probably, since he had fallen into bed. He'd been exhausted then, deliberately so, and had hoped the nightmare would pass him by.

So much for hope.

He sat up. Rummaged in his locker for clean clothes. Struggled into them. Laced up his boots, buckled on his gaiters, stood up. Shut his mind against the memory of the nightmare.

And went back to work.

Chapter 31

As days went, it hadn't been a bad one. The weather had been fine, the sort of bright, clear day that made it difficult to believe that October would soon give way to November. Casualties had been light, so much so that Lilly and Constance had taken a long break at dinner, returning to the ADS at midafternoon to collect what Sergeant Barnes liked to call "me waifs and strays."

The three men in the back of the ambulance were in good spirits; Blighty wounds tended to have that kind of effect. Who wouldn't feel cheerful at the prospect of one or two weeks of bed rest in a base hospital?

"Give us a song, will yeh?"

The appeals from the back of the ambulance brought Lilly sharply back to earth. She looked to Constance, who was at the wheel. "Shall we give them some Gilbert and Sullivan?" Lilly suggested.

"We *could,* but I think they'd rather hear that song all the American boys are singing. How does it go?"

"The lyrics are ridiculous."

"Stop complaining and sing.

"Somewhere in France is the lily,
Close by the English rose;
A thistle so keen, and a shamrock green,
And each loyal flower that grows.
Somewhere in France is a sweetheart—"

At that moment they rounded the crest of the hill. Plumes of black smoke were billowing from the direction of the CCS. It was no ordinary fire that burned, for the smoke was coming from at least three locations. Shell fire, then. As Robbie had told her would happen, sooner or later.

Constance parked the ambulance at the edge of the camp and ran around to the rear of the vehicle. She was back at Lilly's side a moment later. "I told them the camp has been hit, and asked them to stay put. As soon as we know more, we'll come and fetch them."

Arm in arm, they walked in the direction of the reception marquee—or, rather, the remains of the marquee. It had collapsed into a heap of canvas, rope, and jagged, still-smoldering timbers.

"But we were here only an hour ago," Lilly said. Panic surged within her, for what if Robbie had been hurt? Where was he?

"The shells fell right after you left."

The women turned to see Private Gillespie, his hands roughly bandaged, his face blackened by soot and blood.

"Was anyone in the marquee?" Lilly asked.

"The last load of wounded from this morning," he confirmed. "Most of the orderlies. Two nurses. None of the doctors." At that, he looked Lilly straight in the eye.

"What happened to them?" Constance asked.

"No one was killed, thank God. Shell fell just outside the marquee. Some were badly hurt, though."

"And what of the rest of the camp?" Lilly asked. "Is there any other damage?"

"My garage is gone. A corner of the ward tent collapsed when another shell fell just outside it. And there's one dud. See over there, on the far side of the marquee tent? Stay well clear, no matter what. We're waiting for the AOC to defuse it. Assuming they show up, that is."

"We've wounded men in the ambulance," Lilly said. "What shall we do with them?"

"Mess tent. Matron's set up in there. Do you need any help?"

Lilly shook her head. "No; you get back to what you were doing. Are you . . . how are you?"

He smiled, briefly, the white of his teeth flashing against the soot ingrained in his skin. "I'll survive. Was just outside the ward tent when the shell hit. Burst my eardrums, I think, and knocked me over, but I'll be fine."

"Let us know if we can—"

"Matron needs you now. You go to her."

It was hard work, transferring the Tommies from the ambulance to the mess tent. One man was able to walk; the other two, with the help of crutches, and steadying arms, were able to stagger to the relative safety of the makeshift ward.

A jumble of tables flanked its entrance, evidence of the haste in which the tent had been prepared for its new role. Inside, however, all was calm efficiency.

The benches normally used for seating during meals were pushed up against the sides of the tent; they held the walking wounded. Row upon row of stretchers filled the space that remained. Some of the wounded men looked to have been evacuated from the ward tent, while the rest were new arrivals.

Matron spotted the women immediately. Dispensing with any preamble, she handed Lilly and Constance a pair of scissors each and directed them to a line of stretchers.

"These men are waiting to go into surgery. I need you to remove their clothing. All of it off, every bit," she instructed. "This is no time to be missish. There are sheets and blankets to cover them on the table over there. Keep your hands clean."

With that, Lilly and Constance set to work. In minutes their hands were aching from the effort of propelling the scissors through thick woolen material so soaked with sweat, mud, and blood that it might as well have been chain mail.

While Lilly cut along the outer seam of the wounded man's left jacket sleeve, Constance cut along the right. At last they reached his shoulder; what now?

"Let's cut to the collar," Lilly suggested. "We can drag it out from under him after that."

"What about his webbing? Should we try and unfasten all of these straps?"

"No. Cut through everything."

Working together, they managed to pull away the remnants of the jacket. Their charge seemed only vaguely aware of what they were doing, although at one point he opened his eyes, looked at Constance, and smiled. Then he appeared to fall unconscious again.

"Quick, now," Lilly urged. They repeated the exercise for his shirt and singlet, then turned their attention to his trousers. The soldier had been wounded badly in the right thigh; his trouser leg, on that side, had been cut away and replaced by a large field dressing, now sodden with blood.

Lilly began at his waistband, cutting steadily southward until she reached the top band of his puttees, still carefully tucked in place. It would be too difficult to unwind them; best to keep cutting. She snipped through his bootlaces, too, before gently pulling off his left boot.

She looked up to see that Constance had paused, her scissors hovering over the man's undershorts. "Lilly . . . I don't know if I can—"

"You heard what Matron said. Just concentrate on cutting through the material. I'll cover him up so you don't have to look at anything."

"Sorry to be so, ah . . . it's just that I've never seen . . ."

"Nor have I," Lilly reassured her. "But this hardly counts. Hurry up, now; look how many more we have to do."

Chapter 32

It took several hours for Lilly and Constance to complete the task Matron had assigned them. She gave the women a few minutes' respite, which featured a trip to the latrine, fortunately undamaged, and a cup of lukewarm tea, before instructing them to take charge of the walking wounded.

"Offer tea to anyone who seems capable of holding a mug. Make sure none of the head wounds falls asleep. If anyone is having trouble with pain, let me know. Urinals are in the corner."

"I beg your pardon. Did you say . . . ?"

"Urinals, Miss Evans. The enameled jugs on the table. If any of the men need to relieve themselves, that's what they will use. They're far too weak to walk to the latrine. Don't fret; they shouldn't need much help."

Bridget and Annie appeared just as the afternoon turned into evening; they'd been sent to the resuss tent, Lilly learned. When Constance asked them what it had been like, they simply shook their heads.

"You don't want to know," Bridget insisted.

Lilly longed to ask if they had seen Robbie, for there'd been no sign of him all afternoon. Private Gillespie had said that none of the doctors had been hurt, but could he have been mistaken? Could Robbie have been trapped in the wreckage of the reception marquee all along?

It was well past ten o'clock before Miss Jeffries, who had been in the kitchens with Ethel and Rose, excused the WAACs for the evening. The women made for their tent, which stood at the far end of the camp and had been unaffected by the explosions.

In the opposite direction was the ward tent. Did she dare go in search of Robbie? Or should she wait for him to come to her?

He might still be in surgery, but he never went to bed without checking on his patients. She would see if he was there.

Her path took her past the marquee tent, so close to the dud shell that she found herself holding her breath as she walked past. As she drew near, she noticed a flicker of light in one corner of the tent. What if a fire had broken out?

But it wasn't a fire, she soon saw; it was the glow of several kerosene lanterns. She edged closer, moving carefully so as not to trip on the wreckage strewn all about, stopping when she was still safely outside the circle of light. It took a moment for her eyes to adjust to the brightness of the scene, and then long seconds more to adjust to the horror of what she saw.

Private Dixon was lying on the ground, a gauze mask over his nose and mouth. Private Harris crouched by the injured man's head, a bottle of ether at the ready; Nurse Greenhalgh knelt in the dirt, a huge gauze pad in one hand and an enameled basin in the other. Private Gillespie was leaning over them all, a lantern in each hand.

And she saw Robbie, using a scalpel and saw to cut free the mangled remnants of Private Dixon's left leg, which had been pinned to one of the marquee's support timbers by a twisted, blackened strip of shell casing. At Robbie's side was a tray, piled with the bloodied tools of his trade. Lilly's stomach roiled in protest, but she forced herself to look. This was what he did. This was his life.

At last Private Dixon was free. Gillespie and Harris dragged him onto a stretcher, an awkward procedure since Nurse Greenhalgh was pressing the gauze pad to the stump of his leg, and the group shuffled off in the direction of the operating hut.

Robbie pulled off his gloves, letting them fall on top of the surgical instruments. Then he looked up. His eyes met Lilly's without the slightest hesitation.

"What the hell are you doing here?"

"I was worried about you. I hadn't seen you since the shells—"

"I was in surgery all day. I'd just finished when they found Dixon. He'd been buried under the debris." He doused the lanterns, one by one. "Just go, Lilly. Get back to your tent. I'll talk to you later."

He walked away and he didn't look back.

There was nothing she could do now; he was too upset, and rightly so. She'd been a fool to go chasing after him.

She had only taken a few steps in the direction of her tent when the rush of air hit her, knocking her down as roughly, and certainly, as a prizefighter would have done. A wall of sound assaulted her next, filling her ears, her head, her mind with its inescapable baritone roar. Gravel and dirt and mud rained over her, stopping her nose and mouth, forcing her eyes shut.

She tried to take a deep breath but found herself choking on the acrid, burning air. Desperate to escape the onslaught, she rolled herself into a ball, but there was no escape, no way out.

It was hopeless, oh God, it was hopeless. It would bury her, she knew it would, and no one would ever find her.

"Lilly, open your eyes. You need to open your eyes."

Someone was tapping her face, first one cheek, then the other, tapping and tapping—would they never cease?

"Stop, please," she mumbled.

"I'll stop as soon as you open your eyes and look at me. Open your eyes now."

She did so with the utmost reluctance. Robbie was kneeling beside her, covered in mud and dust, but alive and, it seemed, in one piece.

"The dud went off. Thank God you weren't any closer. Lie still, for a moment, until I know you are unhurt."

She said nothing, just stared at him avidly. His face was so very solemn, so weary. Why would he not smile for her? She reached up and traced a tremulous line across his forehead and down his cheek.

Instead of reciprocating, he simply took her hand and placed it at her side. "Lie still, Lilly."

His hands were in her hair, but no trace of passion animated his touch as he searched her scalp for any sign of injury. She thrilled at the feel of his fingers moving gently along her spine and shoulders, then skimming along her limbs, feeling carefully for broken bones or shell-fragment wounds.

He took up the lantern that Constance held out—she, Bridget, and Annie were just behind him—and adjusted the shutter so its light fell directly on Lilly's face.

"Look right at me," he directed. "Don't close your eyes."

Apparently content with what he saw, he handed the lantern back to Constance, stood, then took Lilly's hands and hoisted her to her feet.

Just then, a voice called out in the darkness. "Captain Fraser!"

"I'll be right there," Robbie shouted back. He turned to look at Lilly's friends.

"Miss Evans?"

"Yes, Captain Fraser?"

"I need you to watch over Miss Ashford for me. Don't let her sleep, whatever you do. Keep her warm, give her tea if you like, but do not let her sleep. Understood?"

"Yes, sir."

"Where are you going?" Lilly asked.

"To finish what I started with Dixon. I'll be back once I'm done."

Lilly allowed Constance to lead her into the tent and settle her in bed. She tried to unbutton her coat, but her hands were shaking too badly to manage the buttons. Her friend took over, helping Lilly to shrug out of her clothes and into a nightdress.

"I'm not sure how we'll ever get your skirt and jacket clean," Constance fussed. "Perhaps we'll be able to brush off the worst of it once they're dry."

Lilly nodded, clutching her mug of tea. "Constance?"

"Yes, dear?"

"Can you spare another blanket? I'm so cold."

Constance built Lilly a cocoon of blankets, but it was no use. She was chilled to the marrow, and no matter how hard she tried to calm her mind, tried to tell herself that all was well—she'd only been knocked over; she hadn't been hurt—she couldn't stop the shaking that beset her.

She couldn't stop thinking of the way he had looked at her. The expression on his face, as if he were the one who had been knocked down. Broken.

As if he had given up.

Chapter 33

Robbie stood in his tent, naked, and poured a pitcher of lukewarm water over his head. He'd have committed murder for a proper bath, but the washhouse was tilting like the Tower of Pisa and this was the best he could expect until it was put to rights. At least Matron had let him borrow one of her enamel trays to catch the overflow from his sponge bath.

Working quickly, he scrubbed the grime from his skin and rubbed a bar of carbolic soap through his hair. It stung his scalp in a few places; no doubt he'd been hit by debris when the dud shell had gone off.

He rinsed off the soap, wincing as it ran over the cuts and scratches on his back, toweled himself dry, and dressed in the cleanest of his trousers and shirts.

If only he could simply fall into bed and forget everything. Forget the terror that had consumed him when the shell had gone off and Lilly had been swallowed up by a hurricane of dirt and razor-sharp shell fragments. Forget the danger that stalked her every day, and the role he'd played in bringing her here.

Even worse, he'd *kept* her here. Instead of trying to persuade her to seek another posting, he'd encouraged her at every turn. What were all those letters and clandestine meetings but a way of keeping her close to him?

It had to stop, now, all of it. It had to stop or he would lose whatever shred of sanity he still possessed.

It would stop tonight.

The WAACs had been waiting for him. He'd only just stepped up to the threshold of Lilly's tent when the flap that covered the entrance was pulled back and he was beckoned inside. They were all there, even the two cooks.

"Good evening, ladies. I need to beg a favor of you. May I ask—"

"We were just going to the mess tent, Captain Fraser," one of them interrupted. Was it Annie or Bridget?

"Thank you very much. I won't be long."

The WAACs filed out, a hesitant Miss Evans propelled along by her friends, leaving him alone with

Lilly. He found a chair, drew it near to the head of her cot, and tried not to stare at her. She sat so primly, her blankets drawn up around her hips, her white nightgown the perfect foil to her beautiful dark eyes and hair.

"How is Private Dixon?" she asked.

"He'll live. I managed to save his knee, so that's something. He might even walk again, if he's fitted with a decent prosthetic."

"That's good news," she answered. "Robbie, I am sorry—"

"No," he interrupted. "It is I who should be sorry. I never ought to have encouraged you. The letters, our meetings. It wasn't right."

"I don't understand. Are you upset about earlier? I'm sorry I intruded. It was thoughtless of me."

He shook his head. "It's your being here that isn't right."

"How can you say that? Would you say that of the nurses, or of the other WAACs?"

"No, but—"

"Why should they be given the chance to do their duty, but not me? Why, Robbie?"

He would not say it. Could not confess the truth of his feelings for her, not here, in this terrible place.

He pressed on, determined to convince her. "Lilly, I want—I *need* you to ask for a transfer. There are any number of postings you can take that would allow you—"

"No. I told you when I arrived that I was here to make something of myself. I thought you understood what it means to me, this chance to prove myself."

"I do, Lilly, but what good is it if you're dead?"

"How can you say that to me? You, of all people? Don't you remember what you told me the night of the ball? You said I could do anything I wanted with my life. That we lived in the twentieth century and anything was possible."

"I was wrong."

The color drained from her face; at last he had made an impression on her.

"I see," she said.

"The world we grew up in has changed, Lilly. It has changed out of all knowing. And all that matters, now, is that we survive. Tell me you understand. Tell me you agree."

He dragged the chair closer, meaning to take her hand in his, but she drew back from him as if he repelled her.

"You do see it, don't you? That it's for the best?"

At that she sat up straight and met his gaze. He was astonished to see that anger, not chagrin or sorrow, burned in her eyes.

"It's not for the best. Not my best, at any rate. This is all about you, Robbie. You are worried, you are scared, and you want me to suffer for it."

"Of course I'm afraid," he shot back. "I'm afraid you will be the end of me. You're all I think of, day and night. Everywhere I turn, there you are. Even when I sleep, you're in my dreams. Haunting me. Tormenting me."

"So why did you ask me to write to you? Why did you ask me to go with you to the garage, the night of the ceilidh?"

"I don't know. I thought I could manage it. But how do you manage an obsession? That's what you are. An obsession. And I'm afraid of what you'll do to me. I'm a good doctor, a good surgeon. I know I am. But not if my mind is elsewhere."

"You're reacting to the shock of the attack. You must see that."

"For God's sake, Lilly, give me some credit. A few shells going off isn't enough to unhinge me. But the chance of your being hurt or killed *is*." He dropped to his knees beside her cot. "Until today, it was only an abstraction. A theoretical possibility."

"I wasn't hurt, Robbie."

"Today you weren't. But what about tomorrow? And the day after that?" He bowed his head, running his hands through his hair, pulling at it savagely. "I've been in France for thirty-six months now. That's more than a thousand days of hell, Lilly, and there's no end in sight. A thousand days . . ."

He looked up at her, met her reluctant gaze. He had to say it. Had to make her see. "If I'm to survive this war, I cannot think about anything else apart from the work I do. And that includes you."

At least a minute passed before she spoke. When she did, her voice was eerily calm. "Your mind is quite set on the matter?"

"It is. I'm sorry, Lilly."

"And I am sorry, too. For I cannot do what you ask. As much as I want to help you, I will not go."

A wash of cold swept over him. "Nothing I say will change your mind?"

"Nothing. Forgive me, Robbie."

Had he actually thought she would relent? If so, he was a fool. A fool who could see but one path forward, though it killed him to contemplate it.

He got to his feet and walked away from her, his heart withering in his chest with every step. "Then there is nothing more for us to say to one another. Good-bye, Lilly."

"Good-bye? I just told you I am staying."

"I know." He forced himself not to turn around. "But we are done, you and I. So this is our good-bye."

PART THREE

They march from safety, and the bird-sung joy
Of grass-green thickets, to the land where all
Is ruin, and nothing blossoms but the sky . . .

—SIEGFRIED SASSOON,
  "Prelude: The Troops," 1918

Chapter 34

December 1917

Just before Christmas, Edward wrote to ask if Lilly might join him for a short leave in Saint-Omer. Fortunately, Miss Jeffries was amenable to Lilly's request and granted her two full days, beginning at noon on December 28. It had been her first leave since joining the WAAC nearly nine months earlier.

Miss Jeffries, for all her spit-and-polish approach to the WAACs under her command, must have noticed how miserable Lilly had been in the weeks since the 51st had been shelled. Most likely she attributed it to delayed shock, and shock it was, of a sort. It was a mercy indeed that she knew nothing of Lilly's heartache, or of its cause.

We are done, you and I. We are done. We are done...

Robbie's words sounded constantly in the back of Lilly's mind, a dirge that deadened her spirits and weighted her every step, and no matter what she thought or did, they would not be banished. They haunted her in her sleeping and waking hours, never ceasing, never abating, and though she tried to combat them with words of her own—*it's for the best, you will survive, you must do your duty*—they rang hollow against her heart.

Edward was waiting for her on the platform when she arrived in Saint-Omer late in the afternoon. After embracing her at length, he shouldered her carpetbag and led her through the rain to the tiny, rather shabby premises of the Pension Saint-Bertin, the best that he had been able to manage on such short notice.

But Lilly's room was clean and pretty, with a white linen counterpane on the narrow bed and an eggcup of delicate snowdrops, or *perce-neige*, as the pension's proprietor had called them, on the lace-topped chest of drawers. Best of all, there was enough hot water for her to have a sponge bath before supper.

Edward was little changed from a year ago at Christmas, when she'd last seen him, though he'd shaved off his mustache. He was, Lilly thought, one of the handsomest men she had ever known, and quite possibly the most charismatic. All he had to do was smile and look a person in the eye and he or she fairly leaped to do his bidding. Madame Mercier had been no exception: when she had first greeted them her expression had been dour and unyielding, but Edward had taken her hand in his, thanked her in flawless French for her hospitality, and had proclaimed her home delightful in every respect.

Bowled over by the effect of his regard, Madame Mercier had rewarded them with huge bowls of fish stew and fresh-baked bread for supper, and had even produced a small carafe of white wine. They retreated to the pension's salon afterward, where a fine coal fire had been laid, and Lilly read aloud from *Idylls of the King*, which she had brought along for just that purpose. After a half hour, she set the book aside and turned down the oil lamp on the mantel, and they began to talk, their voices hushed, their faces lit only by the flickering glow of the hearth.

They started with news from home, of which Lilly was entirely ignorant, as neither their parents nor sisters had written to her since her departure from Ashford House. Their aunt Augusta had died some months earlier, Edward informed her, and had left her considerable fortune to the Battersea Dogs Home.

"*All* of it?"

"Every last shilling. Mama was livid. You know how she had been cultivating Aunt Augusta."

"That's one thing I haven't missed," she said. "The way Mama always seems to be angry about something."

"It made for a nice interlude in her letters. Usually she's rabbiting on about how dear everything's become in the shops. As if she's ever set foot in a butcher's in her life."

"She has no sense of the world beyond her own doors, does she?"

"She never has. But she and Papa have been doing their bit for the war, you'll be glad to know." Edward paused, his eyes twinkling. "They had the lawns at Cumbermere Hall dug up last spring and planted out with vegetables and potatoes."

"I don't believe it."

"They hadn't much of a choice. Once the king had the deer park at Windsor plowed up, Papa had to give in, else look like a shirker."

"At least they won't go short of potatoes," Lilly commented, trying and failing to stifle a giggle.

"They won't, will they? But enough of our parents for now, else I'll end up with indigestion. Tell me about Miss Brown instead. How is she?"

"Very well. She had Christmas off this year, her

first proper leave from the hospital in ages, so she went home to her parents'."

"Where is she from again?"

"Somerset. Her father is a prebendary at Wells Cathedral."

"No beau as of yet?" Edward asked, his eyes fixed on the fire.

"Charlotte? Of course not."

"Why do you say that?"

"I don't know," Lilly answered, taken aback by his question. "I suppose because she's never spoken of anyone, not once in all the years I've known her. And she's always seemed so devoted to her work."

"Does she intend to continue work as a nurse after the war?"

"I don't know for certain, for she's never said anything to me, but I don't think so. She's very competent, very good at what she does, but I think she'd rather return to her work with Miss Rathbone in Liverpool."

"I'd forgotten about her rabble-rousing days with the lady politician. Is she still at that hospital in Kensington?"

"The one for neurasthenia patients? Yes."

"It must be bedlam there."

"Not at all. At least, that's what she told me once. It's very quiet, she said. Many of the men can't speak. Some just sit and weep. Some are quite normal until they hear a loud noise, a door slamming, for instance, and then they collapse."

"Sounds dreadful."

"No more dreadful than what you endure."

Lilly stopped short, desperate to ask, to know, but wary of ruining their evening. "I know you don't like to speak of it, but . . ."

"Go ahead. I've drunk enough wine that I might even answer truthfully."

"What is it like? To live there, day in and day out?"

"I don't want to shock you."

"I don't think anything can, not now."

"It doesn't bother me," he said, so quietly that she almost didn't catch his words.

"What? I mean . . . what? How can it not?"

"I don't mean that I *like* it. Far from it. But it doesn't upset me."

"I don't understand. I honestly don't."

"When I joined up, it was because everyone else was doing it. No more. But then I discovered that I was good at it. Being a soldier, that is. Was good at training the men, inspiring them, keeping them going. And that was just during training.

"When they sent us to France, we were thrown into the thick of it straightaway. Lost men at Festubert within weeks, men I'd known all my life. At first, I was worried how I'd manage. Would I crack up? Shame myself in front of my men?

"But it didn't bother me. None of it did. The noise, the smell, the food, the mud, the rats—none of it. Still doesn't. I don't get nervous before a big push, I sleep well enough, I can choke down whatever food they put in front of me."

She thought back to what he'd said a moment before. "Why should I be shocked?"

"Because nothing bothers me, Lilly. *Nothing.* Two days ago one of my lieutenants forgot to duck when he was passing through a shallow stretch of trench. *Ping!* A German sniper got him right through the temple. I was there, only inches away. And as soon as he'd been dragged off, and I'd thrown a bucket of water over the mess his brains had left behind, I went into my dugout, wrote to his widow, and ate my dinner as if nothing had happened."

"It truly didn't affect you?" she whispered.

"I felt badly that Baker had died. But it didn't trouble me in any measurable way. It was just one more death among the hundreds, if not thousands, that I've witnessed."

"Oh, Edward," Lilly said, trying and failing to think of something appropriate to say.

"And the thing is, the fault lies within *me*. If I were a decent man, I'd be writing poetry about the horrors I've seen. It seems as if that's what every other officer on the Western Front is doing. But I'm not a decent man. I'm as shallow and empty as it's possible for any man to be and still have a beating heart in his chest."

"Edward, don't—"

"That's the only true horror of this war, the knowledge of how little horror it holds for me. I've always known I was a shallow bastard. I welcomed it, even. It made everything so much easier to bear. But now," he continued, his voice breaking, "now, when I want to plumb the depths of my soul, I discover I have none."

Desperate to comfort him, Lilly leaned forward and clasped his hands in hers. "Edward, look at me. I know we've always made a joke of it, the way you seemed to sail along without a care in the world, but that's all it was. A *joke*. There's no truth to it. Your not collapsing at the first blast of shell fire doesn't make you shallow. It makes you courageous."

Edward shook his head, his eyes screwed shut, but she pressed on. "Nothing you say can change my opinion of you. I believe you are one of the heroes of this war. What else but courage has kept you at the Front year after year? We both know you could have asked for a staff position behind the lines anytime you wished."

"I never did. Never will."

"Surely you have done enough, suffered enough. Will you not consider it?"

"And leave behind my men? They think me lucky, you know. As if serving under my command offers some kind of protection. Never mind that there's ample evidence to the contrary."

"They would understand."

"They would. They might even forgive me for abandoning them. But how could I forgive myself? If anything were to destroy me, Lilly, that would."

She met his gaze again and in it shone a warning, or perhaps it was a plea. So she held tight to his hands and bent her head so he would not see the tears that gathered in her own eyes.

"Shall I turn up the lamp and read some more Tennyson?" she suggested a few minutes later, once she was certain she wouldn't cry.

"Yes, my darling girl. And thank you."

Chapter 35

As she readied herself for bed, it occurred to Lilly that her brother hadn't once asked after Robbie. Could he have guessed that something had gone wrong between them? Or perhaps her failure to mention his friend had warned Edward away.

It would have been mortifying if Edward had asked, but would also have been such a blessed relief. She hadn't felt able to say anything to her friends, for Robbie had done nothing to them, and it would be unfair to color their impressions of him. But Edward knew Robbie better than nearly anyone else.

She longed to confess the truth of it all to her brother, and in doing so discover what he thought of his friend's actions, not to mention her own. Had she made a mistake? Would it have been better to give in, do as Robbie had begged, and accept a transfer to a less dangerous posting?

No. What was done was done. Further talk would serve only to torment Edward, perhaps even cause a rift between him and his dearest friend. Best to say nothing, bury it away and forget, though forgetting was impossible, the awful night when Robbie had turned away and erased her from his life.

She and Edward both rose with the larks the next morning, eager to make the most of their remaining time together. As luncheon was to be their main meal, Madame Mercier served them a light breakfast of café au lait and tartines, which Edward ate without notice-able enthusiasm.

"I'd give my left arm for a proper cooked breakfast," he grumbled quietly. "Though this is a sight better than the breakfast that'll greet me tomorrow."

"Will you be back on the front lines?"

"Not for a few days. Then we go back for two weeks. I only hope it stops raining soon."

When they'd finished their meal, Lilly presented him with his Christmas gift, a pair of thick woolen socks that she'd knitted herself. "Constance had to help me when I turned the heels, but they're mostly my work. And I didn't drop a stitch!"

After pronouncing himself delighted with his gift, Edward drew a small parcel out of his jacket pocket. "I know it would have been more practical to give you something that would keep you warm or dry, fur-lined gloves or a new pair of Wellingtons, but I thought you might prefer something to read."

It was a leather-bound copy of *Cranford* by Mrs. Gaskell, the pages worn and the gilding on the cover rubbed thin in spots. "I'll confess I wrote to Miss Brown some months ago and asked her to find a book that you would enjoy," he explained. "Is it a good choice?"

"Oh, absolutely. I read it ages ago and loved it. And it's exactly the sort of thing I most want to read. No war, no death, just stories of village life. Thank you, Edward."

"You're most welcome. Now, what do you say to some fresh air?"

A companionable silence hung between them as they walked, arm in arm, along the quiet cobbled streets that flanked the cathedral, and then along the banks of the canal.

"Shall I read some of *Cranford* to you when we get back?" Lilly asked after they'd been walking for nearly an hour.

"Yes, please. Or the Tennyson. It's the sound of your voice that I enjoy."

"I meant to ask earlier—what did you get Helena for Christmas?"

"I'm not sure. I asked Mama to order up a pair of earrings from Garrard's and send them along."

"You didn't."

"I wrote her a letter to go along with it. I'm sure that will be fine."

Feeling decidedly unimpressed with her brother's approach to gift giving, Lilly turned to look up at him, and was astonished when she saw the expression on his face. It was a complete blank, utterly bare of any discernible emotion.

"Edward? Is anything wrong between you and Helena?"

She knew he had heard her, for what else could account for the sudden hesitation in his stride? But he made no response. Only after they'd walked on for several hundred yards did he slow his pace and look down at her.

"It depends on what you mean by 'wrong.' Let's start with this: Is it wrong to force a man—say, for example, your son—to marry a woman he doesn't love? Or how about this: Is it wrong to agree to marry someone you don't love, someone who deserves nothing but happiness, knowing you will probably ruin her life? Even if you're marrying her because you have no choice?"

"Please tell me you're not speaking of yourself and Helena."

"Of course I am. Do you want to know why I agreed to the engagement? Money. I had practically bankrupted myself, and our dear parents knew it. So they proposed a solution to my troubles: they would clear my debts, advance me additional capital, and continue my quarterly allowance, on one condition."

"They didn't. They wouldn't be so cold-blooded."

"In their defense, I think they believed they were helping me. Encouraging me, so to speak. All I had to do was find a suitable girl and pop the question."

"Why Helena?"

"Why not? She was young, pretty, inoffensive. It wasn't so hard."

"So that's why you didn't get married before you left for France."

"That's the one and only favor this war has done me. It got me off the hook, for the duration at least."

"What are you going to do when you return home?"

"I have no idea. I've never let myself think that far ahead."

"Surely it would be kinder to break things off now. I know people would talk, but it would be better than if you waited until you're home."

At this he shook his head decisively. "You're assuming that the war is going to end. And that I'll be alive at the end of it."

Lilly stopped short, the blood rushing from her head, her hands clammy with fear.

"You know I'm right," he added. "Because you see it every day, don't you?"

"You've survived this long with hardly a scratch. You said your men think you lucky—"

"Meaningless."

"But the war is sure to end soon."

"That's what they've been telling us for more than three years. 'One more push and we'll have them.' 'One more ridge and we'll have the Hun on their knees.'"

And then, his voice soft but steely with certainty: "Lilly, I stopped believing years ago."

"What do you mean? In God?"

Edward laughed, a bitter sound that was devoid of mirth. "I can't remember the last time I thought about God. No, I mean I stopped believing I have a future that extends any farther than a day or two ahead of me. Perhaps a week, if we're behind the lines for a spell. But no more than that."

"I don't agree. I believe you will survive. I always have," she insisted, embracing him tightly and knowing, even as she marshaled every ounce of conviction, that she was lying to him.

His arms were strong about her, bestowing comfort, though he was the one who most needed it. "Promise me you will survive," he whispered against her hair. "Endure all of this, go home, and then do everything you always dreamed of doing. No, Lilly. You must listen. I want you to travel the world and go to school and find someone to love. *Promise me*."

"Please, Edward, please don't talk of things like this. I can't bear it."

"I know, darling girl. But it's the only time I'll ever speak of it, so let me finish. I made over my will last year and everything goes to you. You'll have my house, all my belongings, and whatever is in the bank. None of it's entailed; it all goes to you."

She cried for long minutes, letting her tears soak the wool of his uniform jacket, letting his strong arms hold her tight. And then she looked up and saw the expression on his face, as if she had relieved him of an almost unbearable burden.

So Lilly did the only thing she could do. She dug in her coat pocket and found a handkerchief, blew her nose and wiped away her tears, and pasted on her bravest smile.

"Shall we walk back to the pension now?" she asked him. "I'm sure luncheon will be ready soon."

Chapter 36

February 1918

Lilly parked Henrietta in the only spot available, at the very end of the row of ambulances, and descended from the driver's seat as gracefully as her frozen extremities allowed. In good weather it only took about twenty minutes to drive the short distance to the railhead in Merville. Tonight it had taken an hour.

At first she had driven quickly, but sleet and snow had flown in the open sides of the ambulance, covering her in slushy drifts. When she had slowed down, wary of skidding off the road, the snow had responded by settling around her like a mantle, stiffening her hands so she could hardly grip the steering wheel or grasp the gearshift.

Constance was in the ward tent tonight; two days ago the chilblains on her hands had burst and become septic. She hadn't complained, not once, but after she'd fainted in the mess tent, Matron had ordered her to bed until her fever broke.

So Lilly had made the run to the railhead on her own, with two gas cases who had recovered sufficiently to manage the journey to the base hospital in Saint-Omer. It had seemed odd, and awfully lonely, to be perched alone on the hard, high bench that served as a driver's seat.

That one word summed up her life now. Lonely. She had her friends, of course, who did their best to keep her occupied; they knew as well as anyone how difficult the past months had been for Lilly. And she had her letters from Edward and Charlotte.

It had been two and a half months since that night. Ten and a half weeks. Eighty days. It was folly to keep track as she did, but she couldn't bear to stop. If she stopped, that meant it was over. Meant there was no point in counting, since she would have to count forever.

Eighty days since Robbie had said good-bye and walked away. Since then, not one word had passed between them. She had tried to catch his attention, at first, when the hurt of it was still so raw that a glimpse of him was enough to leave her stricken. But he'd ignored her pitiful attempts to engage him, going about his work as if she were invisible. A ghost.

Only once had he responded. She'd been entering the mess tent as he'd been leaving, one of a group, and she'd dared to reach out and pluck at his sleeve. He'd looked at her then, only for an instant, but she would remember it forever. His eyes had burned brightly, almost feverish in their intensity, warning her away.

Lilly had done her best to stay clear of him ever since. It was easy enough, given how many hours she spent on the road to and from the CCS or the nearby railhead. And he always seemed to be in surgery, or hunched over his desk in the ward tent.

Sometimes she saw him walking with Nurse Ferguson, their heads close together as they discussed details of a patient's care. Sometimes she saw them laughing together like old friends, which of course they were. She wished she could hate the pretty Scottish nurse, but the woman was friendly and warm to everyone at the 51st, Lilly in particular. In another lifetime they might have been friends.

She stumbled to her quarters, her footsteps made leaden by the cold. "Please," she muttered to herself, "please let the others have left the kettle on the stove. And please let there be some Bovril left in the jar that Charlotte sent last week."

The others were asleep, but the stove was still warm and the kettle was hissing in the most comforting fashion. Lilly pulled off her leather gauntlets, which stretched to her elbows, then gingerly removed the knitted gloves she wore underneath. She, too, had chilblains, but so far none of them had burst, though they were unbearably itchy.

She rummaged in her locker for the jar of Bovril. A scant teaspoon remained of the savory paste, enough for two or three mugs of beef tea. Best to ration herself to one, for the moment, and see if that tamped down her hunger. Lilly drank it in one go, standing by the stove, then threw caution to the wind and made another. It burned her tongue, but she didn't care; all that mattered was the warmth that had begun to seep, ever so slowly, through her bones.

Turning away from the stove, she began to undress. Not fully, for they all slept in their uniforms in case a call of nature or of duty should wake them. Lilly removed her shearling greatcoat, which she spread over her cot for extra insulation, and her boots, which she wrapped in an old newspaper and placed under the blankets at the foot of her bed. Cold boots in the morn-ing meant cold feet all day.

Lilly woke to gentle hands pushing at her shoulder. She opened one eye, just a crack.

"Bridget? Please don't tell me I've overslept," she groaned.

"Don't worry. We told Miss Jeffries, and she said you were to have a lie-in. Not as if there's much you can do this morning, with Constance off sick. We've kept a bowl of porridge warm for you, and there's a mug of tea as well."

"You're such a dear. I'll get up now. I need to scrape down Henrietta's spark plugs."

"See you at dinner."

Lilly wolfed down her porridge and tea, made a feeble attempt to arrange her hair, and dressed for the day, a simple matter of putting on her coat and boots. Then she set off for the garage, which sat just next to the ruins of its predecessor.

She'd hoped the side door would be open, but it was locked up tight. She'd have to track down Private Gillespie and borrow his key. At this time of day, he'd either be on the road or in the reception marquee. She ran over to it and poked her nose inside its entrance, ready to retreat if Robbie were there. Fortunately, one of the other surgeons was doing triage this morning.

Private Gillespie was on the far side of the tent, talking earnestly with Nurse Taylor. Lilly began to move toward him, tiptoeing between the rows of stretchers so as not to bother any of the men who were waiting for treatment.

"Lady Elizabeth! Is that you?"

One of the wounded men, no more than three yards away, was reaching out to her. She scrambled to his side, her finger at her lips, but it was too late.

"Lady Elizabeth! Do you remember me? Daniel Jenkins. I was second footman at his lordship's house in London."

She didn't have to look up to know that every face in the marquee was turned toward them. "Of course I remember you. But would you mind calling me Miss Ashford? I don't use my . . . that other name anymore."

"Begging your pardon, Miss, ah, Miss Ashford. I knew you was in France, but I'd of never thought to see you here."

It wasn't his fault; how could he have known? But her goose was well and truly cooked, from the sound of the whispers that percolated around the perimeter of the tent. She dared to look up: yes, it was bad. Private Gillespie had heard; so, too, had Nurse Taylor. And

Nurse Bell, Captain Harrison, Captain Mitchell. And, oh bother, Bridget and Annie, who had just walked in.

She dragged her attention back to the young man lying on the stretcher. "I'm sorry to see you've been wounded, Private Jenkins. How are you feeling?"

"Got pipped in the leg, but the doctor said it's not bad. I'll need an operation to get the bullet out. A few weeks on the mend and I'll be as good as new."

"That's wonderful news. Shall I come and visit you in the ward tent later?"

"Only if it's not too much trouble, La—I mean, Miss Ashford. And God bless you, miss. You was always so kind to me and everyone else belowstairs."

Lilly gave him one last smile, patted his hand reassuringly, and stood up. Bridget and Annie were gone; she would have to speak with them later.

But the doctors and nurses, and of course Private Gillespie, still stared at her. There was nothing for it but to look each and every one of them in the eye and smile confidently.

Lilly approached Private Gillespie. "May I have the key to your garage? I need to do some maintenance work on my ambulance."

"Of course, ah . . ."

"Miss Ashford, please. I no longer use the other name. A relic of my life before I came to France."

Lilly took the key he offered her, wishing she could run, feeling her face flushing red with the shame and chagrin of it all, but there was only the one exit from the marquee. To reach it she had to shuffle back along the rows of wounded men, her heavy boots catching again and again on their stretchers or webbing or out-flung limbs.

At last she was free. She stumbled to the garage, her arms clutched tight around her middle, and unlocked the door with trembling hands. Then, alone as never before, she hung her head and covered her face with her hands. And she wept.

Chapter 37

Lilly was rummaging in her pockets for a handkerchief when the door to the garage opened and a face peeped around the threshold. It was Constance.

"What shall I call you? Milady? Although you must admit it sounds awfully old-fashioned."

At that, Lilly burst into tears again. Constance rushed over and enveloped her in a soothing hug, encouraged her to sit down on the bench against the wall, offered up her own handkerchief, and waited for Lilly to regain some measure of composure.

Only then did Lilly remember that her friend was supposed to be resting in bed. "What are you doing here?"

"Matron gave me permission, so don't fuss. When I woke up this morning, the fever was gone. She said I might get back to work, as long as I stay in camp. No driving. And my hands are ever so much better."

"How did you find out?"

"I was just getting out of bed when Bridget and Annie came looking for me. They told me what happened."

"I'm so sorry, Constance. I meant to tell you; I almost did, so many times. But I was worried you would think differently of me. It's just a courtesy title, you know. It has nothing to do with *me*."

Constance reached out and enfolded Lilly in a brief, fierce hug. "It must have been so hard for you. Not being able to talk to any of us about your family, and all of that."

"After the first week or so, I mostly forgot about it. But now . . . now it's spoiled everything."

Constance adopted her sternest expression, the one she used with soldiers who dared to use off-color language in front of her or who were insufficiently courteous to any of the WAACs. "Nonsense. What has it spoiled? You're my friend, Lilly, and nothing can change that. Do you hear me?"

Lilly nodded, not daring to interrupt.

Constance frowned. "Is Lilly Ashford your real name?"

"It is, after a fashion. My real name is Elizabeth Adelaide Sophia Georgiana Neville-Ashford."

"Goodness me. I can see why you prefer the simpler version."

"My parents are very grand. Hence the endless string of names."

"Just who are they, Lilly?"

"The Earl and Countess of Cumberland."

"Your father is an *earl*?"

"I'm afraid so."

"I'd thought a baronet, or something of the sort. An *earl*, you say. Heavens. What about your brother?"

"Edward? He's Viscount Ashford. Captain Ashford for the duration."

"Do *his* friends know?"

"Yes. He would never have been able to hide it. Most of the men who worked on my parents' estate in Cumbria belong to his battalion. But I . . ."

"Yes?" Constance prompted.

"I worried you would think I was just another one of those irritating Lady Bountiful types. Playing at doing her bit and secretly looking down her nose at everyone. So that's why I didn't tell."

"Well, the cat is well and truly out of the bag now. Everyone in camp will know by dinnertime."

"Do you think people will treat me differently?"

"Perhaps at first," her friend admitted. "But when they see you haven't changed, I'm certain they'll come around." She patted Lilly's hand, wincing a little, and stood up decisively. "Now tell me: how shall we spend the rest of this glorious morning?"

"I was going to scrape down Henrietta's spark plugs. But you mustn't help; you'll dirty your bandages."

"I suppose you're right. Shall I keep you company instead? I can fetch the tea and stoke the stove." And then, with a grin, "But only if your ladyship is agreeable."

Lilly made a full confession to Bridget and Annie at dinner, and they accepted the news with good humor.

"It does explain a lot, when you think on it," Annie commented. "You being so prim and proper, like."

"And that hamper you got from your brother. The things in it were right dear, they were. Must've cost him a pretty penny," said Bridget.

"I never meant to—"

"I know it. Annie too. I'm sorry we were so hard on you when we was all of us in Kent. You're just trying to do your bit, same as the rest of us."

Further discussion had to wait for that evening, when they were all tucked in bed, hot bricks at their feet, the tent buffeted by wave after wave of lashing sleet.

"What's it like, then, being a lady?"

Where to begin? "Oh, Bridget, it's wonderful. Simply wonderful. I know that now. Although I'm not sure you'll believe me when I tell you what it was like."

"Go on, then."

"I lived in a palace. I'm not exaggerating; I've been to most of the king and queen's homes and my parents' houses are every bit as grand."

Wondering sighs echoed around the tent.

"I was surrounded by beautiful things, ate delicious food, wore the most divine clothes. Was waited on hand and foot by people whose only thought was the comfort of my family. And I'm ashamed to admit that didn't I do a single day's work until I was past twenty years old."

Annie was the first to respond. "Where did you live?"

"In Belgravia. My family has a house on Belgrave Square. And of course there's our country estate in Cumbria. I much prefer it to London."

"Fancy having two houses," Bridget said.

Lilly hesitated before answering. But she was done with telling half-truths to her friends.

"They, ah . . . they have more than two. There's a hunting and fishing lodge in Scotland, a town house in Bath, another in Brighton. But my parents' favorite homes are Ashford House and Cumbermere Hall."

"What're they like inside?" Constance asked.

"They're big, to begin with. I can't remember exactly how many rooms. I'm not sure anyone has ever counted. Let me try and add them up. There are the drawing rooms, three big ones. The dining room, breakfast room, library, ten principal bedrooms. I'm not counting the bathrooms. There's a ballroom that takes up most of one floor. And of course the kitchens and all the rooms belowstairs. And the servants' bedrooms in the attics. So I would say . . . thirty or forty rooms? Perhaps more?"

"And the London house?" Constance asked.

"Oh, I'm sorry. That *is* the London house. Cumbermere Hall is much bigger. I'm sure there are well over a hundred rooms, perhaps as many as a hundred and fifty."

"All that for one family," Ethel whispered.

"I know. It's rather shameful, isn't it, in this day and age? Of course my parents would never notice such a thing."

"What happened, Lilly? You never speak of them." How like Constance to move to the heart of things so quickly.

"It was two and a half, nearly three years ago. I wanted to work, do my bit for the war effort. But my mother opposed it. She even stole my letters. So I left."

"Where did you go?"

"I went to stay with my friend Charlotte, and then I found a job at the LGOC. First as a painter and then as a clippie. It was difficult at first. I'd never worked before, and I'd so little money—"

A snort came from Bridget's corner of the tent. "A lady like you? No money?"

"I'd hardly a shilling to my name. My father paid for everything. Even now, all I have are my wages."

"So your parents wouldn't let you work?" asked Rose.

"They wouldn't let me go to school either. My mother said my only duty was to marry a suitable man and devote my life to him and our children."

"Were you a debutante, Lilly? All dressed in white, with those feathers in your hair?"

"I'm afraid I was."

"Did you dance with the Prince of Wales?"

"I'm sorry to disappoint, but no." Lilly laughed. "One rarely sees him at Court functions. They're not his sort of thing at all.

"No," she went on, "I hardly danced with anyone. Didn't attract so much as a whiff of interest from any of the young men my mother thought suitable."

A diplomatic silence followed, broken by another question from Annie. "Other than balls and such, what did you do?"

"I can hardly remember. It seems a lifetime ago. Let's see . . . I helped Mama with the estate, visited our tenants, that sort of thing. I spent a lot of time on my own, just reading. When Mama went to Europe, to the spas in Germany, I would go with her."

"Why did you become a WAAC?" Constance asked.

"I'd wanted to do something like this for ages. I had even learned how to drive in the hope that one of the services would take me on. I applied to the VAD and the FANY, but they turned me down. So when I heard about the WAAC, I applied straightaway. Captain Fraser wrote one of my references."

"You mean the Captain Fraser who works here in camp?" gasped Ethel.

"Yes, him. He's my brother's best friend. He convinced me I could do it. But now . . ."

"What happened with him, Lilly?" Of course Constance and the others must have wondered.

"Do you remember the day the camp was shelled, in October? He was so upset. So angry," she said, wiping away the tears that had begun to course down her cheeks. "He told me I had to ask for a transfer. Said that I distracted him, made it impossible for him to do his work."

"Oh, Lilly." Her friends sighed one after the other.

"I told him I wouldn't go. I couldn't bear the idea of going somewhere out of harm's way, miles and miles behind the lines. What good would I be able to do? I'm needed *here*. I'm useful *here*."

"So what did he say?" Bridget prompted.

"He said we were finished; our friendship was finished. And he meant it. He hasn't said a word to me since."

"You're better off without him, duckie."

Lilly shook her head. "No, Annie, I'm not. That's why it's so hard. I miss him so much. I've such lovely memories of his visiting us in Cumbria, back when I was still a girl. He was so different. I don't think he could have been more than twenty, but he was brave enough to speak his mind, even to my mother."

"Why should he be afraid of your mother?" Constance asked.

"She's very grand. More so than the actual queen, you know. Queen Mary is very shy, not regal at all. But Robbie wasn't the slightest bit intimidated by Mama. And she hated him for it."

"Do you hate him now?"

"I don't know, Constance. I . . . I don't know how I feel. I don't want to know, if that makes any sense. Would you mind if we talked about something else? Otherwise I'll never be able to sleep."

"Yes, let's talk about Lilly and the Prince of Wales!"

"Oh, Annie," Lilly groaned. "I already told you that I never danced with him."

"But you have met him, haven't you?"

"Oh, yes. We used to play together when we were little. My parents are great friends with the king and queen. Shall I tell you about our visits to Sandringham and Balmoral?"

It took a long time to sate her friends' curiosity, but Lilly didn't mind. She was happy to answer all of their questions, and recounting her childhood memories made for a pleasant evening.

If only she could share this with Robbie. By now he, too, would have heard that her secret was out. Would he be proud of her? Pleased that she had weathered the ordeal?

She would never know.

Chapter 38

16 Feb. 1918

Dear Robert,

*I'm beginning to worry that something has hap-
pened to you, old friend—not a word, not so much
as a wretched postcard, in more than a month. I
know my battalion has been keeping your lot busy,
but you've never been this silent before.*

*Do you feel in need of a break from all of this?
I've got some leave coming up and I'm weary of
Boulogne and Saint-Omer. What say you to Paris?
For three days, beginning March 10?*

*I did ask Lilly to join us, but apparently she used
up all her leave when she and I went to Saint-Omer
after Christmas and won't be able to get away again*

until May at the earliest. So it would just be the two of us.

As for how I've been, assume the same as ever. Mud, bugs, rats, rain. But the men in my platoon are cheery enough. Probably because the German snipers here are shiftless, or duff shots, or perhaps both, and haven't killed any of us today, or the day before. That's what passes for luck hereabouts.

Edward

It was a tempting offer. No doubt about that. Yet the subject of Lilly would surely come up if he were to spend more than a few minutes in Edward's company. His friend would want to know how his sister was getting on, if she were really able to manage the work, how she was being treated. He might even ask Robbie if she was happy.

What kind of answer could he provide to that question?

If only he could go back in time, to the night of the bombardment, and change what he had said. Not the substance of his words, for he still wished she were far from here. Yet he could have been, ought to have been, less brutal about it.

He couldn't stop thinking about the way she had looked at him, just before he had turned his back on her and walked away. She hadn't believed him at first. Had thought, probably, that she'd misheard. Misunderstood him in some way. And then, once the truth of his intentions had fallen upon her, she had understood, and the hope in her eyes had faded to nothing.

Night after night he dreamed of her at that moment. Sitting as proudly as a queen on her narrow army cot, her unbound hair falling about her shoulders, her work-worn fingers plucking anxiously at the rough wool of the blankets that covered her. She had never been more beautiful.

At first the dream had behaved. He stated his wishes, she acquiesced, and they planned their future together, though that part of the dream was never very clear. Then she kissed him good-bye at the railhead and moved to safety somewhere far behind the lines.

The dream had grown darker. She agreed to the transfer, but only because she wanted to get away from him. Or because she had fallen in love with someone else and wanted to be with him instead.

Worst of all was the dream that had been tormenting him for the past fortnight. In it, they quarreled but never came to an agreement. Her nightdress slipped off one shoulder. He reached out, helplessly, and let his fingers trail along her soft, flawless skin. Felt his heart racing out of his chest and his hands begin to shake, his steady surgeon's hands that never shook, no matter how tired or cold he was.

He pushed her back, roughly, into the cot. Pulled her nightdress above her waist, exposing the milky-white skin of her thighs. He fell on top of her, covered her totally, reveled in her every quiver and sigh.

He asked her if she wanted more. She nodded, her eyes shining with perverse delight. So he reached down, wrenched open his flies, pushed her legs apart, and—

And then he woke up, drenched in sweat, trembling like a fever case, with a rock-solid erection that prevented any easy return to sleep. In a way, it was only fitting. If he couldn't have her in real life, then why should he be able to have her in his dreams?

She even haunted him in his waking hours. He'd seen her that morning, just outside the marquee tent, as she'd been helping to unload her ambulance. She'd been laughing with her friends, singing scraps of Gilbert and Sullivan as she worked, showing not the slightest evidence of fatigue or unhappiness. She was a little pale, admittedly, but it had been a long winter and the sun hadn't shone in what felt like weeks.

They'd walked past each other that morning, at the entrance to the mess tent, and she hadn't so much as looked at him. Just brushed past as if he were of no more interest or importance to her than a gout of mud she'd scraped off her boot.

Her friend Constance had noticed, however, and as usual she'd looked daggers at him. They all did, now, all the WAACs. God only knew what Lilly had told them. The truth, most likely, and that was bad enough.

He read over Edward's letter one more time, then slipped it into his jacket pocket. Time to return to the mountain of charts that needed completing.

The ward tent was nearly empty and, apart from the coughs of one solitary gas case, was blissfully quiet. Robbie found himself making progress, the pile diminishing so steadily that he imagined he might finish all of his paperwork tonight. A rare feat indeed.

The nurses' voices, when they entered, were impossible to ignore. The two of them knew well enough to whisper, but in the silence of the tent they might as well have been shouting from the front of a stage.

"Did you see her face just now? When she asked how you were and you answered, 'Very well, your highness.'" That was Nurse Taylor; a nice enough sort, he thought, but impressionable and easily led.

"I know. White as a sheet. Serves her right for swanning around like she owns the place." That from Nurse Greenhalgh, a first-class nurse but a third-rate person.

He should have known she'd do her best to make Lilly suffer.

At first, when news of Lilly's true background had swept through the camp, he'd been pleased for her. He knew it had pained her, keeping secrets from her friends, so had assumed she would be relieved that it was out in the open. The other WAACs, from what he could tell, had supported her, as had most everyone else in camp, from Private Gillespie to Matron to Colonel Lewis himself.

A few had not. Several nurses, their ringleader Nurse Greenhalgh, had taken it upon themselves to torment Lilly. At first they'd confined themselves to whispered comments as she passed, but when she had made no protest, they'd become bolder, and soon were taunting her directly.

He knew her friends had done their best to defend her, even going so far as to complain to Miss Jeffries on her behalf. He'd overheard the WAAC official's conversation with Matron; it had been impossible to ignore, since it had taken place right in front of his desk.

"Could I trouble you to say something about it? Miss Ashford is one of my best drivers. And she's such a lovely girl. So hardworking."

Matron had been sympathetic. "Of course, Miss Jeffries. I shall speak to them this evening."

He didn't doubt that Matron had chastised them; he knew she was fond of Lilly. Whatever she'd said, though, hadn't worked. Presumably they assumed that Lilly had complained, and that only made them resent her more.

Nurse Williamson, whose shift was just finishing, now approached and joined in. "Speaking of her ladyship, she was in here earlier. Reading to the patients again. Pretending she cared."

He could bear it no more.

"The three of you, come here at once," he demanded, his voice as icy as he could make it. Lady Cumberland would have approved.

The nurses obeyed immediately, arranging themselves in a neat row in front of his desk. He didn't bother to look up.

"You've been warned once already about this, have you not?" He could hear them fidgeting uneasily, wondering how to answer.

"What has Miss Ashford ever done to any of you? Has she injured you in any way? Been rude to you? Has she ever been known to shirk her duty?"

No answer.

"So we're agreed, then, that she's done nothing to provoke you. Can you provide me with any possible justification for your behavior?"

No answer.

At last he looked up. Slowly, deliberately, he looked from one nurse to the next, not troubling to disguise his disgust.

"I'll tell you something now, and I ask you to pass it on to the rest of your wretched cabal. If I hear any of you speak another ill word of Miss Ashford, or if I learn that she has been badly treated again, you will live to regret it. Understood?"

"Yes, Captain Fraser," they whispered, one after the other.

"Then get out of my sight."

He waited until they'd scurried away, then let his head fall into his hands. When would this ever end? Would he ever know peace again?

He thought of the letter in his pocket. It was lunacy to even think of accepting Edward's invitation. Yet he longed to do so, not least of all because he missed his friend.

It would undoubtedly be a glorious three days. Edward would take a suite of rooms at some exclusive hotel and insist on paying the bill. They would go to expensive restaurants, drink gallons of champagne and cognac, be surrounded by beautiful, flirtatious, available women.

It would be three days of heaven, at least for most men. But not for him.

Once, not long ago, he'd had hopes of taking Lilly to Paris. Had daydreamed of the modest hotel where they would stay, on a quiet side street on the Left Bank, and the unpretentious meals they would eat in the neighborhood cafés and brasseries. He'd imagined the lazy walks they would take along the banks of the Seine, or through the Marais.

As for their nights . . . he refused to think of the nights, not now. Would rather be hauled in front of a firing squad at dawn.

It was hard not to give in to regret, though he'd never been a man inclined to question or doubt his decisions. Yet could he have acted differently? Could he have come to some kind of accommodation with her, some way of allowing them both to remain at the 51st?

No. There had been no other way. The insanity of this great and terrible war had dictated it.

Remember how you felt that night, he told himself. The terror that had gripped him when the dud shell had gone off, the god-awful feeling of helplessness and despair when she'd disappeared from sight, had driven him to the edge of madness.

If he were to do his duty, if he were to retain any measure of honor, it had to be this way.

Admit she is lost to you, accept it, and forget.

Chapter 39

O nce, in another life, Lilly wouldn't have thought twice about a cup of tea. What was there to think about? Living with her parents, she'd only had to ring a bell for it to appear, minutes later, perfectly steeped, in a little Limoges pot with matching cup and saucer. She'd had it every day, but not once could she recall ever having looked forward to a cup of tea, really anticipated its arrival, the way a child might wait breathlessly for Christmas or summer holidays.

Here, tea was a lifeline. Sometimes the prospect of a cup of tea was the only thing she had to look forward to in the long hours that separated dawn from dusk. The tea they made on the Primus stove in the garage was never very hot, there was never any milk or sugar, the water they used always tasted faintly of motor oil, and the leaves were used and dried and then used again until they hardly colored the water, but it was tea. And tea meant five minutes of peace.

The tea for their morning break was still steeping when Bridget appeared with the post. "Letters from home for all of us," she announced, passing around the envelopes as quickly as her mittened hands allowed.

The handwriting on the letter she handed Lilly was unfamiliar, but the address was not. Time froze in place as she stared at it, her heart shriveling with dread.

"What's wrong, Lilly?" Bridget asked.

"It's from home. From my father's house in London."

"That's lovely. Perhaps your parents have come round," Constance said.

"I don't recognize the handwriting. There must be some mistake."

"Go ahead and open it, then," urged Bridget.

Lilly tore open the envelope and unfolded the single sheet of paper within.

31, Belgrave Square
London SW1
7 March 1918

Dear Lady Elizabeth,
    His lordship has asked me to write and let you know that he received a telegram from the War Office earlier today informing him that Lord Ash-

ford has been reported missing and is presumed captured or dead. No further details were included in the telegram other than to say Lord Ashford went missing in the early hours of March 3 whilst conducting a raid of the enemy's forward defenses.

I am so very sorry to be the bearer of such tragic news. All of the staff here and at Cumbermere Hall join me in extending their deepest sympathies.

If his lordship receives further details from the War Office and chooses to share such information with me, I will, of course, let you know directly.

Sincerely,
George Maxwell

Missing. Presumed dead.

She fell to her knees, grazing them badly on the garage's rough concrete floor. The letter fluttered out of her grasp and was trampled underfoot as her friends rushed forward to assist her.

They set her on the bench, found a cool cloth for her forehead, brushed away the dust from her skirts. But no one dared to speak.

"It's my brother," Lilly said at last, realizing they were waiting for an explanation. "He's gone missing." Her words hung ominously in the still, close air of the garage.

"So you know only that he's missing? That's all?" Constance clarified. At Lilly's nod, she took her hand and squeezed it hard. "Then you need to hold on to that. He's not dead and that's the important part. You mustn't allow yourself to think otherwise."

How could she not? The sheltered, pampered, idealistic Lilly of 1914 might have believed. Might have dared to hope. But the woman she was now? That woman knew what happened to soldiers who didn't return from no-man's-land.

Yes, there was a chance that he might have been taken prisoner, and she knew she ought to cling to that possibility. But it was far, far more likely that he had been felled by a sniper's bullet, his body lost in the mud or the murky depths of a shell hole.

Hellish images crowded her mind's eye. Edward, hanging on the scalpel-sharp barbed wire that garlanded the barren ground between the lines. Edward, grievously wounded, too weakened to fight off greedily waiting rats and crows. Edward, lost forever to the filth and unspeakable horror of this war.

And then, as quickly as they had come, the images receded. A peculiar kind of clarity descended, and as it washed over her she realized there was something she needed to do. She stood, startling her friends, and dried her eyes.

"What are you doing?" asked Constance.

"Captain Fraser is Edward's dearest friend," Lilly explained. "I know we've been at odds with one another, but he deserves to know. I should hate it if he learned what has happened to Edward from someone else."

Her friends exchanged doubtful glances. "Let me do it," Constance offered. "It will upset you too much."

"Thank you, but no. Edward would expect me to tell Robbie myself. Can you manage without me on this next run?"

"Yes, but—"

"I won't be long."

Lilly retrieved her letter from the garage floor, tucked it in her jacket pocket, and set off across the courtyard to the ward tent.

How should she tell him? *I'm terribly sorry to bother you, but I've had some bad news about Edward.* Or should she get straight to the point? *Edward is missing in action and I thought you should know.*

Inside the ward tent, peace and order prevailed. Matron was at her desk, but the surgeons' desk was empty. Perhaps Robbie was in surgery.

Lilly approached, waiting to speak until Matron looked up from her paperwork.

"Good morning, Miss Ashford."

"Good morning, Matron. I hope I'm not interrupting you."

"Not at all, my dear. Is there anything I can do for you?"

"I'm looking for Captain Fraser. That is . . . I've had some bad news from home, and I wanted to tell him. Captain Fraser is, ah, a family friend."

"I'm so sorry to hear you've had bad news, Miss Ashford. But I'm afraid it will have to wait a day or two. Captain Fraser is on leave."

The veil of clarity that had descended on Lilly began to evaporate. "Ah," she said.

"He's gone to Paris," Matron added. "I gather he was quite looking forward to it. Apparently he was intending to stay with an old school friend. At the Ritz, if you can believe it."

"I see," Lilly said, her voice cracking a little.

It was Edward's Paris trip. The one he had invited her on, and when she couldn't go, he must have instead asked Robbie. "When did Captain Fraser leave?" she asked.

"I believe it was first thing this morning. He'll be back on the twelfth, Miss Ashford."

"Yes, ah . . . thank you, ma'am."

"Would you like to sit down for a moment? I could have one of the nurses bring you a cup of tea. May I ask if the news from home was very grave?"

"It was. My brother has gone missing."

Matron came round the desk, and for a moment Lilly wondered if the older woman was going to embrace her. But she only took Lilly's hands in hers and held them tightly. "I am most sincerely sorry to hear it, Miss Ashford. Now, won't you sit? Just until you have recovered from your shock a little?"

"Thank you, ma'am, but no. I really must get back to work. But thank you for letting me know that Captain Fraser is away."

Lilly stood outside Miss Jeffries's tent, debating the merits of even making her request. She checked her watch again: it was a quarter past ten. The train to Saint-Omer would leave from the railhead in less than an hour. If she were to go to Paris, and tell Robbie what had happened, let him know that Edward would not be joining him, then she had to leave in twenty minutes.

She knocked on the support beam that flanked the entrance to the tent.

"Come in!" rang out a cheery voice from inside. "Good morning, Miss Ashford. Come in, come in. No need to be shy."

"Good morning, Miss Jeffries. I . . ."

"Is anything the matter? I must say, Miss Ashford, you don't look yourself at all."

"I've had some news from home." And then, although she had not been given permission to sit, Lilly dropped into a nearby chair. It was either that or collapse in a heap on the floor.

"Let me get you a cup of tea, Miss Ashford. And please tell me everything."

"Thank you, Miss Jeffries. It's my brother. He's been declared missing in action. I just received a letter from home."

"Oh, my dear. I *am* sorry to hear that."

"I was hoping that I might have a few days, ah, to—"

"Say no more. How long do you need?"

"I beg your pardon?" Wasn't Miss Jeffries going to ask her about what she planned to do? How and where she intended to spend her leave?

"How long do you need? Are forty-eight hours enough? It's not long enough to go home, I'm afraid, but longer leaves need to be approved by the deputy administrator in Boulogne. It will give you a chance to clear your head, however."

"Two days is fine," Lilly answered. "Thank you."

"It's the least I can do. You've been such an asset to the WAAC these past months."

Forty-eight hours. Long enough to make the journey to Paris, tell Robbie the news, and return home. She would have to stay overnight, but it should be easy enough to find a pension near the Gare du Nord.

She wouldn't be staying at the Ritz, for its cheapest rooms were far more than she could afford. Robbie wouldn't want her there, besides.

It occurred to her that he might relent in his disavowal of her once she had told him what had happened to Edward. Might even deign to speak with her for more than a few minutes.

What of it? It would change nothing, and the war of attrition between them would continue. She might hope for a truce, but an armistice?

Not bloody likely.

Chapter 40

S he was kneeling beside her storage locker, trying to decide what to pack, when they tracked her down.

Constance sat on Lilly's cot, her face pale with worry. "Going home won't help your brother. At least wait until you have more news."

"I'm not going home. I'm going to Paris."

"Paris? Why Paris?"

"He's there on leave. Captain Fraser. He and my brother had plans to stay there for a few days."

"You're daft! Being absent without leave—"

"I have permission to go. Miss Jeffries was very nice about it."

The expression on her friends' faces was quite comical. Even the unshockable Annie and Bridget were dumbfounded.

Annie regarded Lilly with admiration. "She's letting you go to Paris? To stay with an officer? Bloomin' 'eck!"

"We didn't talk about the specifics of where I'm going. She offered me two days' leave, and I took it."

"You're taking an awful risk," Constance persisted. "What if you're found out? Ever since the newspapers at home started printing those stories about WAACs being sent home in the family way, the officials here have been on high alert. If anyone sees you with him—"

"That won't happen," Lilly said, her voice as firm as she could make it. "I'm only going there to save him from unnecessary worry."

"It'll take an age to get there," Bridget said. "You'll have to stay overnight."

"I realize that. I shall find a pension near the station, and take the first train back tomorrow."

"I still don't think—" Constance began, but Annie and Bridget shushed her before she could finish.

"Leave off, will you? Let her have her fun. There's no harm in it, as long as she's sensible," said Annie.

"So what are you going to pack?" asked Bridget. "Best to take summat more'n your uniform. Just in case."

"In case of what?"

"In case you end up spending some time with Captain Fraser. Less chance of getting caught out if you're dressed in mufti."

But Constance was not giving up without a fight. "Lilly, don't listen to them. This is madness. If you're so concerned about Captain Fraser, send him a wire at the hotel. I'm sure Miss Jeffries can arrange it. And then you can go to Saint-Omer and have a few days to yourself."

"I know you mean well, Constance, but I need to do this. It's the right thing to do. He and Edward have been friends for so long. No matter our differences, I can't bear the thought of his learning the news from a telegram or letter, as I did."

Lilly turned back to the business of packing for her overnight trip. Rummaging through her locker, she extracted the one civilian dress she had with her, together with a plain pair of court shoes. Once she'd spoken to Robbie, she would have the rest of the day to herself, and she was not going to spend it in her heavy, musty uniform. She found a hat, gloves, a change of underclothes, and her nightgown and added them to the carpetbag.

"Are you sure you don't want to borrow these?" Annie held up a nightgown and matching negligee in a startling hue of emerald green. "They're made of real artificial silk. I'm sure they'll fit."

"You're very kind, Annie, but my nightgown will be fine for tonight. Thanks all the same."

"At least take some jewelry. Here, take my string of pearls. Go on, now."

"That's quite all right—" Lilly protested, but Annie had already tucked them into her carpetbag.

Lilly checked her wristwatch again. Twenty-five minutes before eleven. If she were to catch the train to Saint-Omer, she had to leave now.

"Do you think one of you could give me a lift to the railhead?"

"I'll do it," answered Constance. "It will give me another ten minutes to talk you out of it."

The four WAACs had only just stepped out of the tent when Bridget clapped her hand to her forehead and exclaimed in dismay, "Sorry, everyone. I won't be a minute. Go on without me."

Bridget rejoined them a minute or two later. She looked, Lilly thought, rather like a cat that had been among the proverbial pigeons. What could she be up to?

"Lilly," Bridget whispered, "I have summat for you."

"Yes? What is it?"

"Not so loud. I don't want the others knowing. Stop here while I give it to you." Bridget let Annie and Constance walk on, then passed a rectangular metal tin, about the size of a deck of cards, to Lilly. It was unmarked and curiously light.

"What is this?" she asked, thoroughly mystified.

"It's summat you might need," Bridget explained. "Just in case."

"What on earth are you talking about?"

"It's to protect yourself. Don't worry; Captain Fraser will know what to do."

"Could you please speak plainly?" Lilly asked, more than a little exasperated. If she missed the morning train to Saint-Omer, it would be hours before she could begin her journey. "I really have no idea what you mean."

Before answering, Bridget looked one way, then the other, apparently wanting to ensure she would not be overheard.

"Have you ever heard of a French letter?"

Lilly felt the blood rush to her face. She had an idea, a rather vague one admittedly, but it was enough to shock her.

"Listen to me, Lilly. It might happen that you go and tell Captain Fraser about your brother, and he says thank you and you go your separate ways. But it might *also* happen that you don't leave. And all I'm saying is that it's best to be prepared."

"I . . . I really don't think this is necessary."

"You may be right. And if you are, then no one ever has to know. But if it turns out as I'm right, I'm thinking you'll be glad of this little tin."

For the first few hours of her journey, no matter how hard she tried to forget about it, the presence of the tin in her carpetbag unsettled her. What if there were an accident, and it was discovered among her effects? What if, somehow, Robbie were to learn of it? The prospect of that occurring was so horrifying she could hardly bear to think of it.

From Saint-Omer, she took a second train to Amiens. It arrived ahead of schedule, allowing her enough time to visit the lavatory and buy something to eat. It wasn't much of a lunch, consisting of a single tartine, thickly buttered, of day-old bread, with a cup of bracingly strong black coffee, but it helped to lift her spirits all the same.

The journey from Amiens to Paris took more than two hours, with the train stopping at nearly every crossroads and byway en route. They arrived at the Gare du Nord shortly before four o'clock, and although the sun was getting rather low in the sky, she decided to make the two-mile journey to the Place Vendôme by foot. She didn't have long in Paris and it would be pleasant to see some of it before sunset; and it would also give her a chance to collect her thoughts before she had to face Robbie.

Intent on asking for help, she approached one of the newsagents in the arrivals hall and saw that he had small, folding maps of the central arrondissements for sale. She'd been to Paris before, but always with her mother, and they'd always been driven from place to place; she would need some help to orient herself. The maps were only fifty centimes each, so she bought one and settled herself on a nearby bench, her bag tucked securely behind her knees. The route was straightforward enough: rue de Mauberge to rue La Fayette, left at rue Halévy, then across the Place de l'Opéra to the rue de la Paix, which led straight to the Place Vendôme.

Signs of the war were everywhere, not especially overt, but there all the same. Most of the shopwindows she passed were empty, or filled with somber displays of mourning apparel. Some contained patriotic posters that were so resolute, stolid, and serious that Lilly had to stifle a smile more than once.

"*Économisons le pain en mangeant des pommes de terre,*" one exhorted. "Save on bread by eating potatoes." Or there was the equally earnest "*Semez du blé—c'est de l'or pour la France."* She thought it unlikely that Parisians would be sowing any wheat this growing season, in spite of its being as valuable as gold to France. Poster after poster announced that such-and-such a date would be celebrated as a national day in aid of some worthy group: orphans, the army in Africa, those afflicted with tuberculosis, even the ordinary French soldier, or *poilu.*

Even if there had been any wares for sale in the shopwindows, Lilly would not have found it easy to window-shop, since intricately woven grids of paper ribbon were glued to the glass in what she suspected was an effort to protect against flying glass in the event of an air raid. The effect was curiously attractive, rather as if delicate Moorish screens had been affixed to the shop exteriors. Even the huge windows of the Galeries Lafayette, she saw, had been taped over, and she wondered if similar precautions had been taken to protect the great stained glass dome that crowned the building.

Neat placards had been affixed to most of the buildings she passed: ABRIS À 60 PERSONNES read the first notice she approached. The need for sixty people to shelter in one building seemed mystifying, until she remembered the zeppelin and Gotha raids that had intermittently plagued both Paris and London. The placards must refer to the number of people who could be sheltered in the building's cellars.

She'd been nervous that her uniform, shabby as it had become, might elicit a certain amount of disapproval from passersby, but no one seemed to mind. Instead, most people offered her a smile, some a courteous nod, and a few even stopped to shake her hand and thank her for coming to the aid of France and her people.

She walked past the Opéra, its facade obscured by hoardings and sandbags, and turned onto the rue de la Paix. In the distance she could see the great column at the center of Place Vendôme, its statue of Napoleon still glowering from his perch on its top.

Her carpetbag was beginning to feel terribly heavy, and perspiration had dampened her temples and nape. She shifted the bag to her left arm and quickened her pace. Get it over and done with, she told herself. Then you only need to endure whatever is left of this day.

She approached the front doors of the Ritz, acutely conscious of her disheveled state, but the doorman made a convincing pretense of not noticing.

She marched directly to the front desk, her back as straight as she could make it, so straight that even her mother would have approved.

"*Bonjour, monsieur. Je m'appelle Elizabeth Neville-Ashford. Mon frère—*"

"But of course, Lady Elizabeth. Welcome to the Hôtel le Ritz. The Viscount Ashford has not yet arrived, but Captain Fraser is here already."

"I wonder if—"

"Allow me to ring for one of our footmen. He will show you to Lord Ashford's suite."

"Thank you very much. May I leave my bag here? I won't be staying."

If the concierge was surprised at her request, he betrayed no sign of it. "It would be my pleasure to look after your luggage, Lady Elizabeth. If I am not here when you return, you have only to ask any of the hotel staff and they will retrieve it for you."

With a snap of his fingers, the concierge summoned a waiting footman, who led the way through the sumptuous lobby to the bank of elevators. They made the journey to the fifth floor in silence, a blessing since Lilly wasn't sure how she would have managed to make small talk. As the lift doors opened, she was seized by a nearly overpowering urge to cower inside and refuse to exit. She could still go back; Robbie would never know.

Somehow, as if her body were operating independently of all rational thought, she found herself following the footman down the hall, yard after perilous yard, until at last they were standing in front of the door to the suite Edward had reserved.

Scrabbling in her reticule, which she had thought to extract from her bag, she found a few coins for a tip and waited for the footman to retreat down the corridor.

She waited until she could no longer hear his footsteps. Then she knocked on the door.

Chapter 41

He hadn't expected anyone to knock at the door. He certainly hadn't ordered anything, for the ridiculously lavish suite that Edward had reserved was stocked with enough towels, pillows, toiletries, reading materials, wine, and spirits to last a month, let alone three days. Perhaps it was a mistake.

The knock sounded again. It was not the discreet tap of a servant. He cast aside his newspaper, a copy of yesterday's *Times*, and strode to the door, ready to send whoever it was on their way.

Nothing could have prepared him for the sight of Lilly, her hand raised in midair, interrupted before she could rap on the door a third time.

"Hello, Robbie."

He stood there, staring at her, until he finally remembered his manners. "Hello, Lilly. This is . . ."

"A surprise."

"That it is." Astonishment gave way to delight, and then delight, just as swiftly, was replaced by anger.

"What are you doing here?"

"I apologize for intruding. I won't take long. May I come in for a moment?"

"Why are you here?" he repeated.

"It's Edward. He's missing."

It was true. He knew, from the agony etched on her face, that it was true.

"Christ, Lilly. Come in. Forget how I acted just now. Come in and tell me what has happened."

He directed her to the sofa in the suite's sitting room and returned to the chair where he'd been reading a few moments before. "What happened?"

"I'm not sure. I only found out this morning. Here's the letter from Mr. Maxwell." She extracted an envelope from her reticule and held it out to him. Her hands were shaking.

"It says that Edward was captured on March third," he clarified. "And there's been no news since?"

"As far as I know, nothing." She looked up, her eyes luminous with unshed tears, and in that instant every trace of logic and reason deserted Robbie. He found himself kneeling at her feet, helpless, as she struggled to contain her emotions.

"For the moment I think we ought to assume he is alive," he said, desperate to reassure her. "And you and I both know the Germans are not barbarians. They're known to treat prisoners well, and the Red Cross has access to all of the camps. If Edward has been taken prisoner, your parents will receive news soon enough."

"But what if he wasn't captured? What if he was killed that night? Don't tell me it's not possible. I've heard the Tommies talking. A man can just vanish in no-man's-land. Fall into a shell hole, drown in the mud, be torn to shreds by the machine guns."

He took her shaking hands and stilled them between his own. "Men do disappear, you're right, but usually that happens during a big push. In the heat of battle. Edward was taking part in a raid, if the telegram your parents received was correct. That means he would have been with a small group of his men."

He stood up, not letting go of her hands, and sat next to her on the sofa. "If Edward had been wounded, or even killed, during that raid, his men would never have left him behind. *Never.* So the only logical explanation for his disappearance is that he was taken prisoner."

"Do you really believe that?"

No, he thought. "Yes," he insisted. "And in the absence of any other news, I think you should believe it, too."

He let go of her hands and retreated to the nearby chair. "You must have been traveling for hours, Lilly. And all the while—have you even allowed yourself to cry?"

"No. I had to do this first."

"Why? I don't deserve your consideration."

She laughed, a sharp, almost brittle sound. "Perhaps not, but it's what Edward would expect of me. To leave you here, wondering where he was, not knowing the truth . . . it seemed wrong."

"Thank you, then. What will you do now?"

"Return to camp. Get back to work. What else can I do?"

"Stay," a voice said. His voice.

"But I thought you wanted nothing to do with me." Anger flashed in her eyes, and not a little humor as well. Evidently she was aware of the irony of this moment.

"I was wrong," he admitted. "The way I've treated you . . . it's not right. It's the farthest thing from right."

She said nothing at first, choosing instead to examine the carved tortoiseshell clasp of her reticule. Long seconds passed.

"I see now how wrong I was, how misguided—"

"Enough. I don't want your apologies. As you once told me, life is too short." She stood up. "I must go."

"Don't," he insisted. "There are two bedrooms in this suite, and it's a long way back to Merville."

"I wasn't planning on returning tonight. I'd thought to find a room at a pension near the station."

"But you haven't any luggage."

"I brought my carpetbag. I left it with the concierge." And then she giggled, the sound cleaving through the grim atmosphere of the room. "I thought you might react poorly if it looked as if I were planning to stay."

"God knows what I would have said," he admitted. "But now I want you to stay. This suite is enormous, and there's more than enough room for the two of us."

"I don't know. What will the staff think?"

"I doubt they'll care. They're French, after all." Seeing that she was still wavering, he pointed to a door at the far corner of the sitting room. "At least have a look at your bedroom and bathroom. Then decide."

She walked to the bedroom door and disappeared inside the chamber. He heard a soft gasp, he hoped of delight.

"You really ought to see the bathroom," he called to her.

When Lilly returned to the sitting room a minute or two later, he could swear he saw a look of hunger on her face. He'd had the same reaction when he'd entered the bathroom attached to his own bedroom.

"I suppose it would be a shame to waste all this," she said.

"Absolutely. And Edward paid for it in advance; they told me when I arrived."

"Then I shall stay," she agreed. "Would you mind very much if I had a bath now?"

"Not at all. When you're ready, we can go for a walk and find somewhere for supper. How does that sound?"

"Fine," she said, but there was little enthusiasm in her voice.

She hadn't forgiven him, that was clear enough. Nor did he deserve to be forgiven. It had been a mad idea, asking her to stay, for what would it achieve? They'd spend a pleasant evening together, forget their fears for Edward for a few hours, but then they would return to the 51st and be pulled apart, again, by the same intractable problems: her insistence on remaining in harm's way, despite any number of worthy alternatives, and his conviction that her presence in camp would be his undoing.

It had been foolish of him to ask her to stay, for he could give her nothing. And yet he still wished to comfort her. Protect her, in any way he could. It was so little, what he offered her, that it shamed him.

Tonight he would comfort Lilly; tonight he would try to regain some measure of her regard. The odds of his succeeding were stacked against him; were worse, frankly, than the odds of Edward still being alive. But he would stake his life on them.

What other choice did he have?

Chapter 42

The contrast between the bed Lilly would sleep in tonight and the bed waiting for her back at the 51st could not have been more extreme. Last night, she had slept on a narrow metal cot. Her head had rested on a thin, musty pillow, she had slept in her clothes, and she had kept herself warm by piling her greatcoat and uniform jacket on top of her pitifully thin regulation blankets.

Tonight, however, she would sleep in a huge brass bedstead that could easily accommodate four or five people. She approached it, feeling oddly nervous, and drew back the pale pink counterpane. Underneath were a feather bed, snow-white linens, and six impossibly fluffy down-filled pillows. She replaced the counterpane, smoothing it carefully, and turned to survey the rest of the room.

Intricate tapestry hangings covered the walls, while shell-pink silk draperies, as sumptuous as a ball gown, flanked the windows. A set of French doors, set in the center of the longest wall, gave onto a small balcony with wrought-iron railings and a view of the formal gardens beyond.

The bathroom was just as impressive. One wall was almost entirely taken up with an enormous bathtub, which was fitted with golden taps shaped like swans. A chromed towel rail, warm to the touch, was draped with towels that had been embroidered with the hotel's crest in gold thread. On the walnut vanity, a posy of spring bulbs sat to the left of the sink, while a flight of stoppered glass bottles were arranged to its right.

Lilly approached the vanity and saw that the bottles contained a variety of shampoos, bath essences, and lotions. She made several selections, hardly able to contain her excitement at the prospect of her first hot bath in months. A little gilded chair sat next to the tub, and on it she placed a bar of soap, wrapped in pretty Florentine paper, and two bottles: one of shampoo and one of lily-of-the-valley bath essence. She turned on the taps, tested the water to ensure it was warm enough, and dribbled the scented oil into the stream from the faucet.

It would take an age for the bath to fill, so she wandered back into the bedroom to look for a dressing gown. As she had hoped, there was one in the closet, and she eagerly exchanged it for her smelly, grimy uniform and underclothes. These she folded neatly, tucking her combinations and stockings out of sight, and set the bundle at the end of the bed. She wore no jewelry, apart from her wristwatch, and that she left on the bedside table.

It occurred to her that although she'd lived amid this kind of luxury for most of her life, she'd never truly appreciated it. Certainly she'd never been grateful for it.

Well, she was grateful now.

She returned to the bathroom, where the tub was nearly full. Shedding her dressing gown, she stepped into the tub and sank shoulder-deep into the fragrant water. Then she rested her head against the lip of the tub, where a towel had been placed for just such a purpose, and gave herself up to the bliss of the moment.

Long minutes passed, minutes during which Lilly forced herself to think of nothing. Not Edward, not Robbie, not the war. Only the sensation of being immersed in clean, hot, beautifully scented water.

But she couldn't stop the tears that welled up, unbidden, and carried away what little peace of mind she had left. Robbie had told her to believe, but how could she believe when she knew so well what happened to soldiers lost in no-man's-land? A quick death was the least terrible way in which Edward's life might end: a bullet through the head, or a shell delivering instant oblivion. But what if he were wounded and unable to call for help? What if he did call for help and instead was greeted by an enemy bayonet?

She cried silently, letting her tears fall into the bathwater, willing the panic and dread to leave her in peace, if only for one night. Just one night.

The water cooled a degree or two, prompting her to reach out with one foot and twist on the hot water tap with her toes. As if from a great distance, she heard a knock on the front door of the suite, and the muffled sounds of Robbie speaking to the maid. Her bag must have arrived from downstairs.

With the utmost reluctance she sat up and removed the pins from her hair. It was late in the day to be washing it, for she wouldn't be able to dry it completely before they went out, but the urge to be clean from top to bottom won out.

She knelt in the bath, ducked her head under the water, worked shampoo through her hair, and scrubbed until her scalp was nearly raw. She rinsed it in the bathwater, rubbed in more shampoo, and rinsed again, then reluctantly pulled the stopper from the drain and stepped out of the tub.

She wrapped her hair in a towel, the rest of her in the hotel's dressing gown, and crossed the room to the vanity. It had been ages since she had seen her own reflection: the wash hut in camp had no mirror, and Lilly rarely bothered to borrow the hand mirror that Bridget and Annie shared.

How her mother would despair if she were to see Lilly now. Freckles were sprinkled across her nose and cheekbones, and her complexion still bore faint traces of sun from the summer. Her eyes were a little swollen, but luckily her nose hadn't gone red from all her tears.

She brushed out her hair, using the towel to squeeze out as much moisture as possible. Rather than plait it, she twisted it into a figure eight, which she then secured at the nape of her neck.

Lilly opened the bathroom door and peered out, a little nervous that the maid might have left open the door from the bedroom to the sitting room. It was shut, fortunately, and her bag had indeed been delivered. Not only had it been retrieved from downstairs, but the maid had also unpacked its contents for her. All of its contents.

Her dress hung, neatly pressed, on the closet door.

Her underclothes had also been pressed, and were laid out across the foot of the bed. Her small bag of toiletries, little more than her comb and toothbrush, sat on a bedside table next to her wristwatch and Annie's pearls.

And Bridget's tin? It had been placed on the other bedside table.

If it were possible to die of embarrassment, then Lilly would have expired on the spot. At least Robbie hadn't seen the tin. She snatched it up and stuffed it in the desk drawer, praying she would remember to retrieve it in the morning.

She put on her wristwatch and saw that it was already a quarter past six. Robbie would be wondering what had happened to her. She dressed hurriedly, her fingers fumbling with the buttons that secured the front placket of her dress, then slipped on her shoes. Compared to her boots, they felt like bedroom slippers.

The pearls were one long strand, too low for the middy collar of her gown, so she looped them around her neck several times until they sat nicely. They were artificial pearls, chipped and worn, but they made her feel like a queen all the same. Last of all, she drew on her lace gloves that Nanny Gee had knitted for her years before. They would do a fine job of covering her work-worn hands.

Robbie stood as she walked into the sitting room. "Did you enjoy your bath?" he asked, apparently unconcerned by her lengthy absence.

"You know very well I did," she replied. "Though I apologize for having taken so long."

"I don't mind at all. But you must be ravenous. When did you last eat?"

"This morning, I think. Some coffee and bread."

"So let us find somewhere to eat. Do you want to go downstairs, to the restaurant here? Or would you like to venture farther afield?"

"Would you mind if we found somewhere else to eat? The restaurant here is sure to be very grand. I'd much rather go somewhere more modest."

"I agree," he said. "And it would be a shame for you to see so little of Paris. We'll just have to hope that the air-raid sirens don't sound, otherwise we'll end up spending the evening in someone's cellar."

"I'm ready to go, but my coat and hat aren't where I left them."

"They're here. The maid brought them back a few minutes ago." He indicated a closet door, left ajar, by the entrance to the suite. The woman's coat hanging next to Robbie's greatcoat bore no resemblance to the mud-stained, blood-spattered, embarrassingly scruffy garment that Lilly had shrugged out of less than an hour earlier.

"The staff here are miracle workers," she said, admiring their work. "And the maid rescued my poor hat from the bottom of my bag. It looks quite respectable now."

They walked down the hall to the lift, side by side but never quite touching. Lilly was reminded of the night of the ceilidh, when they had walked away from the reception marquee, its music and its lights, and into the unknowable darkness beyond.

She hadn't dared to reach for his hand that evening, not if there were a chance of anyone seeing. So they'd walked together, yet apart, though she'd longed to take his hand in hers.

The elevator arrived. They were the only passengers, apart from the liveried attendant.

"*Rez-de-chaussée, s'il vous plaît,*" Lilly requested.

There was something rather ridiculous about the way people behaved in lifts, she thought. As if the only way to manage being so closely confined were to pretend the person next to you didn't exist.

Was that what Robbie did now? Was he staring at

the doors, or the back of the attendant's head? Or did he look at her, and ask himself if she would welcome his arm in hers?

Lilly knew she didn't lack for courage. She could even be bold, when occasion demanded. As it did now.

Her eyes still fixed on the lift's doors, she reached out and took his arm, as easily and naturally as if they were a couple married these many years.

But he didn't respond, didn't draw her close as she'd expected. An icicle of despair piercing her through, she began to withdraw her arm, certain she'd ruined their evening before it had properly started.

Only then did his arm tighten around hers. He drew her near, pulling her a little off balance, and she found herself holding her breath, wondering what would follow.

Her answer was the chime of the lift as it reached the main floor, and the serene voice of the attendant.

"Rez-de-chaussée, monsieur, dame."

Chapter 43

As they strolled along the rue de Castiglione, arm in arm, Robbie reflected that he had never in his life been so content. It was absurd, given what had happened to Edward and the general misery of his and Lilly's lives. But he would enjoy the feeling as long as it lasted.

He could see very little of her from this angle, not much more, really, than the sweep of her shoulder in her heavy WAAC overcoat and the indigo-dark velvet of her simple hat. She wore no scarf, so her throat was bare, apart from a triple strand of pearls and a solitary ringlet that had escaped the mass of hair at the nape of her neck. So many women cut their hair, but Lilly had kept hers long, not even adopting a short fringe.

If only he were free to grasp that single curl, encourage it to coil around his finger, let it bounce free again. The night of the ceilidh, her hair had been so soft, and had smelled sweetly of the perfumed soap she used.

He was glad she'd enjoyed her bath, though it had been a long hour indeed for him. His book, a worn copy of *Middlemarch* that he'd already read half a dozen times, hadn't held his attention, and the faint sounds emerging from her bathroom had only served to inflame his beleaguered imagination.

He had tried, sincerely, not to think of Lilly in the bathtub, her hair piled on her head, her skin pink from the water's heat. Yet the image would not budge from his head.

He'd tried desperately not to picture her as she dressed, yet his thoughts had been filled with tantalizing pictures of Lilly in her stockings and combinations, Lilly struggling to button her dress, Lilly brushing and plaiting her hair.

Edward. He had to think of Edward and what he had suffered. Was suffering. If that didn't clear the lascivious images of Lilly from his head, nothing would.

His imaginings, at length suppressed, had been as nothing compared to the reality of the woman who had eventually joined him in the sitting room. She'd abandoned her uniform for a simple dress that buttoned up the front. The color suited her, some pretty shade of blue, that women likely had a name for, but men simply admired. Azure? Cornflower?

The dress, at least to his unschooled eyes, suited her beautifully, not least of all because the neckline dipped low enough in front that he could glimpse the swell of her breasts and the merest shadow of cleavage. The skirt of the dress, drawn close by a buttoned sash, was fitted at the small of her back in such a way that it emphasized the curve of her bottom, and it was all he could do to keep his hands clenched at his sides.

He'd held himself in check, behaved like a gentleman, somehow managed to rein in his baser instincts, and then she had reached for his arm as they stood in the lift.

It had nearly finished him off. Even now, a good ten minutes after they had left the hotel, he was still hard-pressed to come up with anything intelligible to say to her.

"If you're not going to break this silence, then I will," she said, squeezing his arm playfully. "Although I'm not sure what I ought to say."

"It is rather awkward," he admitted.

"No bright ideas?"

"Afraid not. I'm the rustic Scot, after all. You're the one who spent all that time in the drawing rooms of High Society. If anyone can make small talk, it's you."

"Very well," she countered, a slightly artificial note of cheer in her voice. "Tell me about the first time you met Edward."

Memories washed over him, and a grin broke upon his face before he could smooth it away. "I'd arrived at the beginning of Nought Week, before the start of my first term at Oxford, keen as mustard to get started. That's when I learned I'd been assigned to share a set of rooms with the son of an earl. I remember wondering if one of the college officials was a closet socialist and was conducting an experiment on us."

"When did Edward arrive?"

"Oh, well into First Week, I think. Because we shared a set—we each had a bedroom, with a shared sitting room—that meant we also shared a scout. I was terrified of the man at first."

"You, terrified?" she asked, laughing.

"I swear it. Webb had been with the college for nearly forty years, and he was not best pleased to be saddled with the son of a dustman. He told me as much, my first day."

"How uncivil."

"According to him, Lord Edward hailed from the most exalted levels of society. A paragon of aristocratic virtue in every way. My superior in every way. By the time Edward showed up, I was certain I would detest him."

"And yet you didn't."

"Of course not. He shook my hand, looked me in the eye, asked me to call him Edward, and that was that. How could I dislike him? And he was always so much fun."

"I remember, the weekend you visited us in Cumbria, how he kept trying to pull you away from your books."

"It was incessant. And the maddening part was that he always sailed through his exams, though I hardly ever saw him open a book or attend a lecture. I did my best not to envy him, but it was hard at times. I had to work so hard, just to keep my head above water—"

"While he sailed through life. I know." She frowned and looked away. "Did he ever tell you of his troubles?"

"Aye, he did. Not at the time. Later, in a letter to me last year. He told me of the arrangement he'd made with your parents. He appeared resigned to it, but I worried about him. Helena seemed like a pleasant enough girl, but he hardly knew her."

"He still doesn't. And perhaps he never—"

"Don't say it, Lilly. You agreed to hope, until all hope is lost. And I will hold you to it, for tonight at least."

They'd arrived at the end of the rue de Castiglione, so Robbie steered them to the left, along the rue de

Rivoli. Flickering gaslight was their only illumination, for few lights shone from the buildings they passed, and the Jardin des Tuileries, just to the south, had faded into darkness.

As the sun had waned, so too, had the temperature. Robbie found himself longing for the convivial warmth of a restaurant and the restorative powers of food and wine. Lilly seemed warm enough in her coat, but her gloves were thin and her neck was bare.

"Shall we look for somewhere to eat?" he asked.

"Yes, please. I'm famished."

They turned north, onto rue de l'Échelle, then doubled back the way they had come, this time walking along rue Saint-Honoré. But it proved to be a wasteland, gastronomically speaking, though the street itself was pretty enough.

And then they smelled it: the unmistakable aroma of fried onions and roast chicken. Following their noses, they turned onto rue de la Sourdière and discovered a tiny brasserie, its sign so discreet and the lights from its foyer so dim that, if not for the appetizing scents wafting into the street, they would surely have walked past.

Robbie opened the front door for Lilly, ushering her inside. The brasserie's interior was just as it ought to be. The dining room, long and narrow, was brightly lit by burnished brass wall sconces. A buttoned leather banquette stretched the length of one wall, with gilt-framed mirrors hanging above in lieu of artwork. He counted a dozen tables, no more; all full except one. A good sign, he thought.

The lone waiter hurried over, a welcoming smile on his face.

"*Bonsoir, monsieur, dame. Bienvenue à Chez Arnaud.*"

"Thank you," Robbie replied. "Can you accommodate us for dinner?"

"Of course. Anything for our esteemed allies."

He led them to the free table Robbie had noticed, took their coats, and promised to return in a moment with some wine. "I am very sorry but we have not the bread tonight. Because of the new controls, you see."

"The rationing?" Lilly asked.

"Yes, madame. If you have the ration books, I can offer you the bread, but if not . . ."

"Unfortunately, no. We are both working at the Front, with one of the field hospitals," she explained. Her admission had a remarkable effect upon the waiter.

"*Vous êtes une Tommette? Vous travaillez à l'un des hôpitaux pour les soldats blessés? Veuillez attendre un moment.*"

He scurried back to the kitchens, leaving Robbie to wonder what on earth Lilly had said to the man.

She answered before he could ask. "He called me a 'Tommette.' That's what the French call the WAACs, and I suppose any other British woman in uniform. He told us to wait—"

Just then, the waiter emerged from the kitchen, followed closely by a man wearing a long white apron and a chef's toque.

"Monsieur Jérôme would like to thank you for your efforts on behalf of France. He has offered to make you whatever you wish, providing, of course, we have the ingredients." The waiter was beaming from ear to ear; clearly this little brasserie received few visits from foreign soldiers.

Lilly took it upon herself to respond. *"Je vous remercie sincèrement, Monsieur Jérôme. Il y a bien longtemps que nous travaillons très proche au front occidental, et nous n'avons que ce soir à Paris. Je suis certaine que tous vos plats sont délicieux. Je l'aimerais bien si vous nous surpreniez ce soir."*

The chef, evidently astonished by Lilly's command of French, took her hand in his, bestowed a kiss upon it, and rushed back to his kitchens.

"Would you mind letting me know what just happened?" Robbie asked.

"I told them we've both been serving near the Front for a long time, that we only have this one night in Paris, and that we would be delighted with whatever the chef chooses to cook for us. I asked him to surprise us."

"But what if he brings out something exotic?"

"Like what? Escargots or frogs' legs? I doubt it. I'll wager you it will be chicken. Most likely a rather elderly chicken."

He had to laugh. "Do you have any idea how much you've changed? From someone who once looked as if she'd jump at the sight of her own shadow, to . . ."

"To what, Robbie?"

"To a woman who knows her own mind. Who is confident enough to speak to the chef in French. And mean-spirited enough to threaten me with snails for dinner."

"See? You do know some French. Now try this: 'Merci bien pour un repas merveilleux.'"

Chapter 44

As Lilly had predicted, the meal was marvelous. Ignoring the raised eyebrows of the brasserie's other patrons, their waiter—Lilly had discovered his name was Guillaume—first delivered a heaping basket of bread to their table, two stemmed glasses, and a half liter of rough but perfectly drinkable red wine.

Guillaume next deposited a wee pot of something that looked, to Robbie's eyes, disconcertingly like uncooked haggis innards. His alarm faded when Lilly clapped her hands in delight and spread some of the concoction on a slice of baguette.

"*Rillettes!* Oh, Robbie, you must try some."

"What is it?"

"Have you ever had pâté de foie gras? No? Well, this is the countrified version. Rather like potted meat, but much nicer. Do try." She prepared another piece of baguette and handed it to him.

He took a cautious bite, and found it was as delicious as she had promised, tasting richly of goose fat, garlic, and thyme. He washed it down with several mouthfuls of the wine, noting as he did so that the alcohol was going straight to his head. He'd have to take care or risk falling flat on his face the minute they rose from the table.

Their main course arrived: braised rabbit, instead of the chicken that Lilly had predicted, with glazed carrots and a generous heap of scalloped potatoes. Robbie had eaten rabbit often enough as a boy, but it had never tasted like this, the meat so tender he had no need of his knife.

A steady, lulling stream of conversation flowed between them as they ate. They spoke of the peace negotiations taking place between the Bolsheviks and the Central Powers, the effect the Americans were having on the commission of the war, the whisperings that the Germans had developed some new weapon, worse than poison gas, worse than Gotha bombers, to force the Allies into submission. Careful, neutral conversation, suitable for the fragile peace between them.

Guillaume brought them a simple pudding, baked apples with a tiny jug of cream to pour over. To accompany their dessert he offered strong black coffee, which

Robbie alone accepted. Last of all, he produced a bottle of caramel-colored spirits and two small snifters.

"We should like to offer you this, as compliments of the house." The waiter uncorked the bottle and poured two modest measures of liquid into the glasses. "It is our last bottle of Armagnac from the 1890 vintage. I hope you enjoy it."

Robbie took an experimental sip: the brandy was beautifully smooth, the alcohol evaporating on his tongue almost before he could swallow it. Lilly seemed to enjoy it, too, though he noticed she only took the tiniest sips from her glass.

Thinking he might draw strength from the eau-de-vie, he drained his glass and was rewarded by a gratifying sensation of warmth and bravado. They were almost finished with their meal, and soon enough would have to return to the hotel. And then?

"I meant what I said earlier," he said. "I was wrong to adopt the stance that I did."

"I told you I didn't want any apologies," she answered, her eyes on the remaining brandy in her glass.

"Just hear me out," he insisted. "I haven't changed the way I feel. I still wish you would accept a transfer, but I know you won't change your mind. And though you may not believe me, I respect you for it. You are doing your duty, as am I."

"What are you saying, Robbie? That we're friends again? That you'll deign to speak with me when we return to camp?"

He deplored the edge of sarcasm in her voice, though he knew he'd earned it. "Yes. Although I think we'd better not resume our visits to the garage."

"Why? Did anyone else know? Are you worried we might be found out?"

"Not especially. And I don't think anyone knew, so you can put that out of your mind. It's just that I'm not sure I could manage it."

"I don't understand."

"Don't you? Week after week you tried to get me to kiss you, to continue where we left off on the night of the ceilidh."

"And you weren't interested. I understand, Robbie, really I do. I ought not to have persisted as I did."

"I was interested."

"What? I mean . . . what?"

"I was interested. I still am. Those meetings in the garage almost killed me. They certainly pushed me to the brink of insanity."

"What was stopping you? You knew my feel-ings well enough." She looked up, finally, and he was overwhelmed by the unabashed desire he saw in her eyes.

"If it were simple lust," he whispered, hoping to God that no one else in the restaurant spoke English, "and nothing more, then I would have made love to you the night of the ceilidh. But it's not."

He reached for her hands, enfolded them in his. "There's something more than that between us, Lilly, and I have to respect it."

She frowned at him, incomprehension clouding her gaze. "How can you respect it if you deny it? That doesn't make any sense."

"It does if you stop to consider the gulf between us. I can offer you so little, Lilly, certainly far less than you deserve."

"You're speaking to a common worker in the WAAC, Robbie, with hardly a penny to her name. I'm the one who has nothing to offer, apart from myself."

"But when the war is over, and the rift with your parents is repaired—"

"It will never be repaired as long as they deny me the right to live my life as I wish. To work if I wish it, and to serve my country as well."

Shame enveloped him, for his actions over the past months had been no different from those of her parents. When Lilly had stood her ground, when she'd insisted that she had as much right to do her duty as did he, how had he reacted?

He, too, had disowned her.

"I'm sorry," he said. "Truly sorry." Such a pitifully inadequate apology.

"I told you already that I don't want your apologies. What I want is to get on with my life. I'm done with looking backward, saying to myself, 'If only I had done this, my life would be different.' I want to look ahead, not far ahead, not when-the-war-is-over ahead. Just to the next pleasant thing that is waiting for me. It may only be a cup of tea on a cold day, but I'm glad of it all the same. And I wouldn't change a thing about my life in the past year. Nothing, except the break with you."

He found himself agreeing with her. The past was the past, the future was unknowable, but now, this moment, this evening—*that* they could hold in their hands, savor, treasure.

He scanned the dining room, trying to catch the waiter's eye. When, at last, Guillaume looked in their direction, Robbie beckoned him over and asked for their bill.

Guillaume scribbled down a figure on the corner of the brown paper table covering, tore it off, and handed it to Robbie as if it were a card made of the finest bond linen. The entire meal came to nine francs.

Robbie paid up, shook hands with Guillaume, and helped Lilly into her coat, feeling more than a hint of regret as she disappeared into its tentlike embrace. She turned to look up at him, an enigmatic smile on her face. Why was she smiling at him like that? It was so hard to think when she wore that expression; as if she knew all his secrets, but liked him all the same. Liked him more, even.

It was no more than a ten-minute walk, back along rue Saint-Honoré, across the empty expanse of the Place Vendôme, and, finally, to the welcoming embrace of the Ritz. They strolled in silence through the darkened streets, her arm tucked in the crook of his elbow, the silence so profound that he could mark every breath she took. Was it his imagination or had her breathing quickened?

He longed to kiss her now, propriety be buggered. He hadn't exaggerated when he'd told her their meetings in the garage had nearly unhinged him. Knowing she would deny him nothing, but also knowing he had to hold back, had been the purest form of torture.

What was honor compared to the doubt he saw in her eyes? She thought herself undesirable, though the truth, the truth he hadn't dared to tell her, was quite the opposite.

I've never known a woman lovelier than you, he ached to confess. *I've never wanted a woman more than I want you.*

He wished he could say to hell with propriety, to hell with honor, and to hell with everything that stood between them. But he couldn't, not without risking everything Lilly had worked for over the past year. He'd no means of protecting her from the consequences of lovemaking, and no way to find a reliable form of birth control at this late hour.

So he would tell her the truth. Confess that he wanted her but could not, in good conscience, do anything about it. It was sure to be a dispiriting conversation, not least because Lilly, assuming his suspicions were correct, had only the haziest notion of what lovemaking involved. So it would fall to him, lucky man that he was, to explain.

He would explain, make sure she understood, kiss her good night. And then he would retreat to the luxurious, solitary, torturous embrace of the suite's second bedroom.

That, indeed, was what passed for luck from where he stood.

Chapter 45

One sip. She ought to have stopped at one sip of the Armagnac. But it had been so delicious, so unlike any other spirit she had ever tasted. And she hadn't wanted to offend Guillaume and Chef Jérôme.

So she had drunk it down, sip after entrancing sip, and it had gone straight to her head. Yet it didn't seem to be affecting her as did champagne, for she felt perfectly solid on her feet, perfectly in control of herself.

The limitless euphoria that she remembered from evenings when she'd been a bit tipsy was missing, too. In its stead was a singular feeling of anticipation, of nervous excitement. Rather as if she were about to begin a race, and were waiting to hear the starter's pistol go off.

It was a shock to walk through the front doors of the hotel, from the quiet of the darkened streets, and be faced with the noise and lights and convivial atmosphere of the Ritz's opulent lobby. As if sensing her unease, Robbie wasted no time in steering them directly to a waiting lift.

The attendant, recognizing them from earlier, didn't trouble to ask for their floor. Lilly welcomed the silence, though it meant she'd no alternative but to listen to the roar of her heartbeat, so thunderous that she stole a look at Robbie, just the once, to see if he'd noticed.

The lift doors opened and they exited, Robbie pressing a coin into the attendant's hand. She heard the clank and hiss of, but didn't turn to watch, the doors as they closed.

They walked, still arm in arm, to the end of the corridor. He stepped away, and a disagreeable rush of cool air replaced his presence at her side. He unlocked the door, ushered her through, and locked the door behind them.

She thought, then, that he might reach for her, but his hands were busy with the buckles of his Sam Browne belt, which he hung on the hatstand by the door. His uniform jacket, hat, and tie followed, and then he turned to her.

He bent his head, stooping a little, and began to rain kisses on her upturned face. Whisper-soft kisses, never quite landing on her mouth, though one or two grazed the corners of her lips.

She felt her hat being lifted away, then the buttons of her greatcoat coming undone. He took her by the hand and led her to an occasional chair in the sitting room.

As she sat, he knelt before her. She reached out, intending to frame his face with her hands, but he sat back on his heels before she could touch him.

"Robbie," she pleaded.

"I know, Lilly. But we need to stop now."

"You haven't even kissed me yet, not properly. Have I done something wrong?"

"Of course you haven't." He took her hands, pressed kisses to each palm, and bent his head to them, his brow resting on her knees.

"You know that I never expected this," he said. "Never imagined you would be here. So I find myself unprepared . . ."

"Of course you are. So am I." She felt the curve of his smile against her knee, just for an instant, before he looked up.

"I mean unprepared in a practical sense," he clarified. Seeing that she still didn't understand, he pressed on, his discomfort evident in the flush of color along the high planes of his cheekbones. "There are measures I feel obliged to take. But the chemists are all closed at this hour, and I hesitate to ask the concierge. So I'm afraid—"

Not until he said the word *chemist* did she understand. But was she brave enough to admit the truth? She took a deep breath, shut her eyes, and confessed.

"I have it. Them. The measures you are talking about."

Through narrowed eyelids she watched his reaction. If he were to be disgusted, or offended, she was certain she would die of shame.

His eyes widened, but he made no other reaction. Perhaps he thought he had misunderstood.

"Before I left, Bridget gave me a tin. She said it was a French letter. She said it was just in case, and that you would know what to do."

He sat back on his heels, heavily, and his shoulders began to shake.

"Robbie, is anything the matter—"

He looked up, tears at the corners of his eyes, and for a dreadful instant she thought he was crying. And then she noticed how he smiled, as he wiped his eyes, and she realized that he was laughing so hard that he could hardly catch his breath.

"Thank God for Bridget," he gasped. "I wonder if I'll ever have the courage to thank her."

He looked up at Lilly, his expression tender yet grave, and she knew that he had cast his doubts aside.

"Will you come to me?"

She threw herself into his arms, desperate for his kiss, and he responded with a naked fervor that she ought to have found shocking, even alarming. His mouth pressed down on hers, relentlessly pushing her lips apart, his tongue searching inside, seeking some answering contact. She let her tongue dart forward, dip into his mouth, learn the contours of his lips.

He stood, his mouth never leaving hers, and gathered her up as if she were made of swansdown. Striding across the sitting room, he pushed open the door to her bedroom with his shoulder and carried her to the bed. Not until he had set her down did he break their kiss.

He stepped back, mere inches really, but Lilly felt bereft all the same. She was about to stand and reach for him again when he began to undress.

He cast off his leather gaiters, then his boots and socks. Next he pushed his suspenders aside, untucked his shirt, felt at his throat for his collar button. And then he stopped.

"Will you help me?" he asked, his voice husky.

She stood, reaching for the button, and it seemed to her that he held his breath as she undid it.

"And the others?" he prompted.

Her fingers flew over the remaining buttons. When she was done, he held up his wrists so she could undo his cuffs. Without waiting for any further direction, she pushed the shirt off his shoulders and let it drop to the floor.

Feeling wonderfully bold, she pulled off his identity tags, which hung from a thin leather cord around his neck, and moved to unfasten the buttons at the neck of his short-sleeved Henley undershirt. But before she could begin, he pushed her hands away.

She felt his fingers at the nape of her neck, searching carefully for the pins that held her chignon in place. He pulled them out, setting them on the bedside table, and ran his hands through the waterfall of hair that cascaded down her back.

"I had no idea it was so long," he murmured. "Has it never been cut?"

"My mother didn't approve of girls who cut their hair. I thought of cutting it, after I left home, but never got around to it."

He said nothing, just smiled at her, his fingers combing steadily, reverently, through her hair.

"My sisters always had much prettier hair," she said, feeling she ought to fill the silence. "When I was little I longed to look like Alice and Mary."

And still he smiled at her, his thoughts unknowable. She met his gaze, a wisp of worry beginning to coil in her stomach. It was true, what she had said about her sisters. If only she were beautiful, like them—

His touch at the collar of her gown halted all rational thought. There were so many buttons, far more than on his shirt, but he unfastened them all in a matter of seconds. Her dress came open, and then fell away as he eased it off her shoulders.

A tug at her waist told her that he had loosened the string of her single petticoat. It puddled around her shoes, and as she went to step free of it he took her hands to steady her.

It seemed odd to still be wearing her shoes, so she kicked them off, pushing them aside with one foot. Now she wore only her stockings and combinations. They were clean, thank goodness, but bore no resemblance to the pretty lingerie she knew men expected to discover at such moments.

"You don't need satin and ribbons," he said, somehow guessing her thoughts. "You're perfect as you are. Everything about you is perfect."

She steeled herself for the moment when he would begin to unfasten the bodice of her combinations, but instead he sat on the bed and pulled her into his arms, his knees drawn wide so he could embrace her fully.

"Why aren't you wearing a corset?" he asked, his face pressed into the curve of her neck. The stubble on his cheeks felt wonderfully abrasive against her skin.

"I used to. But it got in the way. Do you mind?"

"God, no. Corsets are an abomination."

He pressed a single kiss to the pulse at the base of her throat, his lips a brand upon her skin. Then he pulled away, reached for the hem of his undershirt, and pulled it over his head.

Lilly had never been so close to a man's naked chest. She knew men had nipples, knew they sometimes had hair there, but the difference between knowing something and actually *seeing* it was awfully large.

Hair the color of spun gold covered Robbie's chest, stretching from nipple to nipple and narrowing to a thin line at his navel. She touched him tentatively, marveling at the softness of the hair, at the way it tickled her fingers.

He was so warm. She let her fingers trail along the corded muscles of his shoulders, then his arms, which he spread wide for her, inviting her inspection. Her fingers drifted lower, skipping over the flat planes of his belly, tracing the curve of muscle at one hip, then the other.

His nipples had drawn up on themselves, just as hers did when she was chilled, though it was far from cold in the room. His skin shivered, too, wherever she touched him. Perhaps she was doing something wrong. Perhaps she ought to stop, or wait for him to direct her.

"Lilly?" he asked, his voice gentle. She glanced up and saw that his eyes were closed.

"Yes? I'm getting it all wrong, aren't I?"

"Quite the opposite. Let me hold you some more."

His arms enveloped her, holding her so tightly that it was difficult to breathe properly. She could feel his every breath, almost feel his pulse racing. And she could feel something else, pressing insistently against the juncture of her thighs.

So *this* was what Bridget and Annie talked of after lights-out. *This* was the something that nice girls only discovered the truth of on their wedding night.

"Lilly?" he prompted, his voice infinitely soothing. "Do you know what's next?"

She nodded her head, a little frantically. "Annie and Bridget talk about it, quite often. Although there are some, ah, parts that I'm not entirely sure about. And I was never brave enough to ask."

"It's not the easiest thing to talk about. Few people do."

"What if I make a mistake?"

He laughed, softly, and pressed a reassuring kiss to her mouth. "It's not a maths exam, Lilly. And I promise there's nothing to be frightened of."

"My sisters . . . I overheard them talking about it once. They said it was unpleasant. Revolting, even."

"You should pity them, Lilly. For they'll never know the truth of it." He looked up at her, his eyes glittering. "Now, what about these clothes? Shall we try getting rid of them?"

Chapter 46

He stood, one arm curved about her, and pulled back the bedcovers. Then he picked her up, cradled her briefly in his arms, and laid her upon the bed.

He unbuttoned his flies, turning around as he shrugged off his trousers and undershorts. His bottom was very nice, Lilly thought. Certainly as fine as the bottoms she had seen on the marble statuary in her father's gardens.

What did Annie and Bridget call a bottom again? A bum—that was it. She giggled despite herself. It was a rather comical word, after all.

"I hope that's not at my expense," Robbie said as he stretched out next to her. She closed her eyes, though she was curious to see the rest of him.

"I was thinking of the way Annie and Bridget say 'bum' not 'bottom.' That's all."

"Well, you've seen my bum. Do you want to see the rest of me?"

She nodded, but still could not bring herself to open her eyes.

"Look at me, Lilly. Please."

At last she complied. As long as she kept her eyes on his face and chest, she would be fine.

"I know you're curious, Lilly. There's no need to be shy. Not with me."

She forced herself to look lower, past his navel, her gaze following the skein of golden hair that led toward . . .

Whatever she had expected to see, it had not been *that*. His, his . . . she couldn't bring herself to even think the word for it. His . . . *it*, then.

She'd seen plenty of nudes: her father owned countless portraits and statues in the classical style, and she'd spent many hours wandering through the British Museum with Charlotte. But all the *its* she'd seen before had been inconsequential. Hardly worth noticing. Unthreatening.

"Do I meet with your approval?"

How on earth should she answer? With the truth? That *it* was, frankly, terrifying?

"It's, ah, larger than I expected," she said, hoping he would not be too insulted. But he seemed unaccountably pleased with her comment.

"You're very kind." Seeing that she did not share his good humor, he began to stroke her hair. "Are you worried?"

"A little. Will it . . . will it hurt?"

"Yes," he answered gravely. "But only for a bit. And if you want to stop, at any point, we will stop."

Still he stroked her hair, not moving to touch her anywhere else. Long seconds dragged by. Just what would happen next? What would he do?

Her answer came with the touch of his hand at the bodice of her combinations. One, two, three, the tiny buttons came free, and then he was easing the soft cotton down her shoulders, down and down until she knew, without looking, that her breasts lay bare to his gaze.

He said nothing, offered no compliment, but his sigh of admiration was enough. He bent his golden head, his lips dancing over her collarbone, then lower and lower, until they closed over a nipple and he began to suckle at her breast. It was shocking and alarming. It was wonderful.

With every soft pull of his mouth, her unease abated, replaced by an unfamiliar sensation. She felt warm, as if she were bathed in sunlight, only the sunlight was coming from within, from a place at the very center of her.

She felt his hand beneath her, and she realized he was pulling off her combinations. His mouth left her breast as he turned to unclasp her stockings from the garters at her knees, long seconds that left her bereft and restless. She shifted, squirmed, desperate for him to continue.

"Robbie . . ."

He made no answer, simply returned to her breasts. She felt the delicious rasp of his stubbled cheeks against one breast, then the other; then the surprise and delight of his clever fingers, tweaking and pulling and delicately pinching at her nipples.

"Bridget's tin—where is it?"

"In the drawer of the writing desk."

He rolled away, leaving her trembling, alone, but returned before she could grow cold. She felt the edge of the mattress depress as he sat down, his back to her.

She heard him open the tin, heard the sound of paper unfolding. More sounds, entirely mysterious to her, followed.

"May I ask . . . what *is* a French letter?"

He laughed softly, still intent on whatever task needed to be accomplished before they could continue.

"It's a sheath that I wear. Some are made of rubber, but this one is of lambskin. I wear it to ensure you won't fall pregnant."

If only he knew how little she really knew. He turned, caught a glimpse of her face, and she knew then that he understood the depth of her ignorance.

"When a man makes love to a woman, he leaves behind some . . . ah, some seeds. Those seeds can help make a baby. This sheath will prevent me from leaving behind the seeds."

"I see," she said, still not entirely clear about how, exactly, the seeds would be left behind. That had not been part of Bridget and Annie's primer. "How do—"

"I'm happy to tell you, but wouldn't you prefer that I show you?"

Apparently satisfied with the French letter, he stretched out upon the bed again. He turned her toward him, so they lay face-to-face, and began to caress her back, his fingers drawing circles upon her skin. The circles twined lower, then lower, until they spiraled over the curve of her bottom and the sweep of her thigh.

And then she felt his fingers at the backs of her knees, soothing the ticklish skin there, leaving behind shivers as he skimmed along the line where her legs pressed together, wooing them open.

A nice girl would have clamped her legs together, begged him to remove his questing fingers. Then again, a nice girl would not be lying naked in bed with a man who wasn't her husband. She left her legs as they were.

It was hard not to flinch, though, when she felt his precise, confident touch sweep over her hip, trace along the crease at the top of her thigh, and, even more shockingly, brush over the triangle of hair that flanked it.

And then the mad urge to shrink away simply vanished, replaced by a surge of curiosity that engulfed every instinct she had. Something was happening to her, something so new, so remarkable, that she feared it all might end before she discovered the truth of it.

"What is . . . ?" she whispered.

"It's supposed to be like this. Don't worry, Lilly. Just let it happen."

She closed her eyes and gave herself over to the astonishing sensations his fingers were producing. He had pushed between the hidden folds between her legs, into a place so unknown to Lilly that she had no name for it.

A nearly unbearable sense of something was building, rushing toward her. But even as she rose to meet it, pushing wildly against his fingers, it eluded her. Nothing ought to feel this wonderful. Nothing had ever felt this wonderful before.

He'd taken his hand away—why had he stopped? She opened her mouth, the question on her lips, but before she could speak he kissed her and the words were lost.

He rolled her onto her back, kneeling between her thighs, pushing them wide, and she felt his touch between her legs again.

"This is the part that will hurt, Lilly. Are you—"

"Don't stop," she ordered, hoping she sounded more confident than she felt.

She felt his fingers, beautifully gentle, but then they were replaced by something else, and it was pushing inside her, inside a place she had scarcely known existed, and it hurt, hurt terribly, and she was so disappointed that tears rushed to her eyes.

He kissed them away, murmured soft endearments to her, but he didn't stop, just kept pushing forward, and she felt something pulling, tearing, giving way. He was really inside her now, which had to be impossible, for how could *it* fit all the way inside?

She was trying not to squirm; she knew, from the conversation between her sisters she had overheard, that men disliked it when women complained about lovemaking. So she lay as still as she could and waited for him to finish.

He had stopped moving, now that he was buried inside her, and when she opened her eyes she realized that he was looking at her, an expression of heartfelt guilt on his face.

"I'm so sorry, my darling. I promise it will get better."

She nodded, wanting to be brave. The important thing was to please him; she knew that much.

He leaned to the side, taking his weight on one elbow, and just as she began to wonder what he was doing she felt his hand searching between them, and then an electric jolt of awareness as his thumb touched her *there*.

He brushed his thumb back and forth, hardly moving it at all, caressing her so delicately that a feather would have felt rough in comparison. Not for an instant did he stop; and so the feeling built and built within her, until she had very nearly forgotten about the pain and the disagreeable sensations of a minute before.

His hips pulled away from her, and then pushed back, and she realized with a jolt that the pain was gone, or if not gone then set aside. All that mattered was the feeling of his hand between them, and the insistent, mesmerizing friction of him, of Robbie, as he moved within her.

She clutched at him, her fingernails digging into his back, but he didn't seem to notice, didn't so much as flinch.

Everything seemed to gather within her, every beautiful touch and sensation and thought, until it was a tight, tiny sphere, revolving within her, threatening to shatter at any moment.

"Lilly, open your eyes. Look at me."

"Robbie, I—"

"This is perfect. You are perfect. Let it happen."

So she was meant to embrace it, then. A deep breath, a plunge into the pool, like the time she'd jumped into the lake at Cumbermere Hall when she was little.

A breath, a heartbeat, and then an implosion, deep inside, as the feeling spiraled outward, carrying her up and up. It was so intense, so all-consuming, that she feared she wouldn't be able to bear it.

Her reaction seemed to have affected him, for he was pushing into her faster than before, harder than before, and she knew he was about to reach the place she had just discovered.

"Lilly," he gasped. "My Lilly."

He rolled onto his side, taking her with him, his arms embracing her so tightly that she could feel the tremors coursing through him, the raging torrent of his heartbeat, the erratic rhythm of his breath.

She lay still, not wanting to disturb him, content to rest in his arms as he recovered.

"Lilly?"

"Yes?"

"Thank you."

He dropped a kiss on her mouth and another on the tip of her nose, and then pulled away from her.

"Don't fret," he soothed. "I'll be back in a moment."

She heard the pad of his feet on the carpet as he walked to the bathroom, then the sound of water running. She didn't attempt to move; the sense of lassitude enveloping her was too great an impediment.

The sweep of a warm washcloth across her inner thigh told her he had returned. "Shall I?" he asked. "Or are you feeling shy?"

She shook her head, though in truth she was feeling shy again. He washed her carefully, sponging away the flecks of blood between her legs, pressing the cloth to her like a warm compress.

"You'll be a bit sore tomorrow," he told her. "I am sorry."

"And I'm not," she retorted. "That was . . ."

"Yes?"

"As you said. Perfect."

Chapter 47

He'd forgotten to switch off the desk lamp. Much later, well into the wee hours, its light woke him. Hovering at the edge of his dreams, remote and golden, it beckoned him, teased him, and at last he opened his eyes, though it was nowhere close to dawn. He lay in the half-light, blinking sleepily, reluctant to free himself from the cobweb remnants of his dreams.

Robbie looked down, to the woman nestled in his arms, and felt his chest constrict at the sight of her. He knew he ought to feel some sense of remorse about what they'd just done. What *he* had done, if he were honest about it.

She'd been a virgin; had known nothing, or close to nothing, of the mechanics of lovemaking. He had taken that from her, without the protection of his name or even the promise of his name. He had made love to the sister of his dearest friend even as that friend was lost, lying dead or slowly dying, in the horrific wastes of no-man's-land.

And he hadn't even thought to tell Lilly that he loved her.

He'd been nervous, of course. He'd never made love to a virgin before, and had been preoccupied with making the experience a pleasurable one for her. His roster of romantic conquests was slight compared to that of most men his age, or so he imagined. In the main, they had consisted of nurses at the London, modern women with a healthy interest in sex and an understandable disdain for the career-ending confines of marriage.

Marriage. The only honorable thing to do, now that he had compromised Lilly so thoroughly, was to ask her to marry him. He'd never before considered marriage; had never met anyone with whom he could imagine spending a lifetime. And yet, as much as he yearned for her, he couldn't shake the fear that it was the wrong thing to do.

He had come far, it was true. To his peers, he was a respectable professional man, a surgeon with a promising future ahead of him. A successful member of the upper middle class. But he was also the son of a dustman and a laundress, born in a slum tenement in Glasgow. A man with no family, no fortune, no connections. A man with nothing to offer but himself.

And his postwar prospects were limited. He had a gentleman's agreement with the chief of surgery at the London Hospital that a position would be waiting for him when he returned, but no more than that. And he'd no savings to speak of, for he'd long sent every spare shilling he had to his mother.

If he and Lilly were to marry, it would be years before they could afford a house of their own. Until then, they'd have to lease a property. No mansion in Belgravia for them, but perhaps they might be able to afford the rent on a house in one of the garden suburbs. If they were very careful with money, they might be able to keep a maidservant. But Lilly would probably have to do most of the cooking on her own, and care for their children without the help of a nursemaid.

Perhaps she wouldn't mind. Perhaps after living so simply, so roughly, she might be content with a modest, middle-class life.

Or she might be well and truly sick of it, and more than ready to return to the bosom of her family and the life of privilege they offered. She was angry with them still, but that was certain to fade in time. If that were the case, his offer of marriage could only cause her grief, for she would forever be pulled between two worlds, never properly belonging to either.

Enough with this useless speculation, he told himself. Switch off that lamp and get back to sleep.

He slipped out of the bed, doing his best not to jostle her, but had taken only a few steps when he heard her stir.

"What are you doing out of bed?"

"I was just going to switch off the light," he explained, looking back.

She shook her head. "Can we leave it on? Please? I want to be able to see you."

She smiled at him, a dimple appearing in her cheek, and he felt his heart flip-flop in response.

He didn't require any further encouragement. A second later he was back in bed, Lilly spooned in his arms, her bottom pressed against his groin. Compounding that distraction was the proximity of her breasts to his free arm, which she had insisted on pulling around her. If he were to twist his wrist, just a little, he could cup her left breast in his hand, then tweak the nipple of her right breast with his thumb.

He'd had every intention of leaving her alone for the rest of the night. It was the decent thing to do, especially in light of how sore she must surely be. But he wasn't made of stone, and the feel of her lush body pressed against him was so enthralling, so distracting, that it threatened to eclipse all rational thought.

"Lilly," he said, hoping she did not notice how strangled his voice sounded, "I think we need to talk."

She twisted in his arms so she could face him, her expression serious. Alarmingly serious. The heady sensations of a moment before evaporated almost instantly.

"Of course we do. How do you think we will manage it?"

"Manage what?"

"We must agree on what we will do when we return to camp."

She was right. "I suppose I shall have to learn how to bear it," he ventured. "I don't suppose there's any way I can convince you to return to England?"

She offered him a gentle, troubled smile. "I can't go back, Robbie. You know that.

"And even if I were to return to London," she went on, "there's no guarantee I'd be safe there. You know, better than most people, how uncertain life can be. I could fall ill, or be run down while crossing the street, or a zeppelin might drop a bomb on my lodgings—"

"But the risk of something happening is so much greater here," he insisted.

"Perhaps it is, but I accept it, Robbie. I truly do. It's the price I must pay in order to do my duty."

They stared at each other, her words hanging in the air. *Duty.* Why should such an abstraction interfere with their happiness?

"Did you read much poetry when you were in school?" she asked. It took him a moment to recover from his surprise and formulate a response.

"Some. The classics, mostly. Virgil, Homer. Why do you ask?"

"Did you ever read 'Dover Beach'?"

"Yes, as it happens. My English tutor loved Matthew Arnold."

"It's my favorite poem. But I never understood it, not properly, until now."

"What do you mean?" he asked, mystified by the turn their conversation had taken.

"Everything the poet knows, everything he is certain about, is slipping away from him. So what does he do? He turns to the one he loves. 'Let us be true to one another,' he says. The world may be crumbling to ashes, he tells her, but he is still certain of love."

Her eyes bright with unshed tears, she framed his face with her hands. "I love you. I've always loved you. Even when you hated me, I loved you still."

He silenced her with a kiss, as gentle as he could

make it, and then pulled back so he could look in her eyes. "I never hated you," he told her, willing her to believe. "Not for one instant did I hate you. And I would give anything to take away the hurt my disgraceful behavior caused you.

"I love you, Lilly. I wish I could offer you more, more than just myself. You deserve—"

"Look at me," she commanded. "*You* are all I have ever wanted. It has always been you."

"I—"

"There is nothing I would change about you. *Nothing.* You need to know that. When the war is over, we will be together. No matter what, we will be together."

She was smiling, her eyes dancing with fierce, unalloyed delight, and he found himself smiling back, giddy with gratitude and another emotion he could not at first identify.

And then he knew. As he looked in her eyes, her lovely hazel eyes that regarded him with adoration, he knew the feeling for what it was, though he'd never been graced with it before.

It was joy.

Chapter 48

Lilly woke at dawn, her mind awhirl with all that had happened, tragic and good, in the past twenty-four hours. Her first thought was of Edward. If only she could believe that he was awake, *alive*, able to see the pale glow of dawn as it softened the sky. Her heart yearned for it, ached for the certainty of knowledge, but war had a way of strangling such hopes.

She turned to face Robbie, who lay on his back, sound asleep, one hand flung over his brow. His face was so dear, so familiar, as if he'd been hers forever and not a matter of hours. It would be so marvelous to have more time with him, time to explore the truce they'd established and the promises they'd made. But she was expected back in camp before the end of the day and, given how irregularly the trains had been running, she had to leave before midday in order to ensure she wouldn't be late.

Rather than wake him right away, she tiptoed to the bathroom and ran herself a scalding-hot bath, immersing herself up to her neck until the water was tepid and her fingers were as wrinkled as a walnut. Unwilling to put on her uniform right away, she dressed in her nightgown and the same hotel dressing gown she'd borrowed the night before, then returned to the bedroom and drew wide the draperies to let in the thin winter sun. Robbie stirred, stretched, and came awake almost instantly. No doubt it was a skill he had perfected while at the CCS.

"Good morning, Lilly. Have you been awake for long?"

"About an hour. I took a shockingly long bath. Now we need to order breakfast, and then I need to be on my way."

"I'll come with you to the station."

"I'm glad of it. Shall I ring downstairs now? What do you want?"

"Coffee. Can't think what else."

Their coffee, in the form of huge bowls of café au lait, was delivered in minutes, and was accompanied by a basket of croissants and *pains aux amandes*. And then, the hour growing late, Lilly retreated to the bedroom to dress and pack. Less than a day earlier, her uniform had felt like a second skin to her; now it lay heavily on her shoulders, its chafing wool and unflattering cut unwelcome burdens. But at least it was clean.

When she returned to the sitting room, Robbie was dressed, too, and as ever he looked impossibly handsome in his uniform and greatcoat.

"Do you want me to come back with you?" he asked. "If anyone should notice we've returned together, I can simply say I ran into you on the train. It wouldn't be an out-and-out lie."

"No," she insisted. "You've earned every minute of your leave. I want you to stay here and enjoy the best of everything the Ritz can supply. And you must go to bed early tonight and catch up on your sleep. Promise?"

"I promise. I'll miss you, though."

"And I you. Shall we go?"

Rather than call for a taxi, they retraced the path Lilly had taken the day before, arm in arm, hardly speaking, preparing themselves for the moment of parting. The streets were quiet, empty, but had they been teeming with crowds she wouldn't have noticed. She saw only him.

She bought her ticket, asked about and was informed of the platform she required. They had abandoned all attempts at propriety now, Robbie's arm about her shoulders, his head bent to kiss the top of her head. A whistle blew, a swath of soldiers moved toward the platform, and it was time to go.

Lilly lifted her face to his, closing her eyes only when she felt his hands in her hair, smoothing it back lightly, then the welcome weight of his mouth on hers. She wrapped her arms around him, hugging him fiercely, and then she picked up her bag and took a step back.

"I'll see you tomorrow."

"Yes. Lilly, I—"

"No time. We'll talk when you return. We'll find a way."

The journey home took nearly ten hours, for she missed her first connection in Amiens and then had to wait in Saint-Omer while repairs to a shelled-out stretch of rail line took place. Constance and the others were already in bed when she returned, but no sooner had she poked her nose through the front flap of their quarters than the lantern was lighted, the kettle was set to boil, and her friends began their interrogation.

"Where did you stay?" Constance asked.

"In a hotel, not far from the station." It wasn't a complete lie; the Ritz was a hotel, and it was within walking distance of the Gare du Nord.

"What happened when he saw you? What did he say?"

"He was upset, quite upset with me. But then I explained what had happened to Edward and he was lovely after that. Very civil."

"So you told him and left?" Constance pressed.

"Not precisely. I told him, we talked at length, and we agreed—I suppose he agreed—that we ought not to remain at odds. Then we went to dinner."

"I like the sound of that!" said Bridget.

Lilly didn't dare look at her, for the truth of what had happened after dinner was likely written all over her face. Instead, she unfastened her uniform jacket and folded it neatly over the end of her cot. "We talked about Edward, mostly. And that's really all there is to tell."

With difficulty she stifled a yawn. "Would you all mind if we finished talking tomorrow? It took so long to get back—"

"Of course," said Constance soothingly. "Besides, Sergeant Barnes said the next few days are going to be bad. Says he can feel it in his bones, like an old lady with rheumatism. So we'd best sleep while we can."

They were awake again less than five hours later. It was the sound of the guns that roused them: no longer a distant rhythm as familiar as a heartbeat, but a wildly discordant clamor only marginally more frightening than the ominous silences with which it alternated.

Robbie was late in returning, only landing back in camp well after midnight the following day; apparently the rail lines to Saint-Omer had all been shelled, as had most of the roads, and he'd been forced to catch one lift after another until he was within walking distance of Merville. This information she gleaned from Nurse Ferguson, as they stood in line in the mess tent early one morning, for Robbie himself had disappeared into the operating hut within minutes of his return and had barely emerged since.

In the month that followed, Lilly caught only fleeting glimpses of him, usually as he crouched next to stretchers while performing triage in the reception marquee. Paris was soon a distant memory, a half-remembered interval of light and delight from another life, another world.

She knew Robbie was spending twenty hours or more at a stretch in surgery. When he slept, it was only for an hour or two, on a cot that Matron had dragged next to the surgeons' desk in the ward tent, before rousing himself and returning to work. For her part, Lilly spent every waking moment on the road to the

ADS. When the bombardment worsened, at the end of March, they began to evacuate patients to the 33rd CCS in Saint-Venant.

The following fortnight passed by in a nightmarish, arduous blur. With the nearby rail lines shelled into oblivion, the wounded had to be evacuated by ambulance. If Lilly had ever thought herself exhausted before, she knew now that she had been wrong.

This was exhaustion. Up at dawn's first light, back and forth and back again to Saint-Venant, a five- or ten-minute break for dinner, then on and on and on until she could hardly prop herself upright behind Henrietta's steering wheel.

One day, when this was all over, when the enemy had been beaten back and the Front was secure and she'd had the chance to sleep for more than an hour or two at a stretch, she would let herself think of Paris, of Robbie, of all that waited for them once the war was done.

Until then, her eyes burning, her brain begging for sleep, she allowed herself but a single thought.

Drive.

Chapter 49

Merville, France
April 11, 1918

A thousand miles. In less than a fortnight she had driven more than a thousand miles, endlessly circling the tangled skein of craters and mud that had once been the five-mile stretch of road between Saint-Venant and Merville.

Laid out in a straight line, how far could those miles have taken her? Far enough to silence the guns? To dry the mud that caked her boots and skirts? A thousand miles away, would she still hear the cries of the wounded men she drove to safety, or the piteous stillness of those who could not be saved?

This morning she had begun work at half-past five. It was now—she checked her watch by the light of the moon—nearly three in the morning. And she had one final journey to make, tonight, before she could rest.

She was hurrying back to Henrietta, ready to top up the radiator with the can of water she'd just filled, when the night was fractured by the whistle and whine of yet another approaching shell. It struck the ground no more than two hundred yards away, its impact close enough to force the can of water out of her suddenly nerveless fingers, but it didn't knock her down. It would take a direct hit to do that.

She wiped the dust off her face with her sleeve, picked up the water can, which by some miracle had landed more or less upright, and filled the radiator. Then she hurried back to the ward tent to help her final two passengers of the night into the front cab of her ambulance. Stretcher-bearers, they'd been gassed the night before in no-man's-land, where they'd been sent to retrieve the fallen.

Three men already lay on stretchers in the back, their skin and eyes horribly blistered by mustard gas, their lungs flayed. Their eyes might heal, and their skin, but they would never draw an easy breath again. If they lived. If she could bring them to safety.

Turning, she caught sight of Robbie for the first

time that day. He'd just come out of the operating hut, his surgeon's gown sodden with blood. Seeing her, he faltered, but only for a moment; time was too precious now.

Their eyes met. She steeled herself to hold his gaze, though she feared she might collapse under the weight of his regard. She had hoped she would see him before she left; had prayed for this moment. But no armor could ever have shielded her from its torment, so raw and fierce that she thought she might faint from the agony of it.

Lilly had been in France for more than a year, and in all that time she had never been afraid. Anxious, yes. Worried, sad, even despairing, but never afraid.

She was afraid now. It wasn't the shelling, or the dread and certain knowledge that the enemy had broken through the lines mere miles away. It was the fact that nearly a dozen men still lay, waiting for their turn in an ambulance, in the ward tent.

And her ambulance was the last one to leave that night.

And Robbie would refuse to go until every last one of the wounded men under his care had been evacuated. Would be taken prisoner rather than abandon them.

She longed to say something to him, some words of comfort or affection. Longed to tell him again how she loved him.

Instead she ran across the yard, her heart racing, and was enveloped in the shelter of his arms. For one beautiful instant she let him hold her, then she tipped back her head for his fierce, desperate kiss.

She stepped away, gently pulling her hands from his grasp. He nodded, his eyes grave. He knew, as well as she did, what this moment meant.

And then it was over. She ran back to her ambulance, cranked the engine to life, dragged herself up behind the steering wheel, and drove away into the night. Into the dark.

She urged the ambulance forward, hardly daring to switch out of first gear. The miles inched past, marked only by the groans of her passengers and the distancing roar of the guns.

It had been many months since she had prayed, truly prayed. But she prayed now, the words tumbling mutely from her lips. *He has done his duty, has never once failed in his duty. Please, God, please let Robbie survive, though others perish. Please let him survive. Please oh please oh please—*

She heard the whistle first. High-pitched, sharp, insistent. A dull thud as the shell tore apart the road. The heart-stopping knowledge of what was to come. And then a wave of heat and dirt and screaming metal swept over Lilly and the five men she'd hoped to save.

The ambulance careened across the road, reached the mud-filled ditch at the side, trembled at its precipice, and toppled over.

She woke to pain. Pain so knife-sharp it made her long for the darkness again. She was on the ground; at least it felt like the ground, all cold and wet and shingled with pebbles. Rain beat down on her face. She turned her head and saw that someone was kneeling, in the mud, next to her.

"Lilly, it's Constance. I'm here."

Constance. Relief flooded over her. "What happened?"

"You were late arriving. Really quite late. So we drove out to search for you. It's a miracle you weren't killed by that shell."

"Men in my ambulance . . ." Whose voice was that, so reedy, pale, insubstantial?

"They're out. We got them out. But, Lilly, your leg is pinned. Under the ambulance. They're working to free you now. It will only be a minute or two."

Lilly peered into the darkness, trying to see her friend's face. "Constance? Where are you?"

"I'm here, Lilly. I'm holding your hand."

"So cold."

"I know. I'm so sorry. I promise we'll have you in a warm bed in no time."

"Robbie . . ." Lilly licked her lips, which felt parched despite the rain. "Where is he?"

"I don't know, Lilly. I haven't seen him."

"Tell him . . ."

"Yes, Lilly?" Constance was leaning over her now, straining to hear.

"Forgive . . . forgive . . ."

And then, the words dying in her throat, she was swept backward, gently backward, into a tide of ink-dark, tender, blessed unknowing.

Chapter 50

It was a near thing, in the end. He and Matron had been huddled in the ward tent with the few patients who had been left behind; eleven in total, all postoperative. All were stable enough for evacuation, but since there were no more ambulances, they'd nothing to do but wait for the Germans to arrive. At least Lilly was gone, safely away to Saint-Venant, and finally out of danger.

The crunch of tires on the graveled yard outside the ward tent came sooner than he'd expected. He didn't bother to get up; best to stay where he was and wait for the inevitable. His service pistol was still in his locker; any kind of resistance would be madness, especially with the lives of Matron and the patients at stake.

Robbie had certainly not expected to see Private Gillespie's face appear at the tent's entrance. So it was not the Germans, come to bayonet them where they sat, after all.

"What are you doing here?" Matron asked.

"Colonel Lewis let me take one of the Dennis lorries. I thought I might be able to fetch the lot of you. But we haven't much time. Come on with you, now."

Robbie needed no further encouragement. While Matron helped the few men who could stand, he and Gillespie ferried stretcher after stretcher to the lorry, which was at least double the size of a typical ambulance. It was a tight squeeze, in the end, but they fit everyone inside, as tightly and uncomfortably as sardines in a tin.

The journey to Saint-Venant took something like forever, for Private Gillespie had to slow the lorry almost to a halt whenever they encountered shell craters, else risk a shattered axle. And the rain hammered down on them so relentlessly that it was impossible to see more than a few feet ahead.

At one point they passed the wreckage of an ambulance, not unlike the reliable little Ford that Lilly drove, but its driver and passengers had vanished. He hoped they'd found shelter from the rain and the bombs.

The 33rd CCS, which had evacuated to Saint-Venant a few weeks before, had set up shop in an old convent. No sooner had Gillespie pulled the lorry to a halt than the wounded men in its rear were being carried inside.

Robbie stood in the rain, not sure of what to do next. He really had been so certain that he would be taken prisoner. Perhaps he would see if he could find Lilly, discretion be damned.

"So you made it after all."

Robbie turned and saw that Colonel Lewis was approaching him.

"Thank you, sir, for sending the lorry. They'd have had us otherwise."

"Thank Gillespie. He was the one who insisted. Damn near ordered me. Said he could do it, and he was right."

"Well, I'm grateful all the same. To you and to Private Gillespie."

"I do have some bad news."

Robbie was instantly alert. It must be someone he knew; one of his colleagues, perhaps.

"It's Miss Ashford, I'm afraid. No, don't say anything. I don't need to know."

"What is it? What has happened to her?"

Robbie felt the ground tipping and tilting under his feet. Not now, not now. He had to keep his wits about him. Had to know the truth of it, no matter how unbearable.

"Good God, man, are you all right?"

"Yes, yes. I'm fine. Just tell me what happened."

"There was a crash. A shell fell directly in her path as she was driving here, not two hours ago. Compound fracture to her left leg, but the artery wasn't compromised. And a lacerated spleen."

"So she's alive?"

"Of course she's alive. Didn't I say so already? No?"

"Where is she now? I must see her—"

"She's still in surgery. Harrison is handling it. He's set her leg already and is taking out her spleen now. But she's stable, she's tolerating the anesthetic well, and she's been transfused. So you've nothing to worry about."

"I . . ."

"Get some rest, now. I'll send someone to let you know as soon as she's awake."

With that, Colonel Lewis slapped Robbie on the back, shook his hand, and marched away, leaving him alone on the convent's muddy cobbled courtyard. Get some rest, the OC had said. As if that were possible now.

A hand touched his elbow. "Captain Fraser? It's me, Constance. You look terrible. Let me get you a cup of tea."

He allowed her to lead him inside, to a small chapel attached to the main sanctuary, and sat down when she indicated he should.

"I'll be back in a moment. Don't even think of getting up," she warned.

The cup of tea she brought him was hot and black and he wasn't sure he would be able to drink it. But he forced it down and was relieved when it stayed put.

"Please tell me what happened, Miss Evans," he said, his voice hardly more than a whisper.

"She'd almost made it. Was less than a mile away. But a shell fell in the road, directly in front of her. When she swerved to avoid it, the ambulance tipped into the ditch at the side of the road. She was pinned beneath it; her leg was pinned. I'm not sure for how long. Perhaps half an hour."

Constance took a sip of her own tea, and Robbie saw that her hands were trembling. "She regained consciousness for a minute or two. I was at her side. She wanted me to tell you—"

Her voice broke, her shoulders shaking, and Robbie was moved to take her hand in his. "She wanted you to forgive her," Constance said. "She didn't say why. Just asked you to forgive her."

An icy fist of shame and regret tightened itself around Robbie's heart. She had thought she was dying, and in that moment she had asked him to forgive her for the very things that had made him love her.

It was her courage, her tenacity, her conviction that she must do her duty, no matter the consequences to herself. That was why he loved her.

He fished in his tunic pocket, searching for the little box he had carried with him, day and night, since his return from Paris. Without opening it, he pressed the box into Constance's hand.

"What do you think of this? Do you think she'll like it?"

Constance opened it, gasping as she saw the ring inside. He didn't have to look at it again to know its every detail. Instead of a diamond, the ring's central stone was a sapphire, a quarter-inch square, the same ink-dark, fathomless blue of the lochs in which he had swum and fished as a boy. A delicate row of seed pearls, set in gold, framed the gem. The gold was an unusual color, rich and coppery, and he'd thought it would look lovely against Lilly's ivory skin.

"When I was in Paris with Lilly, I had almost a day to myself after she left. I saw this in a jeweler's window. It seemed perfect for her. Although it's not very grand, as engagement rings go . . ."

Constance shook her head. "It *is* perfect for her. She'll adore it."

"I'd meant to give it to her straightaway, but the shelling had already begun when I returned. For a month now I've been trying to find a time to be alone with her, but we never had a chance."

"You'll have a chance very soon. Do you want another cup of tea?"

"I'm fine. Thank you for your help."

"Are you sure you'll be all right?"

"Once I've seen Lilly. Only then."

Chapter 51

I t seemed a shame to wake up. That was the first thought that crossed Lilly's mind as she emerged from the most delicious fog of oblivion. Everything was so wonderfully vague, as if the edges of the world had been smudged by a giant eraser, or a veil had been drawn over her eyes.

She let herself float in the agreeable fog for a while, slowly becoming more and more aware of her rather confusing surroundings.

To begin with, she seemed to be in a church. More specifically, she was lying in bed in a church. That was certainly quite odd.

She was lying on white linen sheets, she realized. It had been months since she had felt sheets against her skin, apart from that single night at the Ritz, of course.

Perhaps she and Robbie could return there one day. It really had been so lovely. And the bed in her room had been awfully comfortable. But first she probably ought to sort out where she was now.

Could it be that she'd died, and was in heaven? That would explain the ecclesiastical architecture. And possibly also the white sheets. But if this were heaven, why did her side hurt so much? And her leg?

She looked to her right, and saw that another cot had been arranged parallel to hers. The man in it appeared to be sleeping, and there was a large bandage wrapped around his head. If only he were awake; she could ask him where they were.

She turned her head to her left, and saw another man, his back against the wall, his head lolling against his shoulder. He, too, seemed to be asleep.

There was something familiar about this man. He had such pretty golden hair, though it was mussed and needed a good brushing. And his clothes were covered with blood; were simply soaked in the stuff. She decided that, just as soon as he woke up, she would tell him he needed a bath.

She stared at him, comprehension beginning to clear

the fog from her mind. It was . . . Robbie. That was his name. He loved her; yes, that was it. He loved her, and she loved him. And she'd been so worried about him, so fearful he would be captured by the Germans, and sent to a prisoner-of-war camp, and she might never see him again—

But what was he doing sitting here? He knew they couldn't risk being seen together, otherwise she'd be sent home by Miss Jeffries. She had to wake him, now, or they'd surely be seen.

Before she could say anything, or even move, he was at her side, was stroking her hair, and she saw there were tears in his eyes.

"My throat," she wheezed. "So dry."

"I know, darling. Let me lift you a little so you can have a sip of water. But just a sip."

He braced her up, held a mug to her lips, and let her take one small sip, then another. "That's all for now," he ordered. "You can have more in a minute or two. How do you feel?"

"Sore," she mumbled. "Where am I?"

"You're in the post-op ward in Saint-Venant. Set up, for the moment, in the convent's sanctuary."

"There was a crash," she said, suddenly remembering.

"Yes. All the men in your ambulance are safe, so don't fret about them. They're alive because of you.

Private Gillespie says that most any other driver would have driven right into the exploding shell. He's very proud of you, Lilly. As am I."

"Why is my leg so sore? And my side?"

"Your leg was pinned in the wreck. But it's still there, so don't worry about that. It's in a splint now. Your side hurts because your spleen was lacerated. It had to come out."

She thought about this a moment. "What's a spleen?"

He smiled and squeezed her hand. "It's nothing you can't live without, I promise."

"I suppose I shall have to take your word for it." It occurred to her that he wasn't meant to be here at all.

"How did you escape? We were all so certain that you'd be captured."

"Your Private Gillespie came to our rescue. He badgered Colonel Lewis into letting him have one of the lorries. We all got out, every last one of us."

"I hope you thanked him," she said.

"I will when I see him next. Now, Lilly, how are you feeling? How is the pain?"

"It's getting worse, but don't give me anything for it. Not yet. Not before you tell me what is going to happen."

"If I could do anything to prevent—"

"They're sending me home, aren't they?"

Robbie nodded, his expression filled with regret. "In a day or two, as soon as you can be moved, you'll be evacuated to one of the base hospitals. Abbéville has been shelled, so it will probably be Boulogne."

"And back to England after that."

"I'm afraid so, yes. But I spoke to Miss Jeffries while you were sleeping, and she says they will keep you on, at least until the end of the war. You'll still have your wages, so you won't have to go back to your parents."

"Perhaps I can lodge with Mrs. Collins again, once I'm out of hospital. She might have room."

"It won't be for long," he added. "Only until the war is over and I'm back in London."

She stared at him, not entirely certain she understood what he was talking about.

"I meant to ask you this weeks ago. Had meant to give you this."

Robbie held up a small leather box, then, seeing she hadn't the strength to take it from him, opened it for her. When she saw the ring inside, she began to cry.

"Will you marry me, Lilly?"

She nodded, the tears running unchecked down her face. "Yes," she whispered.

"I can't promise you anything grand," he told her. "I'd like to go back to the London, continue my work there. I haven't much money, but there's enough for a house. And I was thinking that you could go to university, if you like. We could hire tutors for you, just to help you get through the entrance exams, and then—"

"But don't you want children?" she interrupted, her head reeling at the mention of school.

"Of course I do. But you're only twenty-four. We have plenty of time. Time enough for you to discover what you really want out of life. Just as long as I get to come along with you."

"Oh, Robbie. I don't know what to say. Apart from yes."

"You already said yes."

"So I did. But we both know it's not official until you kiss me."

At that he rose up on his knees, leaned across the cot, and kissed her tenderly. Only when he moved away did she see they were no longer alone.

Constance was standing at the end of the cot, and just behind her Lilly could see Bridget, Annie, Matron, Private Gillespie, Captain Mitchell, and Miss Jeffries; nearly all of the friends she had made over the past months.

They began to applaud and cheer, the sound building and building as people came to see what all the fuss was about, were told about the love story that had taken place at the 51st, and then began to clap as well.

It was mortifying and it was wonderful and it was, suddenly, all too much for her.

"Robbie?" she asked.

"I'll send them away in a minute. But let them sing your praises for a moment more. You deserve it."

Then he kissed her again, kissed her until the world and everything in it fell away. And she was alone at last, at long last, with her Robbie.

Epilogue

London
January 1919

Most evenings, Lilly didn't bother to take the Underground home from work, for it only took an hour to walk from Whitehall, where she was working as a clerk for the Imperial War Graves Commission, to her lodgings in Camden Town. It was safer, too, for influenza still stalked the streets of London, and one of the surest ways to fall ill was to jam oneself into a crowded carriage full of sneezing, coughing strangers.

For six months now, ever since her discharge from hospital, she'd been seconded to the War Graves Commission as a clerk. Her work, in the main, consisted of answering letters from people seeking the graves of their loved ones. Most of the time she was unable to help, for thousands upon thousands of graves in France and Belgium had no marking on their headstone, apart from the devastating explanation KNOWN UNTO GOD.

Just yesterday, however, she'd located the grave of a young captain, lost not far from where Edward had last been seen, and had been able to send directions to his parents. It had been a rare and bittersweet moment of success.

Today had been a long day, occupied by fruitless searches through filing cabinets and the depressing task of advising one family after another that the commission had no news as yet of their loved one's grave, but would certainly advise if and when such information were to be discovered.

She was tired and out of sorts and it was raining, so rather than walk home she had tied a fresh muslin mask over her nose and mouth and had taken the Northern Line home to Camden Town, her thoughts occupied by plans for her and Charlotte's supper. Sardines on toast? Beans on toast? It was washday, too, so Mrs. Collins might have boiled a pudding in the copper when she was done with the linens. She always shared some with her girls, and something sweet at the end of a long day would be welcome indeed.

Last July, their landlady had been overjoyed to welcome Lilly back, wasting no time in informing all the neighbors that Miss Ashford had gone to France and come home crippled by wounds. Never mind that Lilly's limp was almost imperceptible; the drama of the story was what counted.

Mrs. Collins may have been an interfering busybody, but she had a good heart and Lilly was fond of her. And she refused to even contemplate the idea of returning to live with her parents, though they had softened toward her of late.

Perhaps it had been the shock of losing Edward. Perhaps it had been the realization that their daughter had almost died in the ambulance crash. Whatever the reason, they had astonished Lilly by appearing at her hospital bedside not long after her return from France. Although visitors had been officially discouraged because of the flu, somehow Mama and Papa, looking rather comical in the butter-muslin masks that everyone was forced to wear, had finagled their way onto the ward where she was recuperating.

It had been an awkward conversation, full of lengthy, fraught silences. And the atmosphere hadn't improved when Lilly had informed them she and Robbie were to be married upon his return from France.

When she'd been discharged from hospital in July,

her parents had invited her to come and live with them. Much to their surprise, she had declined, though she'd attempted to do so as tactfully as possible. She did pay a visit to Ashford House each Wednesday, sharing supper with them in the breakfast room. It was a chore in which she took little pleasure, for the loss of Edward had broken both her parents, leaving them mere shells of the people they had once been.

The house had become unutterably gloomy, more like a tomb than a home, with the curtains perpetually drawn and a permanent shrine to Edward set up in the front hall. His portrait, draped in black, was propped on a walnut table in the center of the foyer. His medals were arranged on a velvet-lined tray, which in turn was flanked by half a dozen framed photographs.

For her part, Lilly could not bear to admit that Edward was dead, though no news had ever come to explain his fate. Even after the Armistice, when prisoners began to return from the camps where they'd been held, her parents hadn't heard from Edward, nor had any account of his whereabouts been forwarded to them.

It had been two months since peace had been declared, two months to the day. She and Charlotte had passed the evening at home, sitting by the fire in her room, a half-empty bottle of sherry their replacement for champagne. They had toasted the war's end quietly, without jubilation, for what was there to celebrate? Millions had died on the battlefields; millions more were dying as the Spanish flu swept around the world.

Back in August, back when influenza had been the sort of thing that only made one miserable for a week, she and Charlotte had fallen ill. They'd both been confined to bed for a few days, feverish and racked with pain, but that had been the worst of it. At the 51st, which had been relocated to Coyecque, nearly everyone, Robbie included, had caught the flu in the early summer. None of her friends there had died, although some of the weaker patients had succumbed.

The influenza that struck England in the autumn was an altogether more lethal and frightening disease. It killed in hours; it killed strong young men and women, people who had survived the war and ought to have lived for many more years; and it emptied London's streets and public places as not even the zeppelins and Gotha bombers had managed to do. Roads and sidewalks had been sprayed with disinfectant, masks had been as ubiquitous as hats, and handshakes had become a thing of the past. But still the epidemic had rolled on, striking down thousands upon thousands of Londoners in October and November alone.

And then, in December, fewer people had died, and

it seemed that fewer still were dying in January. No one could pinpoint the reason; certainly no treatment had emerged to beat back the disease. Likely enough it would roar back again, an enemy retreating so it might regroup and attack again.

The flu had kept Robbie in France for longer than she had expected, for after the Armistice he'd been sent to one of the base hospitals in Saint-Omer, where nearly all the staff had fallen ill; and then on to Belgium, where similar conditions prevailed.

He had told her not to be frightened for him, since he was quite certain that, having been sick in the summer, he had acquired a degree of immunity to the second wave of contagion. He had also warned her that the tonics, potions, and remedies being touted for their flu-repellent properties were nothing more than quack medicine. Vinegar, quinine, spirits, morphia: all were useless. The only thing that worked, in his opinion, was frequent hand washing, avoidance of large gatherings, and the use of a mask when forced into close quarters with other people.

His letters arrived frequently, each one ending with a promise to return to her soon, but they were never long enough, and included few details of his work. Altogether it was terribly dispiriting, for it had been nine months since they'd been parted. How long would it be before she saw him again?

Her train had arrived at Camden Town. She made her way outside, pulling off her mask as she left the station, and walked west through darkened side streets. Arriving home, she opened the front door and crouched to remove her boots. Before she had so much as loosened a lace, her landlady came rushing down the hall.

"There you are!"

"Good evening, Mrs. Collins. How was your day?"

"Nice enough, thank you for asking. A telegram's come for you, not a half hour ago. Thought you'd want to see it straightaway."

She took it from Mrs. Collins, tore open the envelope, and read the single sheet inside.

ABOUT TO BOARD FERRY TO DOVER. WILL ARRIVE VICTORIA STATION HALF PAST SIX 11 JAN. LONGING TO SEE YOU. ROBBIE.

"What time is it, Mrs. Collins?"

"It's just gone six o'clock, my dear. Is anything the matter?"

"Not at all. It's Captain Fraser—he's coming home!"

"When does he arrive?"

"In a half hour. I'll never make it to Victoria on time," Lilly fretted.

"There's sure to be a taxi or two outside the Underground station," Mrs. Collins reminded her. "Run up there and hop in. Do you have enough to cover the fare?"

"I think so. Oh, Mrs. Collins—I look a fright!"

"Never mind that, be off with you. And wear your mask!"

A panicked dash, back the way she had come, to the Underground station, then a flash of despair when she saw that the taxi rank outside was deserted. A moment later a motorcar came round the corner, by luck a taxi, and Lilly hailed it with a wild wave and a most unladylike whistle, with no regard for what passersby might think.

Twenty minutes later, just as the station clock at Victoria struck the half hour, she reached the barrier as Robbie's train pulled into Platform Three. At first it was hard to see much of anything, what with the clouds of steam still swirling around the platform and the jostling, anxious crowd that surrounded her. Little by little the air cleared, and the people around her found their loved ones, greeted them, and departed.

It dawned on Lilly, then, that perhaps she'd missed

him; perhaps he'd missed the train in Dover. It was perfectly possible that he'd been delayed.

She might as well return home and wait for another telegram. Wait, though her heart was breaking from the agony of having already waited so long.

She'd made up her mind to leave, and was about to turn on her heel and walk away, when a man emerged from the very last carriage, so far away that she could see nothing of his features. He reached back into the carriage, extracted some bags, and then, hailing one of the station attendants, turned his attention back to the carriage interior.

Another man alighted, somewhat awkwardly, and even from where she stood Lilly could see that his right trouser leg was pinned up. Taking a set of crutches from the first man, he began to move down the platform, slowly, painstakingly, still so distant that she could see nothing of his face.

But there was something about the way the first man moved, the way he walked, and though Robbie had said nothing of traveling with a friend, a flame of hope ignited inside her.

Ignoring the protestations of the attendant standing guard at the barrier, she ducked under the gate and rushed toward the men on the platform. They were still in the shadows, so it was impossible to be sure, but it might be Robbie after all.

As the men passed under the light that marked the halfway point of the platform, she saw that the first man was Robbie, come home to her at last. And then, a fraction of a second later, the second man came into the light.

It was Edward, his dear face so sad and tired and old that she knew, oh God, she knew that his missing leg was the least of his injuries.

Tearing off her mask, she ran forward and flung her arms around him, though he was still holding his crutches and unable to embrace her in return.

"I thought . . . I always hoped . . ."

"I know, darling girl. I know."

"But how? We had no news. How is this possible?"

"Robbie found me. I was lost, even to myself. But he found me."

She turned to the man she loved, still not quite believing, and threw herself into his arms, her tears blinding her. He wiped them away tenderly, all the while whispering words of endearment to her.

"I don't understand," she said at last.

"I couldn't come home without him. So I decided I would have to find him first. Or at the very least discover what had happened."

"So all these months . . ."

"When I wasn't working I was searching for Edward. They discharged me in December, but I had to try."

"How long have you known?"

"A few weeks." Robbie looked to Edward, as if seeking permission to speak further. "Edward was still quite unwell when I found him. I ought to have told you, let you know somehow. But Edward—"

She put her fingers to his lips and shook her head. "Not now. Now I only want one thing from you."

A smile, almost shy, lit up his face. "And what might that be?"

"A kiss."

"Here? In public? With you still in uniform? Someone might see," he said teasingly. "What will your superior officers say?"

"Bother the lot of them. Haven't you heard, Captain Fraser? The war ended months ago."

Acknowledgments

I offer my sincere thanks to the following for their assistance:

The staff of the Great War Archive (Oxford), Collections Canada (Library and Archives Canada), the Imperial War Museum, National Archives (UK), the National Library of Scotland, and the Toronto Reference Library for their assistance as I researched this book.

Deborah Cooke, former writer-in-residence at the Toronto Public Library, for her very helpful advice regarding an early draft of this book.

Aaron Orkin, Division of Emergency Medicine, University of Toronto; Eric Webber, Department of Surgery, University of British Columbia; and Farah Valimohamed, Department of Anesthesiology, Royal

Columbian Hospital, for their informed critiques of my descriptions of Great War–era surgery, anesthesiology, and postoperative care.

Professor Stuart Robson and professor Mariel Robson for their painstaking review of this novel at all stages.

My agent, Kevan Lyon, who saw the potential in Lilly's story, found it a home at William Morrow, and talked me off the ledge every time I started to panic. I am honored by your belief in me.

My editor, Amanda Bergeron, for her sensitive and insightful approach at all stages of the editorial process, and for her warm support for me personally. Her colleagues at William Morrow and HarperCollins have also been a delight to work with, and I am most grateful for their assistance.

My dear friend Kelly Smith Wayland, who persuaded me to try again when I'd given up hope, as well as Denise Beaton, Rena Boniza, Jane Dimoff, Jane Evans, Elizabeth Felgueiras, Kelly Fruhauf, Ana Nascimento, and Jennifer Milligan. I am so grateful for your friendship and constant support.

Members of my family, both near and far, who have been my greatest cheerleaders, in particular Stuart, Mariel, and Molly; Regina and Gino; Sean, Maggie, and Grace; Michela, Jonathan, Emma, and Chiara;

Terry and Graham; and John and Bunny. My grandmother Nikki Moir broke down many barriers in her own career as a journalist and was a key source of inspiration for me.

My late mother, Wendy Robson, who gave me my first copy of *Testament of Youth*, and instilled in me a passion for historical fiction that even graduate school could not extinguish.

My sister, Kate Robson, who was the first to read this book back when it was nothing more than a ridiculously elaborate outline. It would likely still be an outline if not for her relentless and unwavering encouragement. I owe everything to her.

My children, Matthew and Daniela, who were patient and loving as I worked on this book, and who have evinced nothing but delight and pride in its being published. You are my life, my light, and my joy.

But the greatest part of my thanks must go to my husband, Claudio. You're Italian, not Scottish; you have brown eyes, not blue; you're an engineer, not a surgeon. But I never would have found Robbie without you.